SEARCH FOR ATLANTIS

an original
graphic novel

WRITTEN BY
Shea Fontana

ART BY
Yancey Labat

COLORS BY
Monica Kubina

LETTERING BY
Janice Chiang

SUPERGIRL BASED ON THE CHARACTERS CREATED BY JERRY SIEGEL AND JOE SHUSTER.
BY SPECIAL ARRANGEMENT WITH THE JERRY SIEGEL FAMILY.

D0485295

DC SUPER HERO GIRLS: SEARCH FOR ATLANTIS. Published by DC Comics, 2900 W. Alameda Avenue, Burbank, CA 91505. GST # is R125921072.
Printed by Cenveo, Richmond, VA, U.S.A. 8/24/18. ISBN: 978-1-4012-8353-7

SUSTAINABLE FORESTRY INITIATIVE
Certified Chain of Custody
Promoting Sustainable Forestry
www.sfiprogram.org
SFI-00484

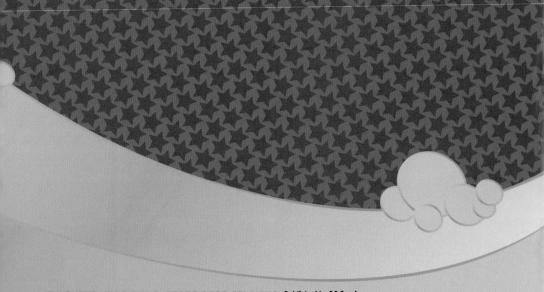

TABLE OF CONTENTS

ROLL CALL

SUPER HERO HIGH SCHOOL

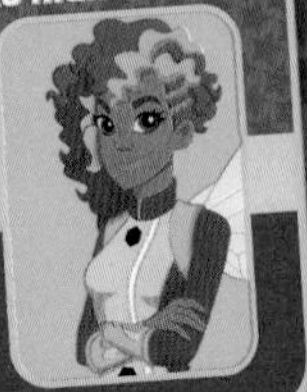

BUMBLEBEE

SUPERPOWERS
Enhanced strength, flight, ability to shrink, stinger blasts

SUPER HERO HIGH SCHOOL

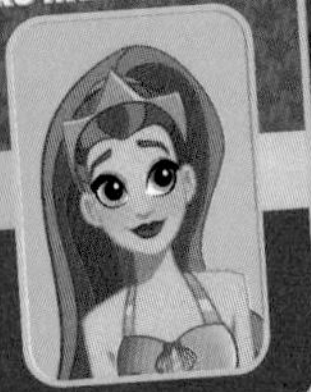

MERA

SUPERPOWERS
Ability to breathe in water or air, control over water, enhanced strength

SUPER HERO HIGH SCHOOL

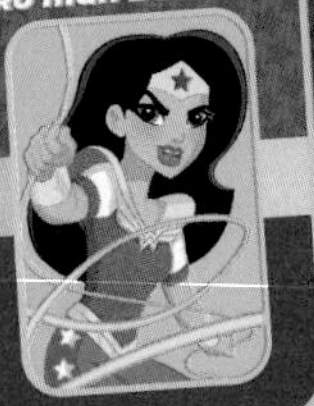

WONDER WOMAN

SUPERPOWERS
Super-strength, flight, near-invincibility, super-athleticism

SUPER HERO HIGH SCHOOL

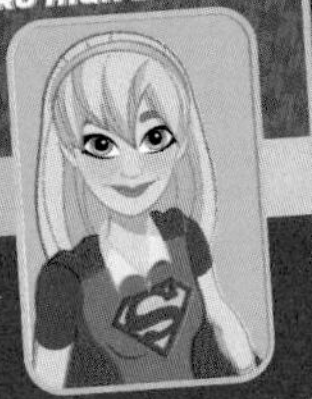

SUPERGIRL

SUPERPOWERS
Super-strength, flight, invincibility, super-hearing, heat vision, X-ray vision

SUPER HERO HIGH SCHOOL

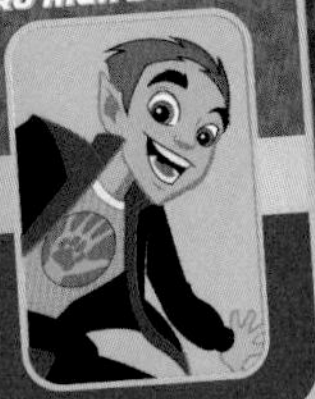

BEAST BOY

SUPERPOWERS
Shape-shifting into any animal form, world-class slacking

SUPER HERO HIGH SCHOOL

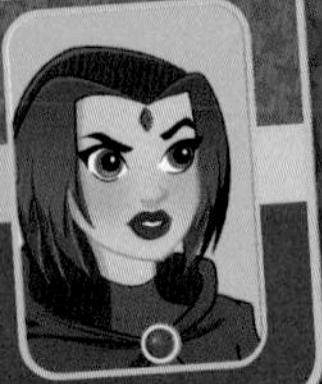

RAVEN

SUPERPOWERS
Empath power, teleportation, flight

SUPER HERO HIGH SCHOOL

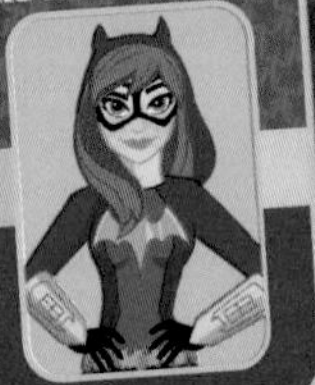

BATGIRL

SUPERPOWERS
Computer genius, expert martial artist, photographic memory, legendary detective skills

SUPER HERO HIGH SCHOOL

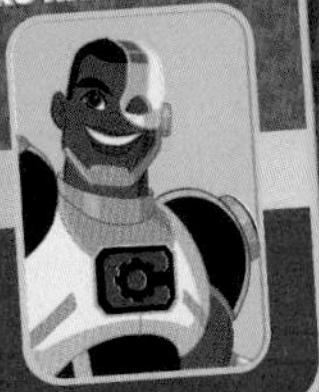

CYBORG

SUPERPOWERS
Advanced technological implants, enhanced strength

SUPER HERO HIGH SCHOOL

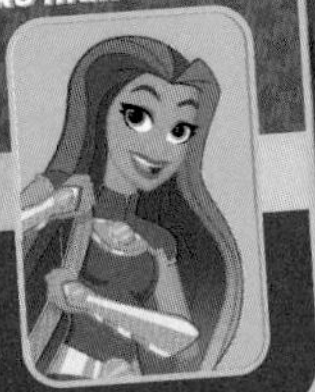

STARFIRE

SUPERPOWERS
Flight, super-strength, ability to shoot starbolts from her hands

SUPER HERO HIGH SCHOOL

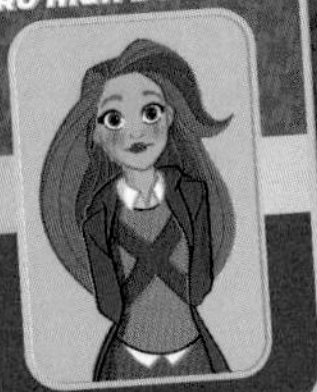

MISS MARTIAN

SUPERPOWERS
Flight, shape-shifting, mind-reading, invisibility, super-strength

SUPER HERO HIGH SCHOOL

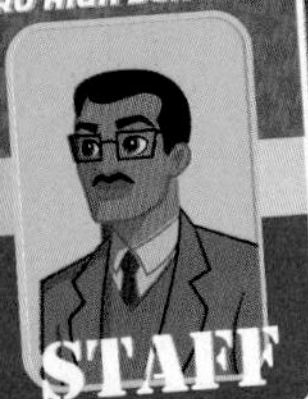

LUCIUS FOX

Professor of Weaponomics

STAFF

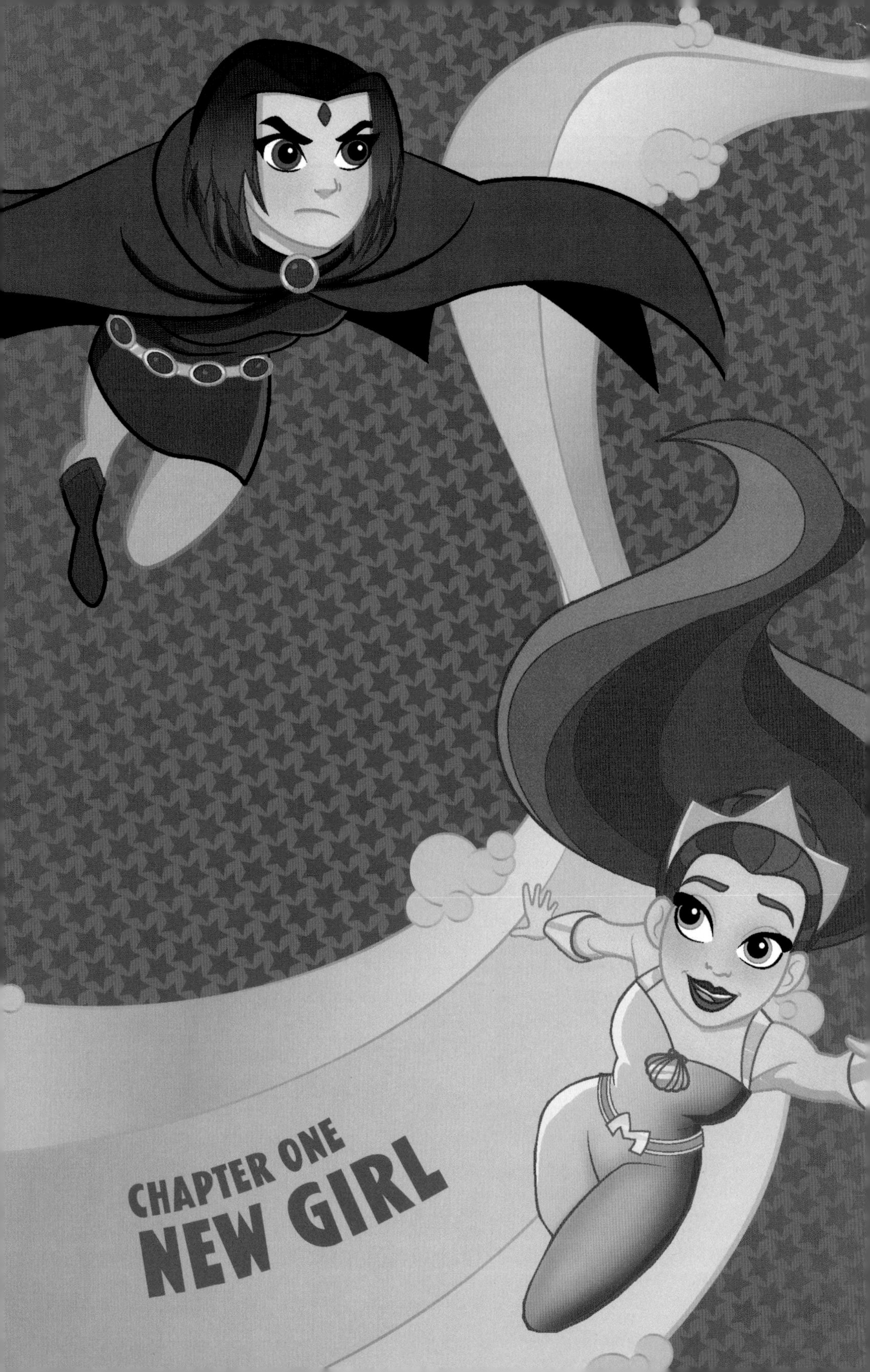

CHAPTER ONE
NEW GIRL

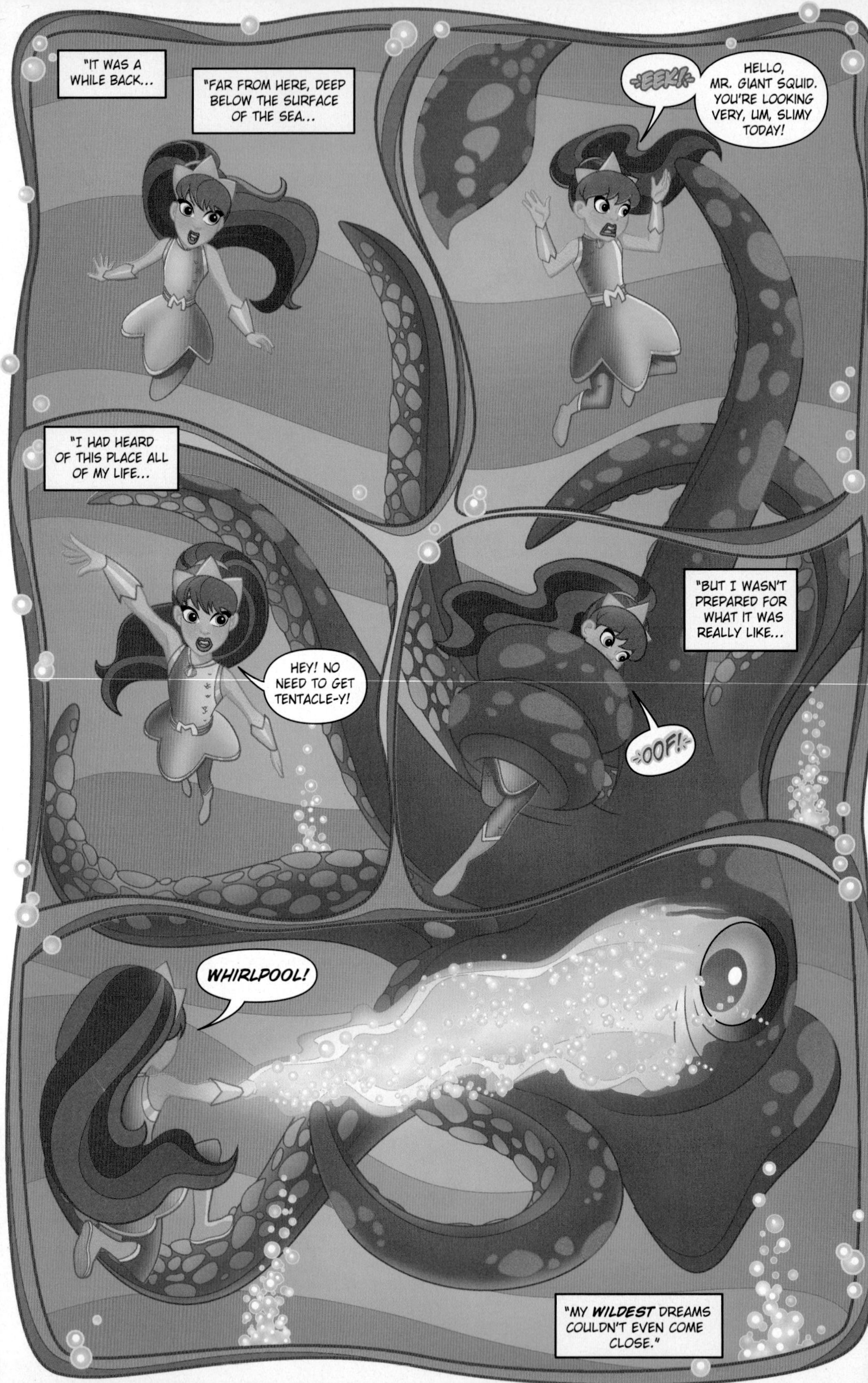
"IT WAS A WHILE BACK...
"FAR FROM HERE, DEEP BELOW THE SURFACE OF THE SEA...
EEK!
HELLO, MR. GIANT SQUID. YOU'RE LOOKING VERY, UM, SLIMY TODAY!
"I HAD HEARD OF THIS PLACE ALL OF MY LIFE...
HEY! NO NEED TO GET TENTACLE-Y!
"BUT I WASN'T PREPARED FOR WHAT IT WAS REALLY LIKE...
OOF!
WHIRLPOOL!
"MY WILDEST DREAMS COULDN'T EVEN COME CLOSE."

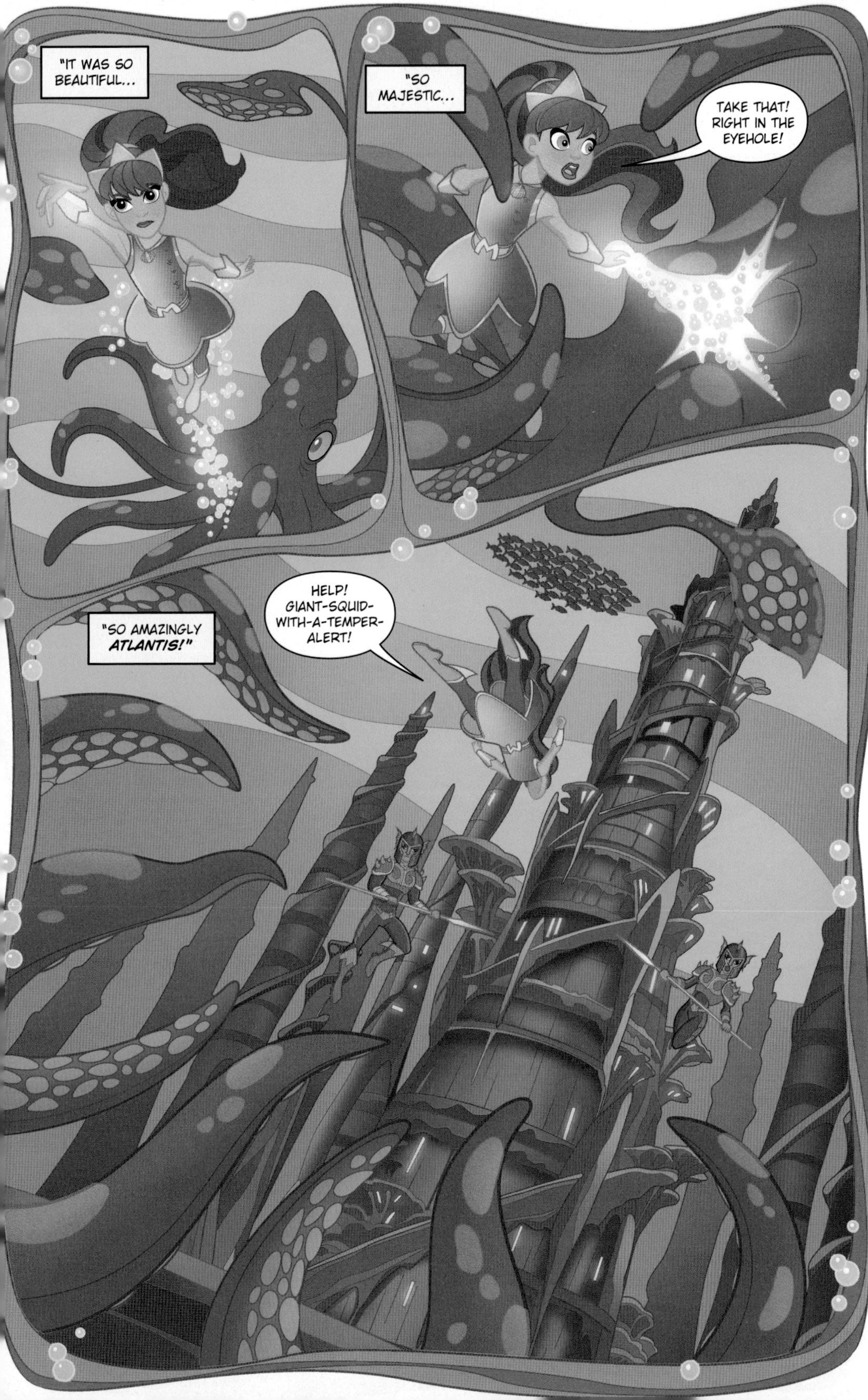
"IT WAS SO BEAUTIFUL...
"SO MAJESTIC...
TAKE THAT! RIGHT IN THE EYEHOLE!
"SO AMAZINGLY ATLANTIS!"
HELP! GIANT-SQUID-WITH-A-TEMPER-ALERT!

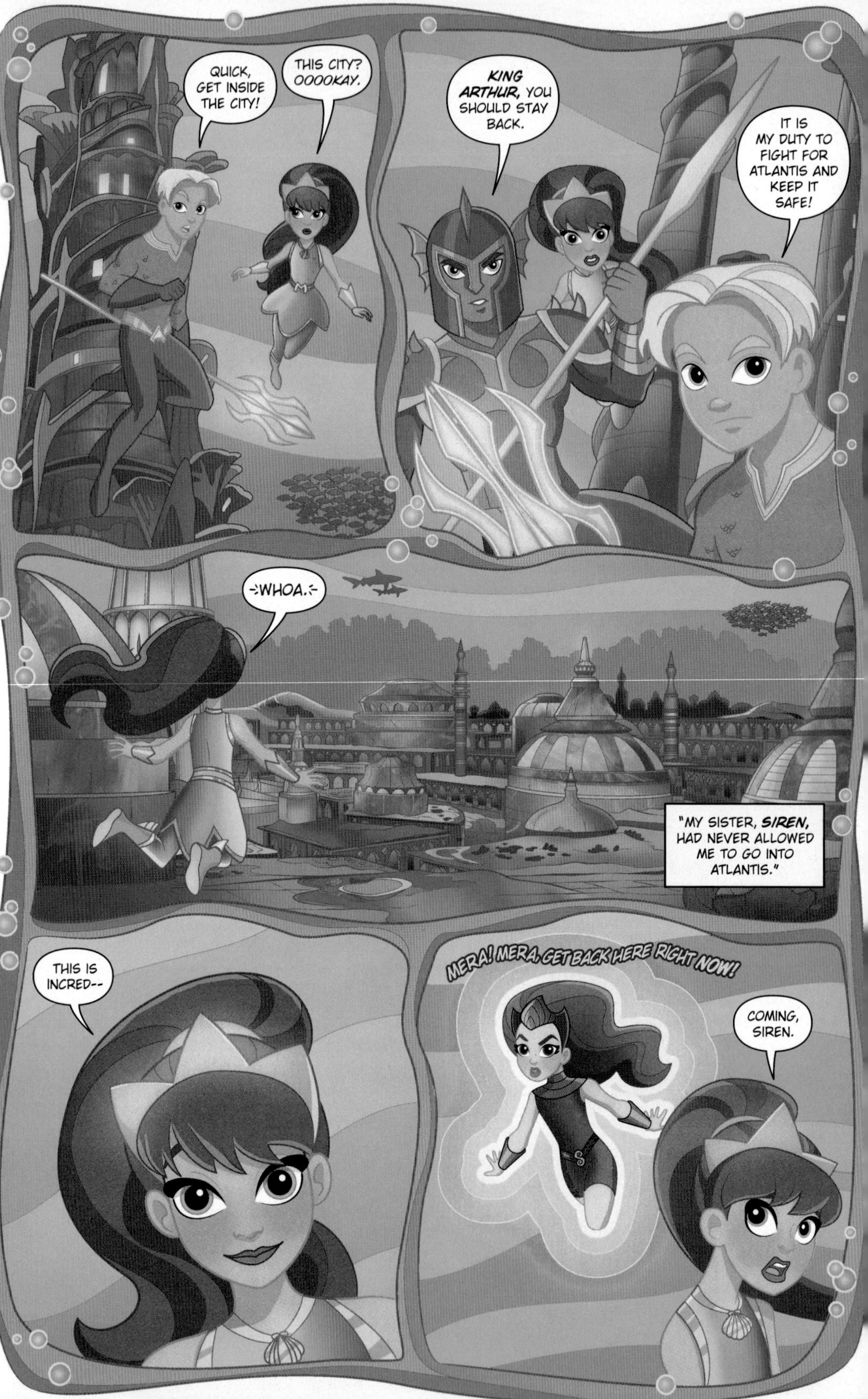
QUICK, GET INSIDE THE CITY!
THIS CITY? OOOOKAY.
KING ARTHUR, YOU SHOULD STAY BACK.
IT IS MY DUTY TO FIGHT FOR ATLANTIS AND KEEP IT SAFE!
WHOA.
"MY SISTER, SIREN, HAD NEVER ALLOWED ME TO GO INTO ATLANTIS."
THIS IS INCRED--
MERA! MERA, GET BACK HERE RIGHT NOW!
COMING, SIREN.

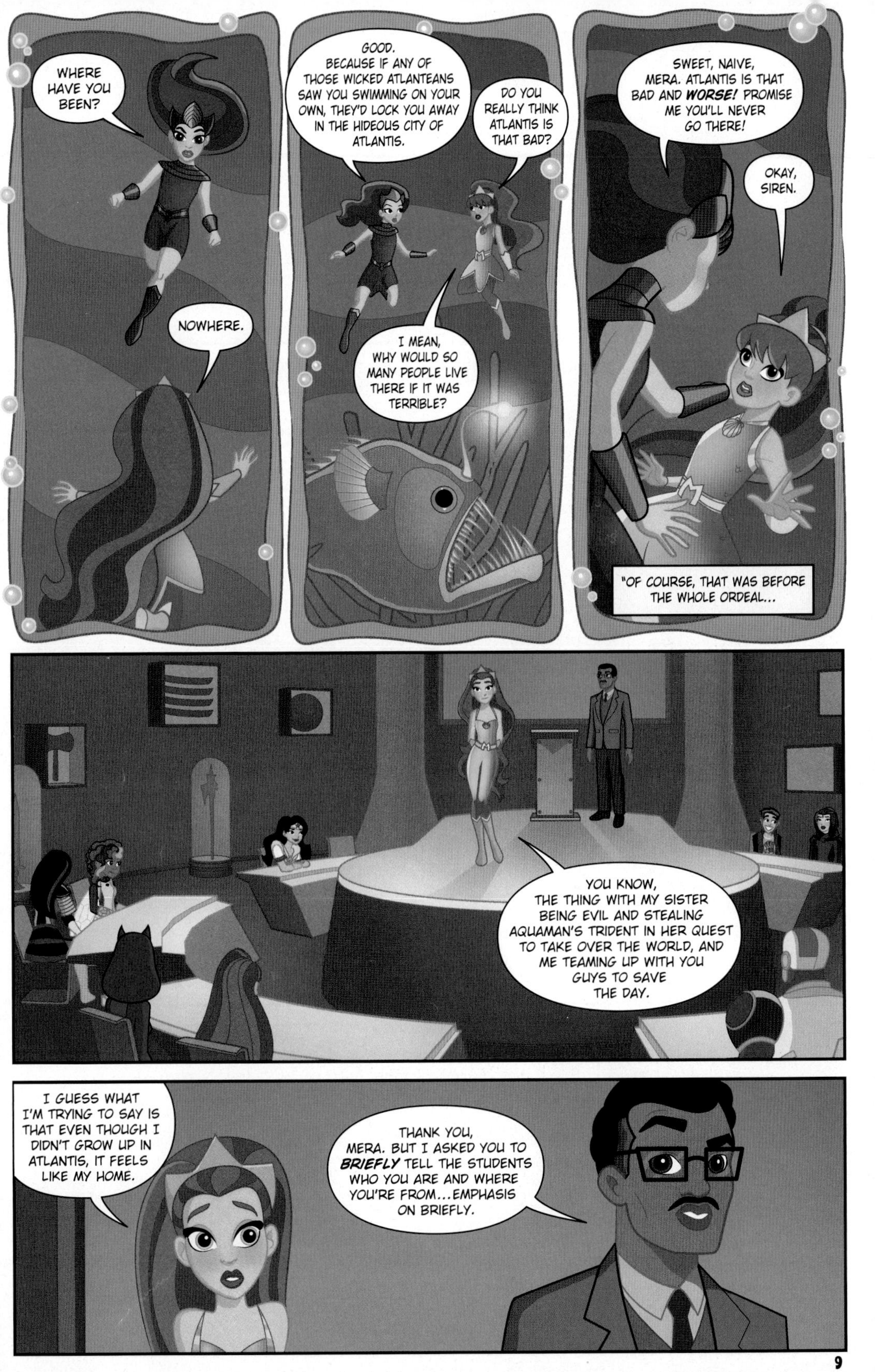
WHERE HAVE YOU BEEN?
NOWHERE.
GOOD. BECAUSE IF ANY OF THOSE WICKED ATLANTEANS SAW YOU SWIMMING ON YOUR OWN, THEY'D LOCK YOU AWAY IN THE HIDEOUS CITY OF ATLANTIS.
DO YOU REALLY THINK ATLANTIS IS THAT BAD?
I MEAN, WHY WOULD SO MANY PEOPLE LIVE THERE IF IT WAS TERRIBLE?
SWEET, NAIVE, MERA. ATLANTIS IS THAT BAD AND **WORSE!** PROMISE ME YOU'LL NEVER GO THERE!
OKAY, SIREN.
"OF COURSE, THAT WAS BEFORE THE WHOLE ORDEAL...
YOU KNOW, THE THING WITH MY SISTER BEING EVIL AND STEALING AQUAMAN'S TRIDENT IN HER QUEST TO TAKE OVER THE WORLD, AND ME TEAMING UP WITH YOU GUYS TO SAVE THE DAY.
I GUESS WHAT I'M TRYING TO SAY IS THAT EVEN THOUGH I DIDN'T GROW UP IN ATLANTIS, IT FEELS LIKE MY HOME.
THANK YOU, MERA. BUT I ASKED YOU TO ***BRIEFLY*** TELL THE STUDENTS WHO YOU ARE AND WHERE YOU'RE FROM...EMPHASIS ON BRIEFLY.

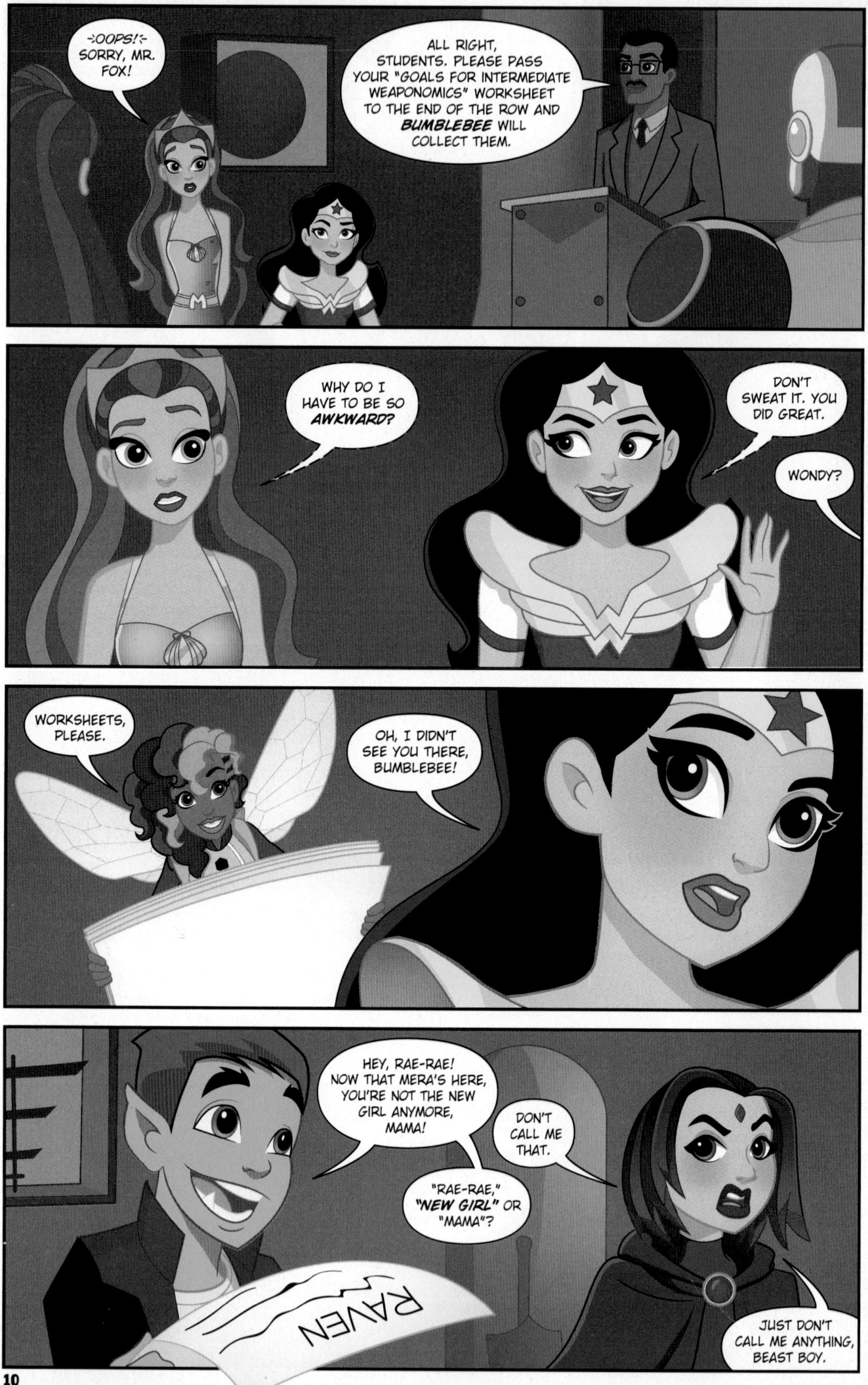
-OOPS!- SORRY, MR. FOX!
ALL RIGHT, STUDENTS. PLEASE PASS YOUR "GOALS FOR INTERMEDIATE WEAPONOMICS" WORKSHEET TO THE END OF THE ROW AND BUMBLEBEE WILL COLLECT THEM.
WHY DO I HAVE TO BE SO AWKWARD?
DON'T SWEAT IT. YOU DID GREAT.
WONDY?
WORKSHEETS, PLEASE.
OH, I DIDN'T SEE YOU THERE, BUMBLEBEE!
HEY, RAE-RAE! NOW THAT MERA'S HERE, YOU'RE NOT THE NEW GIRL ANYMORE, MAMA!
DON'T CALL ME THAT.
"RAE-RAE," "NEW GIRL" OR "MAMA"?
JUST DON'T CALL ME ANYTHING, BEAST BOY.
RAVEN

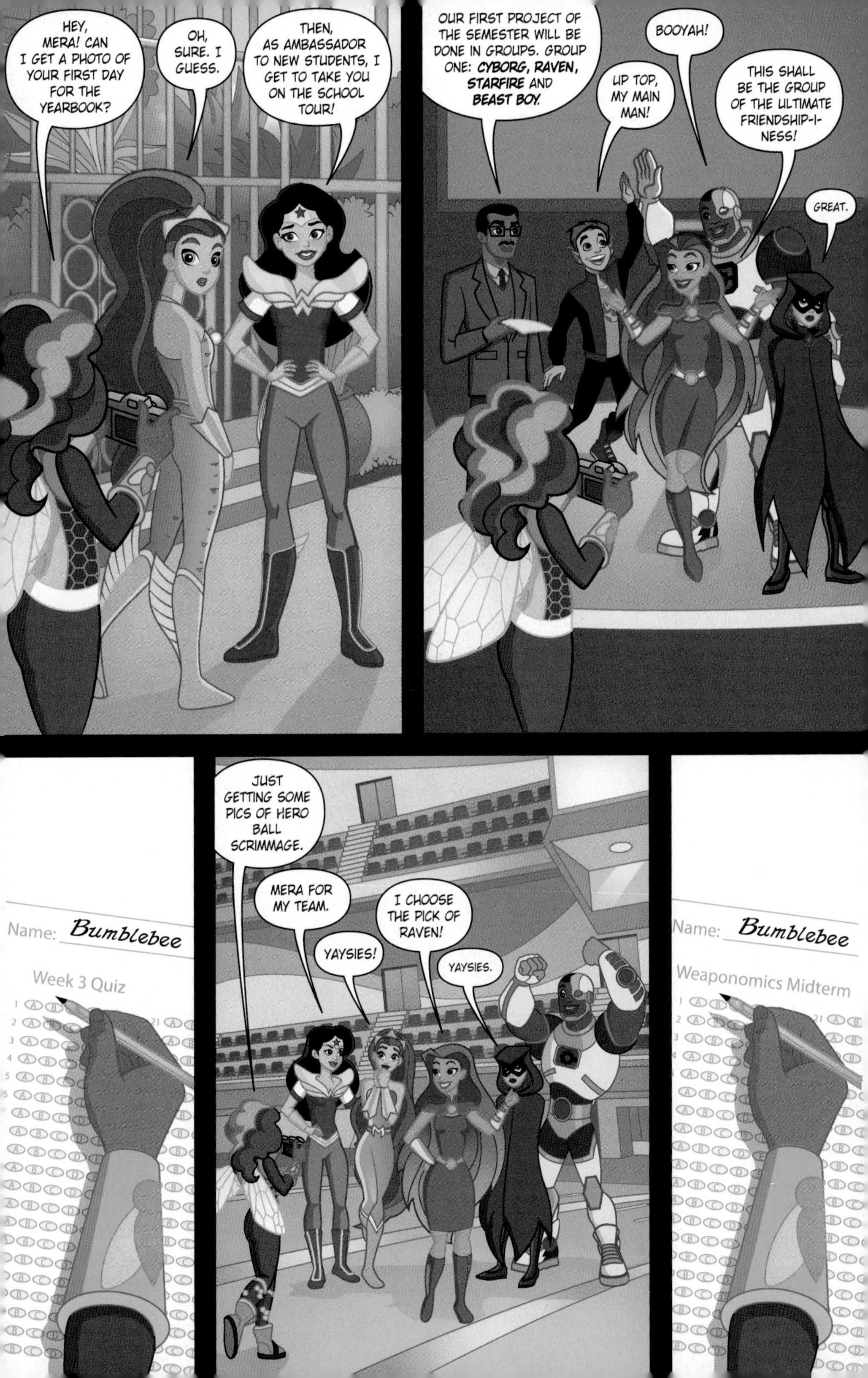

HEY, MERA! CAN I GET A PHOTO OF YOUR FIRST DAY FOR THE YEARBOOK?
OH, SURE. I GUESS.
THEN, AS AMBASSADOR TO NEW STUDENTS, I GET TO TAKE YOU ON THE SCHOOL TOUR!
OUR FIRST PROJECT OF THE SEMESTER WILL BE DONE IN GROUPS. GROUP ONE: CYBORG, RAVEN, STARFIRE AND BEAST BOY.
UP TOP, MY MAIN MAN!
BOOYAH!
THIS SHALL BE THE GROUP OF THE ULTIMATE FRIENDSHIP-I-NESS!
GREAT.
Name: Bumblebee
Week 3 Quiz
JUST GETTING SOME PICS OF HERO BALL SCRIMMAGE.
MERA FOR MY TEAM.
YAYSIES!
I CHOOSE THE PICK OF RAVEN!
YAYSIES.
Name: Bumblebee
Weaponomics Midterm

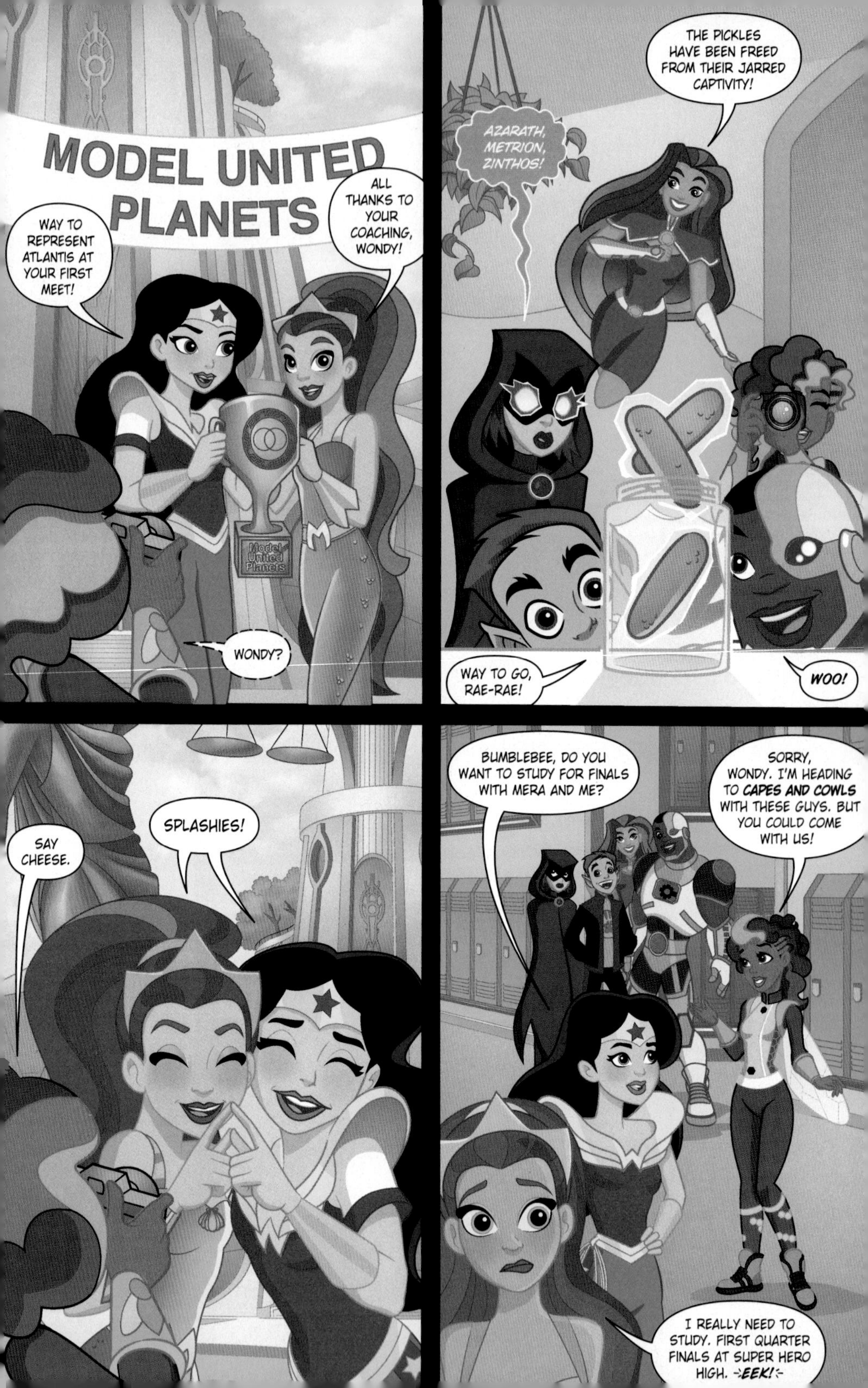
MODEL UNITED PLANETS
WAY TO REPRESENT ATLANTIS AT YOUR FIRST MEET!
ALL THANKS TO YOUR COACHING, WONDY!
Model United Planets
WONDY?
AZARATH, METRION, ZINTHOS!
THE PICKLES HAVE BEEN FREED FROM THEIR JARRED CAPTIVITY!
WAY TO GO, RAE-RAE!
WOO!
SAY CHEESE.
SPLASHIES!
BUMBLEBEE, DO YOU WANT TO STUDY FOR FINALS WITH MERA AND ME?
SORRY, WONDY. I'M HEADING TO CAPES AND COWLS WITH THESE GUYS. BUT YOU COULD COME WITH US!
I REALLY NEED TO STUDY. FIRST QUARTER FINALS AT SUPER HERO HIGH. EEK!

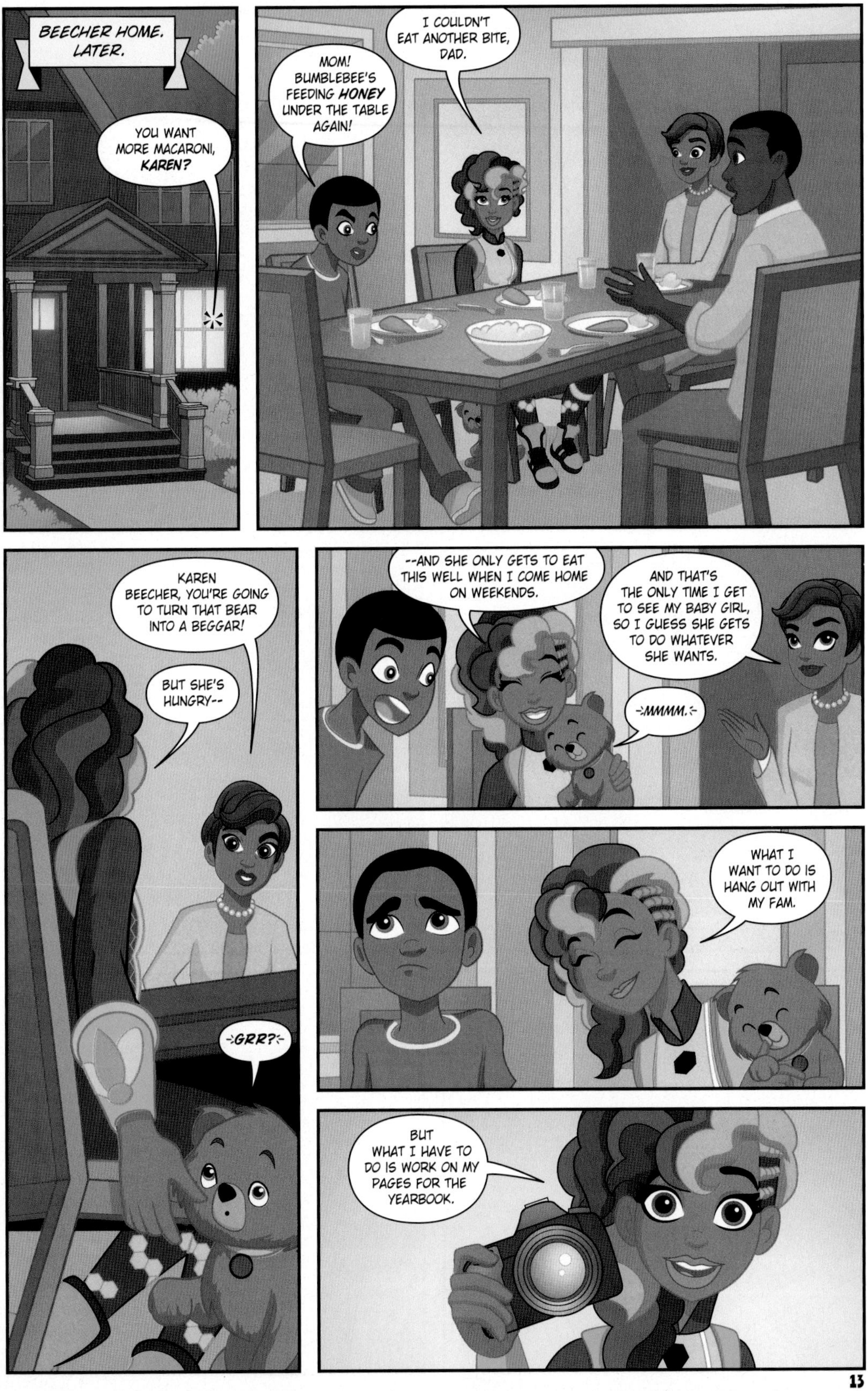
BEECHER HOME. LATER.
YOU WANT MORE MACARONI, KAREN?
MOM! BUMBLEBEE'S FEEDING HONEY UNDER THE TABLE AGAIN!
I COULDN'T EAT ANOTHER BITE, DAD.
KAREN BEECHER, YOU'RE GOING TO TURN THAT BEAR INTO A BEGGAR!
BUT SHE'S HUNGRY--
GRR?
--AND SHE ONLY GETS TO EAT THIS WELL WHEN I COME HOME ON WEEKENDS.
AND THAT'S THE ONLY TIME I GET TO SEE MY BABY GIRL, SO I GUESS SHE GETS TO DO WHATEVER SHE WANTS.
MMMM.
WHAT I WANT TO DO IS HANG OUT WITH MY FAM.
BUT WHAT I HAVE TO DO IS WORK ON MY PAGES FOR THE YEARBOOK.

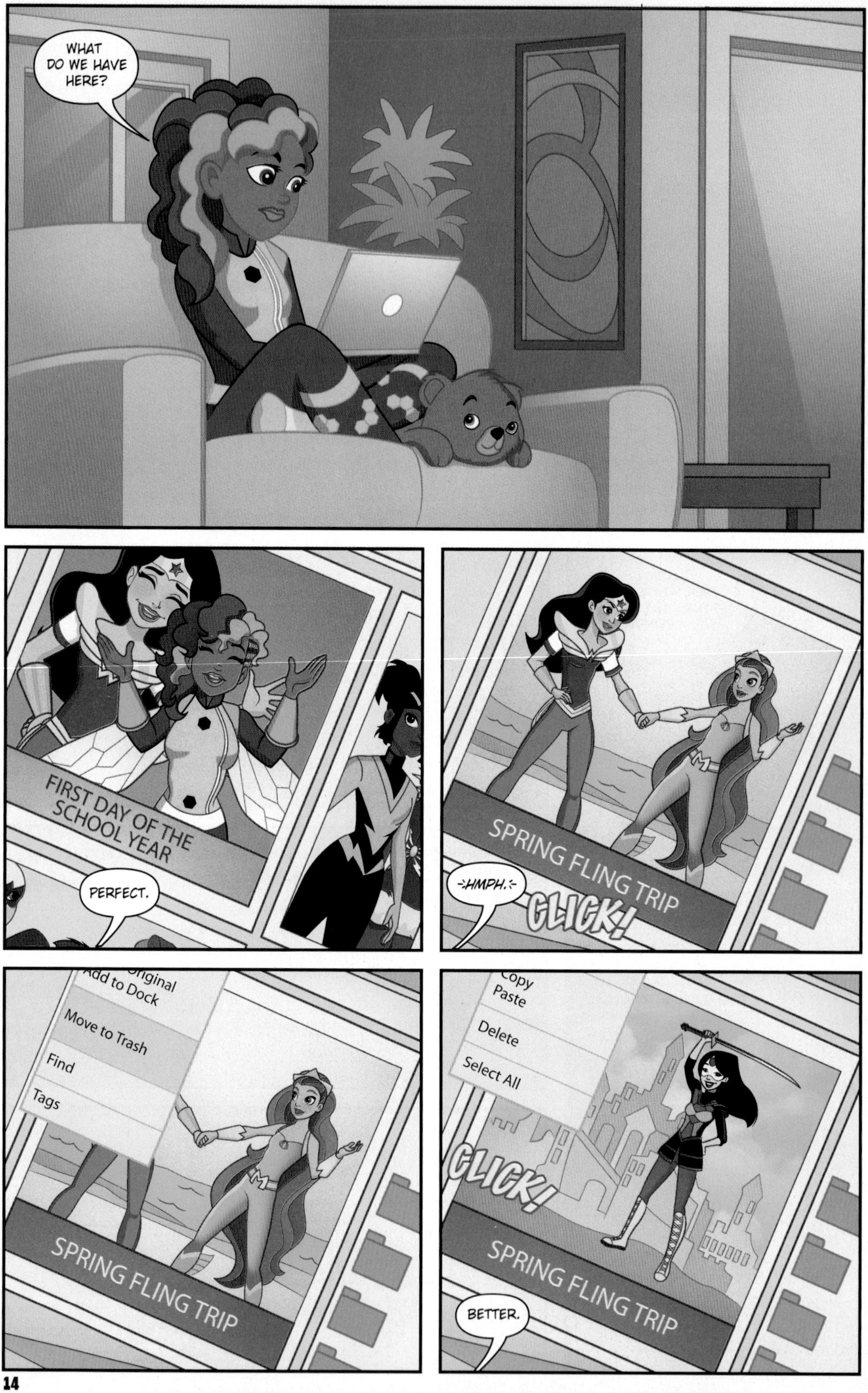
WHAT DO WE HAVE HERE?
FIRST DAY OF THE SCHOOL YEAR
PERFECT.
SPRING FLING TRIP
HMPH.
CLICK!
Original
Add to Dock
Move to Trash
Find
Tags
SPRING FLING TRIP
Copy
Paste
Delete
Select All
CLICK!
SPRING FLING TRIP
BETTER.

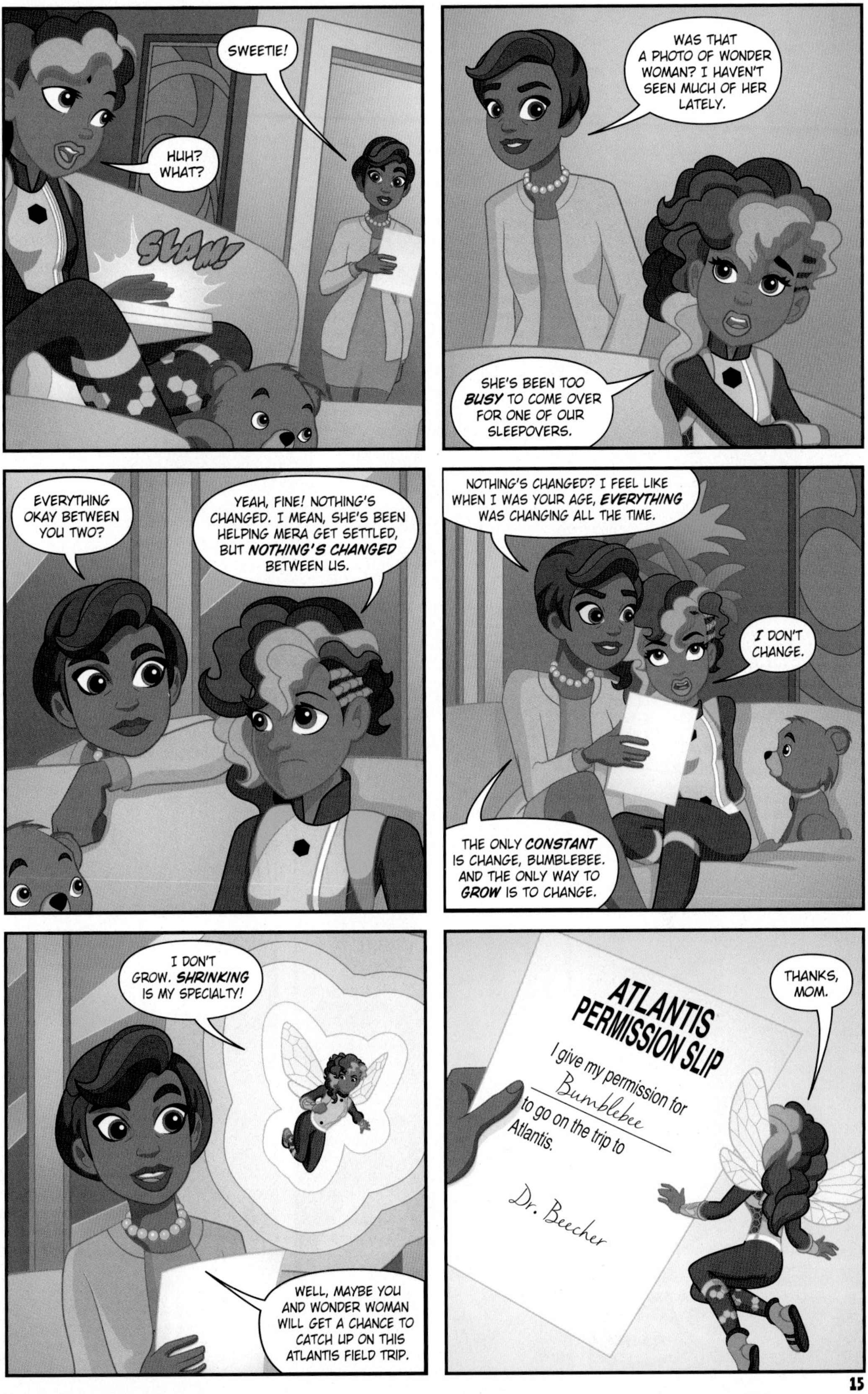

SWEETIE!
HUH? WHAT?
SLAM!
WAS THAT A PHOTO OF WONDER WOMAN? I HAVEN'T SEEN MUCH OF HER LATELY.
SHE'S BEEN TOO BUSY TO COME OVER FOR ONE OF OUR SLEEPOVERS.
EVERYTHING OKAY BETWEEN YOU TWO?
YEAH, FINE! NOTHING'S CHANGED. I MEAN, SHE'S BEEN HELPING MERA GET SETTLED, BUT NOTHING'S CHANGED BETWEEN US.
NOTHING'S CHANGED? I FEEL LIKE WHEN I WAS YOUR AGE, EVERYTHING WAS CHANGING ALL THE TIME.
I DON'T CHANGE.
THE ONLY CONSTANT IS CHANGE, BUMBLEBEE. AND THE ONLY WAY TO GROW IS TO CHANGE.
I DON'T GROW. SHRINKING IS MY SPECIALTY!
WELL, MAYBE YOU AND WONDER WOMAN WILL GET A CHANCE TO CATCH UP ON THIS ATLANTIS FIELD TRIP.
ATLANTIS PERMISSION SLIP
I give my permission for Bumblebee to go on the trip to Atlantis.
Dr. Beecher
THANKS, MOM.

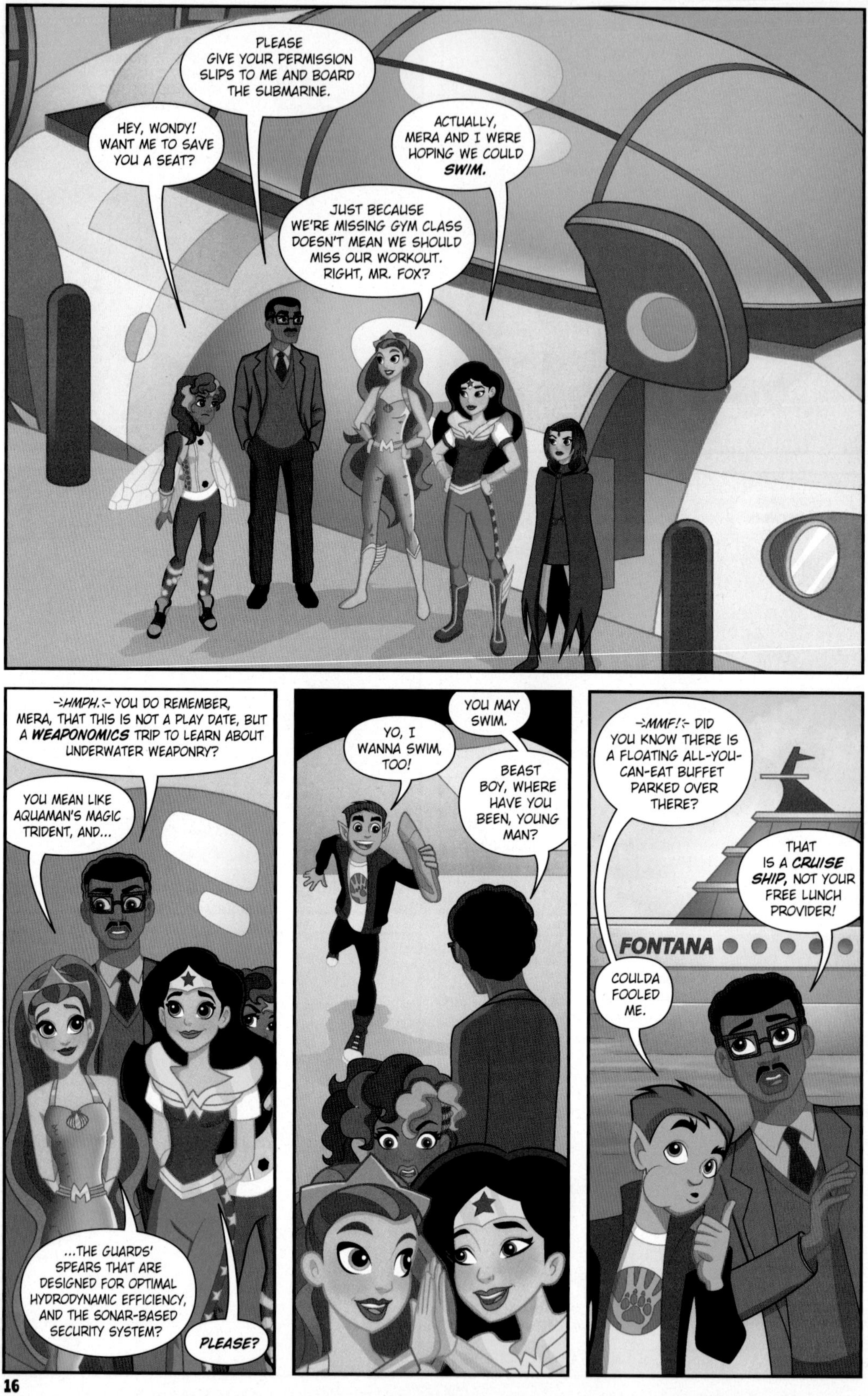
PLEASE GIVE YOUR PERMISSION SLIPS TO ME AND BOARD THE SUBMARINE.
HEY, WONDY! WANT ME TO SAVE YOU A SEAT?
ACTUALLY, MERA AND I WERE HOPING WE COULD SWIM.
JUST BECAUSE WE'RE MISSING GYM CLASS DOESN'T MEAN WE SHOULD MISS OUR WORKOUT. RIGHT, MR. FOX?
HMPH. YOU DO REMEMBER, MERA, THAT THIS IS NOT A PLAY DATE, BUT A WEAPONOMICS TRIP TO LEARN ABOUT UNDERWATER WEAPONRY?
YOU MEAN LIKE AQUAMAN'S MAGIC TRIDENT, AND...
...THE GUARDS' SPEARS THAT ARE DESIGNED FOR OPTIMAL HYDRODYNAMIC EFFICIENCY, AND THE SONAR-BASED SECURITY SYSTEM?
PLEASE?
YOU MAY SWIM.
YO, I WANNA SWIM, TOO!
BEAST BOY, WHERE HAVE YOU BEEN, YOUNG MAN?
MMF! DID YOU KNOW THERE IS A FLOATING ALL-YOU-CAN-EAT BUFFET PARKED OVER THERE?
FONTANA
THAT IS A CRUISE SHIP, NOT YOUR FREE LUNCH PROVIDER!
COULDA FOOLED ME.

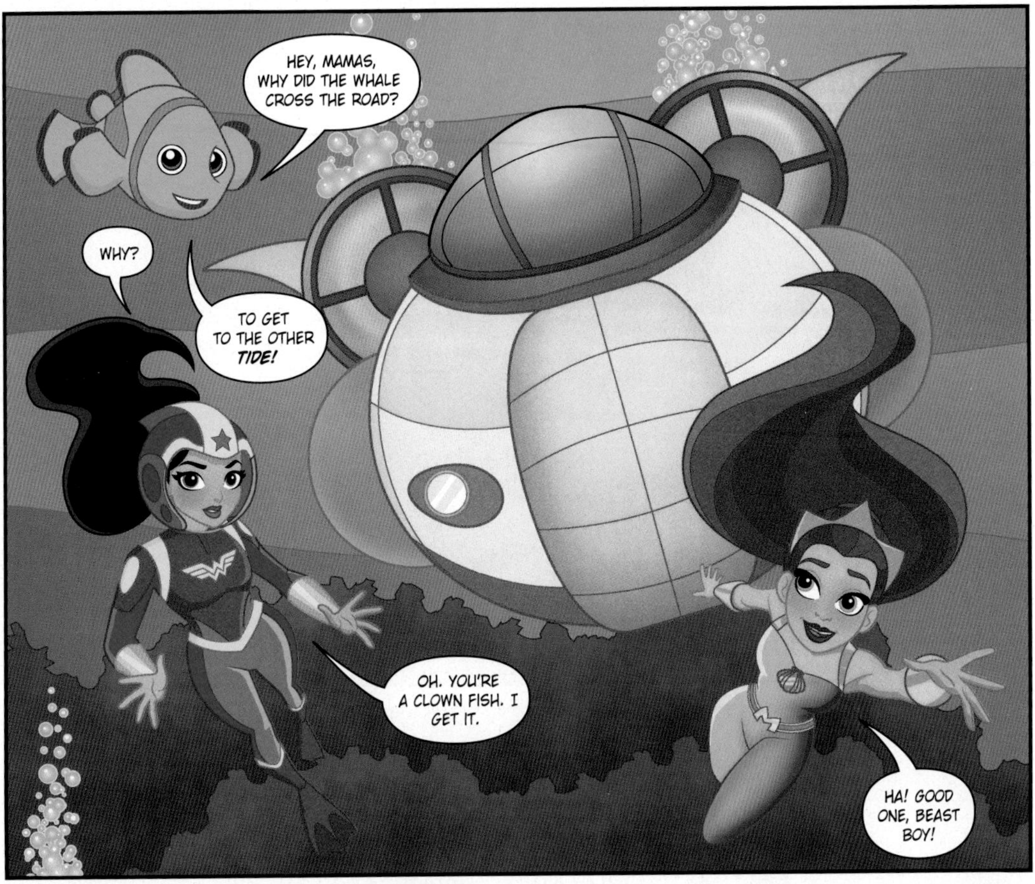
HEY, MAMAS, WHY DID THE WHALE CROSS THE ROAD?
WHY?
TO GET TO THE OTHER *TIDE!*
OH. YOU'RE A CLOWN FISH. I GET IT.
HA! GOOD ONE, BEAST BOY!

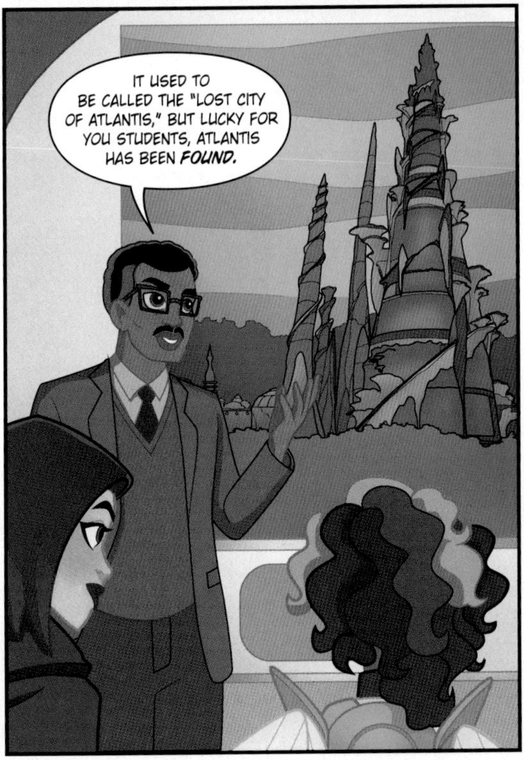
IT USED TO BE CALLED THE "LOST CITY OF ATLANTIS," BUT LUCKY FOR YOU STUDENTS, ATLANTIS HAS BEEN *FOUND.*

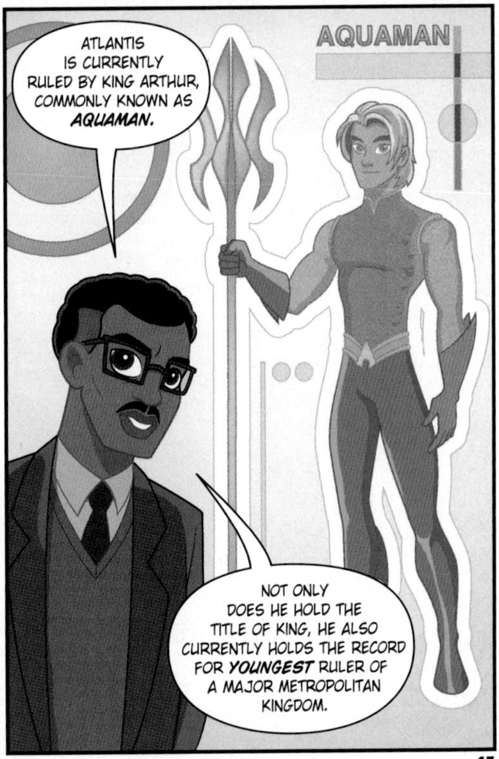
AQUAMAN
ATLANTIS IS CURRENTLY RULED BY KING ARTHUR, COMMONLY KNOWN AS *AQUAMAN.*
NOT ONLY DOES HE HOLD THE TITLE OF KING, HE ALSO CURRENTLY HOLDS THE RECORD FOR *YOUNGEST* RULER OF A MAJOR METROPOLITAN KINGDOM.

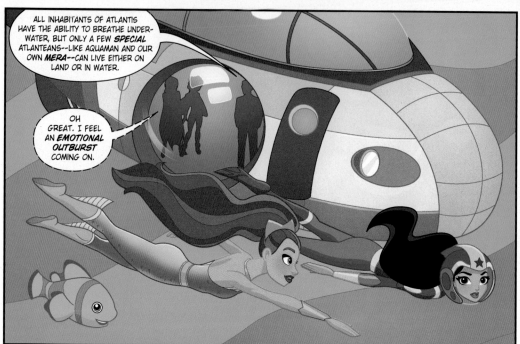

ALL INHABITANTS OF ATLANTIS HAVE THE ABILITY TO BREATHE UNDER-WATER, BUT ONLY A FEW *SPECIAL* ATLANTEANS--LIKE AQUAMAN AND OUR OWN *MERA*--CAN LIVE EITHER ON LAND OR IN WATER.

OH GREAT. I FEEL AN *EMOTIONAL OUTBURST* COMING ON.

EXCUSE ME, BUMBLEBEE, BUT MY EMPATH POWERS CAN'T HANDLE WHAT YOU METROPOLIS KIDS CALL "ALL THE FEELS." SO IF YOU'RE GOING TO *BREAK DOWN*, CAN YOU AIM IT OUT THE WINDOW?

SORRY, RAVEN.

IT'S JUST THAT WONDER WOMAN AND I HAVE BEEN *BEST FRIENDS* EVER SINCE HER FIRST DAY AT SUPER HERO HIGH.

AND *I* HAVEN'T GONE ANYWHERE, BUT SHE'S ALL THE WAY OUT--

CRASH!

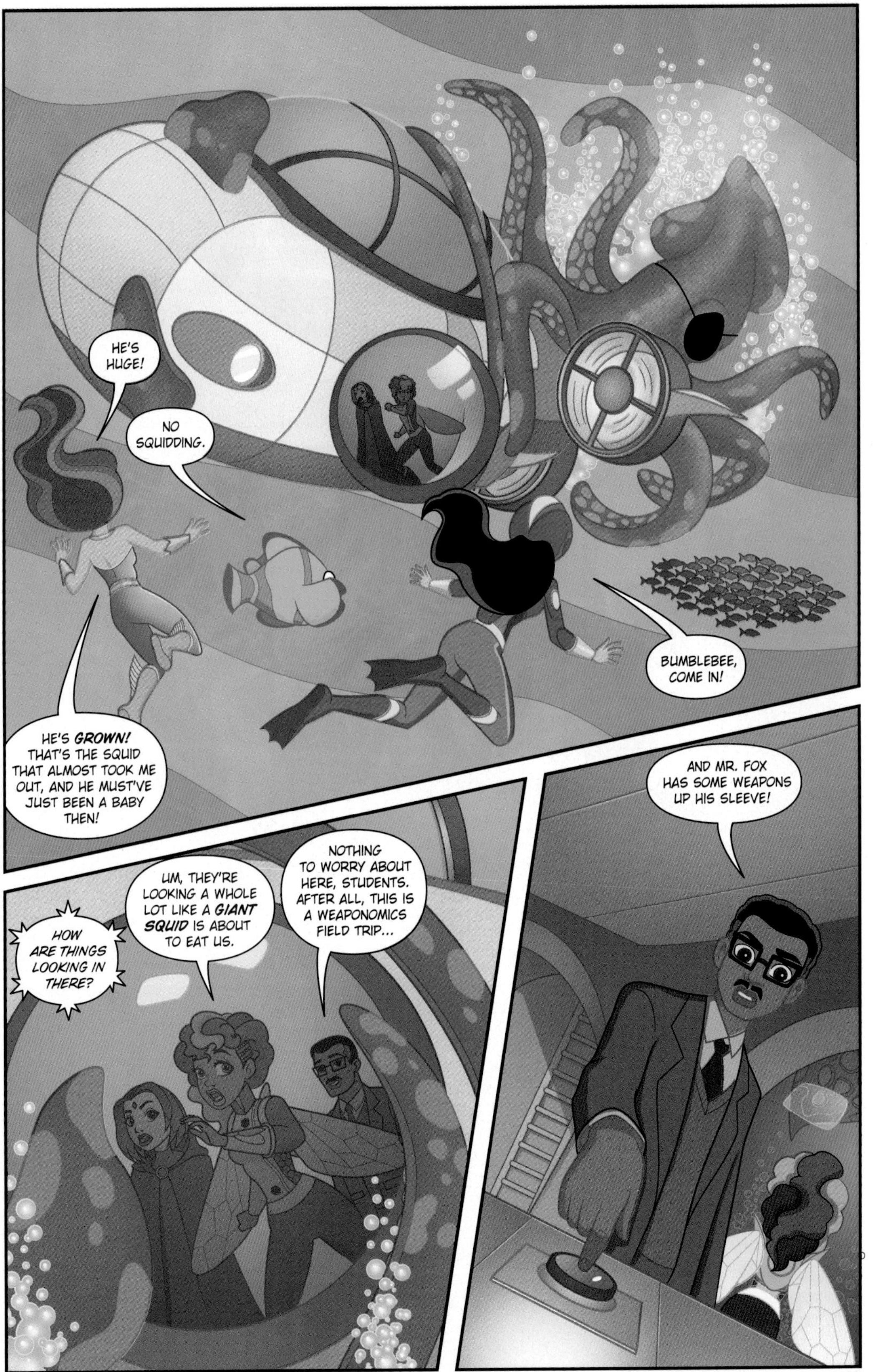
HE'S HUGE!
NO SQUIDDING.
BUMBLEBEE, COME IN!
HE'S GROWN! THAT'S THE SQUID THAT ALMOST TOOK ME OUT, AND HE MUST'VE JUST BEEN A BABY THEN!
HOW ARE THINGS LOOKING IN THERE?
UM, THEY'RE LOOKING A WHOLE LOT LIKE A GIANT SQUID IS ABOUT TO EAT US.
NOTHING TO WORRY ABOUT HERE, STUDENTS. AFTER ALL, THIS IS A WEAPONOMICS FIELD TRIP...
AND MR. FOX HAS SOME WEAPONS UP HIS SLEEVE!

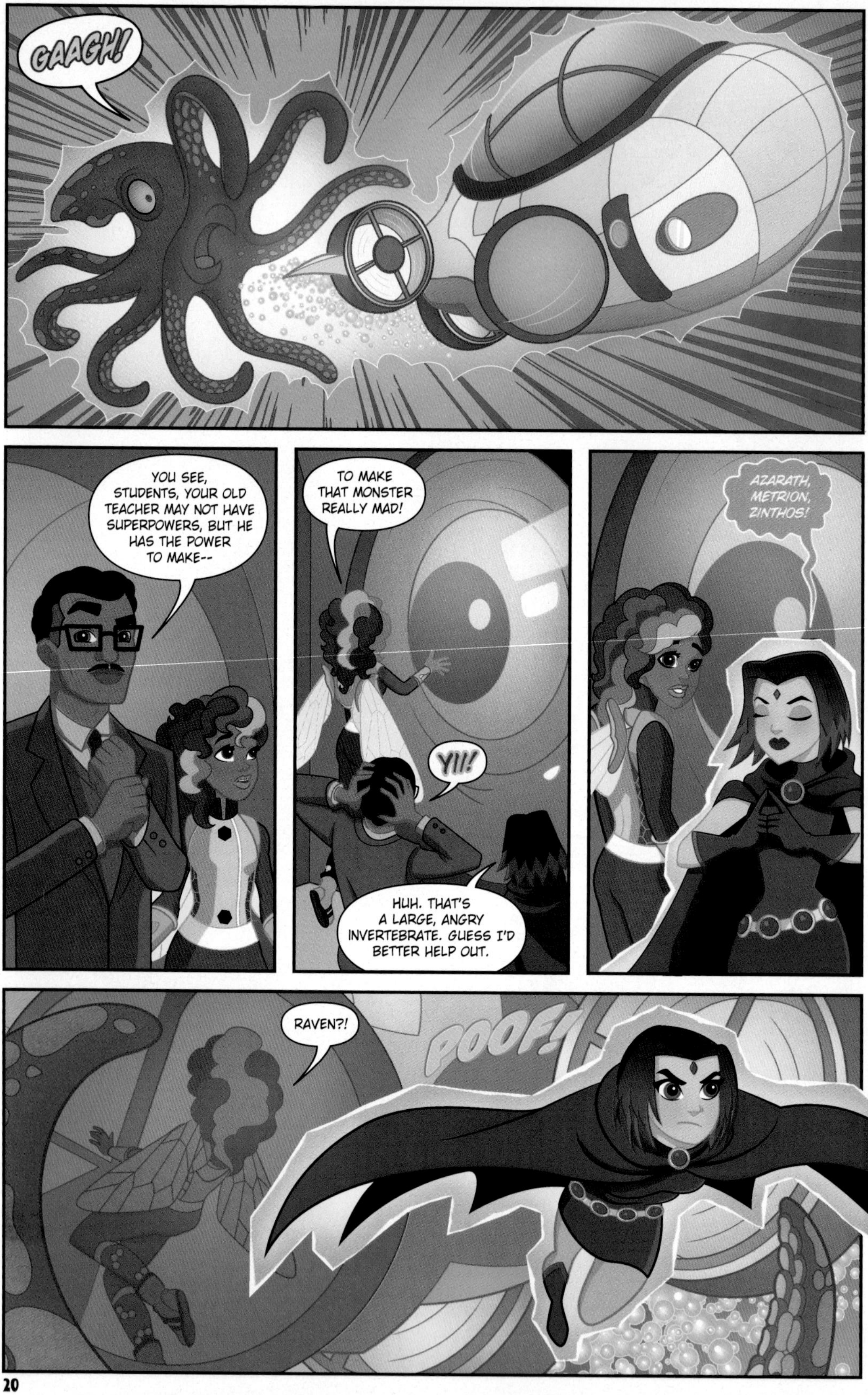
GAAGH!
YOU SEE, STUDENTS, YOUR OLD TEACHER MAY NOT HAVE SUPERPOWERS, BUT HE HAS THE POWER TO MAKE--
TO MAKE THAT MONSTER REALLY MAD!
YII!
HUH. THAT'S A LARGE, ANGRY INVERTEBRATE. GUESS I'D BETTER HELP OUT.
AZARATH, METRION, ZINTHOS!
RAVEN?!
POOF!

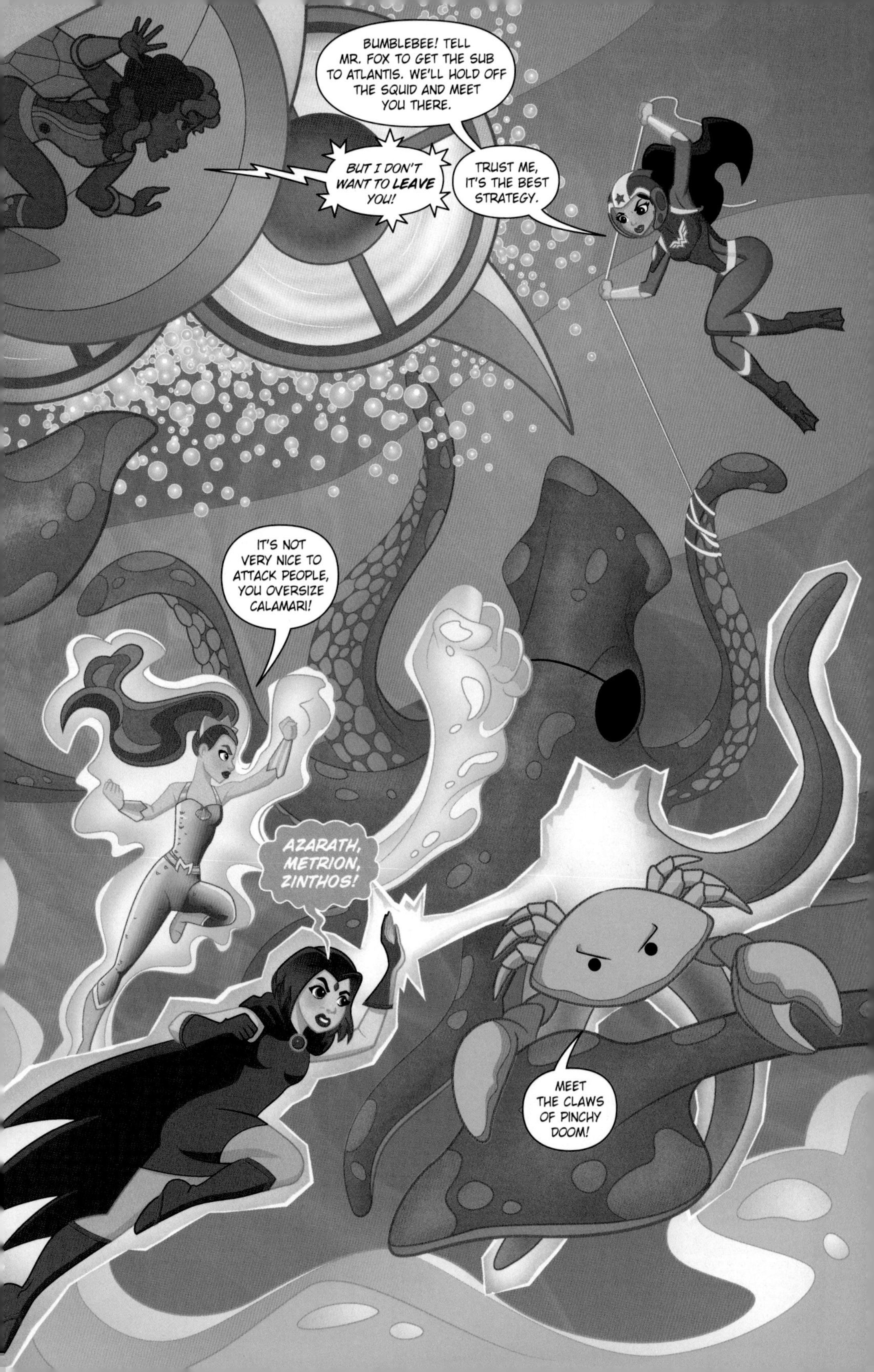
BUMBLEBEE! TELL MR. FOX TO GET THE SUB TO ATLANTIS. WE'LL HOLD OFF THE SQUID AND MEET YOU THERE.
BUT I DON'T WANT TO **LEAVE** YOU!
TRUST ME, IT'S THE BEST STRATEGY.
IT'S NOT VERY NICE TO ATTACK PEOPLE, YOU OVERSIZE CALAMARI!
AZARATH, METRION, ZINTHOS!
MEET THE CLAWS OF PINCHY DOOM!

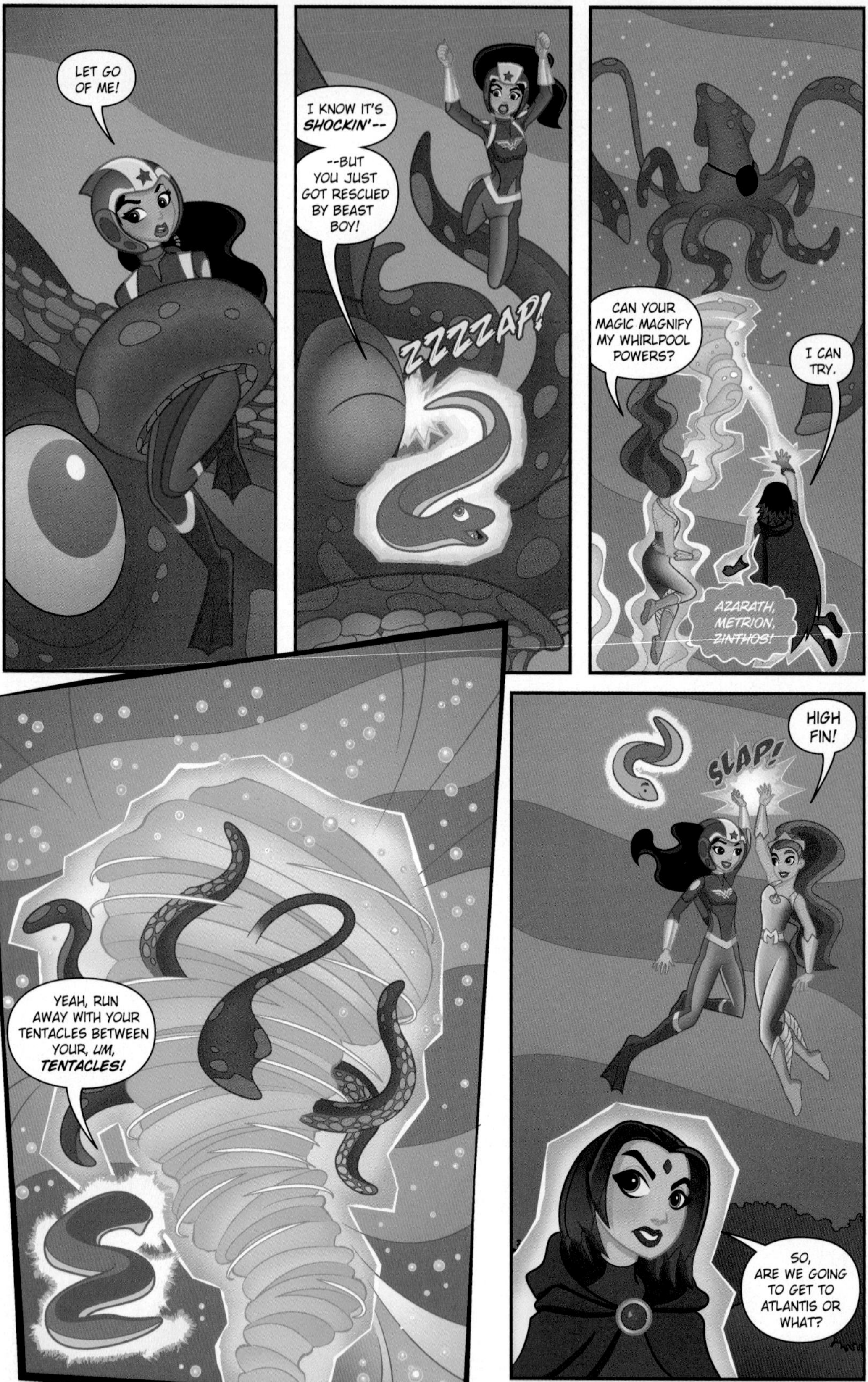
LET GO OF ME!
I KNOW IT'S SHOCKIN'--
--BUT YOU JUST GOT RESCUED BY BEAST BOY!
ZZZZZAP!
CAN YOUR MAGIC MAGNIFY MY WHIRLPOOL POWERS?
I CAN TRY.
AZARATH, METRION, ZINTHOS!
YEAH, RUN AWAY WITH YOUR TENTACLES BETWEEN YOUR, UM, TENTACLES!
HIGH FIN!
SLAP!
SO, ARE WE GOING TO GET TO ATLANTIS OR WHAT?

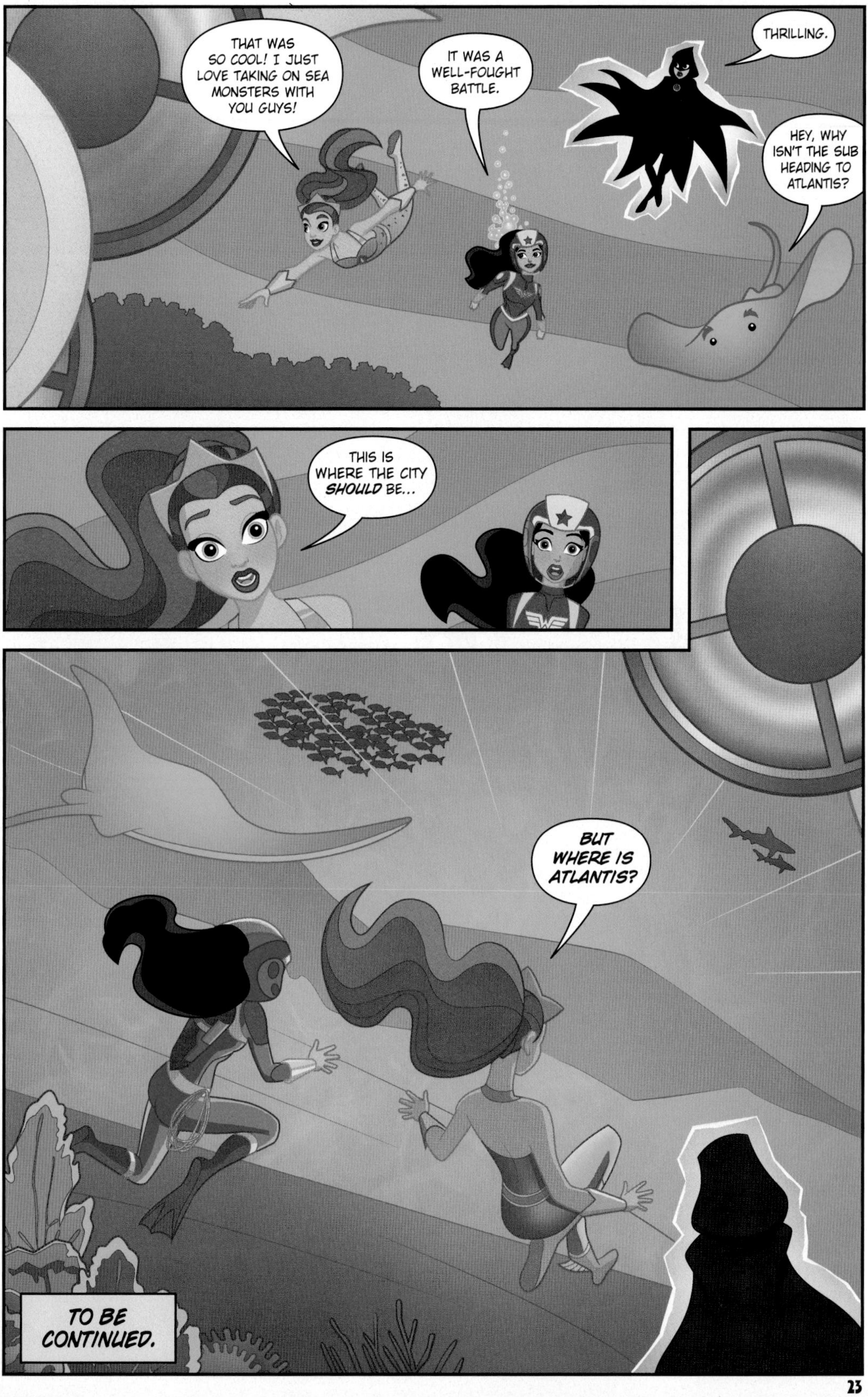
THAT WAS SO COOL! I JUST LOVE TAKING ON SEA MONSTERS WITH YOU GUYS!
IT WAS A WELL-FOUGHT BATTLE.
THRILLING.
HEY, WHY ISN'T THE SUB HEADING TO ATLANTIS?
THIS IS WHERE THE CITY *SHOULD* BE...
BUT WHERE IS ATLANTIS?
TO BE CONTINUED.

CHAPTER TWO
MARTIAN IN THE MIDDLE

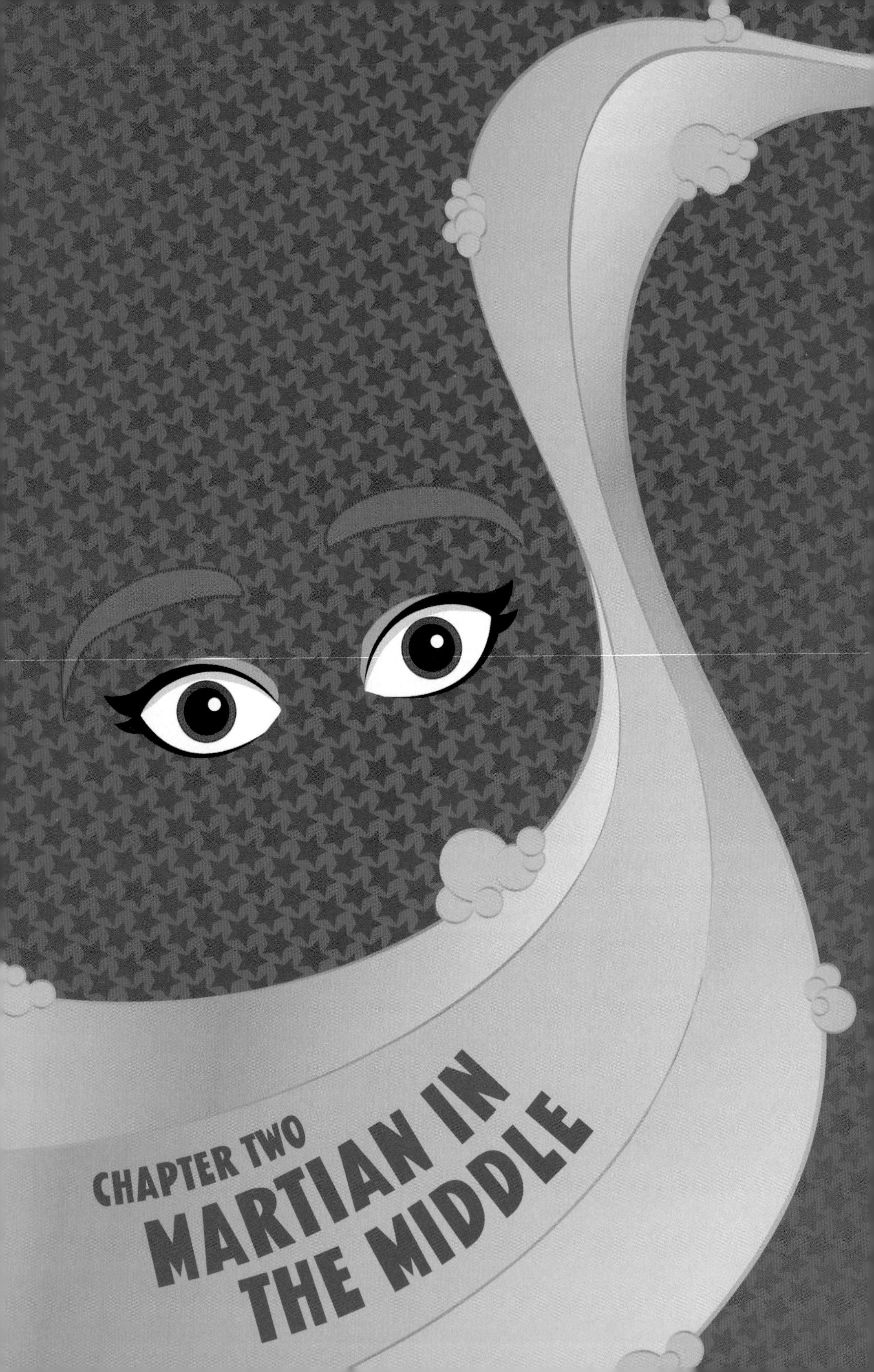

ATLANTIS IS MY HOME! HOW CAN IT JUST **DISAPPEAR?**

THIS **TASK FORCE** IS WORKING ON IT, MERA. AND I THINK I'VE UNCOVERED SOMETHING SIGNIFICANT.

SATELLITE FOOTAGE FROM TWO DAYS AGO. ALL SHIPS ENTERING THE WATER WERE ACCOUNTED FOR BY THE COAST GUARD **EXCEPT** THIS ONE.

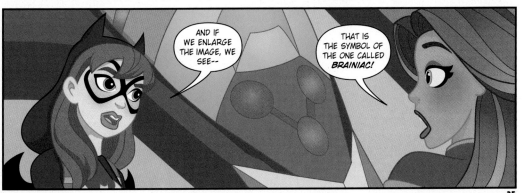

AND IF WE ENLARGE THE IMAGE, WE SEE--

THAT IS THE SYMBOL OF THE ONE CALLED **BRAINIAC!**

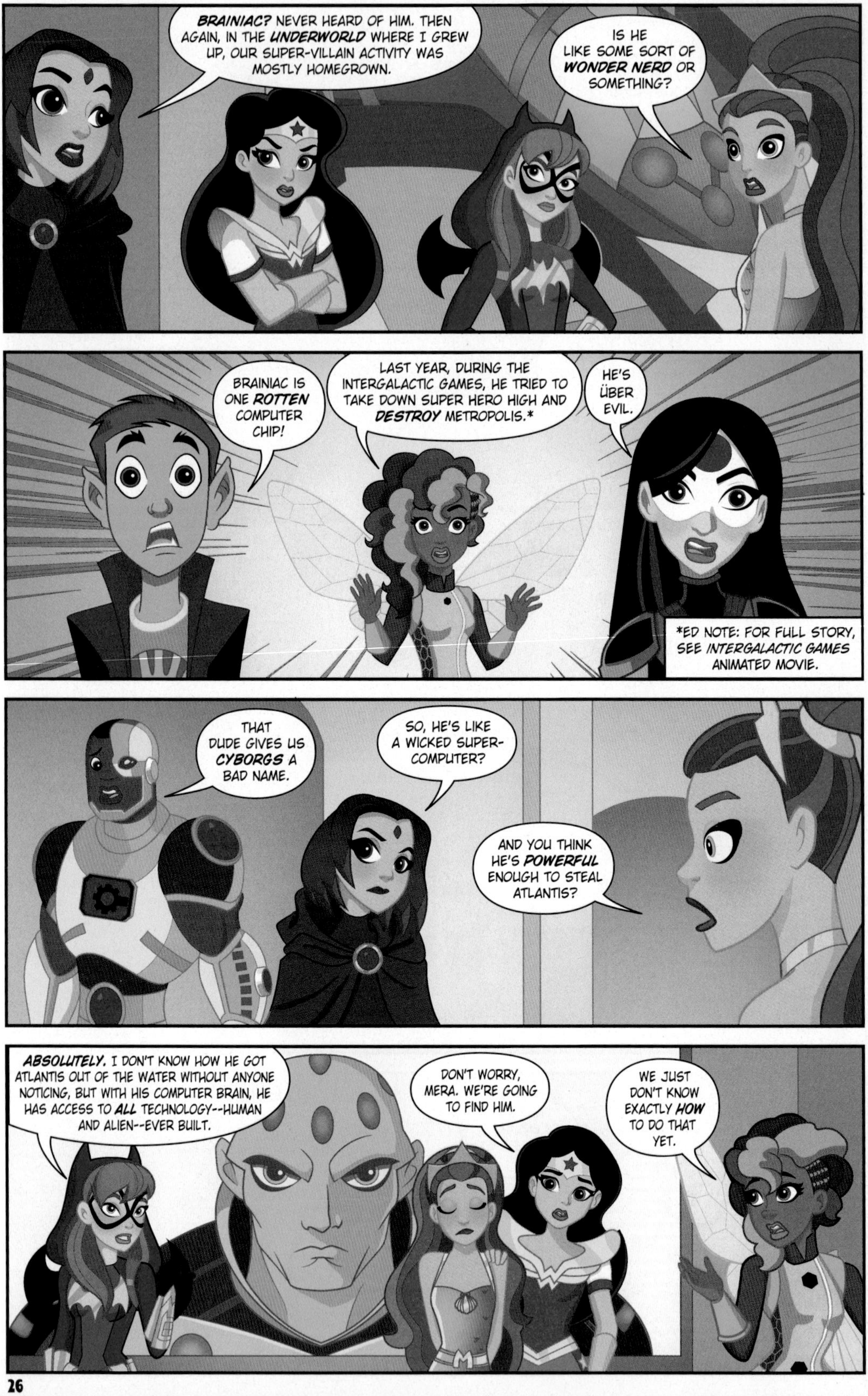

BRAINIAC? NEVER HEARD OF HIM. THEN AGAIN, IN THE UNDERWORLD WHERE I GREW UP, OUR SUPER-VILLAIN ACTIVITY WAS MOSTLY HOMEGROWN.
IS HE LIKE SOME SORT OF WONDER NERD OR SOMETHING?
BRAINIAC IS ONE ROTTEN COMPUTER CHIP!
LAST YEAR, DURING THE INTERGALACTIC GAMES, HE TRIED TO TAKE DOWN SUPER HERO HIGH AND DESTROY METROPOLIS.*
HE'S ÜBER EVIL.
*ED NOTE: FOR FULL STORY, SEE INTERGALACTIC GAMES ANIMATED MOVIE.
THAT DUDE GIVES US CYBORGS A BAD NAME.
SO, HE'S LIKE A WICKED SUPER-COMPUTER?
AND YOU THINK HE'S POWERFUL ENOUGH TO STEAL ATLANTIS?
ABSOLUTELY. I DON'T KNOW HOW HE GOT ATLANTIS OUT OF THE WATER WITHOUT ANYONE NOTICING, BUT WITH HIS COMPUTER BRAIN, HE HAS ACCESS TO ALL TECHNOLOGY--HUMAN AND ALIEN--EVER BUILT.
DON'T WORRY, MERA. WE'RE GOING TO FIND HIM.
WE JUST DON'T KNOW EXACTLY HOW TO DO THAT YET.

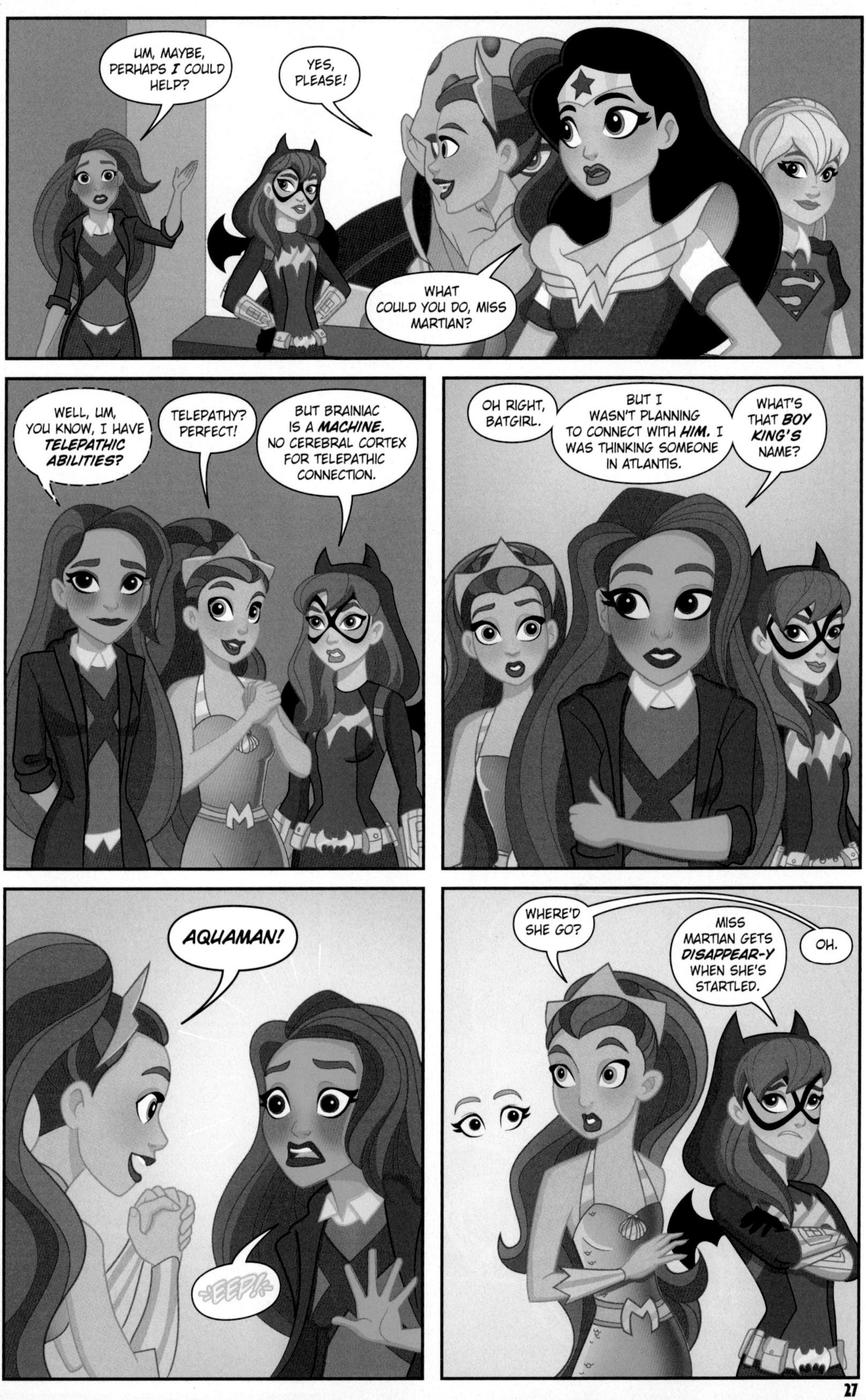
UM, MAYBE, PERHAPS I COULD HELP?
YES, PLEASE!
WHAT COULD YOU DO, MISS MARTIAN?
WELL, UM, YOU KNOW, I HAVE TELEPATHIC ABILITIES?
TELEPATHY? PERFECT!
BUT BRAINIAC IS A MACHINE. NO CEREBRAL CORTEX FOR TELEPATHIC CONNECTION.
OH RIGHT, BATGIRL.
BUT I WASN'T PLANNING TO CONNECT WITH HIM. I WAS THINKING SOMEONE IN ATLANTIS.
WHAT'S THAT BOY KING'S NAME?
AQUAMAN!
EEP!
WHERE'D SHE GO?
MISS MARTIAN GETS DISAPPEAR-Y WHEN SHE'S STARTLED.
OH.

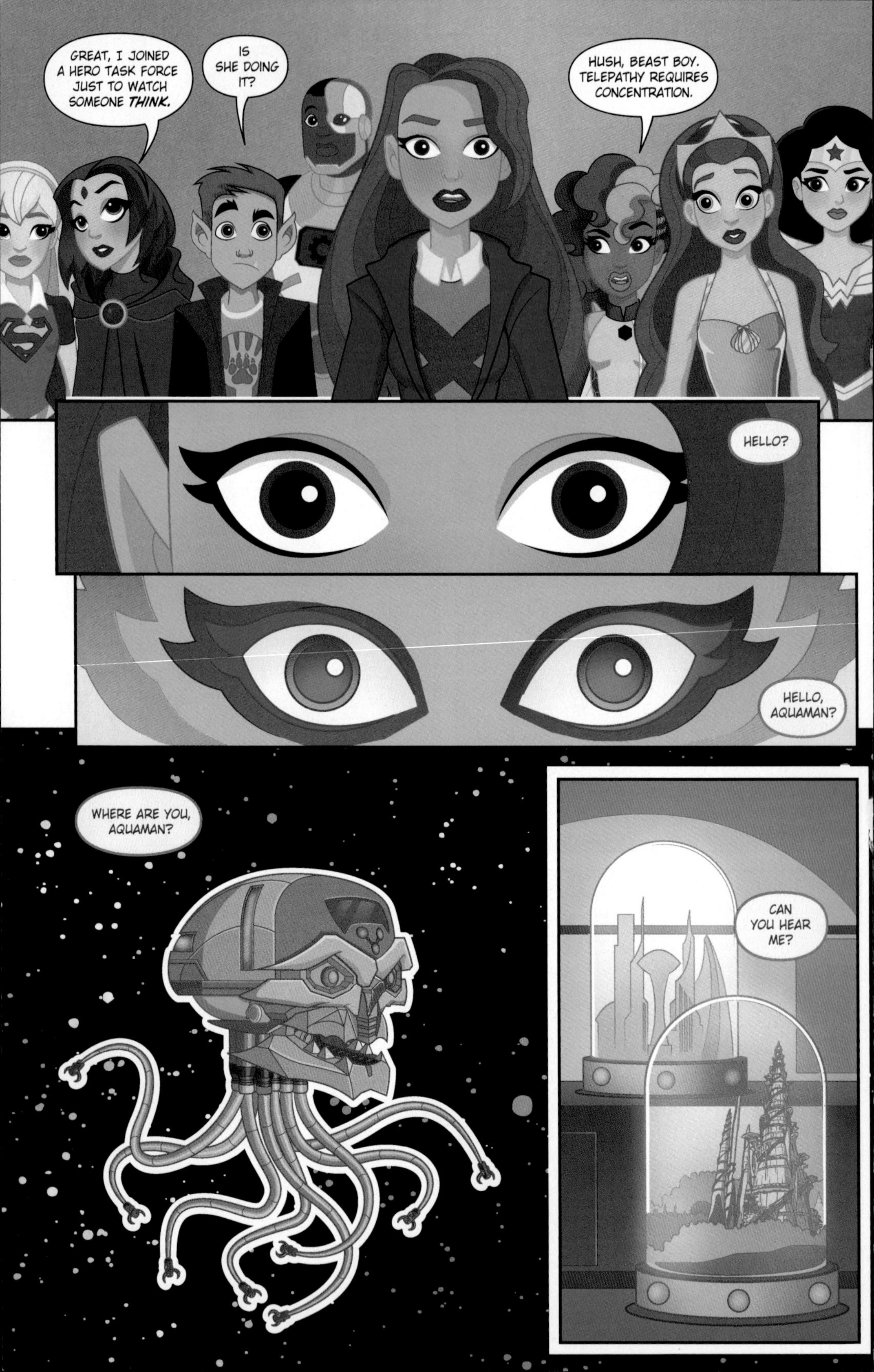
GREAT, I JOINED A HERO TASK FORCE JUST TO WATCH SOMEONE **THINK.**
IS SHE DOING IT?
HUSH, BEAST BOY. TELEPATHY REQUIRES CONCENTRATION.
HELLO?
HELLO, AQUAMAN?
WHERE ARE YOU, AQUAMAN?
CAN YOU HEAR ME?

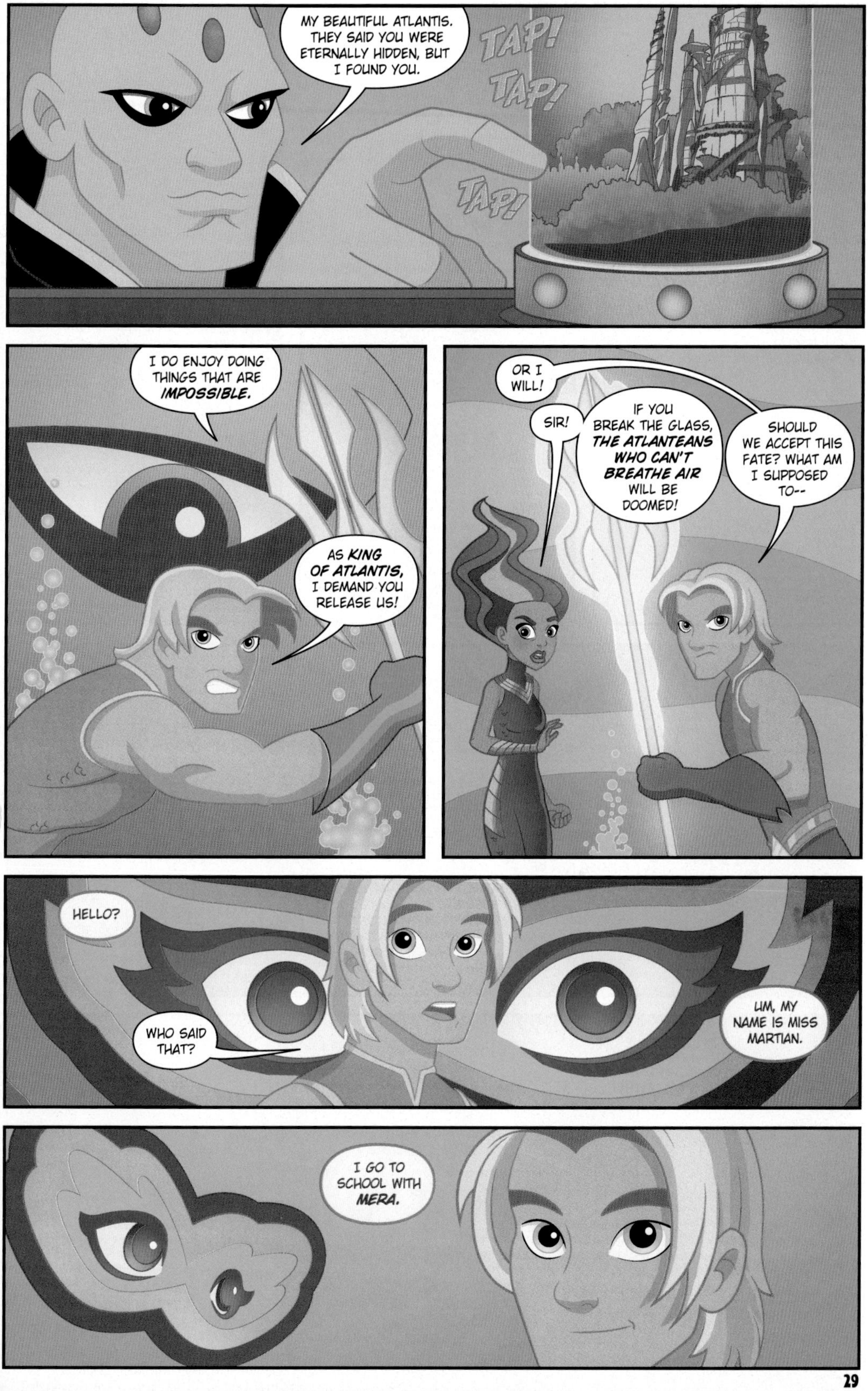
MY BEAUTIFUL ATLANTIS. THEY SAID YOU WERE ETERNALLY HIDDEN, BUT I FOUND YOU.
TAP! TAP! TAP!
I DO ENJOY DOING THINGS THAT ARE ***IMPOSSIBLE.***
AS ***KING OF ATLANTIS,*** I DEMAND YOU RELEASE US!
OR I WILL!
SIR!
IF YOU BREAK THE GLASS, ***THE ATLANTEANS WHO CAN'T BREATHE AIR*** WILL BE DOOMED!
SHOULD WE ACCEPT THIS FATE? WHAT AM I SUPPOSED TO--
HELLO?
WHO SAID THAT?
UM, MY NAME IS MISS MARTIAN.
I GO TO SCHOOL WITH ***MERA.***

KING ARTHUR, WHAT IS IT?

I HEAR ONE OF MERA'S FRIENDS. SHE'S TELEPATHIC.

WE'RE GOING TO HELP YOU. WHAT HAPPENED?

BRAINIAC HAD A SHRINK RAY--HE SHRUNK US, SHRUNK THE WHOLE CITY! HE HAS A COLLECTION OF CITIES IN BOTTLES.

MAY I SEE THROUGH YOUR EYES?

IF THAT WILL HELP, OKAY.

DOOP. DOOP.

INCOMING CALL: AR RO

AH, MY OLD TRADING COHORT.

BLIP. BLOP!!

KANJAR RO, IT HAS BEEN SOME TIME SINCE YOU LAST ACQUIRED SOMETHING GOOD ENOUGH FOR ME TO PURCHASE.

WELL, MY FRIEND, I THINK YOU WILL FIND THAT CHANGED! I HAVE BEEN SCOURING THE GALAXIES FOR TRINKETS THAT WOULD INTEREST A DISCERNING GENTLEMAN SUCH AS YOURSELF.

WHAT HAVE YOU FOUND?

AH, YOU KNOW AS WELL AS I THAT ONE SHOULD NOT SAY SUCH THINGS OVER GALACTIC TRANSMISSION!

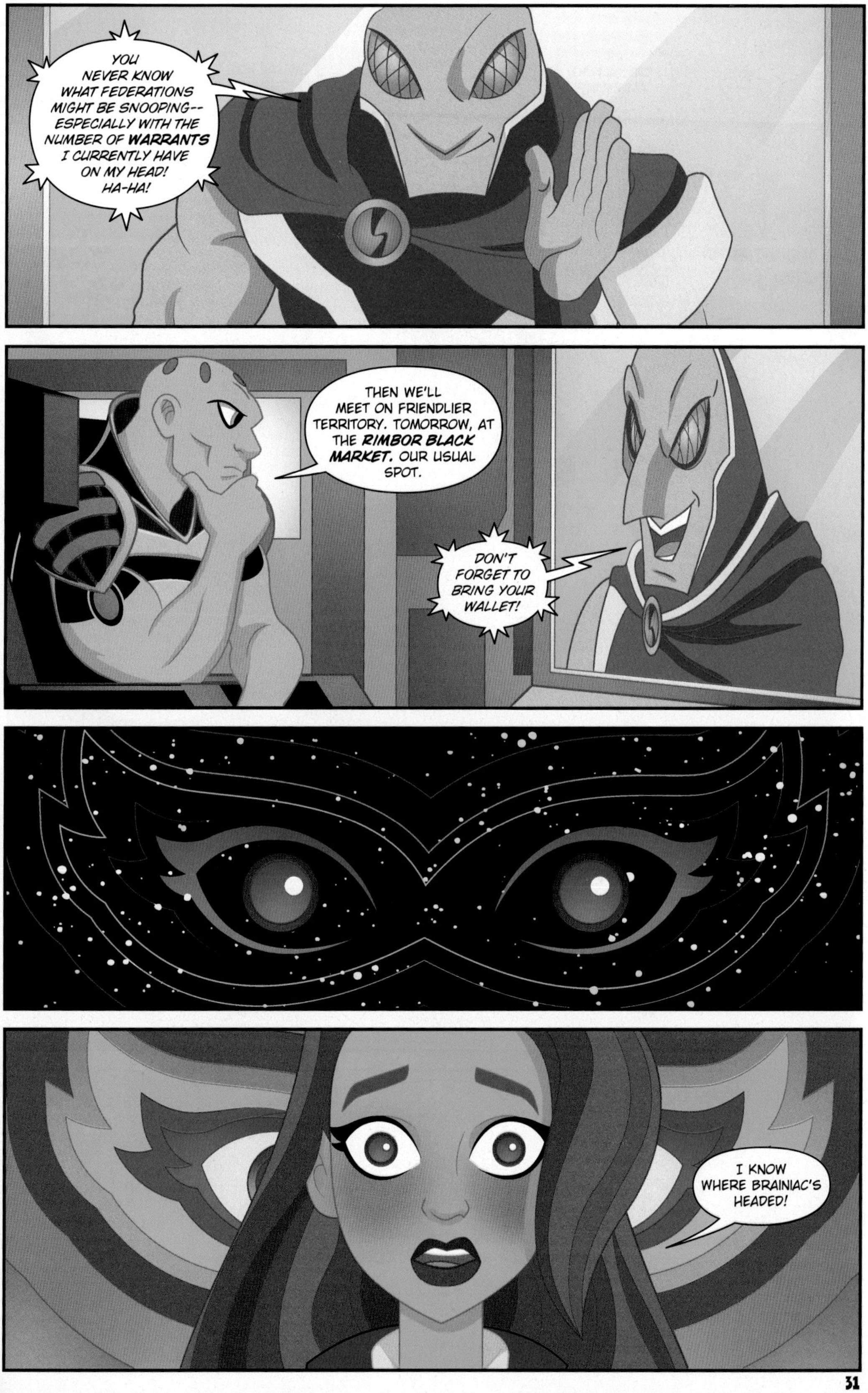
YOU NEVER KNOW WHAT FEDERATIONS MIGHT BE SNOOPING-- ESPECIALLY WITH THE NUMBER OF WARRANTS I CURRENTLY HAVE ON MY HEAD! HA-HA!
THEN WE'LL MEET ON FRIENDLIER TERRITORY. TOMORROW, AT THE RIMBOR BLACK MARKET. OUR USUAL SPOT.
DON'T FORGET TO BRING YOUR WALLET!
I KNOW WHERE BRAINIAC'S HEADED!

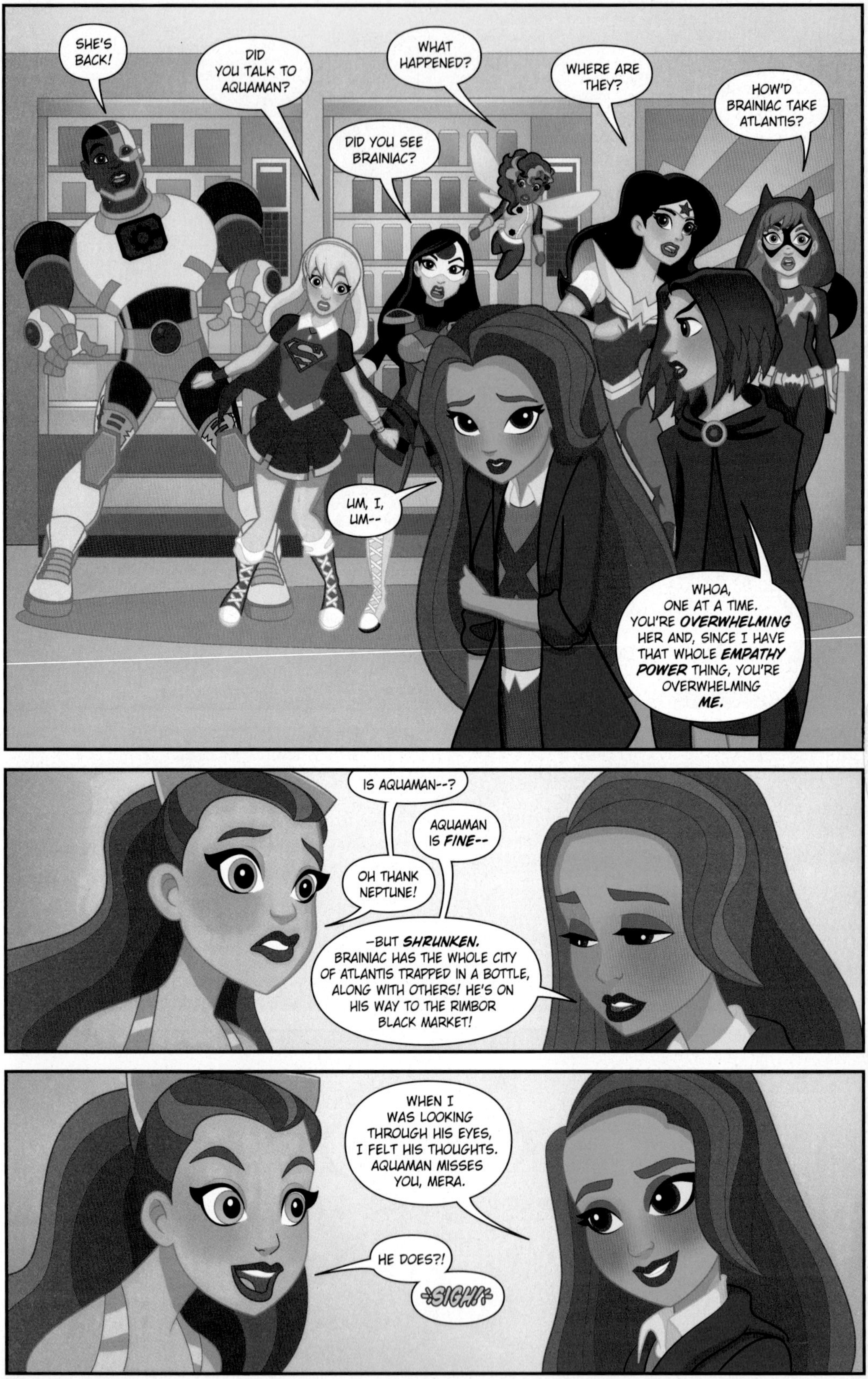
SHE'S BACK!
DID YOU TALK TO AQUAMAN?
WHAT HAPPENED?
DID YOU SEE BRAINIAC?
WHERE ARE THEY?
HOW'D BRAINIAC TAKE ATLANTIS?
UM, I, UM--
WHOA, ONE AT A TIME. YOU'RE **OVERWHELMING** HER AND, SINCE I HAVE THAT WHOLE **EMPATHY POWER** THING, YOU'RE OVERWHELMING **ME.**
IS AQUAMAN--?
AQUAMAN IS **FINE--**
OH THANK NEPTUNE!
--BUT **SHRUNKEN.** BRAINIAC HAS THE WHOLE CITY OF ATLANTIS TRAPPED IN A BOTTLE, ALONG WITH OTHERS! HE'S ON HIS WAY TO THE RIMBOR BLACK MARKET!
WHEN I WAS LOOKING THROUGH HIS EYES, I FELT HIS THOUGHTS. AQUAMAN MISSES YOU, MERA.
HE DOES?!
SIGH!

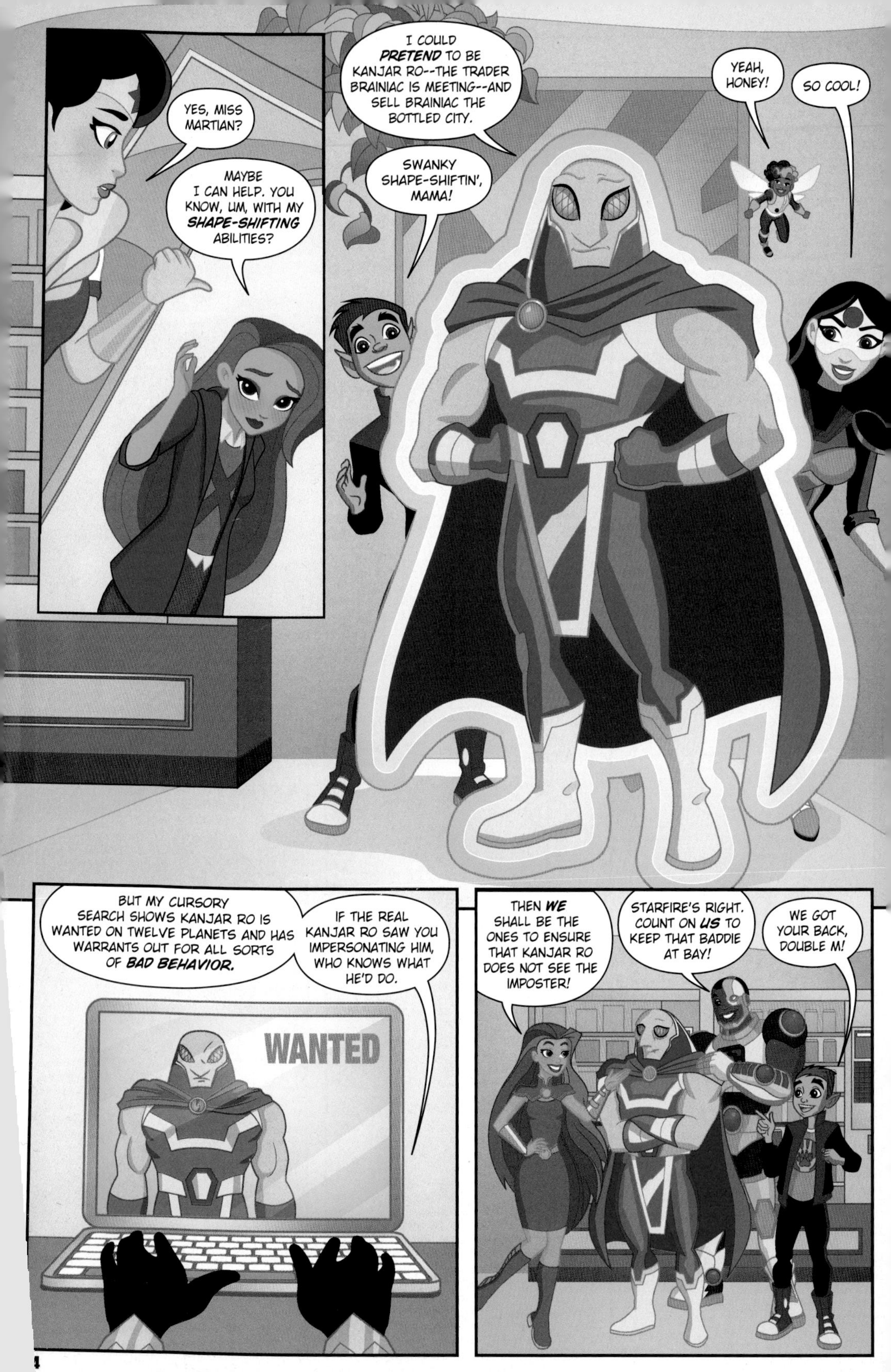
YES, MISS MARTIAN?
MAYBE I CAN HELP. YOU KNOW, UM, WITH MY SHAPE-SHIFTING ABILITIES?
I COULD PRETEND TO BE KANJAR RO--THE TRADER BRAINIAC IS MEETING--AND SELL BRAINIAC THE BOTTLED CITY.
SWANKY SHAPE-SHIFTIN', MAMA!
YEAH, HONEY!
SO COOL!
BUT MY CURSORY SEARCH SHOWS KANJAR RO IS WANTED ON TWELVE PLANETS AND HAS WARRANTS OUT FOR ALL SORTS OF BAD BEHAVIOR.
IF THE REAL KANJAR RO SAW YOU IMPERSONATING HIM, WHO KNOWS WHAT HE'D DO.
WANTED
THEN WE SHALL BE THE ONES TO ENSURE THAT KANJAR RO DOES NOT SEE THE IMPOSTER!
STARFIRE'S RIGHT. COUNT ON US TO KEEP THAT BADDIE AT BAY!
WE GOT YOUR BACK, DOUBLE M!

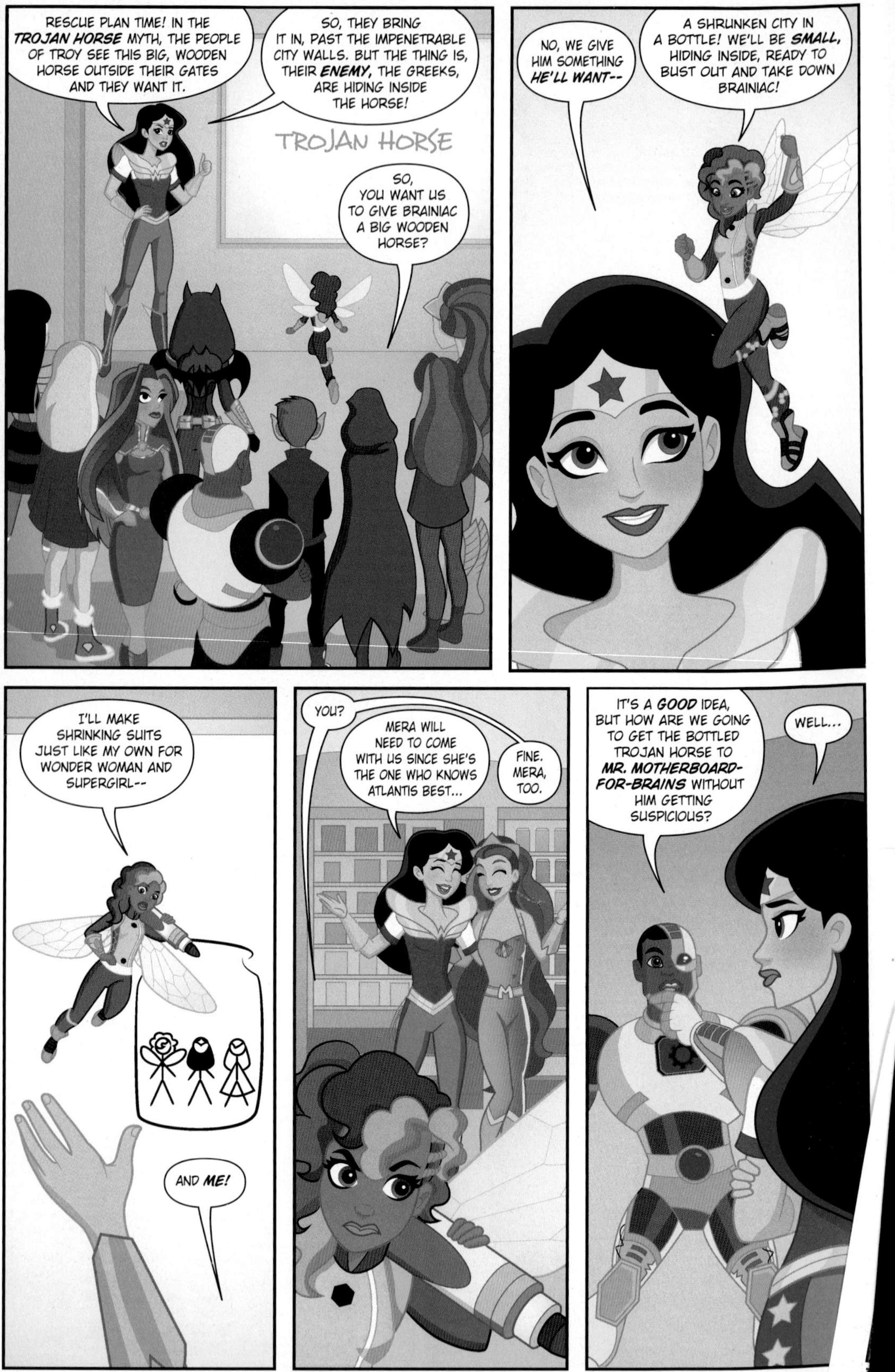
RESCUE PLAN TIME! IN THE TROJAN HORSE MYTH, THE PEOPLE OF TROY SEE THIS BIG, WOODEN HORSE OUTSIDE THEIR GATES AND THEY WANT IT.
SO, THEY BRING IT IN, PAST THE IMPENETRABLE CITY WALLS. BUT THE THING IS, THEIR ENEMY, THE GREEKS, ARE HIDING INSIDE THE HORSE!
TROJAN HORSE
SO, YOU WANT US TO GIVE BRAINIAC A BIG WOODEN HORSE?
NO, WE GIVE HIM SOMETHING HE'LL WANT--
A SHRUNKEN CITY IN A BOTTLE! WE'LL BE SMALL, HIDING INSIDE, READY TO BUST OUT AND TAKE DOWN BRAINIAC!
I'LL MAKE SHRINKING SUITS JUST LIKE MY OWN FOR WONDER WOMAN AND SUPERGIRL--
AND ME!
MERA WILL NEED TO COME WITH US SINCE SHE'S THE ONE WHO KNOWS ATLANTIS BEST...
YOU?
FINE. MERA, TOO.
IT'S A GOOD IDEA, BUT HOW ARE WE GOING TO GET THE BOTTLED TROJAN HORSE TO MR. MOTHERBOARD-FOR-BRAINS WITHOUT HIM GETTING SUSPICIOUS?
WELL...

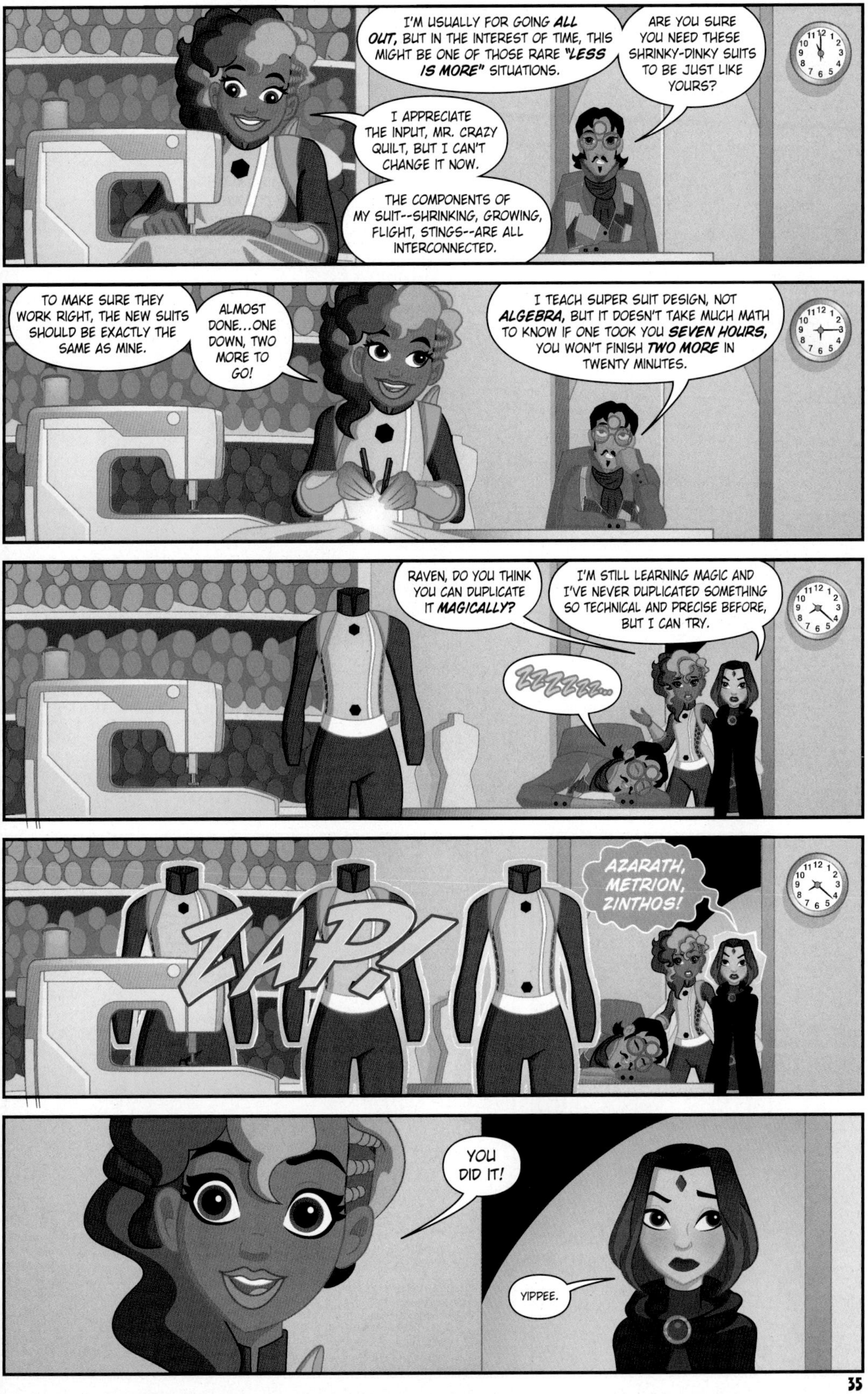
I'M USUALLY FOR GOING ALL OUT, BUT IN THE INTEREST OF TIME, THIS MIGHT BE ONE OF THOSE RARE "LESS IS MORE" SITUATIONS.
ARE YOU SURE YOU NEED THESE SHRINKY-DINKY SUITS TO BE JUST LIKE YOURS?
I APPRECIATE THE INPUT, MR. CRAZY QUILT, BUT I CAN'T CHANGE IT NOW.
THE COMPONENTS OF MY SUIT--SHRINKING, GROWING, FLIGHT, STINGS--ARE ALL INTERCONNECTED.
TO MAKE SURE THEY WORK RIGHT, THE NEW SUITS SHOULD BE EXACTLY THE SAME AS MINE.
ALMOST DONE...ONE DOWN, TWO MORE TO GO!
I TEACH SUPER SUIT DESIGN, NOT ALGEBRA, BUT IT DOESN'T TAKE MUCH MATH TO KNOW IF ONE TOOK YOU SEVEN HOURS, YOU WON'T FINISH TWO MORE IN TWENTY MINUTES.
RAVEN, DO YOU THINK YOU CAN DUPLICATE IT MAGICALLY?
I'M STILL LEARNING MAGIC AND I'VE NEVER DUPLICATED SOMETHING SO TECHNICAL AND PRECISE BEFORE, BUT I CAN TRY.
ZZZZZZ...
AZARATH, METRION, ZINTHOS!
ZAP!
YOU DID IT!
YIPPEE.

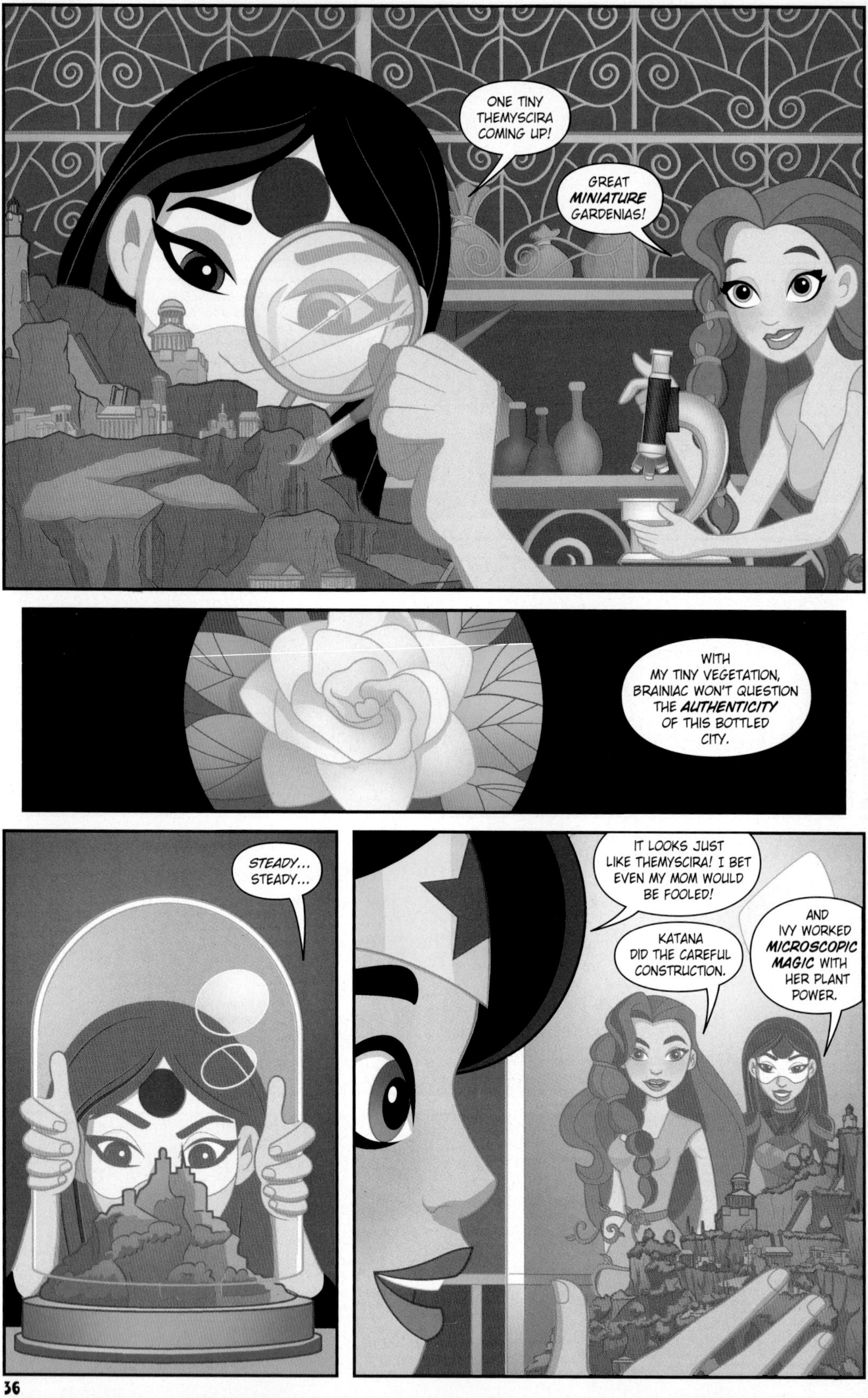
ONE TINY THEMYSCIRA COMING UP!
GREAT *MINIATURE* GARDENIAS!
WITH MY TINY VEGETATION, BRAINIAC WON'T QUESTION THE *AUTHENTICITY* OF THIS BOTTLED CITY.
STEADY... STEADY...
IT LOOKS JUST LIKE THEMYSCIRA! I BET EVEN MY MOM WOULD BE FOOLED!
KATANA DID THE CAREFUL CONSTRUCTION.
AND IVY WORKED *MICROSCOPIC MAGIC* WITH HER PLANT POWER.

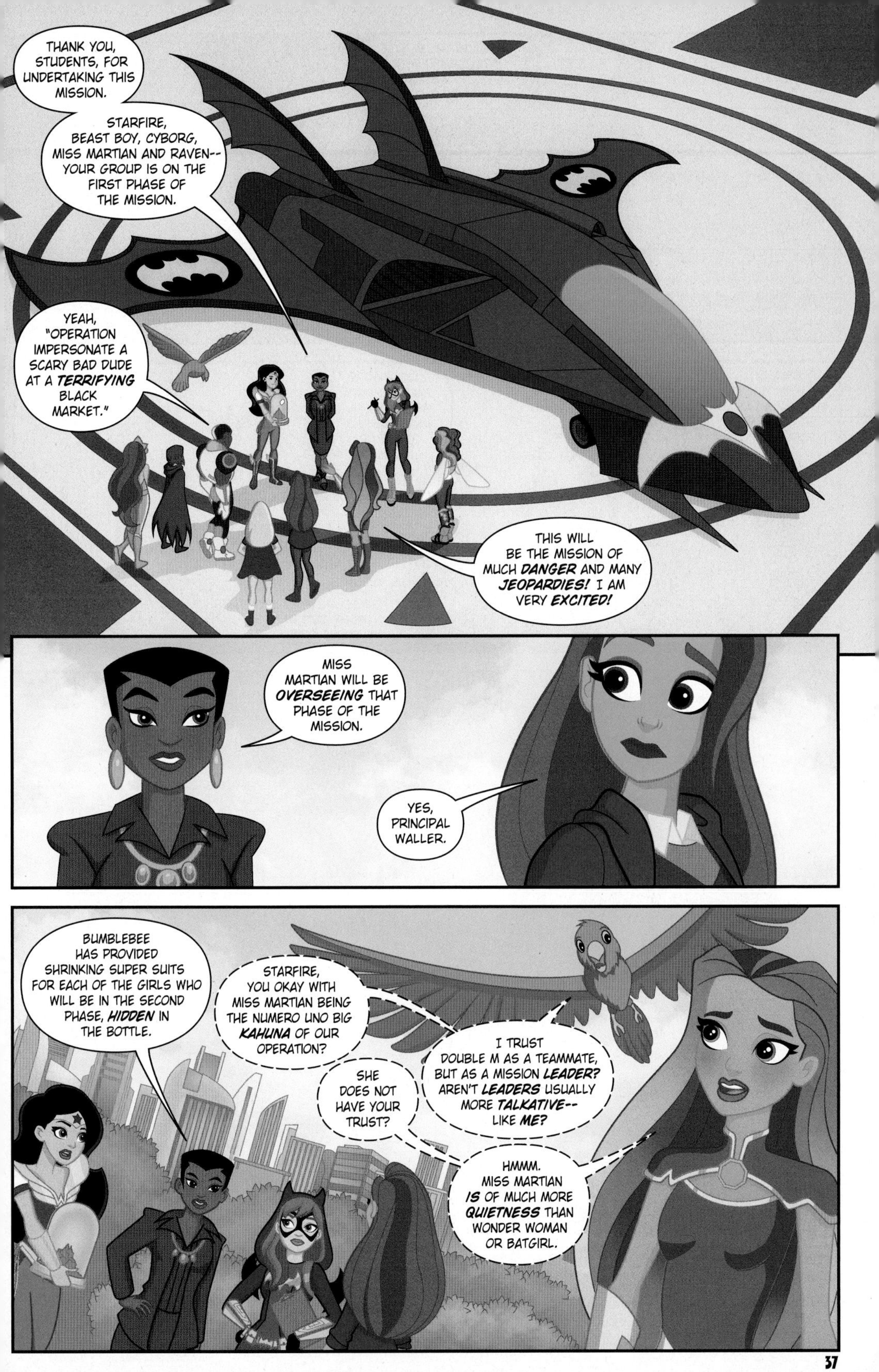
THANK YOU, STUDENTS, FOR UNDERTAKING THIS MISSION.
STARFIRE, BEAST BOY, CYBORG, MISS MARTIAN AND RAVEN-- YOUR GROUP IS ON THE FIRST PHASE OF THE MISSION.
YEAH, "OPERATION IMPERSONATE A SCARY BAD DUDE AT A TERRIFYING BLACK MARKET."
THIS WILL BE THE MISSION OF MUCH DANGER AND MANY JEOPARDIES! I AM VERY EXCITED!
MISS MARTIAN WILL BE OVERSEEING THAT PHASE OF THE MISSION.
YES, PRINCIPAL WALLER.
BUMBLEBEE HAS PROVIDED SHRINKING SUPER SUITS FOR EACH OF THE GIRLS WHO WILL BE IN THE SECOND PHASE, HIDDEN IN THE BOTTLE.
STARFIRE, YOU OKAY WITH MISS MARTIAN BEING THE NUMERO UNO BIG KAHUNA OF OUR OPERATION?
I TRUST DOUBLE M AS A TEAMMATE, BUT AS A MISSION LEADER? AREN'T LEADERS USUALLY MORE TALKATIVE-- LIKE ME?
SHE DOES NOT HAVE YOUR TRUST?
HMMM. MISS MARTIAN IS OF MUCH MORE QUIETNESS THAN WONDER WOMAN OR BATGIRL.

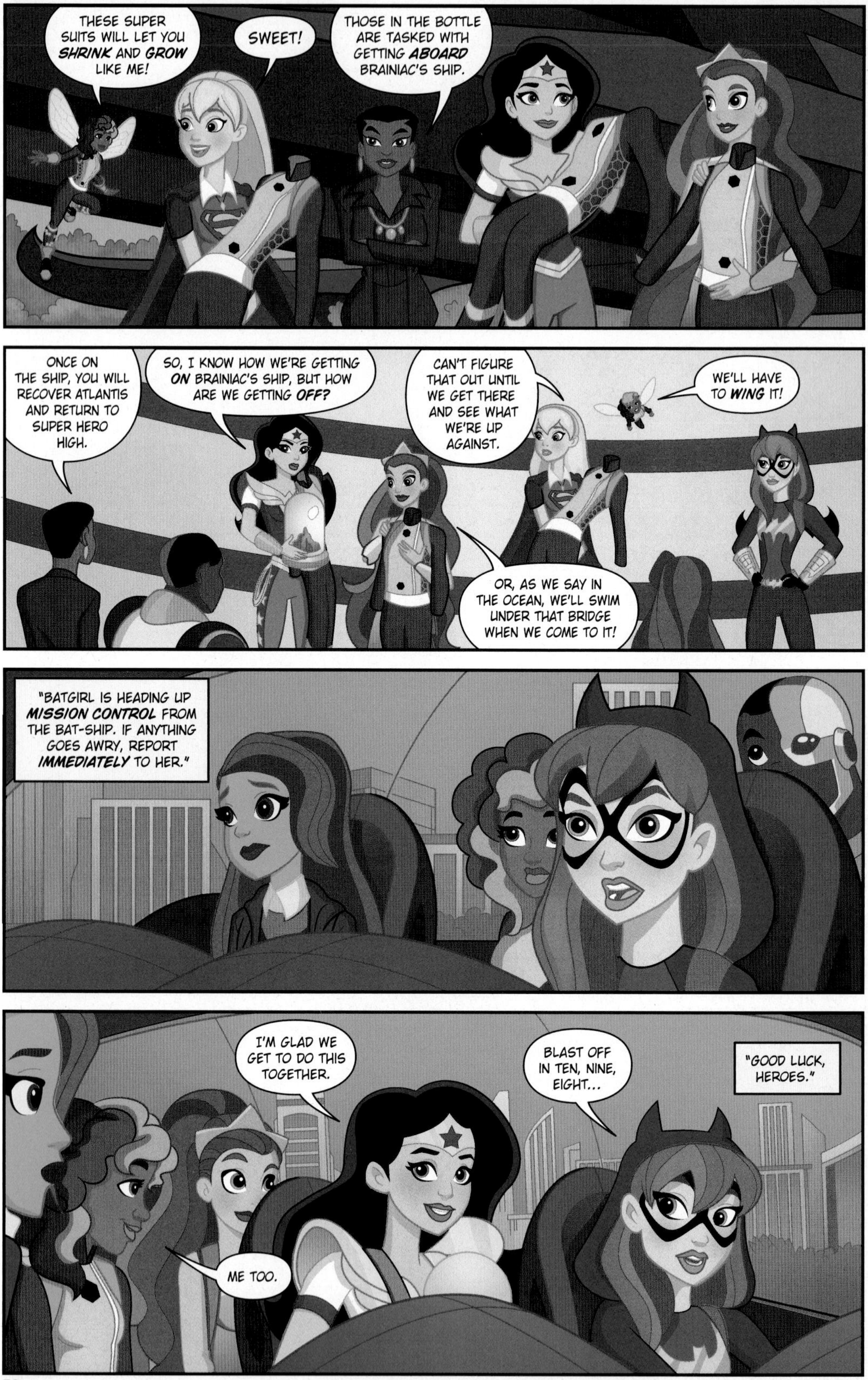
THESE SUPER SUITS WILL LET YOU SHRINK AND GROW LIKE ME!
SWEET!
THOSE IN THE BOTTLE ARE TASKED WITH GETTING ABOARD BRAINIAC'S SHIP.
ONCE ON THE SHIP, YOU WILL RECOVER ATLANTIS AND RETURN TO SUPER HERO HIGH.
SO, I KNOW HOW WE'RE GETTING ON BRAINIAC'S SHIP, BUT HOW ARE WE GETTING OFF?
CAN'T FIGURE THAT OUT UNTIL WE GET THERE AND SEE WHAT WE'RE UP AGAINST.
WE'LL HAVE TO WING IT!
OR, AS WE SAY IN THE OCEAN, WE'LL SWIM UNDER THAT BRIDGE WHEN WE COME TO IT!
"BATGIRL IS HEADING UP MISSION CONTROL FROM THE BAT-SHIP. IF ANYTHING GOES AWRY, REPORT IMMEDIATELY TO HER."
I'M GLAD WE GET TO DO THIS TOGETHER.
ME TOO.
BLAST OFF IN TEN, NINE, EIGHT...
"GOOD LUCK, HEROES."

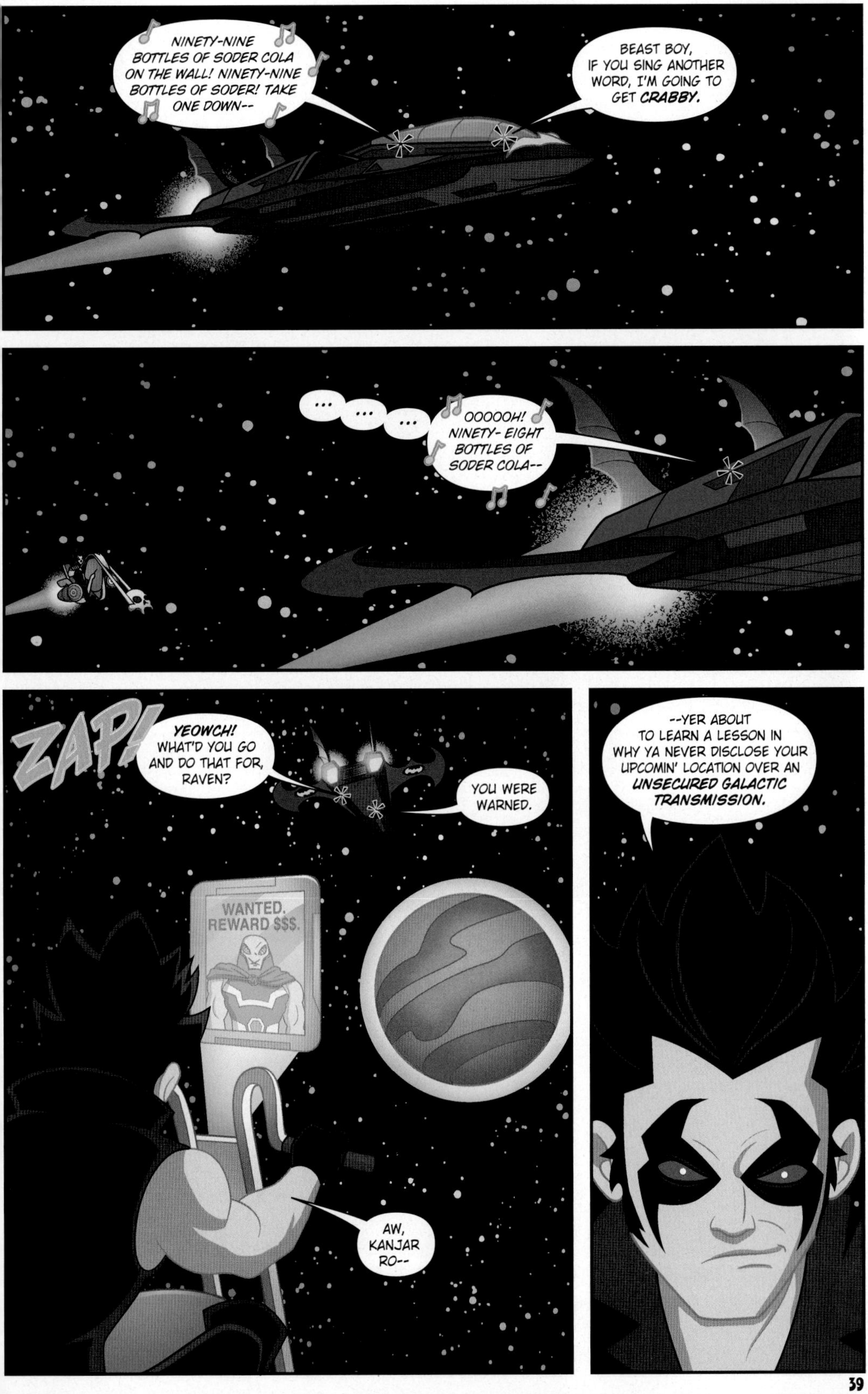
NINETY-NINE BOTTLES OF SODER COLA ON THE WALL! NINETY-NINE BOTTLES OF SODER! TAKE ONE DOWN--
BEAST BOY, IF YOU SING ANOTHER WORD, I'M GOING TO GET CRABBY.
...
...
...
OOOOOH! NINETY- EIGHT BOTTLES OF SODER COLA--
ZAP!
YEOWCH! WHAT'D YOU GO AND DO THAT FOR, RAVEN?
YOU WERE WARNED.
WANTED. REWARD $$$.
AW, KANJAR RO--
--YER ABOUT TO LEARN A LESSON IN WHY YA NEVER DISCLOSE YOUR UPCOMIN' LOCATION OVER AN UNSECURED GALACTIC TRANSMISSION.

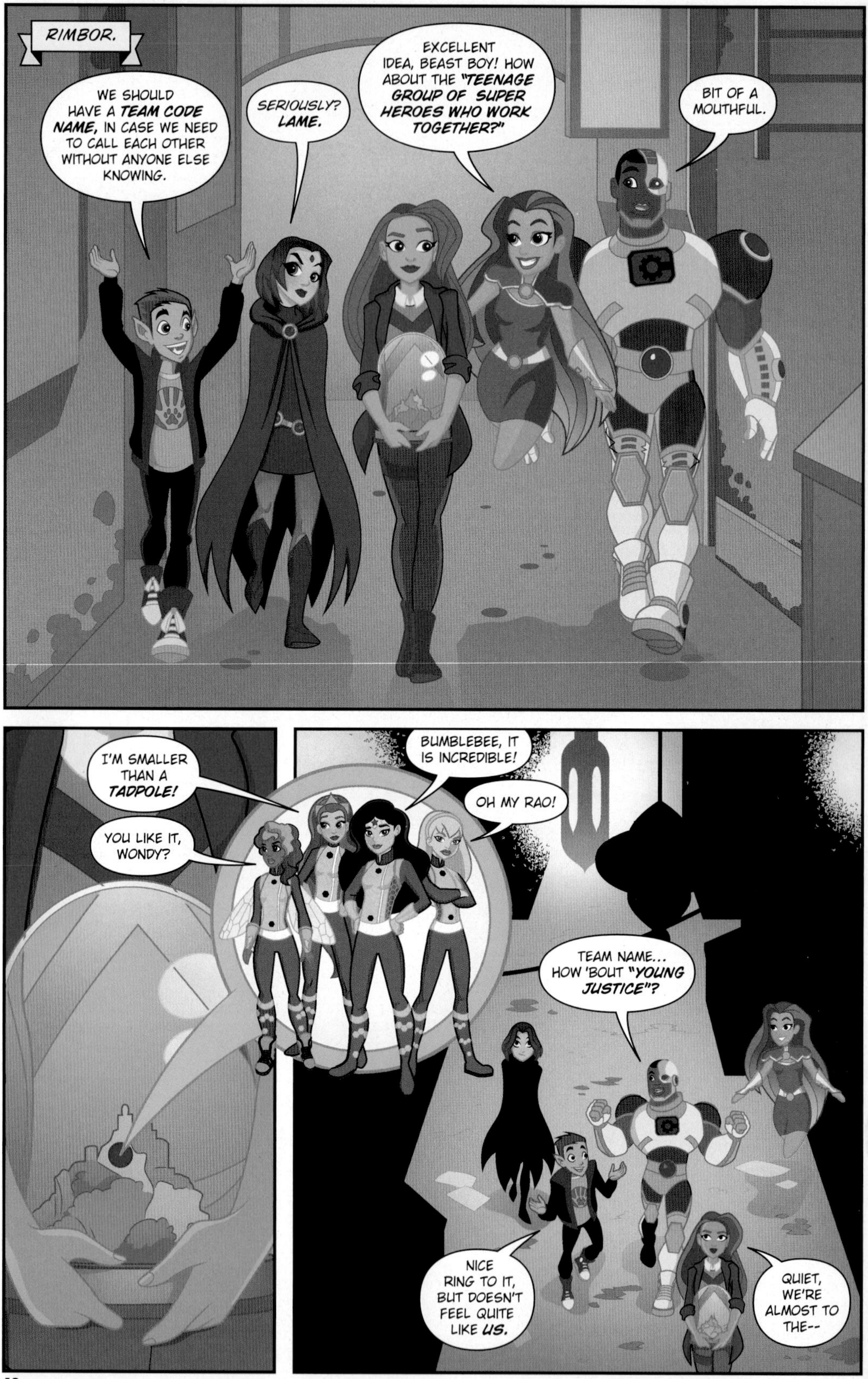
RIMBOR.
WE SHOULD HAVE A TEAM CODE NAME, IN CASE WE NEED TO CALL EACH OTHER WITHOUT ANYONE ELSE KNOWING.
SERIOUSLY? LAME.
EXCELLENT IDEA, BEAST BOY! HOW ABOUT THE "TEENAGE GROUP OF SUPER HEROES WHO WORK TOGETHER?"
BIT OF A MOUTHFUL.
I'M SMALLER THAN A TADPOLE!
YOU LIKE IT, WONDY?
BUMBLEBEE, IT IS INCREDIBLE!
OH MY RAO!
TEAM NAME... HOW 'BOUT "YOUNG JUSTICE"?
NICE RING TO IT, BUT DOESN'T FEEL QUITE LIKE US.
QUIET, WE'RE ALMOST TO THE--

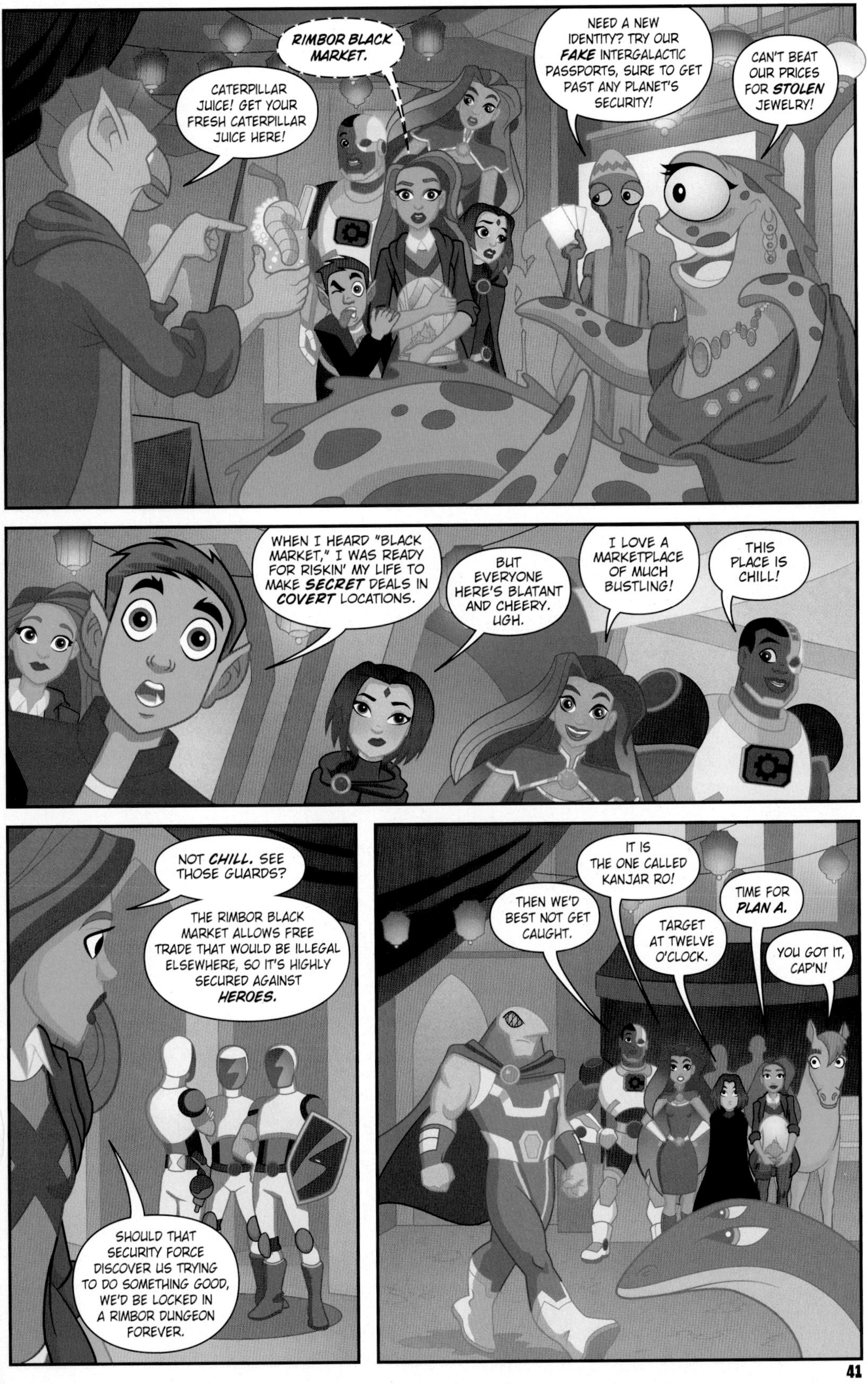
RIMBOR BLACK MARKET.
CATERPILLAR JUICE! GET YOUR FRESH CATERPILLAR JUICE HERE!
NEED A NEW IDENTITY? TRY OUR FAKE INTERGALACTIC PASSPORTS, SURE TO GET PAST ANY PLANET'S SECURITY!
CAN'T BEAT OUR PRICES FOR STOLEN JEWELRY!
WHEN I HEARD "BLACK MARKET," I WAS READY FOR RISKIN' MY LIFE TO MAKE SECRET DEALS IN COVERT LOCATIONS.
BUT EVERYONE HERE'S BLATANT AND CHEERY. UGH.
I LOVE A MARKETPLACE OF MUCH BUSTLING!
THIS PLACE IS CHILL!
NOT CHILL. SEE THOSE GUARDS?
THE RIMBOR BLACK MARKET ALLOWS FREE TRADE THAT WOULD BE ILLEGAL ELSEWHERE, SO IT'S HIGHLY SECURED AGAINST HEROES.
SHOULD THAT SECURITY FORCE DISCOVER US TRYING TO DO SOMETHING GOOD, WE'D BE LOCKED IN A RIMBOR DUNGEON FOREVER.
THEN WE'D BEST NOT GET CAUGHT.
IT IS THE ONE CALLED KANJAR RO!
TARGET AT TWELVE O'CLOCK.
TIME FOR PLAN A.
YOU GOT IT, CAP'N!

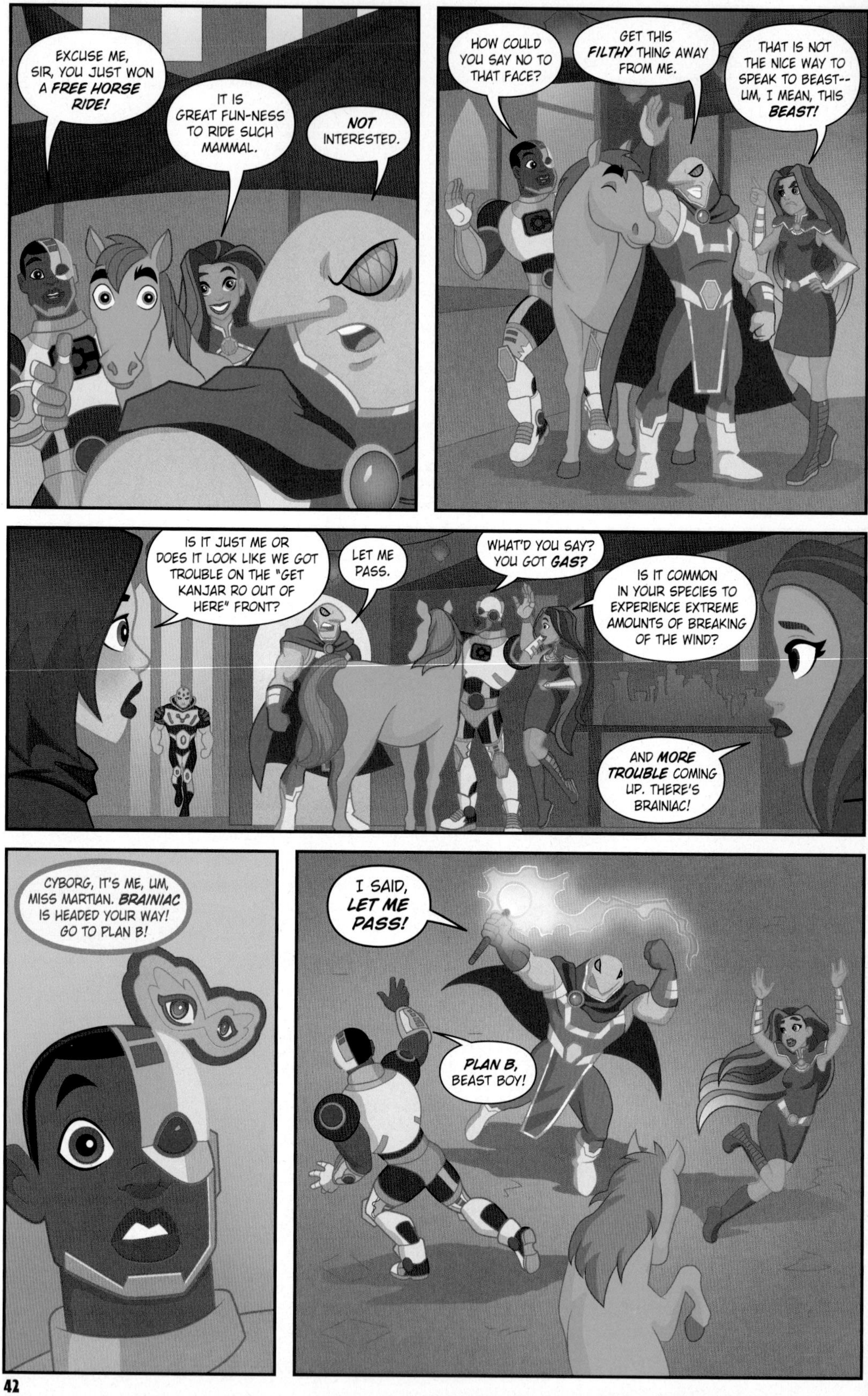
EXCUSE ME, SIR, YOU JUST WON A FREE HORSE RIDE!
IT IS GREAT FUN-NESS TO RIDE SUCH MAMMAL.
NOT INTERESTED.
HOW COULD YOU SAY NO TO THAT FACE?
GET THIS FILTHY THING AWAY FROM ME.
THAT IS NOT THE NICE WAY TO SPEAK TO BEAST-- UM, I MEAN, THIS BEAST!
IS IT JUST ME OR DOES IT LOOK LIKE WE GOT TROUBLE ON THE "GET KANJAR RO OUT OF HERE" FRONT?
LET ME PASS.
WHAT'D YOU SAY? YOU GOT GAS?
IS IT COMMON IN YOUR SPECIES TO EXPERIENCE EXTREME AMOUNTS OF BREAKING OF THE WIND?
AND MORE TROUBLE COMING UP. THERE'S BRAINIAC!
CYBORG, IT'S ME, UM, MISS MARTIAN. BRAINIAC IS HEADED YOUR WAY! GO TO PLAN B!
I SAID, LET ME PASS!
PLAN B, BEAST BOY!

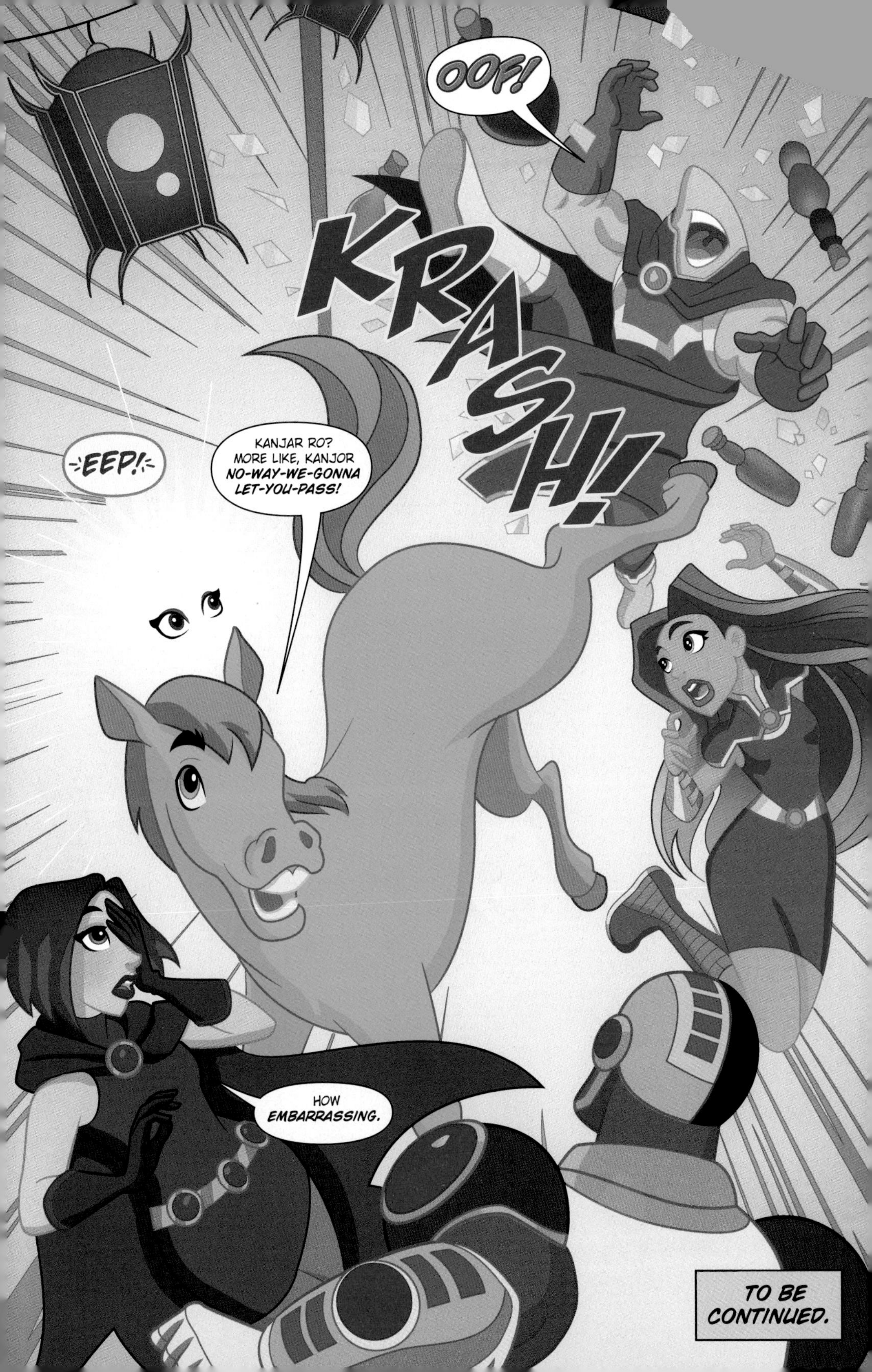
OOF!
KRASH!
-EEP!-
KANJAR RO? MORE LIKE, KANJOR NO-WAY-WE-GONNA LET-YOU-PASS!
HOW EMBARRASSING.
TO BE CONTINUED.

CHAPTER THREE
SMALL WONDER

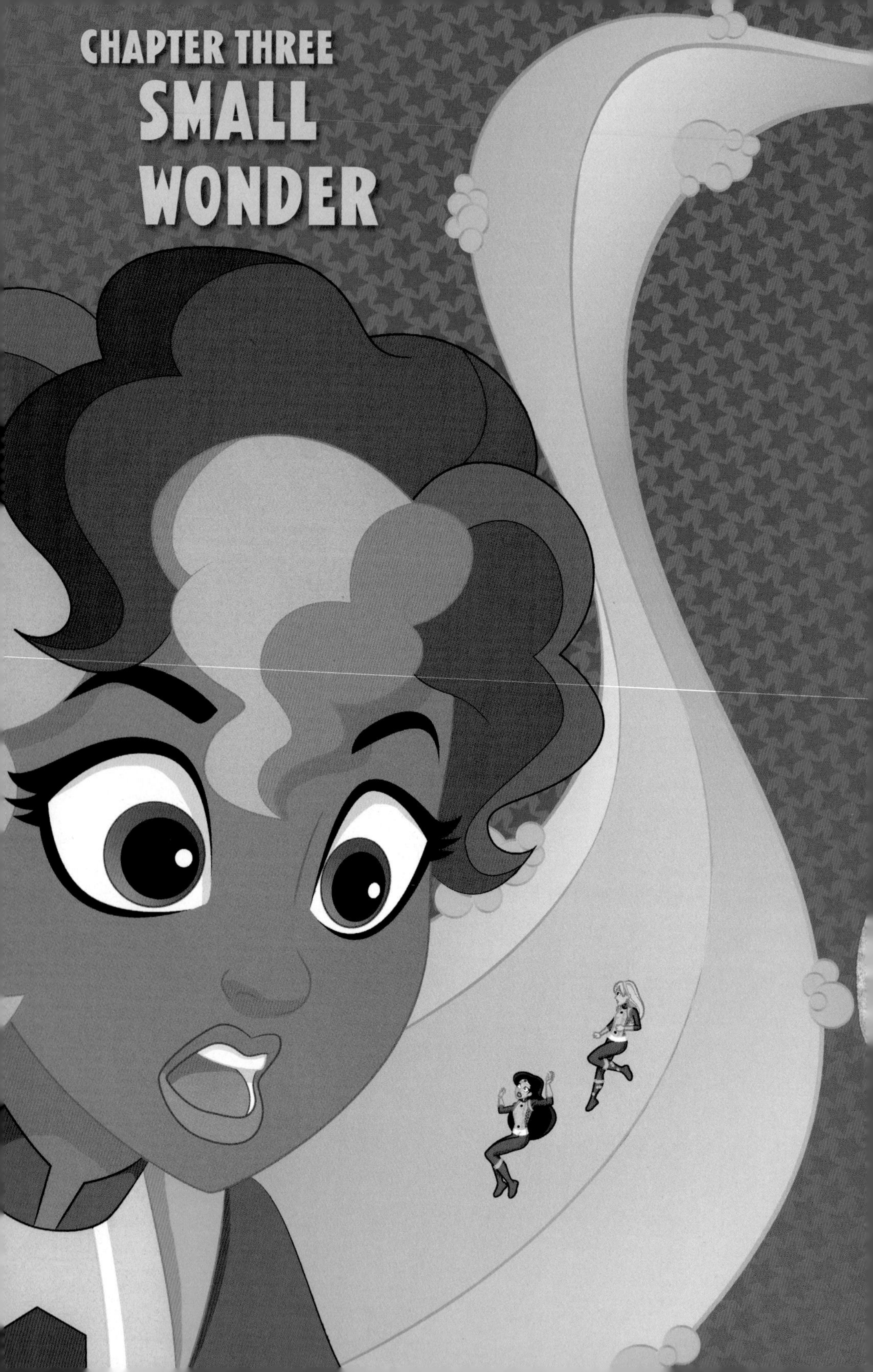

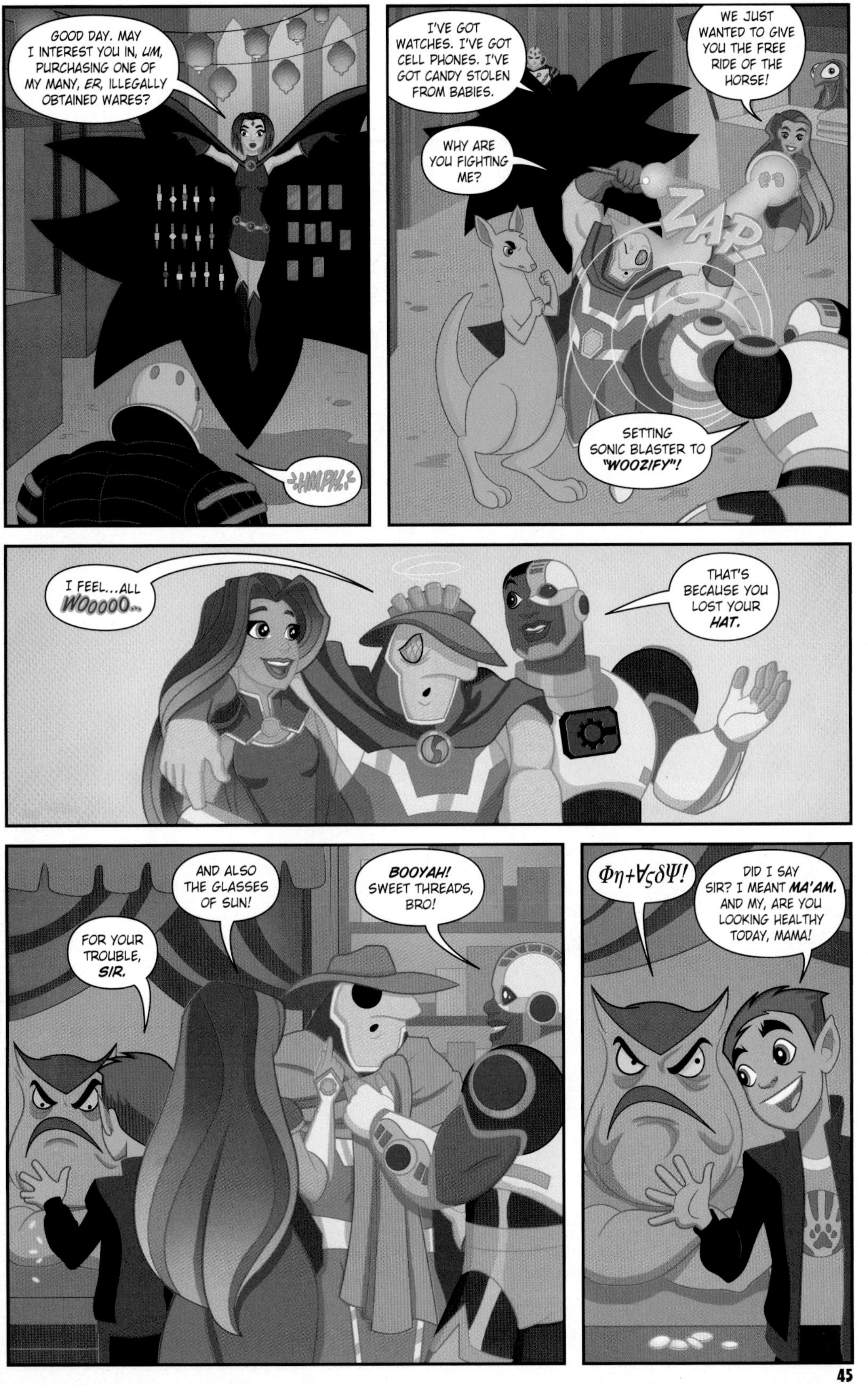
GOOD DAY. MAY I INTEREST YOU IN, UM, PURCHASING ONE OF MY MANY, ER, ILLEGALLY OBTAINED WARES?
HMPH.
I'VE GOT WATCHES. I'VE GOT CELL PHONES. I'VE GOT CANDY STOLEN FROM BABIES.
WHY ARE YOU FIGHTING ME?
WE JUST WANTED TO GIVE YOU THE FREE RIDE OF THE HORSE!
ZAP!
SETTING SONIC BLASTER TO "WOOZIFY"!
I FEEL...ALL WOOOOO...
THAT'S BECAUSE YOU LOST YOUR HAT.
FOR YOUR TROUBLE, SIR.
AND ALSO THE GLASSES OF SUN!
BOOYAH! SWEET THREADS, BRO!
Φη+∀ƽδΨ!
DID I SAY SIR? I MEANT MA'AM. AND MY, ARE YOU LOOKING HEALTHY TODAY, MAMA!

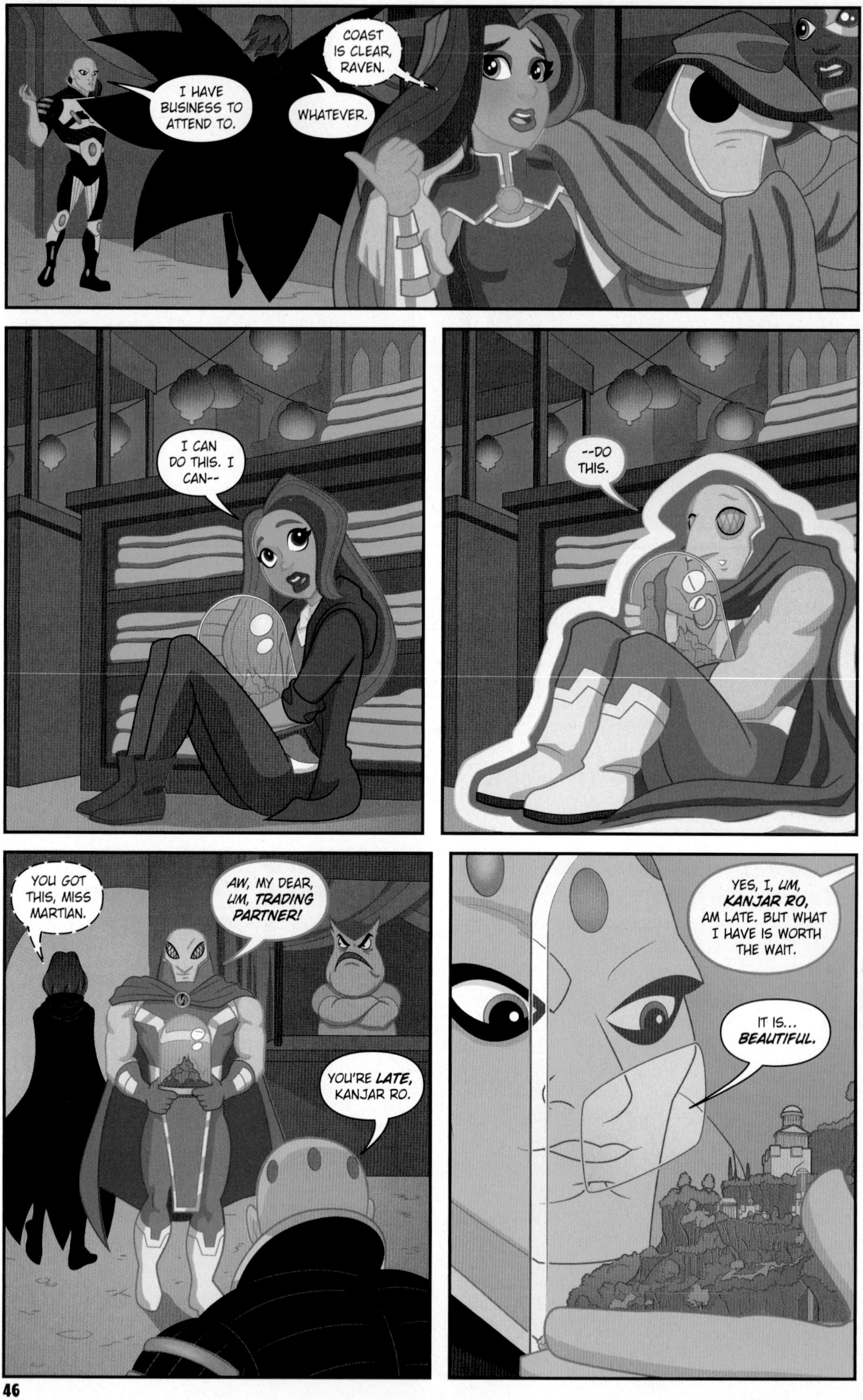

I HAVE BUSINESS TO ATTEND TO.
WHATEVER.
COAST IS CLEAR, RAVEN.
I CAN DO THIS. I CAN--
--DO THIS.
YOU GOT THIS, MISS MARTIAN.
AW, MY DEAR, UM, TRADING PARTNER!
YOU'RE LATE, KANJAR RO.
YES, I, UM, KANJAR RO, AM LATE. BUT WHAT I HAVE IS WORTH THE WAIT.
IT IS... BEAUTIFUL.

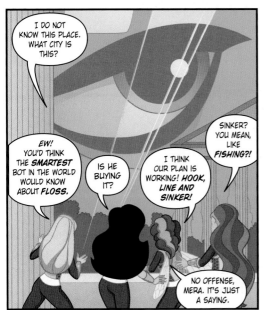

I DO NOT KNOW THIS PLACE. WHAT CITY IS THIS?

EW! YOU'D THINK THE **SMARTEST** BOT IN THE WORLD WOULD KNOW ABOUT **FLOSS**.

IS HE BUYING IT?

I THINK OUR PLAN IS WORKING! **HOOK, LINE AND SINKER!**

SINKER? YOU MEAN, LIKE **FISHING?!**

NO OFFENSE, MERA. IT'S JUST A SAYING.

THEY CALL IT THEMYSCIRA.

THEMYSCIRA? ACCORDING TO MY DATABASE, THAT IS AN EARTH CITY, OF THE GRECIAN EMPIRE.

YES. IT WAS **MAGICALLY HIDDEN** BY THE GODS SO NO OUTSIDER COULD SEE IT. WHICH MEANS, NO ONE WILL BE MISSING IT.

HOW DID YOU GET IT?

I CANNOT DIVULGE THE **SOURCE** OF MY ACQUISITIONS. JUST AS I WILL NEVER REVEAL WHO **BUYS** THEM.

WHY DO YOU THINK I WOULD WANT SUCH A THING?

IT IS MY JOB TO KNOW THE PARTICULAR, EVEN **ECCENTRIC, TASTES** OF MY CLIENTELE.

BUT IF YOU'RE NOT INTERESTED, I'M SURE THERE ARE OTHER--

NO! I'LL **TAKE** IT!

47

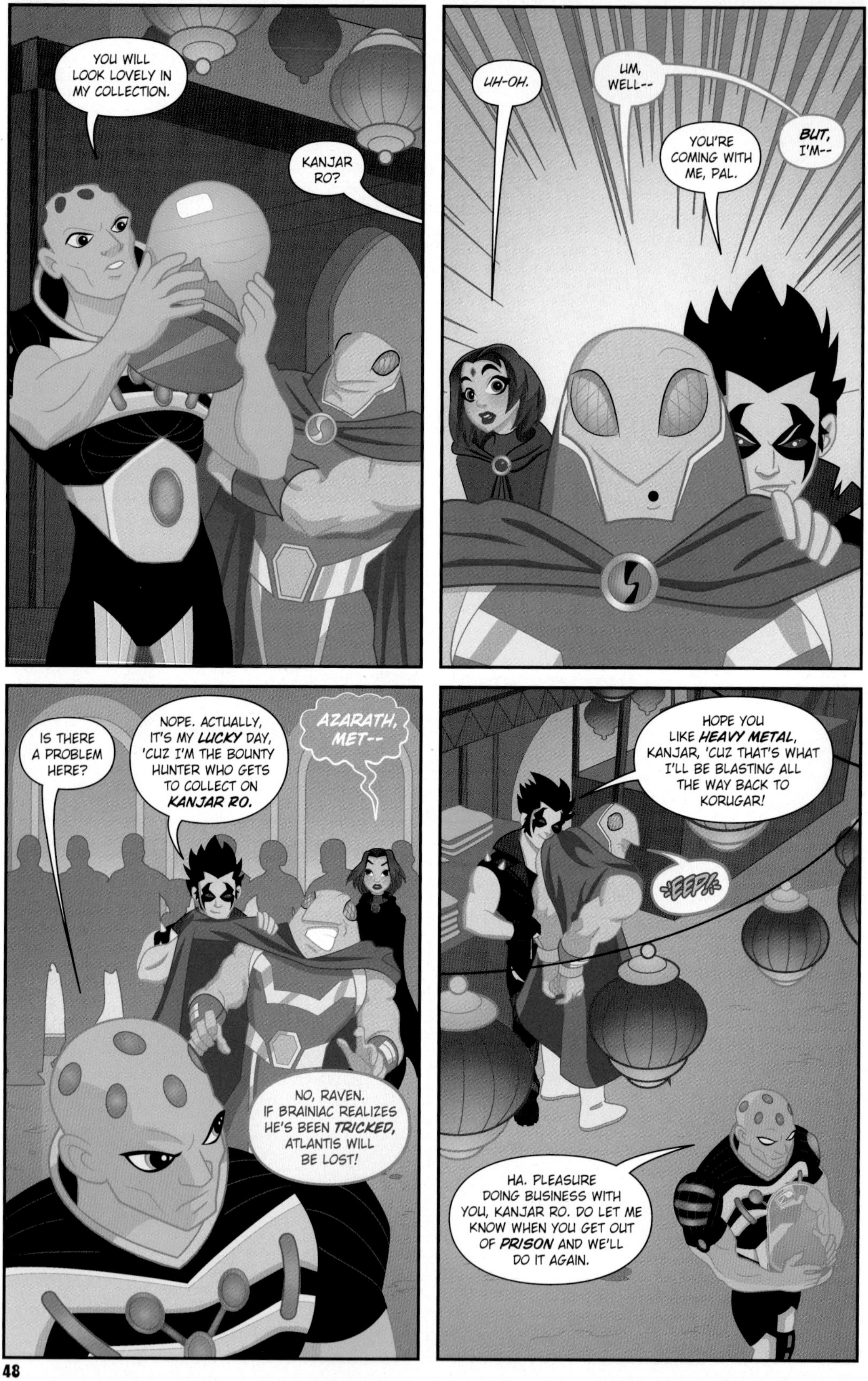
YOU WILL LOOK LOVELY IN MY COLLECTION.
KANJAR RO?
UH-OH.
UM, WELL--
YOU'RE COMING WITH ME, PAL.
BUT, I'M--
IS THERE A PROBLEM HERE?
NOPE. ACTUALLY, IT'S MY LUCKY DAY, 'CUZ I'M THE BOUNTY HUNTER WHO GETS TO COLLECT ON KANJAR RO.
AZARATH, MET--
NO, RAVEN. IF BRAINIAC REALIZES HE'S BEEN TRICKED, ATLANTIS WILL BE LOST!
HOPE YOU LIKE HEAVY METAL, KANJAR, 'CUZ THAT'S WHAT I'LL BE BLASTING ALL THE WAY BACK TO KORUGAR!
EEP!
HA. PLEASURE DOING BUSINESS WITH YOU, KANJAR RO. DO LET ME KNOW WHEN YOU GET OUT OF PRISON AND WE'LL DO IT AGAIN.

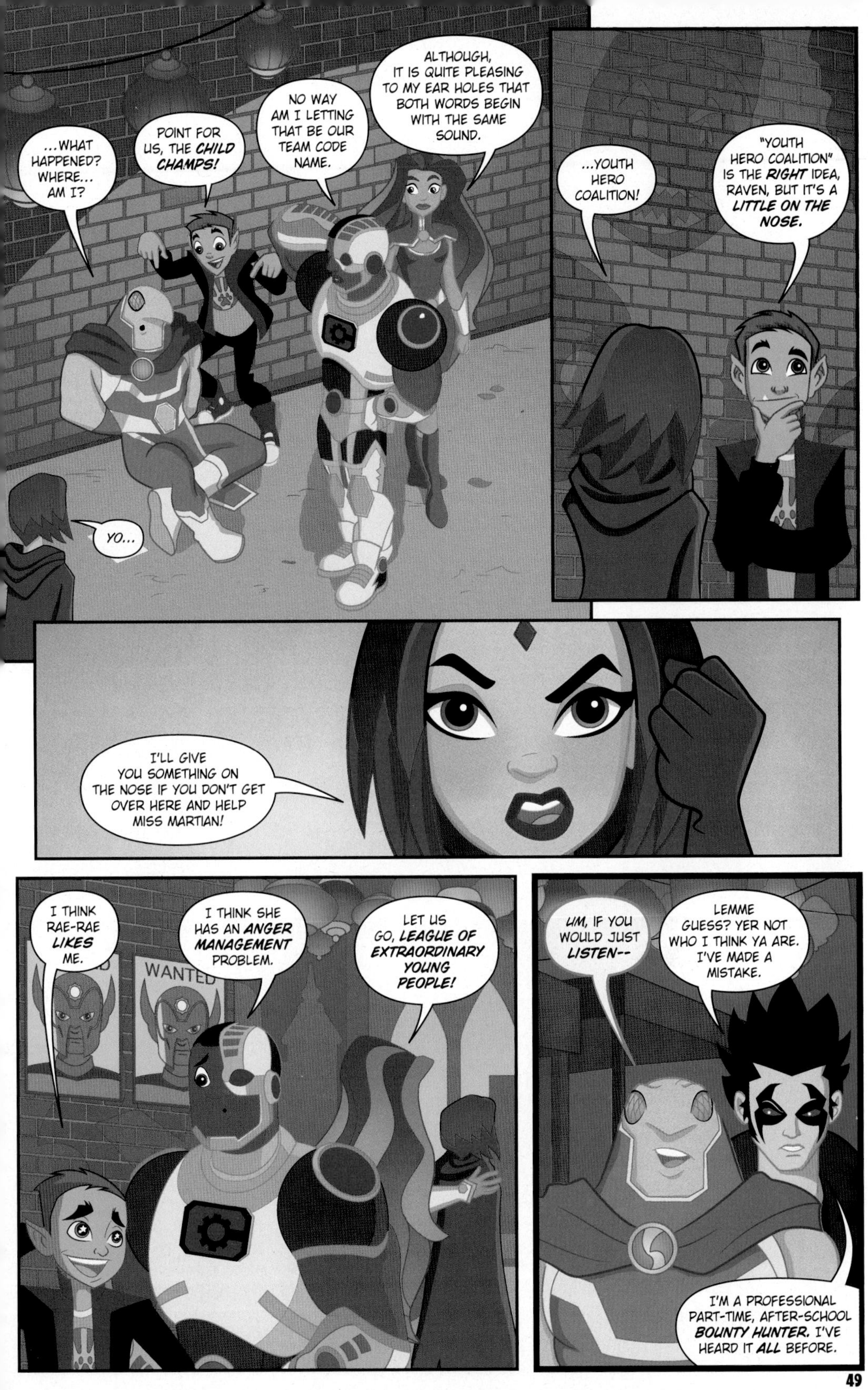
...WHAT HAPPENED? WHERE... AM I?
POINT FOR US, THE CHILD CHAMPS!
NO WAY AM I LETTING THAT BE OUR TEAM CODE NAME.
ALTHOUGH, IT IS QUITE PLEASING TO MY EAR HOLES THAT BOTH WORDS BEGIN WITH THE SAME SOUND.
YO...
...YOUTH HERO COALITION!
"YOUTH HERO COALITION" IS THE RIGHT IDEA, RAVEN, BUT IT'S A LITTLE ON THE NOSE.
I'LL GIVE YOU SOMETHING ON THE NOSE IF YOU DON'T GET OVER HERE AND HELP MISS MARTIAN!
WANTED
I THINK RAE-RAE LIKES ME.
I THINK SHE HAS AN ANGER MANAGEMENT PROBLEM.
LET US GO, LEAGUE OF EXTRAORDINARY YOUNG PEOPLE!
UM, IF YOU WOULD JUST LISTEN--
LEMME GUESS? YER NOT WHO I THINK YA ARE. I'VE MADE A MISTAKE.
I'M A PROFESSIONAL PART-TIME, AFTER-SCHOOL BOUNTY HUNTER. I'VE HEARD IT ALL BEFORE.

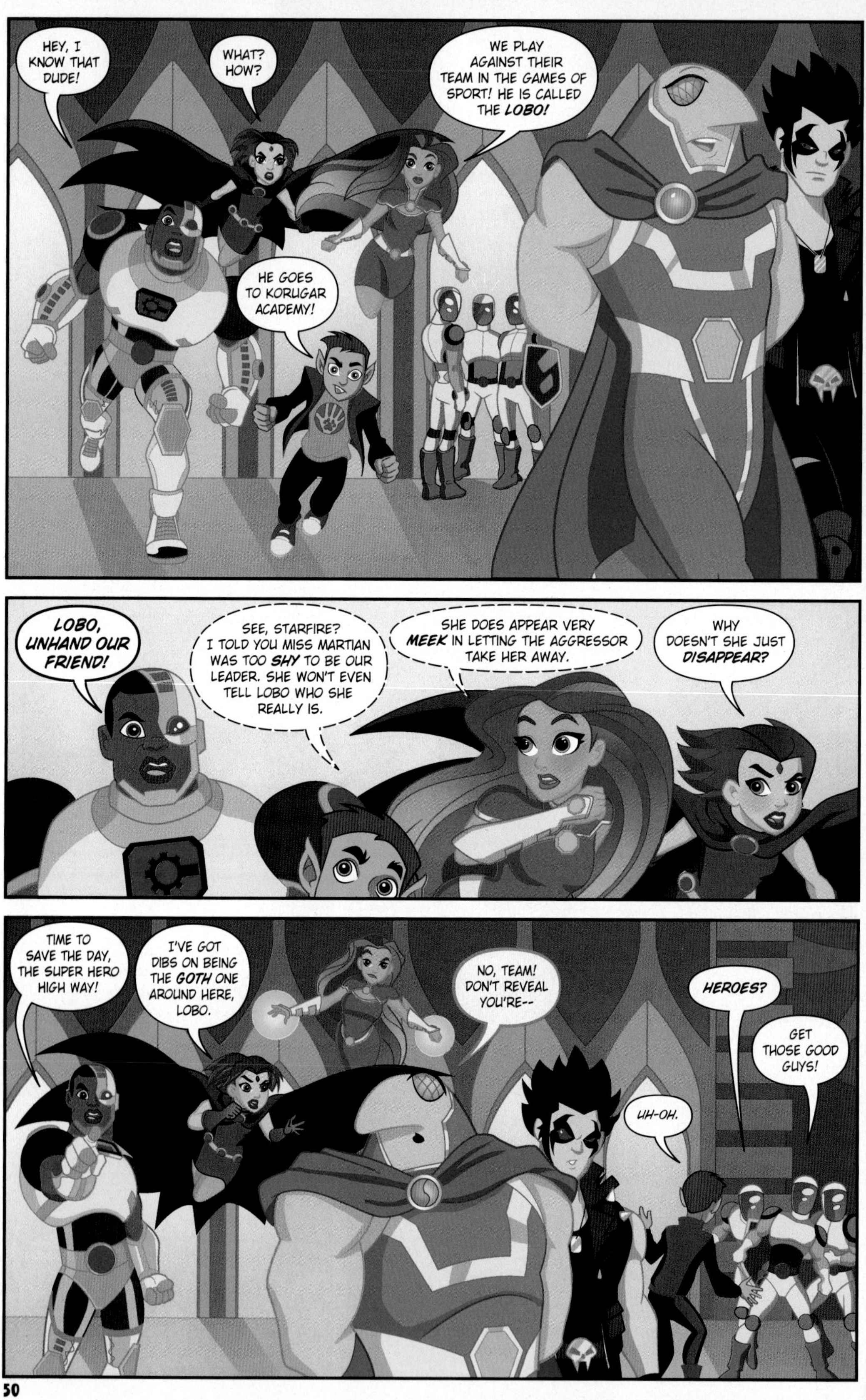
HEY, I KNOW THAT DUDE!
WHAT? HOW?
WE PLAY AGAINST THEIR TEAM IN THE GAMES OF SPORT! HE IS CALLED THE LOBO!
HE GOES TO KORUGAR ACADEMY!
LOBO, UNHAND OUR FRIEND!
SEE, STARFIRE? I TOLD YOU MISS MARTIAN WAS TOO SHY TO BE OUR LEADER. SHE WON'T EVEN TELL LOBO WHO SHE REALLY IS.
SHE DOES APPEAR VERY MEEK IN LETTING THE AGGRESSOR TAKE HER AWAY.
WHY DOESN'T SHE JUST DISAPPEAR?
TIME TO SAVE THE DAY, THE SUPER HERO HIGH WAY!
I'VE GOT DIBS ON BEING THE GOTH ONE AROUND HERE, LOBO.
NO, TEAM! DON'T REVEAL YOU'RE--
HEROES?
GET THOSE GOOD GUYS!
UH-OH.

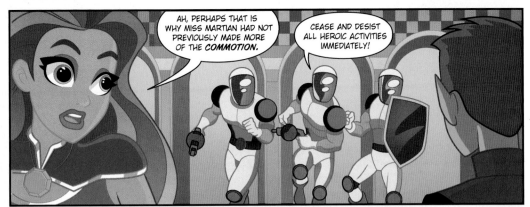

AH, PERHAPS THAT IS WHY MISS MARTIAN HAD NOT PREVIOUSLY MADE MORE OF THE **COMMOTION.**

CEASE AND DESIST ALL HEROIC ACTIVITIES IMMEDIATELY!

THAT'S NOT WHO YOU THINK IT IS, LOBO!

PLEASE, CYBORG. I HAD A PLAN--

YER JUST TRYIN' TO GET MY BOUNTY FOR YERSELF!

AZARATH, METRION, ZINTHOS!

ZAP!

I DO NOT APPRECIATE YOUR ATTEMPTS TO CAUSE ME BODILY INJURY!

OOF!

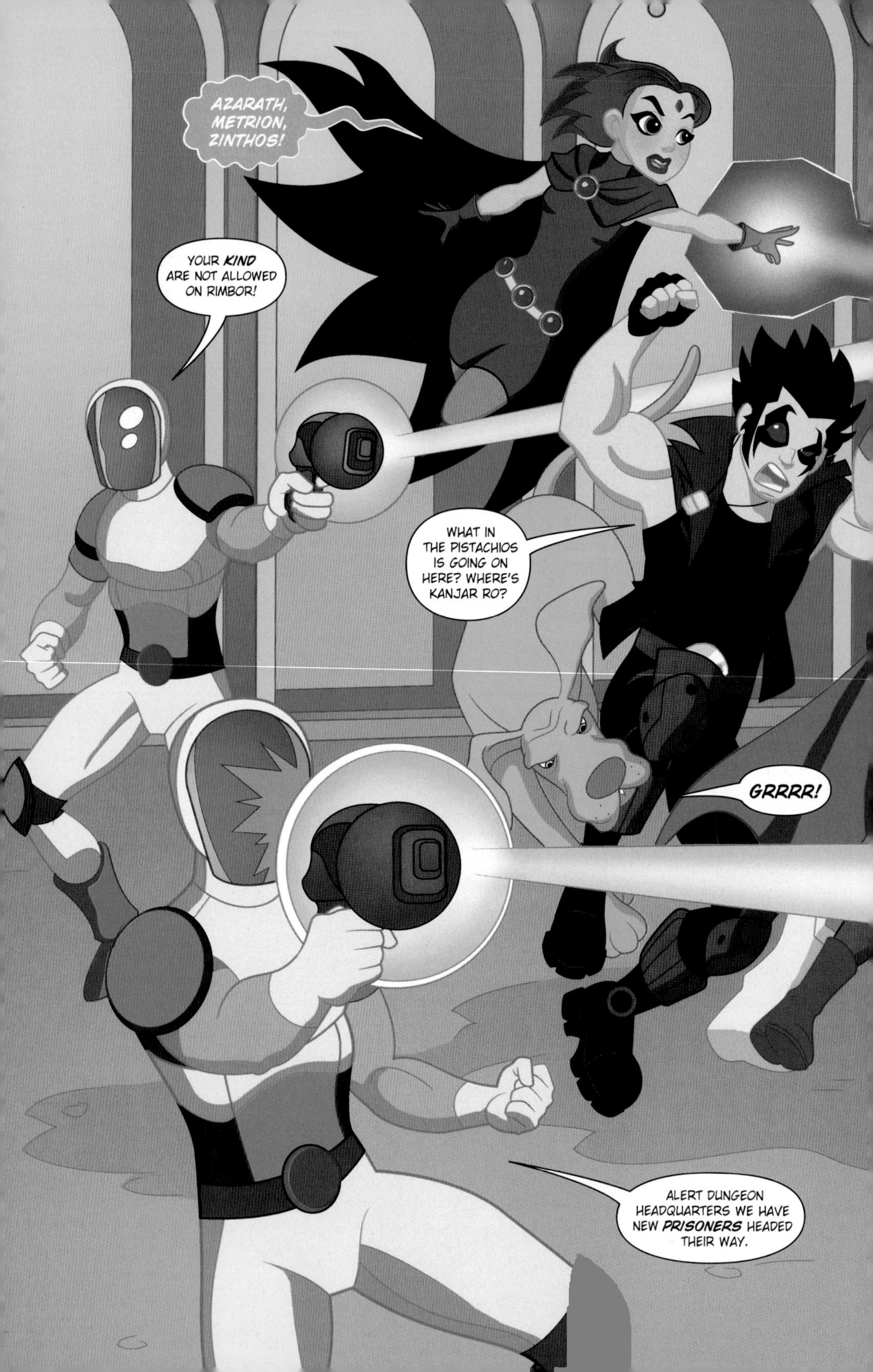
AZARATH, METRION, ZINTHOS!
YOUR KIND ARE NOT ALLOWED ON RIMBOR!
WHAT IN THE PISTACHIOS IS GOING ON HERE? WHERE'S KANJAR RO?
GRRRR!
ALERT DUNGEON HEADQUARTERS WE HAVE NEW PRISONERS HEADED THEIR WAY.

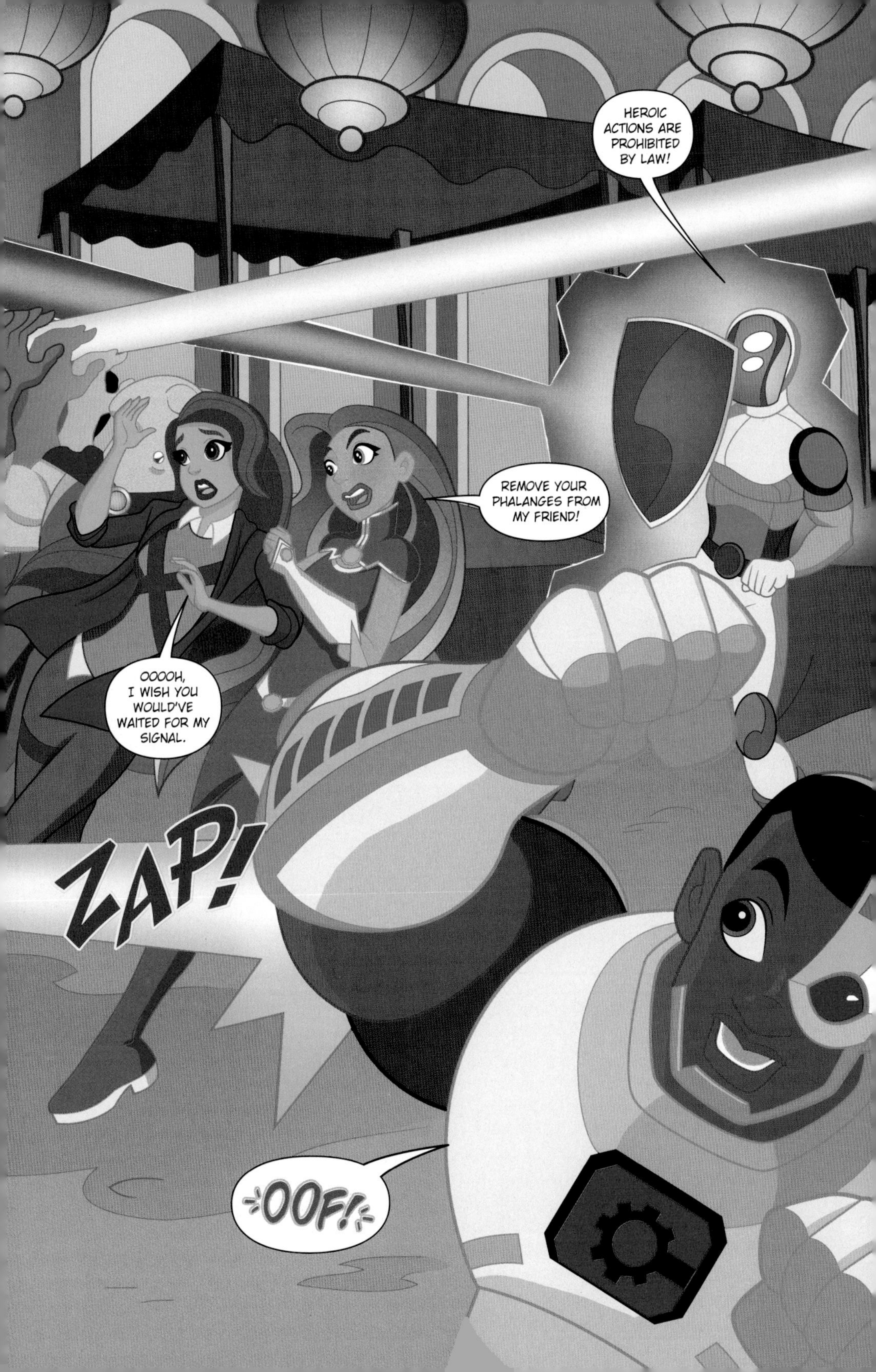
HEROIC ACTIONS ARE PROHIBITED BY LAW!
REMOVE YOUR PHALANGES FROM MY FRIEND!
OOOOH, I WISH YOU WOULD'VE WAITED FOR MY SIGNAL.
ZAP!
OOF!

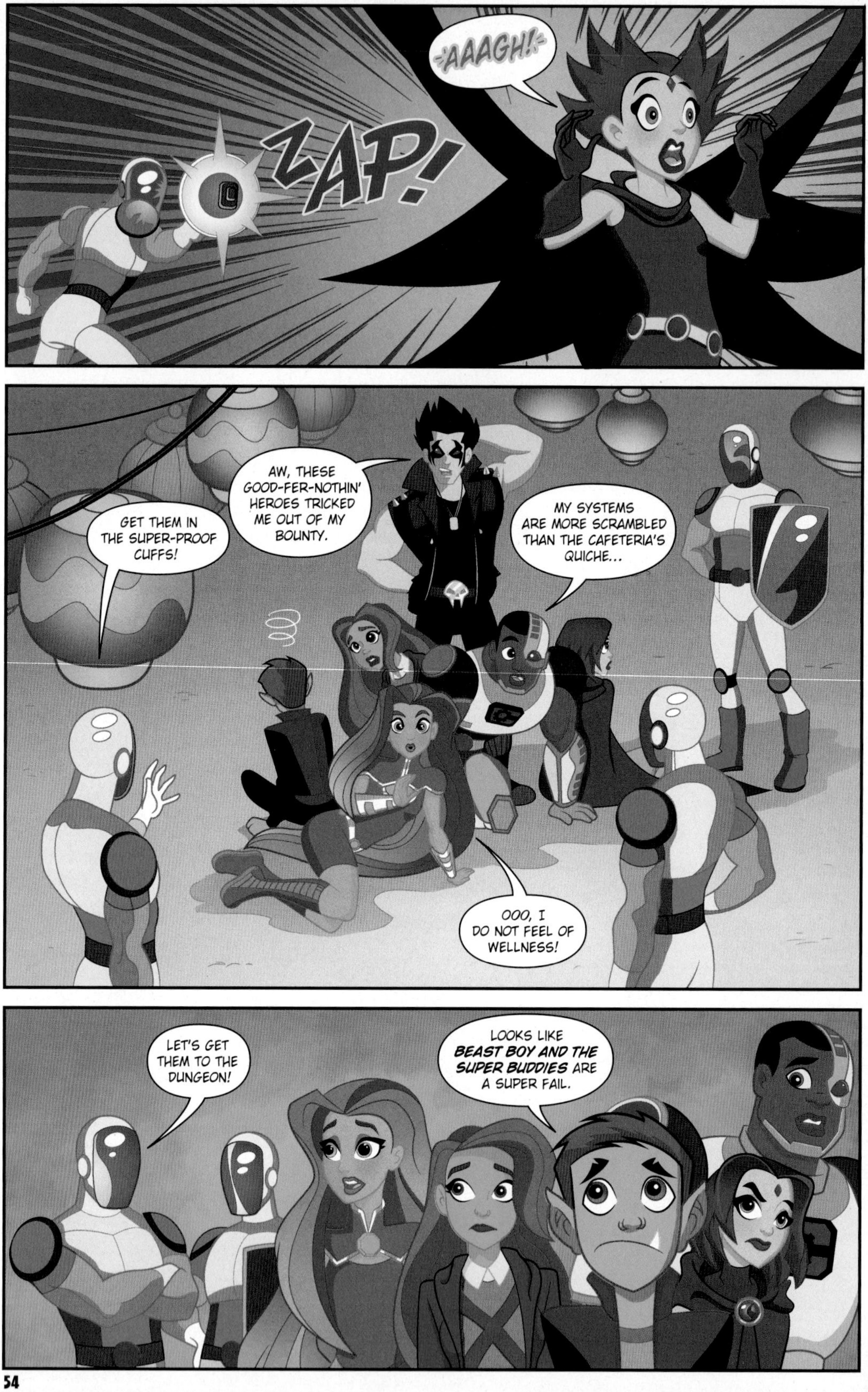
ZAP!
AAAGH!
GET THEM IN THE SUPER-PROOF CUFFS!
AW, THESE GOOD-FER-NOTHIN' HEROES TRICKED ME OUT OF MY BOUNTY.
MY SYSTEMS ARE MORE SCRAMBLED THAN THE CAFETERIA'S QUICHE...
OOO, I DO NOT FEEL OF WELLNESS!
LET'S GET THEM TO THE DUNGEON!
LOOKS LIKE ***BEAST BOY AND THE SUPER BUDDIES*** ARE A SUPER FAIL.

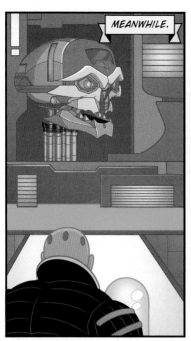

PERFECT! HERE YOU WILL BE FOR THE REST OF ETERNITY, *NEVER CHANGING*, FROZEN IN TIME--

--REMAINING PRECISELY THE WAY YOU ARE AT THIS MOMENT.

GET READY FOR SOME *MAJOR MODIFICATIONS*, BOLT-BRAIN!

JUDGING BY WHAT I COULD SEE ON THE WAY IN, ATLANTIS SHOULD BE NEARBY.

BUT GETTING THERE AMOEBA-SIZED IS GOING TO TAKE *FOREVER!*

THAT'S WHY WE'RE GOING TO KICK IT UP TO BEE-SIZE!

SUPERGIRL, ARE YOU SURE BRAINIAC CAN'T SEE US?

POSITIVE.

GIRLS, TAKE YOUR SUITS UP A NOTCH AND *GROW* ON MY COUNT. ONE, TWO--

THREE!

WOW! THIS SUIT IS *OFF THE HOOK!* ISN'T THIS AWESOME, WONDY?

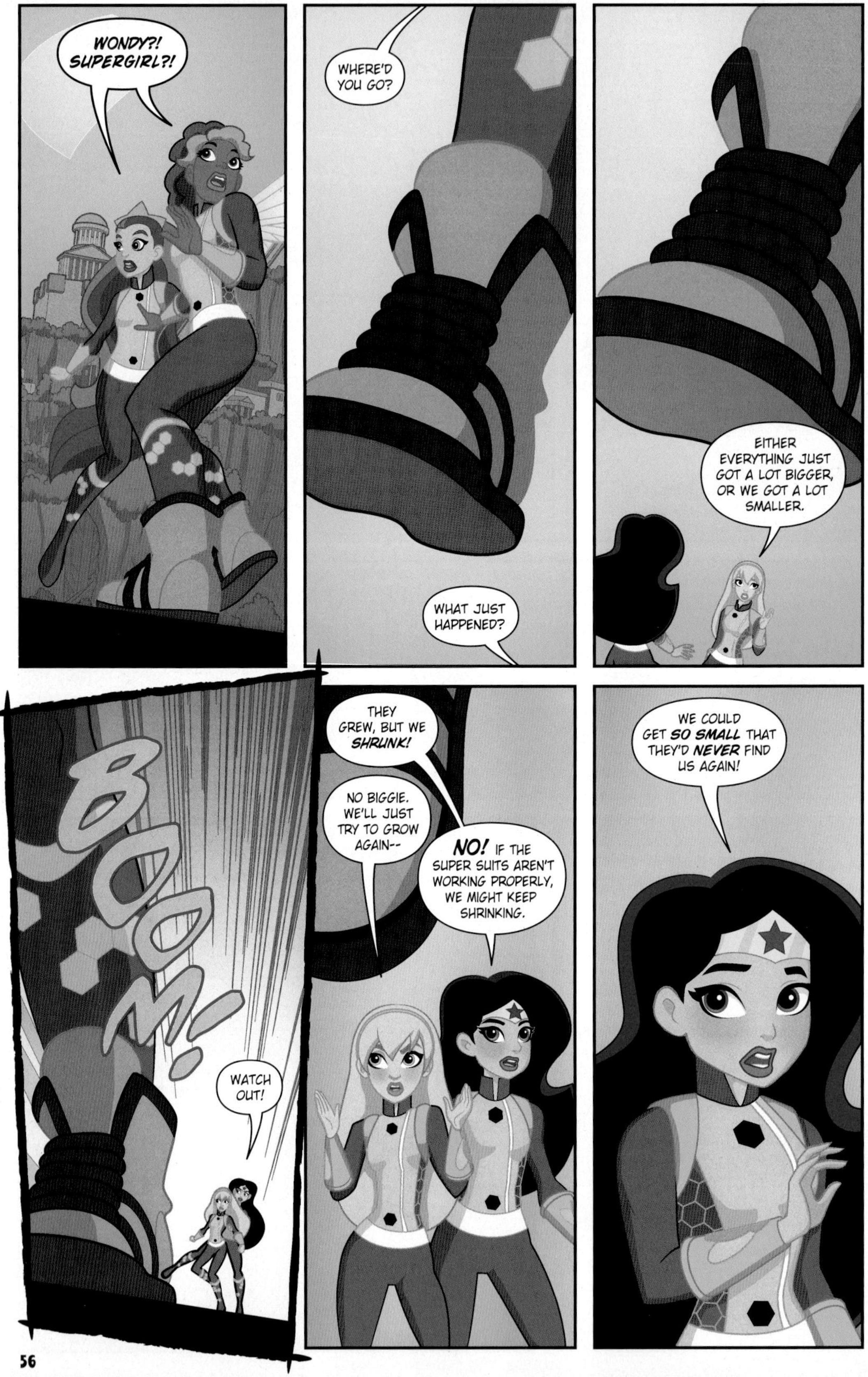
WONDY?! SUPERGIRL?!
WHERE'D YOU GO?
WHAT JUST HAPPENED?
EITHER EVERYTHING JUST GOT A LOT BIGGER, OR WE GOT A LOT SMALLER.
BOOM!
WATCH OUT!
THEY GREW, BUT WE SHRUNK!
NO BIGGIE. WE'LL JUST TRY TO GROW AGAIN--
NO! IF THE SUPER SUITS AREN'T WORKING PROPERLY, WE MIGHT KEEP SHRINKING.
WE COULD GET SO SMALL THAT THEY'D NEVER FIND US AGAIN!

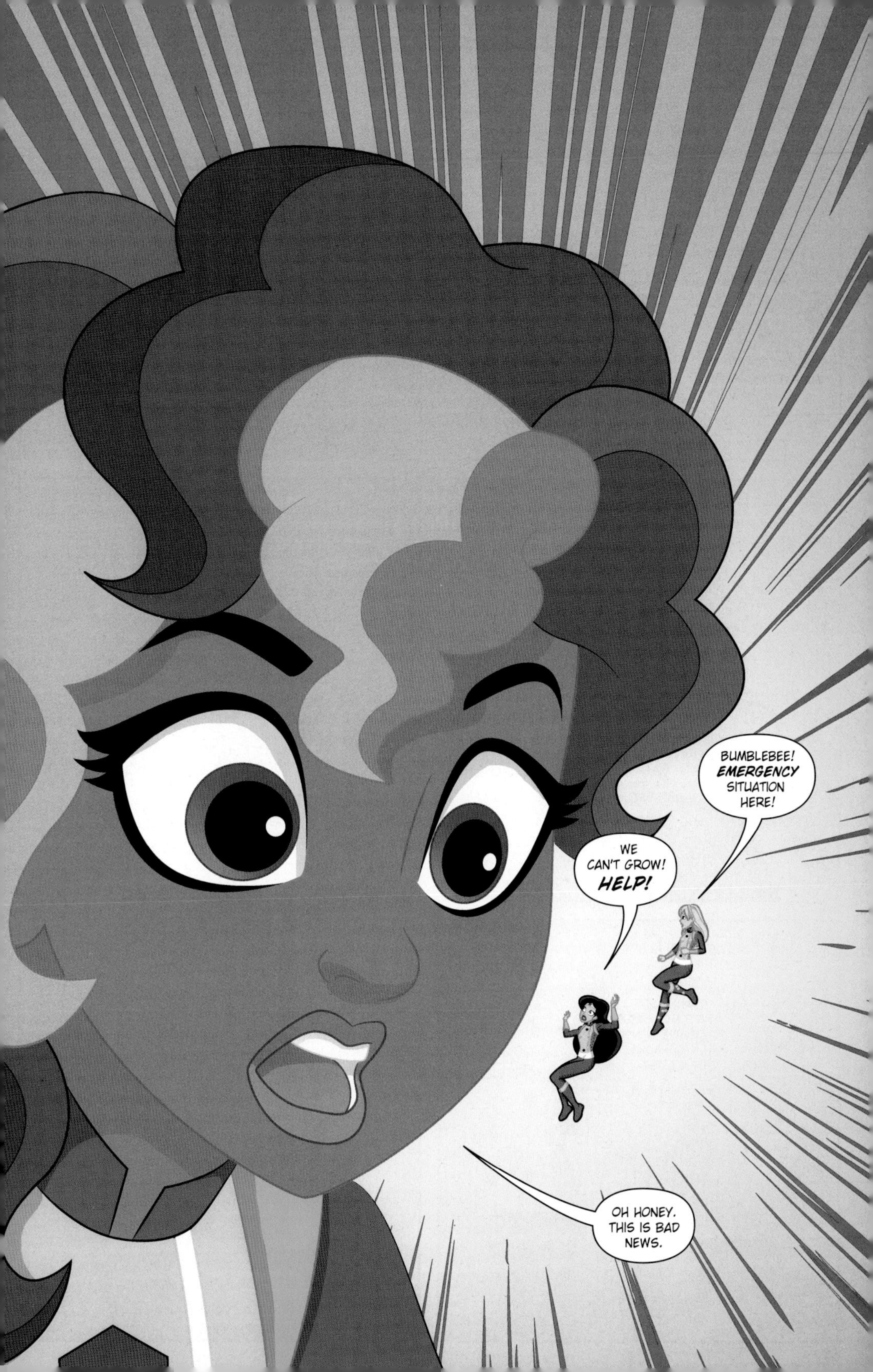
BUMBLEBEE! EMERGENCY SITUATION HERE!
WE CAN'T GROW! HELP!
OH HONEY. THIS IS BAD NEWS.

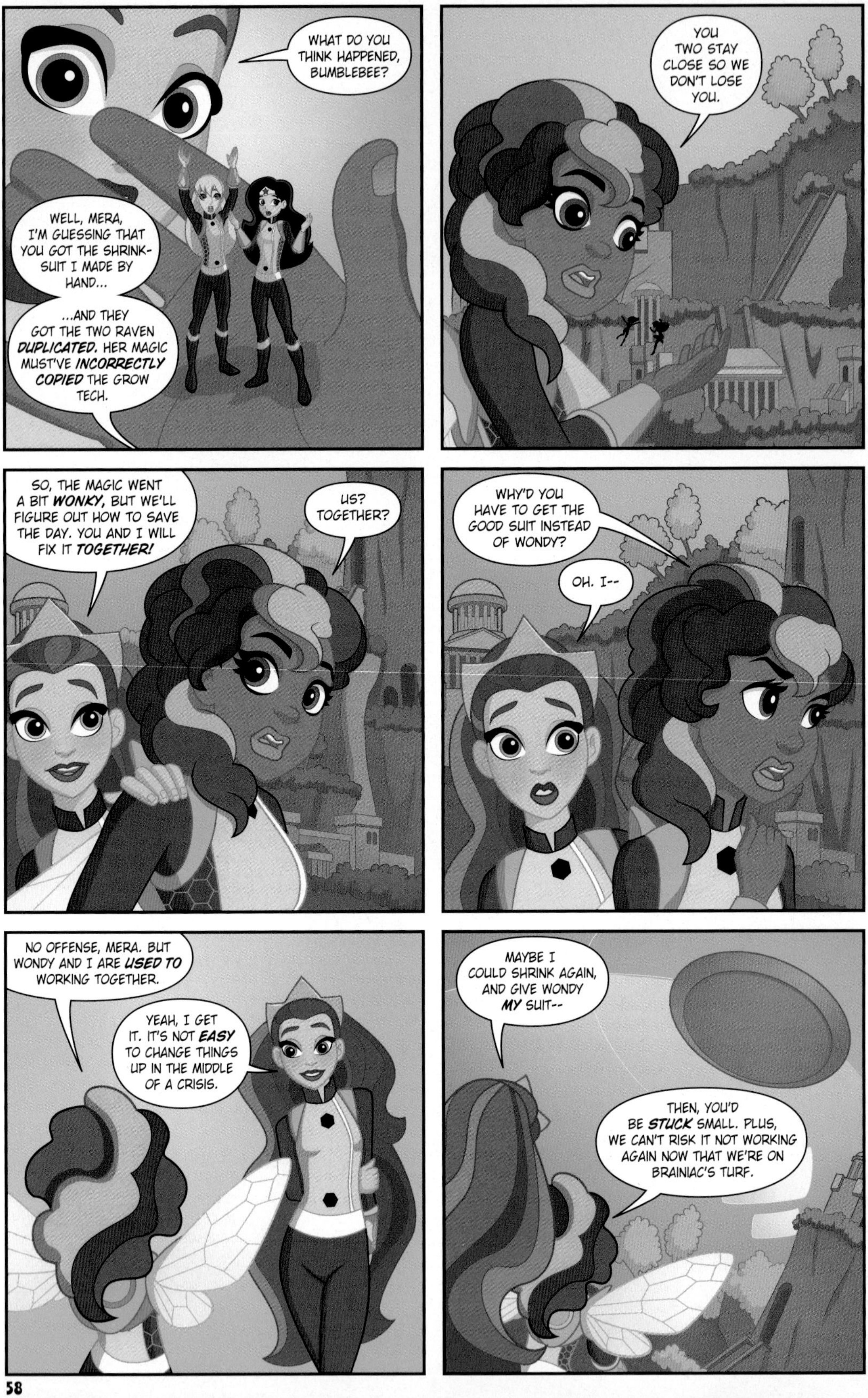
WHAT DO YOU THINK HAPPENED, BUMBLEBEE?
WELL, MERA, I'M GUESSING THAT YOU GOT THE SHRINK-SUIT I MADE BY HAND...
...AND THEY GOT THE TWO RAVEN DUPLICATED. HER MAGIC MUST'VE INCORRECTLY COPIED THE GROW TECH.
YOU TWO STAY CLOSE SO WE DON'T LOSE YOU.
SO, THE MAGIC WENT A BIT WONKY, BUT WE'LL FIGURE OUT HOW TO SAVE THE DAY. YOU AND I WILL FIX IT TOGETHER!
US? TOGETHER?
WHY'D YOU HAVE TO GET THE GOOD SUIT INSTEAD OF WONDY?
OH. I--
NO OFFENSE, MERA. BUT WONDY AND I ARE USED TO WORKING TOGETHER.
YEAH, I GET IT. IT'S NOT EASY TO CHANGE THINGS UP IN THE MIDDLE OF A CRISIS.
MAYBE I COULD SHRINK AGAIN, AND GIVE WONDY MY SUIT--
THEN, YOU'D BE STUCK SMALL. PLUS, WE CAN'T RISK IT NOT WORKING AGAIN NOW THAT WE'RE ON BRAINIAC'S TURF.

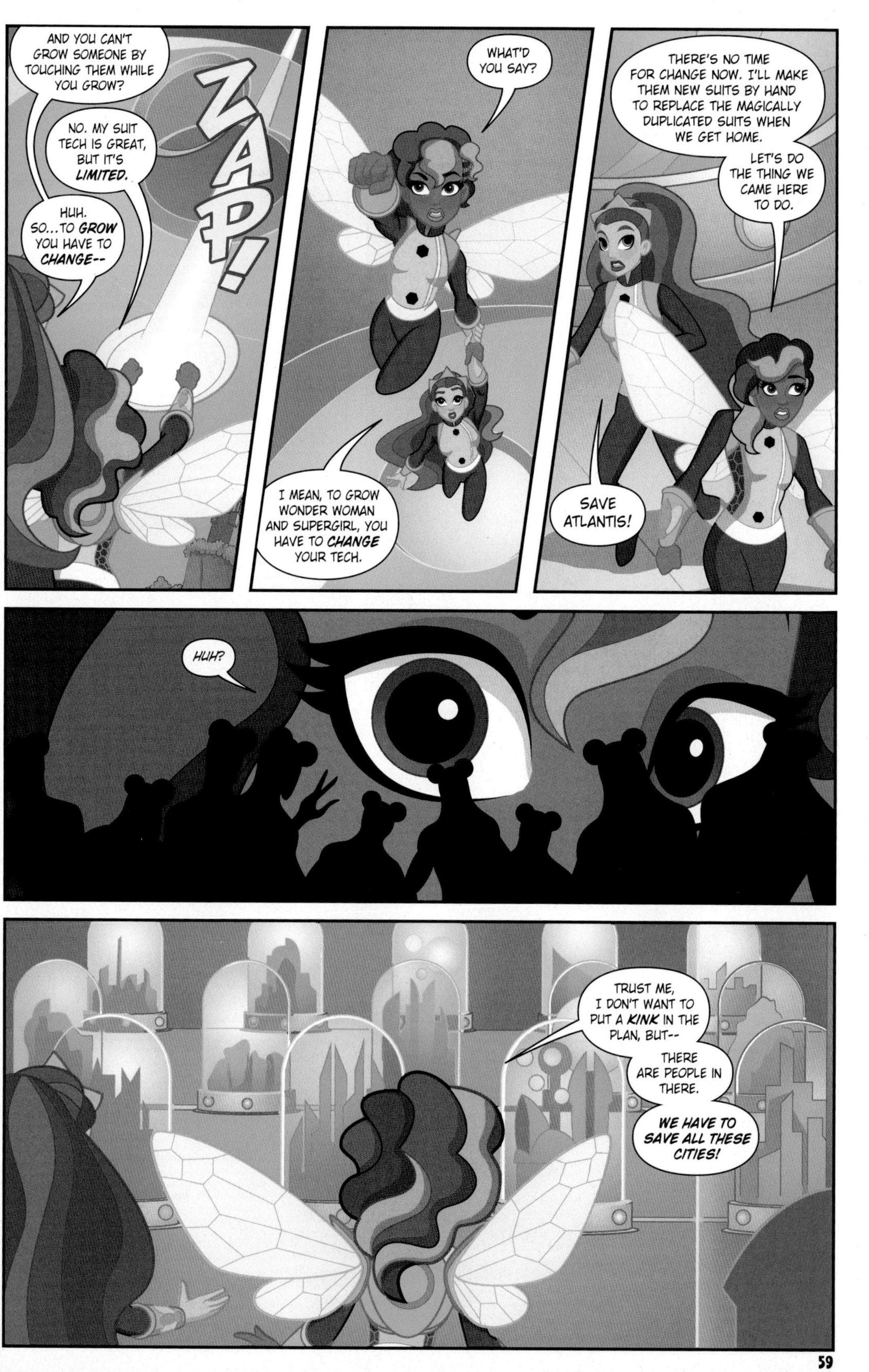
AND YOU CAN'T GROW SOMEONE BY TOUCHING THEM WHILE YOU GROW?
NO. MY SUIT TECH IS GREAT, BUT IT'S *LIMITED.*
ZAP!
HUH. SO...TO *GROW* YOU HAVE TO *CHANGE--*
WHAT'D YOU SAY?
I MEAN, TO GROW WONDER WOMAN AND SUPERGIRL, YOU HAVE TO *CHANGE* YOUR TECH.
THERE'S NO TIME FOR CHANGE NOW. I'LL MAKE THEM NEW SUITS BY HAND TO REPLACE THE MAGICALLY DUPLICATED SUITS WHEN WE GET HOME.
LET'S DO THE THING WE CAME HERE TO DO.
SAVE ATLANTIS!
HUH?
TRUST ME, I DON'T WANT TO PUT A *KINK* IN THE PLAN, BUT--
THERE ARE PEOPLE IN THERE.
WE HAVE TO SAVE ALL THESE CITIES!

HOW ARE WE GOING TO GET OUT OF HERE WITH ALL THESE BOTTLES, MERA?

MERA?

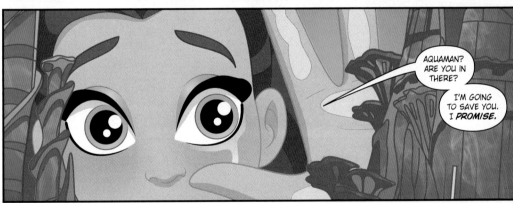

AQUAMAN? ARE YOU IN THERE?

I'M GOING TO SAVE YOU. I *PROMISE.*

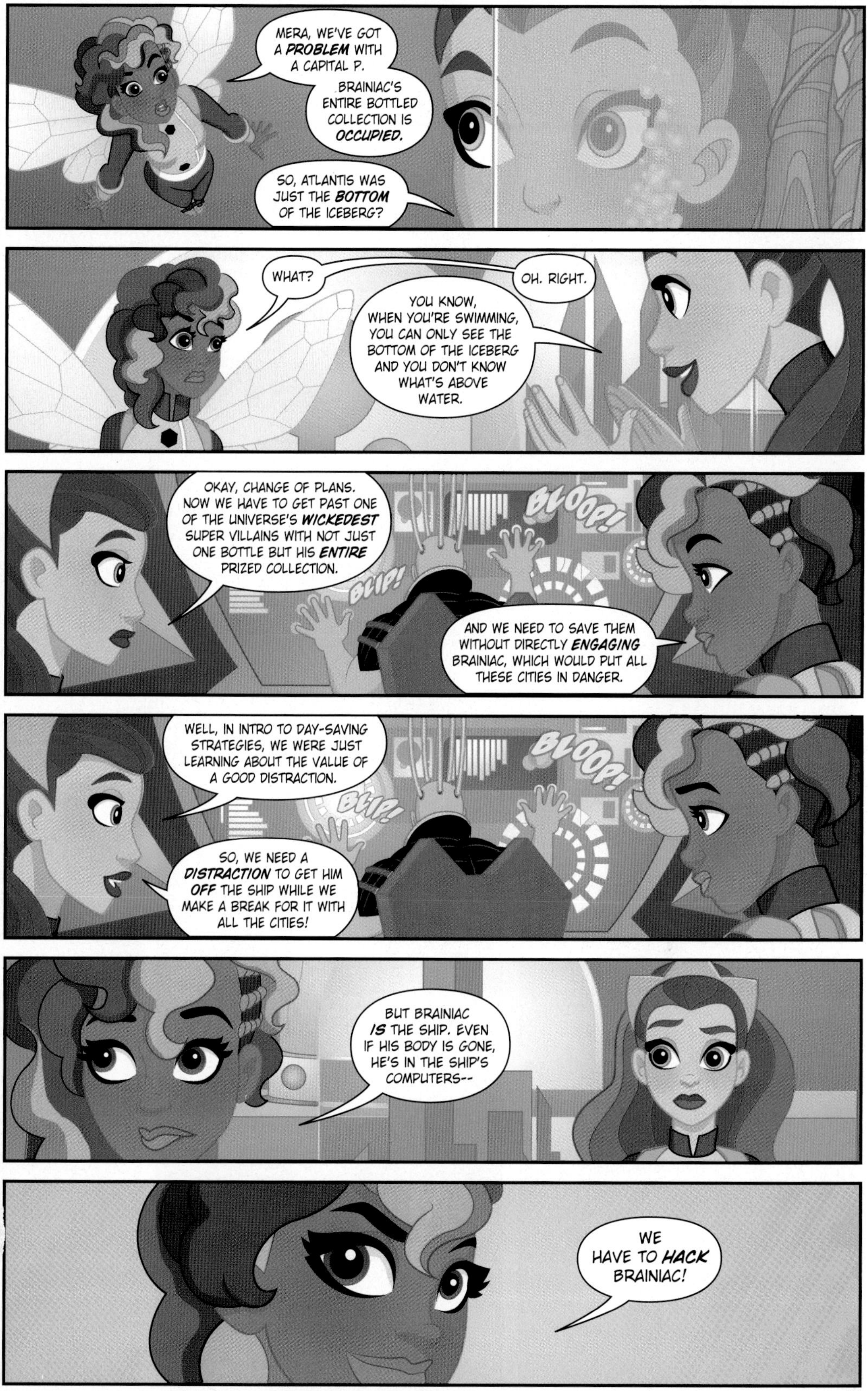

MERA, WE'VE GOT A ***PROBLEM*** WITH A CAPITAL P.
BRAINIAC'S ENTIRE BOTTLED COLLECTION IS ***OCCUPIED.***
SO, ATLANTIS WAS JUST THE ***BOTTOM*** OF THE ICEBERG?
WHAT?
OH. RIGHT.
YOU KNOW, WHEN YOU'RE SWIMMING, YOU CAN ONLY SEE THE BOTTOM OF THE ICEBERG AND YOU DON'T KNOW WHAT'S ABOVE WATER.
OKAY, CHANGE OF PLANS. NOW WE HAVE TO GET PAST ONE OF THE UNIVERSE'S ***WICKEDEST*** SUPER VILLAINS WITH NOT JUST ONE BOTTLE BUT HIS ***ENTIRE*** PRIZED COLLECTION.
BLOOP!
BLIP!
AND WE NEED TO SAVE THEM WITHOUT DIRECTLY ***ENGAGING*** BRAINIAC, WHICH WOULD PUT ALL THESE CITIES IN DANGER.
WELL, IN INTRO TO DAY-SAVING STRATEGIES, WE WERE JUST LEARNING ABOUT THE VALUE OF A GOOD DISTRACTION.
BLOOP!
BLIP!
SO, WE NEED A ***DISTRACTION*** TO GET HIM ***OFF*** THE SHIP WHILE WE MAKE A BREAK FOR IT WITH ALL THE CITIES!
BUT BRAINIAC ***IS*** THE SHIP. EVEN IF HIS BODY IS GONE, HE'S IN THE SHIP'S COMPUTERS--
WE HAVE TO ***HACK*** BRAINIAC!

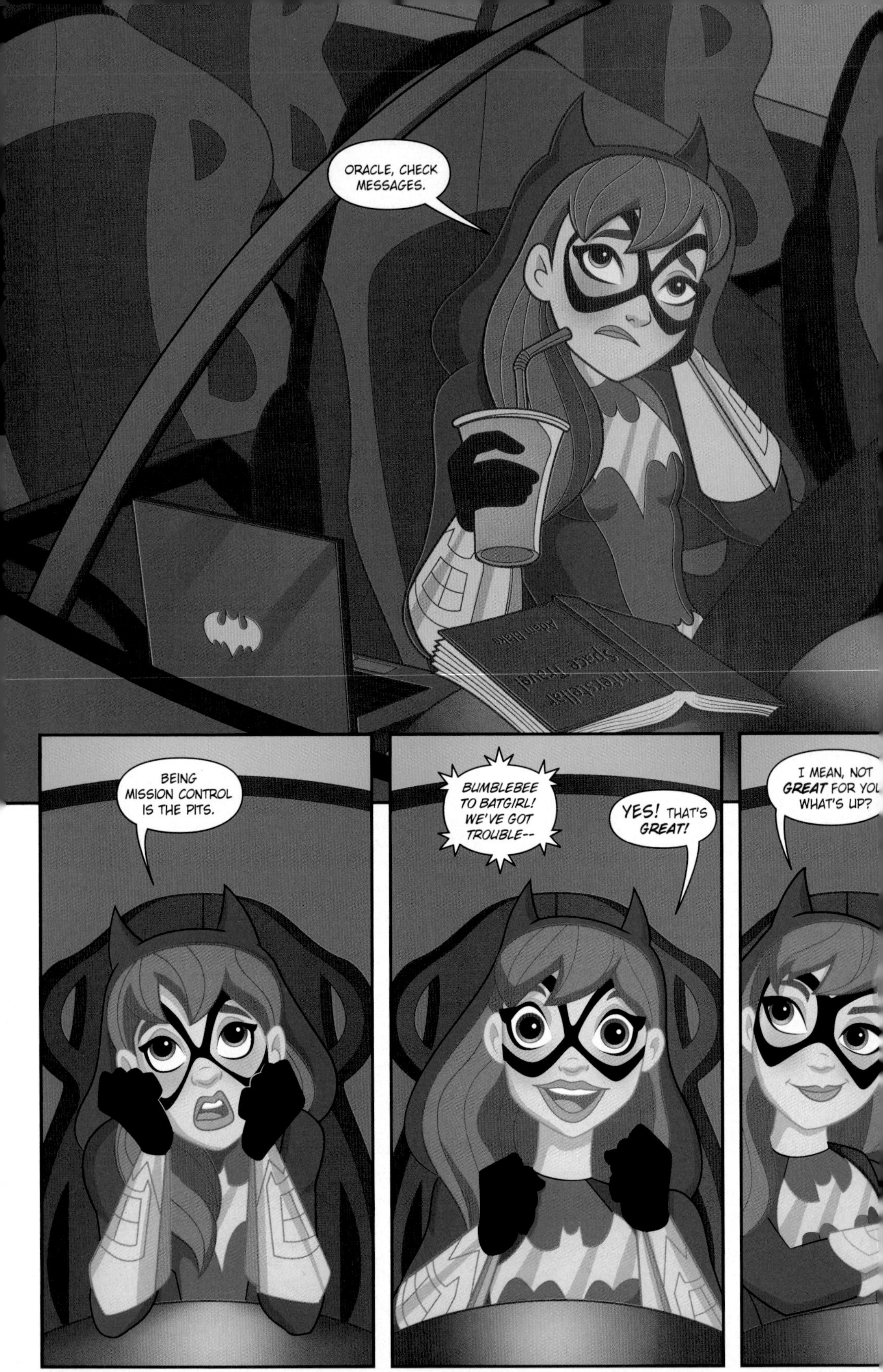
ORACLE, CHECK MESSAGES.
Interstellar Space Travel
Adam Blake
BEING MISSION CONTROL IS THE PITS.
BUMBLEBEE TO BATGIRL! WE'VE GOT TROUBLE--
YES! THAT'S GREAT!
I MEAN, NOT GREAT FOR YO
WHAT'S UP?

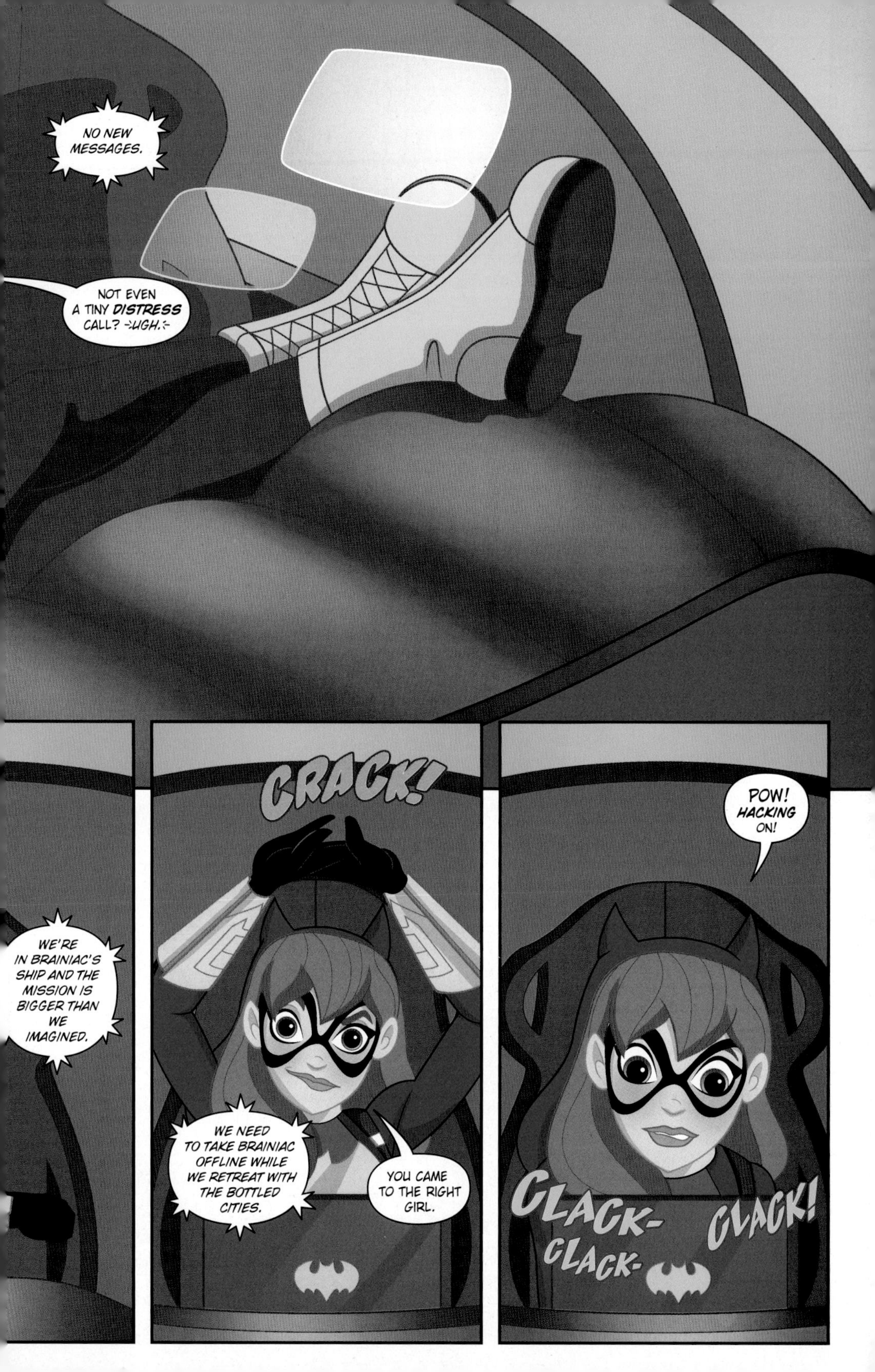
NO NEW MESSAGES.
NOT EVEN A TINY DISTRESS CALL? -UGH.-
WE'RE IN BRAINIAC'S SHIP AND THE MISSION IS BIGGER THAN WE IMAGINED.
CRACK!
WE NEED TO TAKE BRAINIAC OFFLINE WHILE WE RETREAT WITH THE BOTTLED CITIES.
YOU CAME TO THE RIGHT GIRL.
POW! HACKING ON!
CLACK-
CLACK-
CLACK!

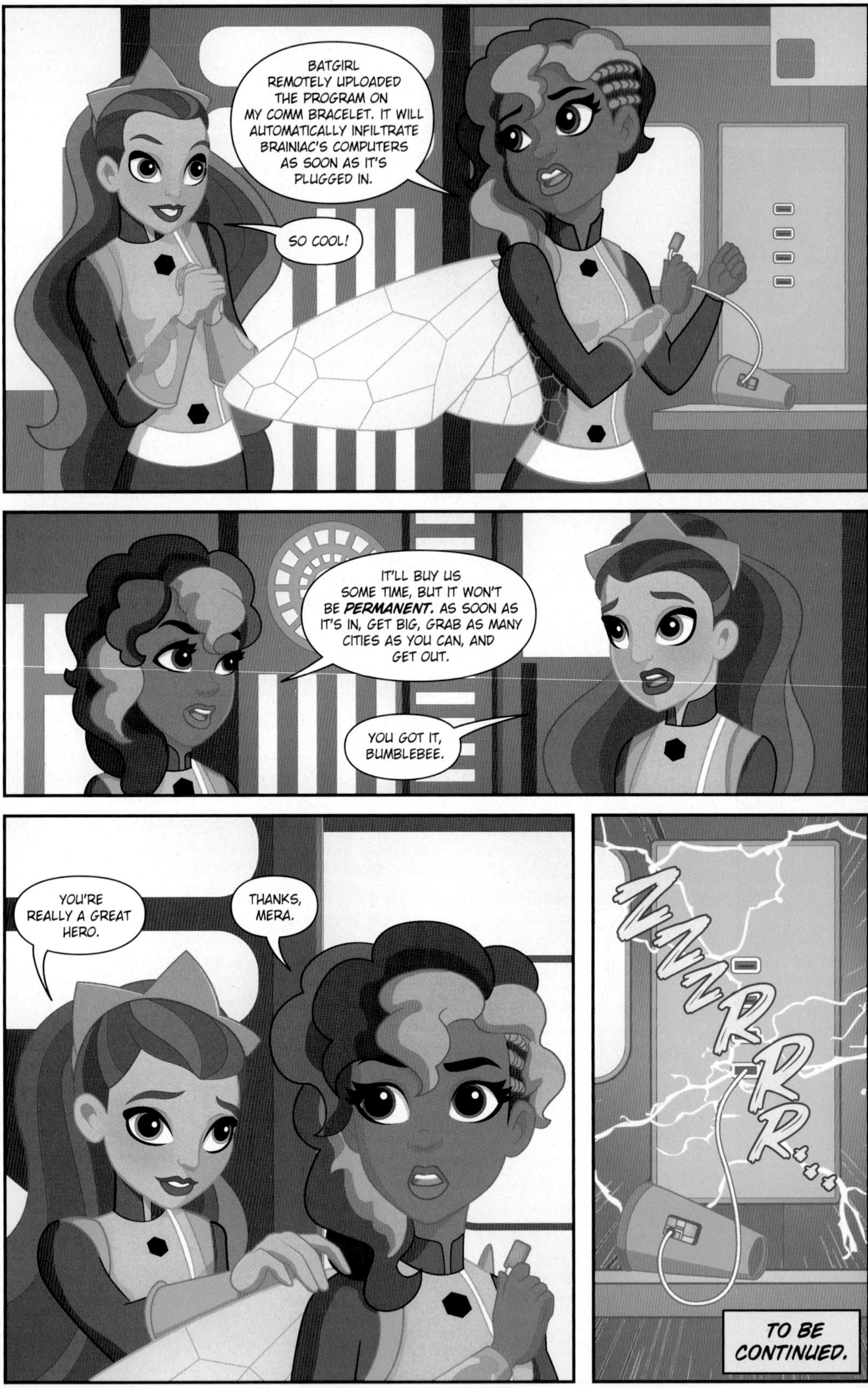
BATGIRL REMOTELY UPLOADED THE PROGRAM ON MY COMM BRACELET. IT WILL AUTOMATICALLY INFILTRATE BRAINIAC'S COMPUTERS AS SOON AS IT'S PLUGGED IN.
SO COOL!
IT'LL BUY US SOME TIME, BUT IT WON'T BE ***PERMANENT.*** AS SOON AS IT'S IN, GET BIG, GRAB AS MANY CITIES AS YOU CAN, AND GET OUT.
YOU GOT IT, BUMBLEBEE.
YOU'RE REALLY A GREAT HERO.
THANKS, MERA.
ZZZZRRR...
TO BE CONTINUED.

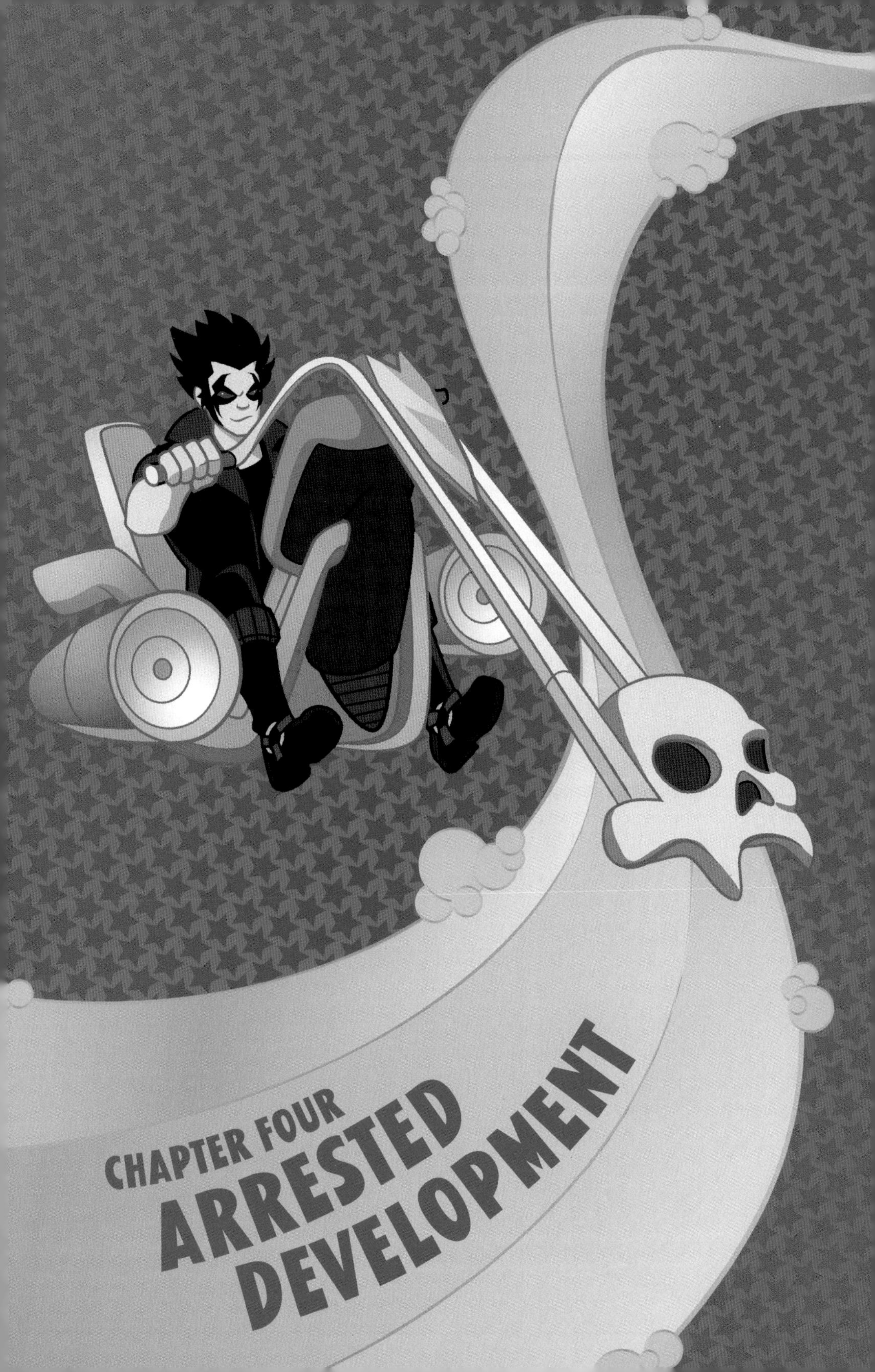
CHAPTER FOUR
ARRESTED
DEVELOPMENT

RUNNING SOFTWARE UPDATE.

I DID NOT INITIATE A SOFTWARE UPDATE!

CLACK!

CLACK!

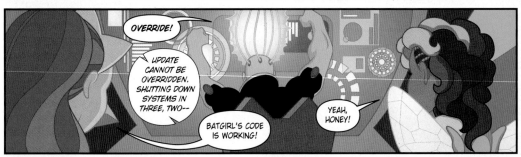

OVERRIDE!

UPDATE CANNOT BE OVERRIDDEN. SHUTTING DOWN SYSTEMS IN THREE, TWO--

BATGIRL'S CODE IS WORKING!

YEAH, HONEY!

BUT--

ONE.

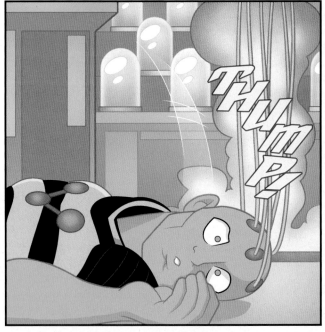

THUMP!

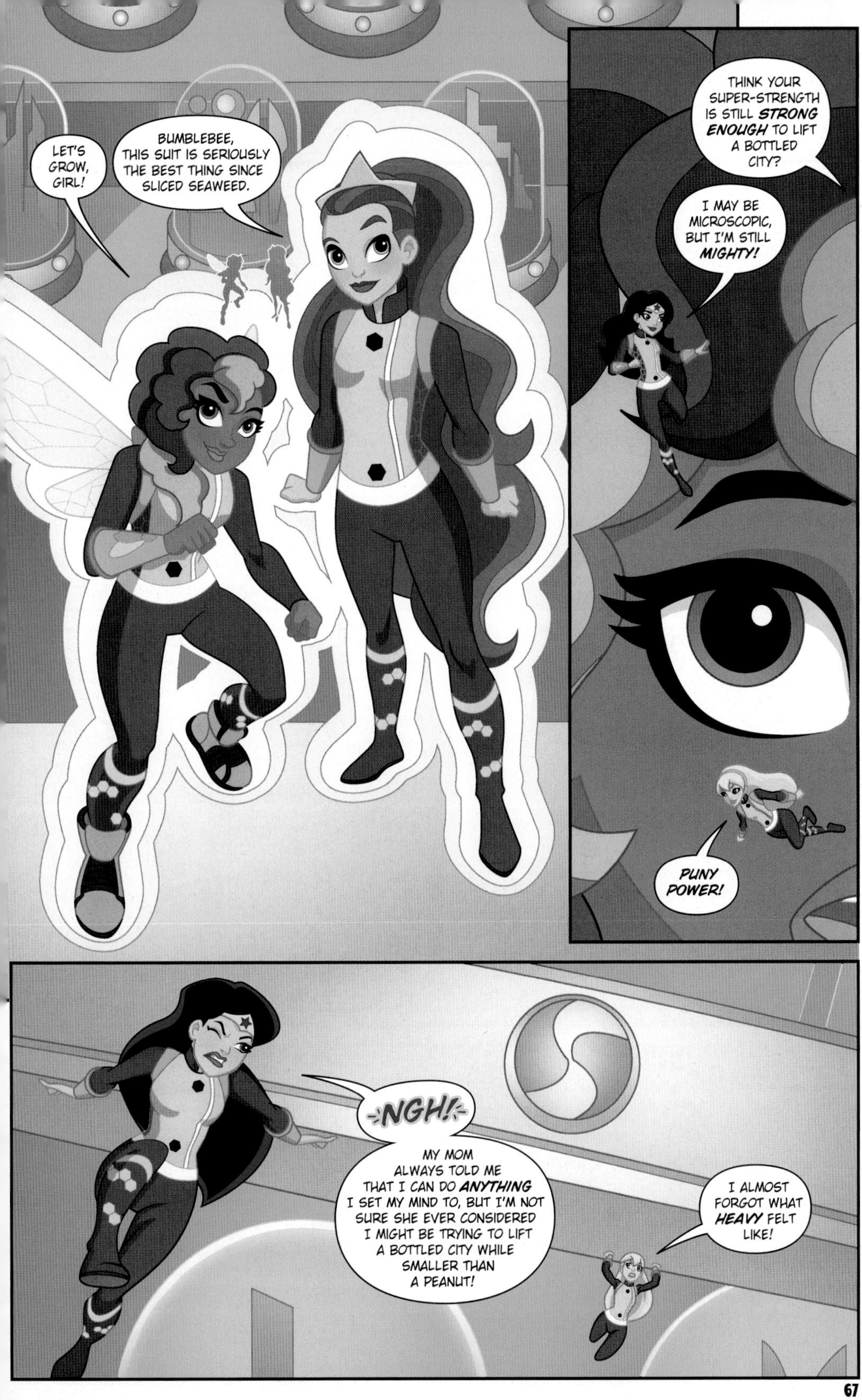

LET'S GROW, GIRL!
BUMBLEBEE, THIS SUIT IS SERIOUSLY THE BEST THING SINCE SLICED SEAWEED.
THINK YOUR SUPER-STRENGTH IS STILL STRONG ENOUGH TO LIFT A BOTTLED CITY?
I MAY BE MICROSCOPIC, BUT I'M STILL MIGHTY!
PUNY POWER!
-NGH!-
MY MOM ALWAYS TOLD ME THAT I CAN DO ANYTHING I SET MY MIND TO, BUT I'M NOT SURE SHE EVER CONSIDERED I MIGHT BE TRYING TO LIFT A BOTTLED CITY WHILE SMALLER THAN A PEANUT!
I ALMOST FORGOT WHAT HEAVY FELT LIKE!

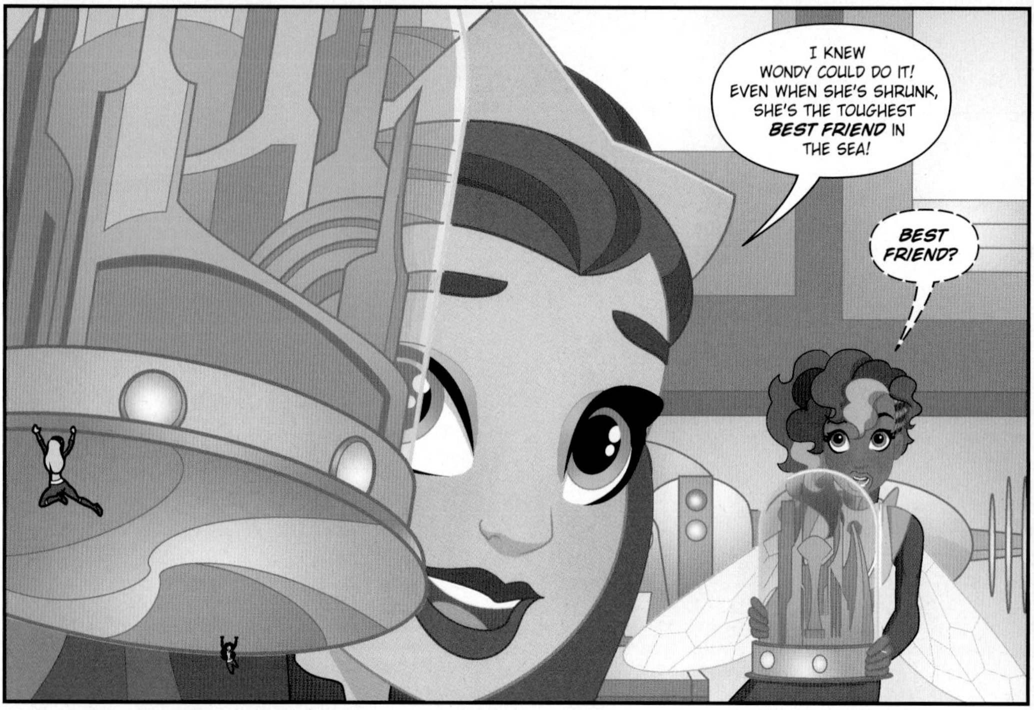
I KNEW WONDY COULD DO IT! EVEN WHEN SHE'S SHRUNK, SHE'S THE TOUGHEST **BEST FRIEND** IN THE SEA!
BEST FRIEND?

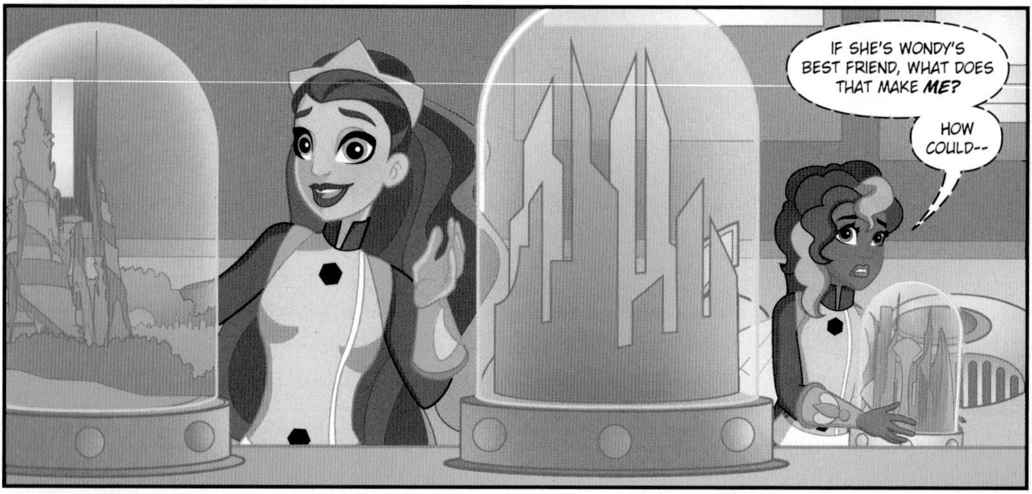
IF SHE'S WONDY'S BEST FRIEND, WHAT DOES THAT MAKE **ME?**
HOW COULD--

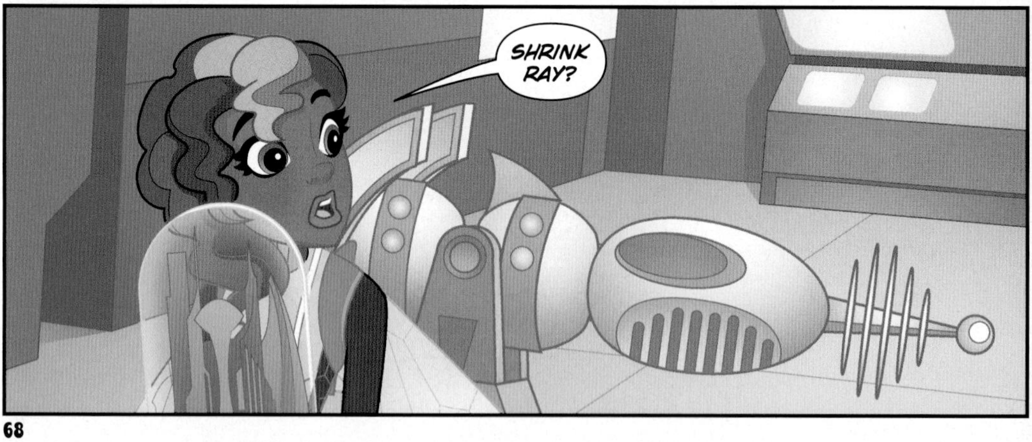
SHRINK RAY?

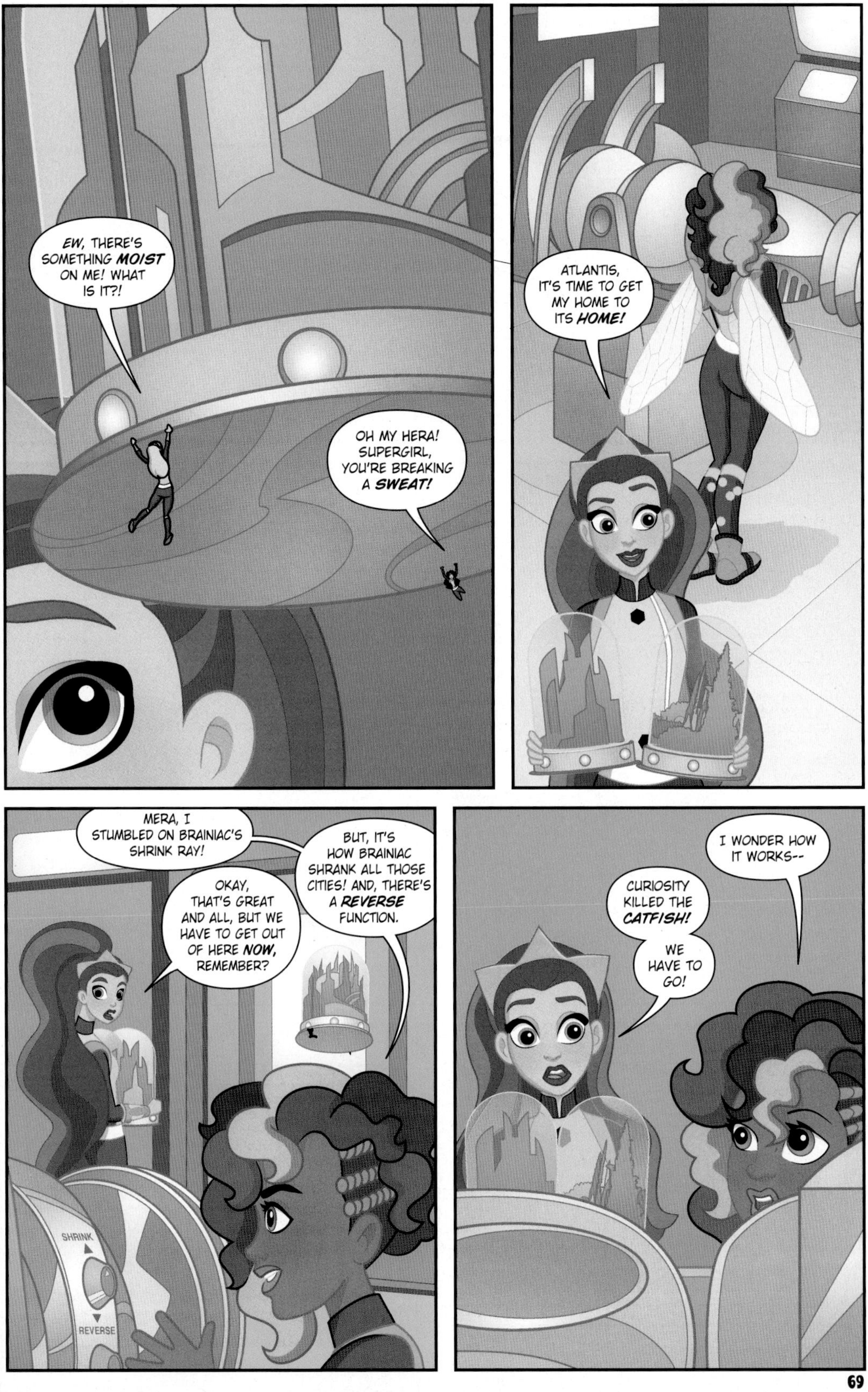
EW, THERE'S SOMETHING MOIST ON ME! WHAT IS IT?!
OH MY HERA! SUPERGIRL, YOU'RE BREAKING A SWEAT!
ATLANTIS, IT'S TIME TO GET MY HOME TO ITS HOME!
MERA, I STUMBLED ON BRAINIAC'S SHRINK RAY!
OKAY, THAT'S GREAT AND ALL, BUT WE HAVE TO GET OUT OF HERE NOW, REMEMBER?
BUT, IT'S HOW BRAINIAC SHRANK ALL THOSE CITIES! AND, THERE'S A REVERSE FUNCTION.
SHRINK
REVERSE
I WONDER HOW IT WORKS--
CURIOSITY KILLED THE CATFISH!
WE HAVE TO GO!

ERRRR! MERA, WE **NEED** THE SHRINK RAY! UNLESS YOU'RE OKAY WITH AN EXTRA-EXTRA-EXTRA SMALL **SWEETHEART.**

AQUAMAN? HE'S **NOT** MY SWEETHEART. WE JUST HANG OUT SOMETIMES, WHEN I'M IN ATLANTIS--

EVERYONE KNOWS YOU LIKE HIM!

WE'LL NEED TO **REVERSE** THE SHRINKING ONCE WE GET THESE CITIES BACK WHERE THEY BELONG.

BUT YOU'RE AN **ENGINEER** WHO SPECIALIZES IN SIZE CHANGE.

YOU CAN JUST MAKE SOMETHING TO GROW THEM!

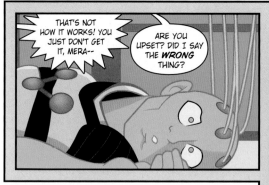

THAT'S NOT HOW IT WORKS! YOU JUST DON'T GET IT, MERA--

ARE YOU UPSET? DID I SAY THE **WRONG** THING?

SORRY, I'M STILL NEW TO LAND-WALKER ETIQUETTE.

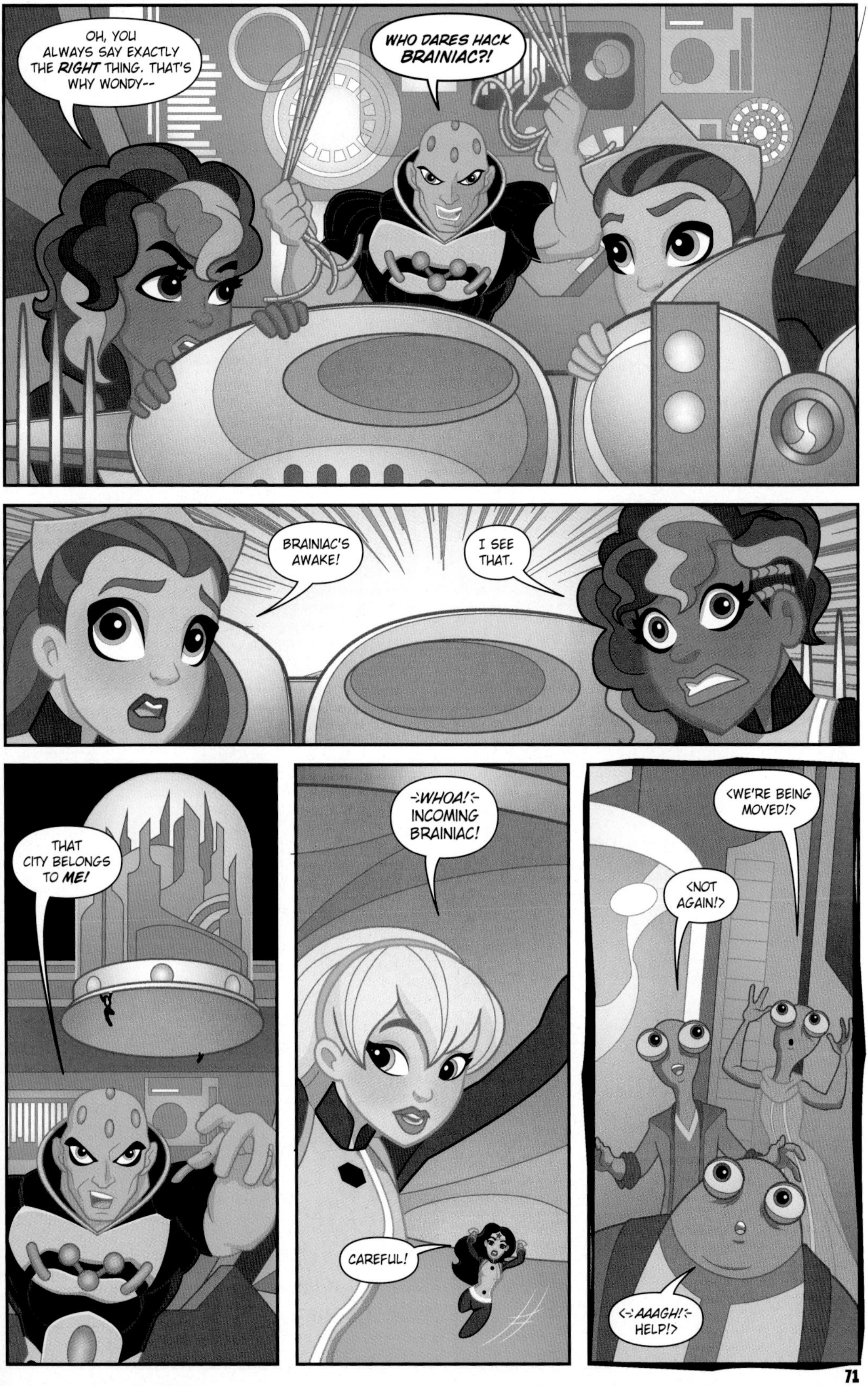
OH, YOU ALWAYS SAY EXACTLY THE RIGHT THING. THAT'S WHY WONDY--
WHO DARES HACK BRAINIAC?!
BRAINIAC'S AWAKE!
I SEE THAT.
THAT CITY BELONGS TO ME!
WHOA! INCOMING BRAINIAC!
CAREFUL!
<WE'RE BEING MOVED!>
<NOT AGAIN!>
<AAAGH! HELP!>

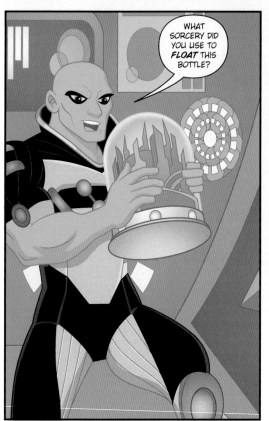

WHAT SORCERY DID YOU USE TO *FLOAT* THIS BOTTLE?

I DON'T DO *SORCERY.* JUST ELECTRIC ST--

NO! IF YOU HIT THE BOTTLE, ALL THOSE PEOPLE INSIDE WILL BE *LOST!*

JUST BECAUSE I'M LITTLE, DOESN'T MEAN I'M GOING TO GIVE UP!

PUT DOWN THAT CITY, YOU OVERGROWN *CALCULATOR!*

Life-forms Detected. Kryptonian: 1. Amazon: 1.

Current Status: Students of Super Hero High.

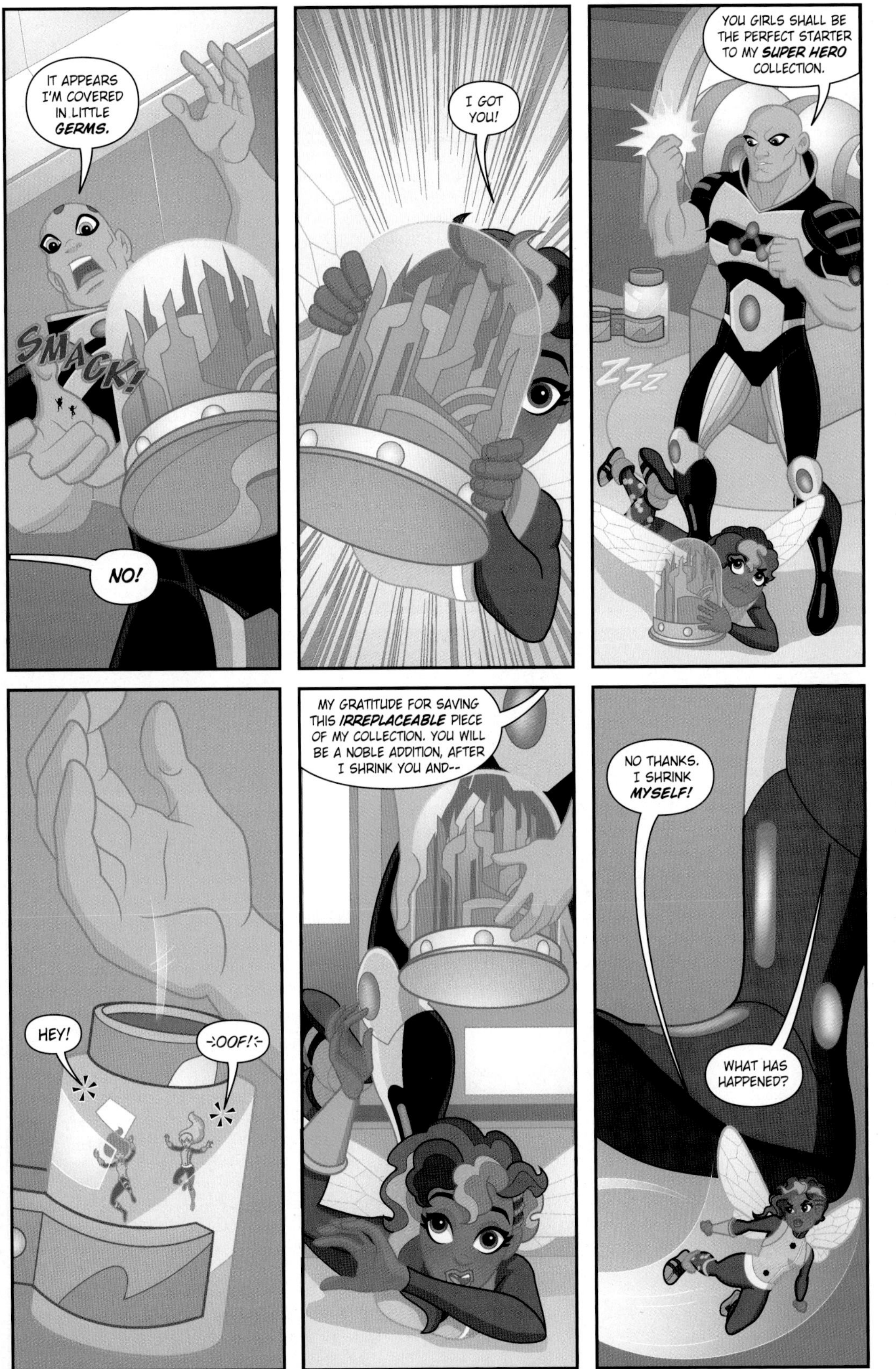
IT APPEARS I'M COVERED IN LITTLE GERMS.
SMACK!
NO!
I GOT YOU!
YOU GIRLS SHALL BE THE PERFECT STARTER TO MY SUPER HERO COLLECTION.
ZZZ
HEY!
-OOF!-
MY GRATITUDE FOR SAVING THIS IRREPLACEABLE PIECE OF MY COLLECTION. YOU WILL BE A NOBLE ADDITION, AFTER I SHRINK YOU AND--
NO THANKS. I SHRINK MYSELF!
WHAT HAS HAPPENED?

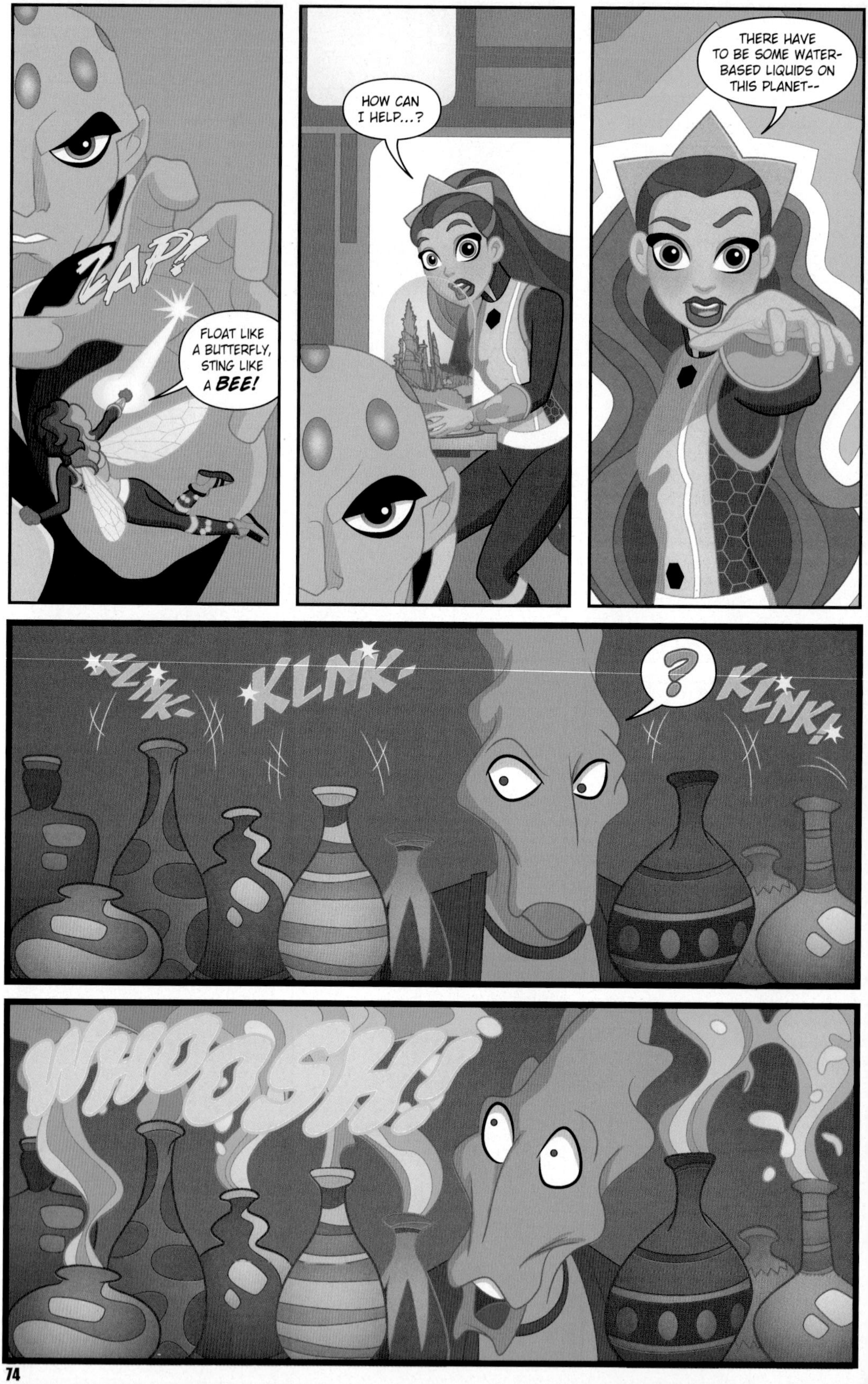

ZAP!
FLOAT LIKE A BUTTERFLY, STING LIKE A **BEE!**
HOW CAN I HELP...?
THERE HAVE TO BE SOME WATER-BASED LIQUIDS ON THIS PLANET--
KLNK-
KLNK-
?
KLNK!
WHOOSH!

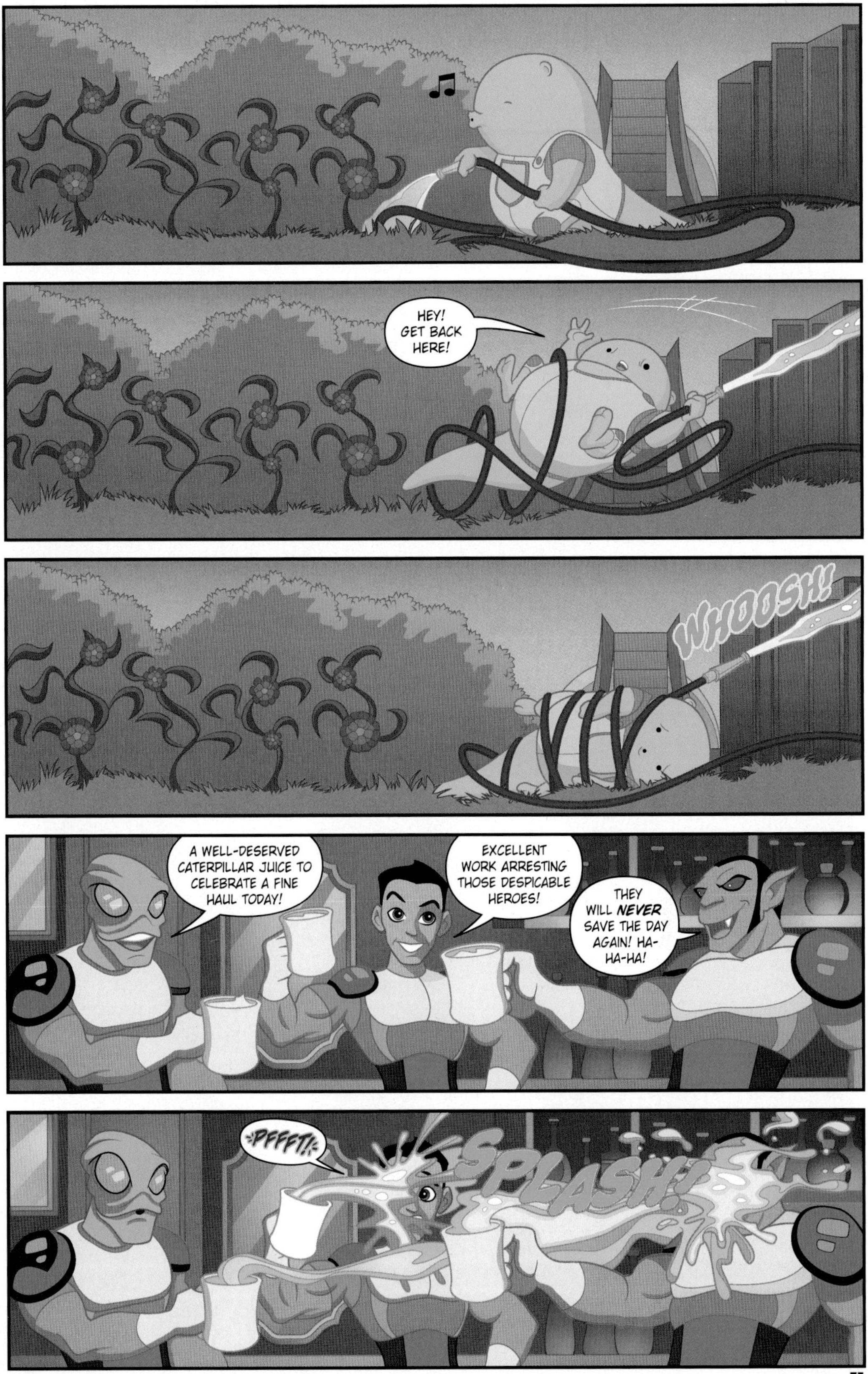
HEY! GET BACK HERE!
WHOOSH!
A WELL-DESERVED CATERPILLAR JUICE TO CELEBRATE A FINE HAUL TODAY!
EXCELLENT WORK ARRESTING THOSE DESPICABLE HEROES!
THEY WILL **NEVER** SAVE THE DAY AGAIN! HA-HA-HA!
PFFFT!
SPLASH!

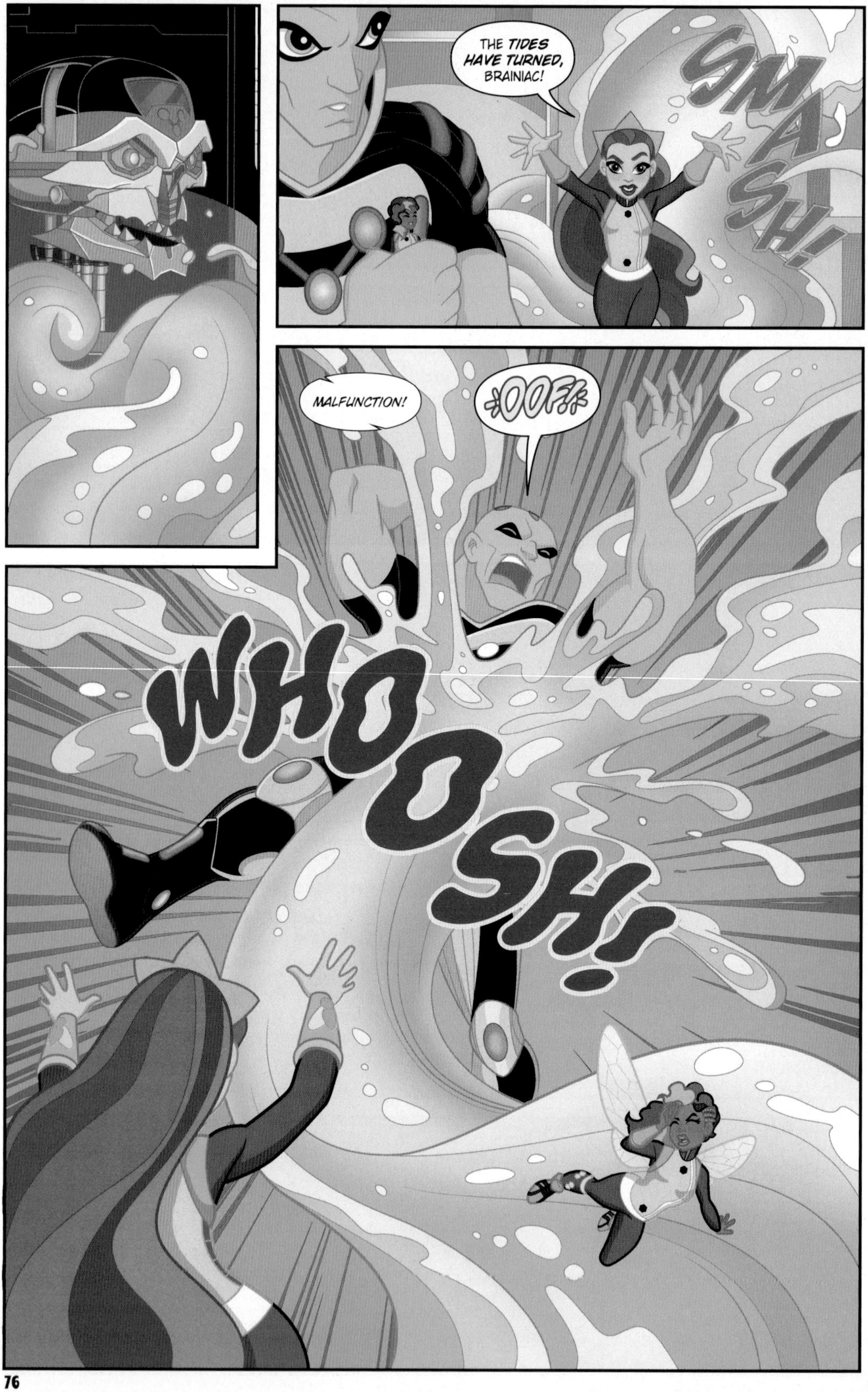
THE TIDES HAVE TURNED, BRAINIAC!
SMASH!
MALFUNCTION!
OOF!
WHOOSH!

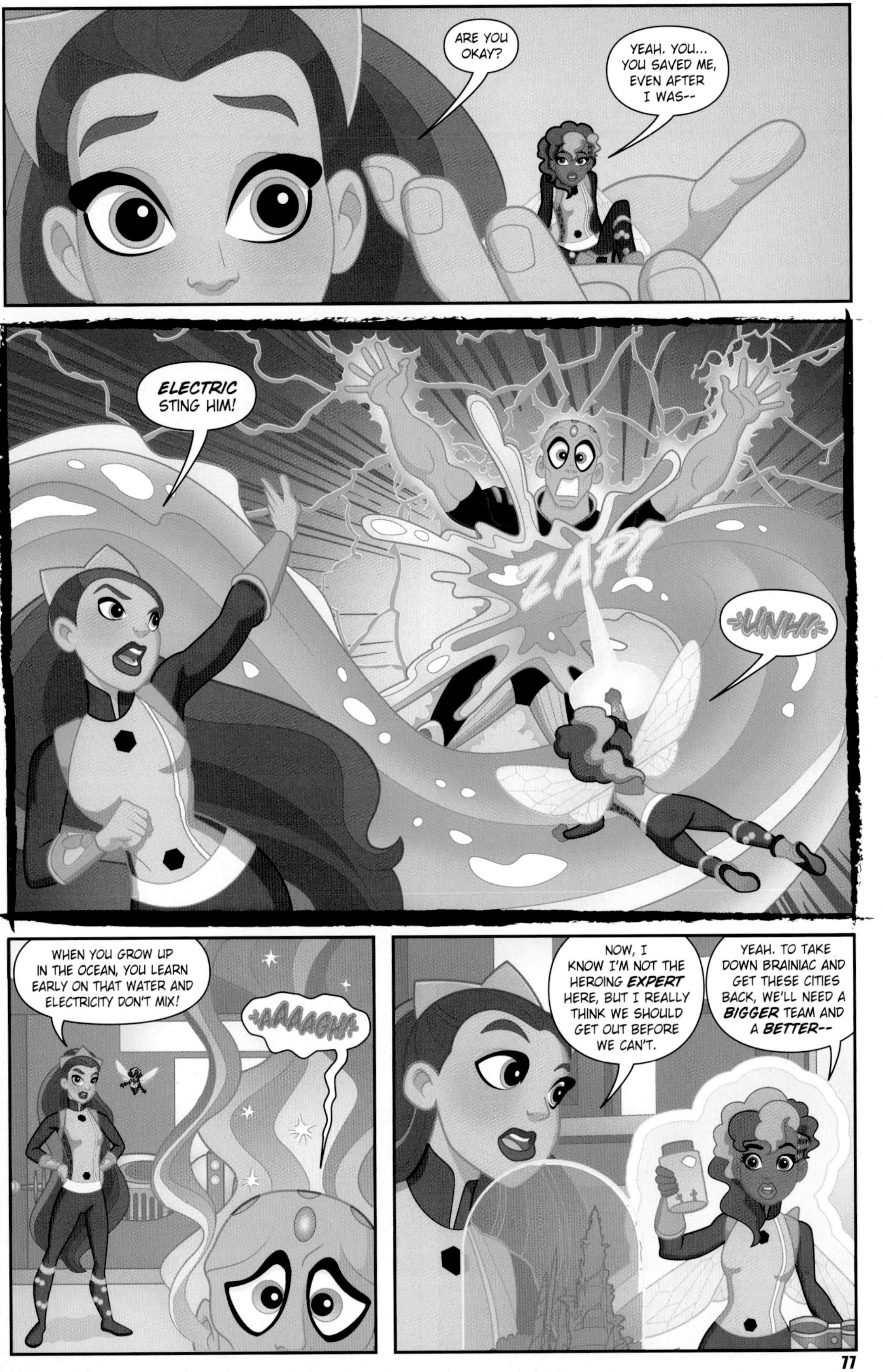

ARE YOU OKAY?
YEAH. YOU... YOU SAVED ME, EVEN AFTER I WAS--
ELECTRIC STING HIM!
ZAP!
-UNH!-
WHEN YOU GROW UP IN THE OCEAN, YOU LEARN EARLY ON THAT WATER AND ELECTRICITY DON'T MIX!
-AAAAGH!-
NOW, I KNOW I'M NOT THE HEROING *EXPERT* HERE, BUT I REALLY THINK WE SHOULD GET OUT BEFORE WE CAN'T.
YEAH. TO TAKE DOWN BRAINIAC AND GET THESE CITIES BACK, WE'LL NEED A *BIGGER* TEAM AND A *BETTER*--

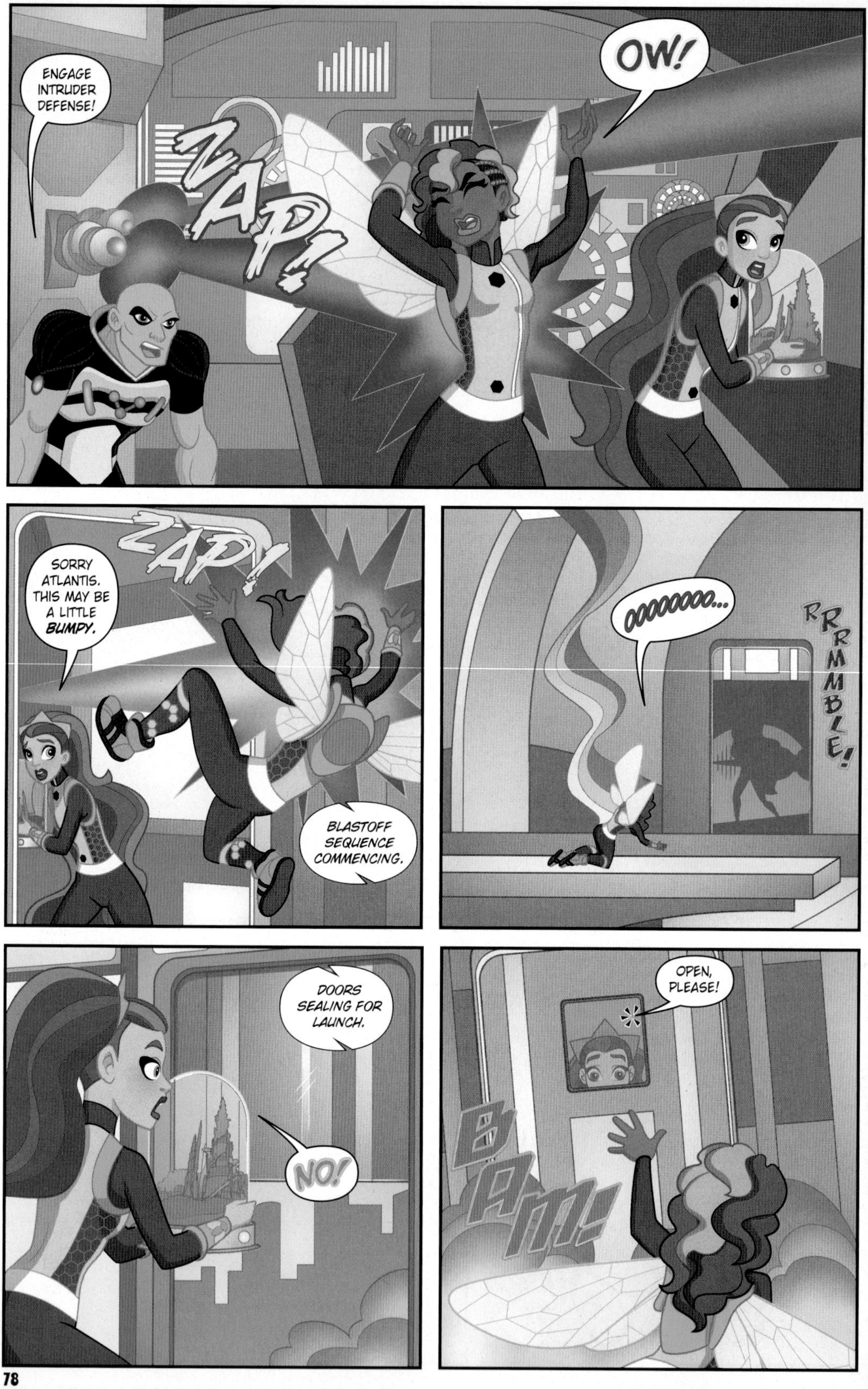
ENGAGE INTRUDER DEFENSE!
ZAP!
OW!
SORRY ATLANTIS. THIS MAY BE A LITTLE BUMPY.
ZAP!
BLASTOFF SEQUENCE COMMENCING.
OOOOOOOO...
RRRMMBLE!
DOORS SEALING FOR LAUNCH.
NO!
OPEN, PLEASE!
BAM!

WONDER WOMAN? SUPERGIRL? MERA?

STOP!

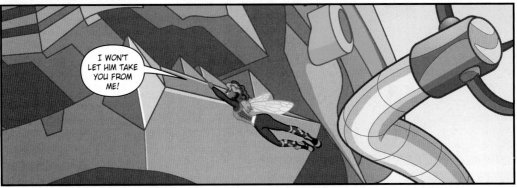

I WON'T LET HIM TAKE YOU FROM ME!

WHOOSH

MY WING--

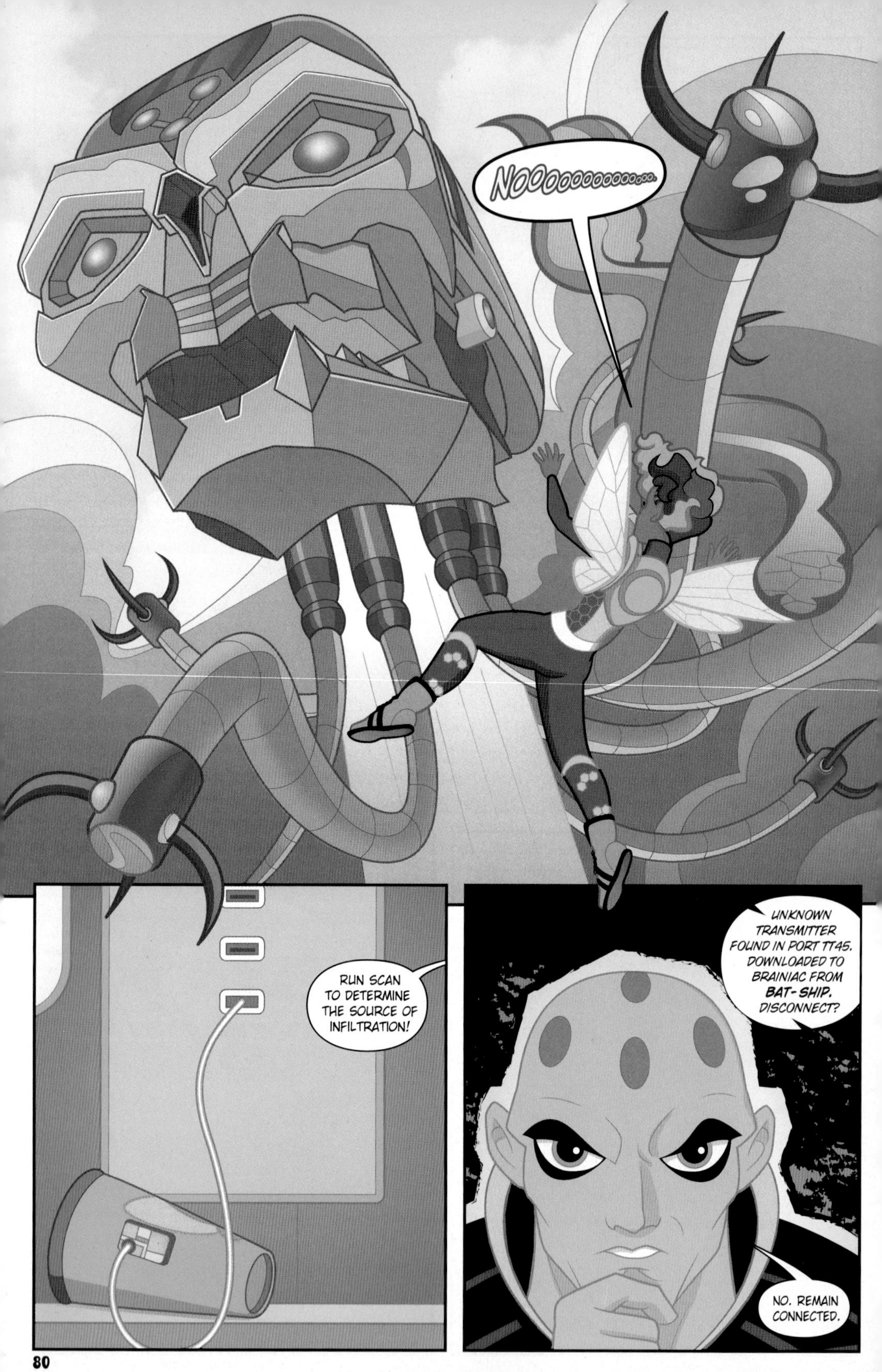
NOOOoooooooooooo...
RUN SCAN TO DETERMINE THE SOURCE OF INFILTRATION!
UNKNOWN TRANSMITTER FOUND IN PORT TT45. DOWNLOADED TO BRAINIAC FROM BAT-SHIP. DISCONNECT?
NO. REMAIN CONNECTED.

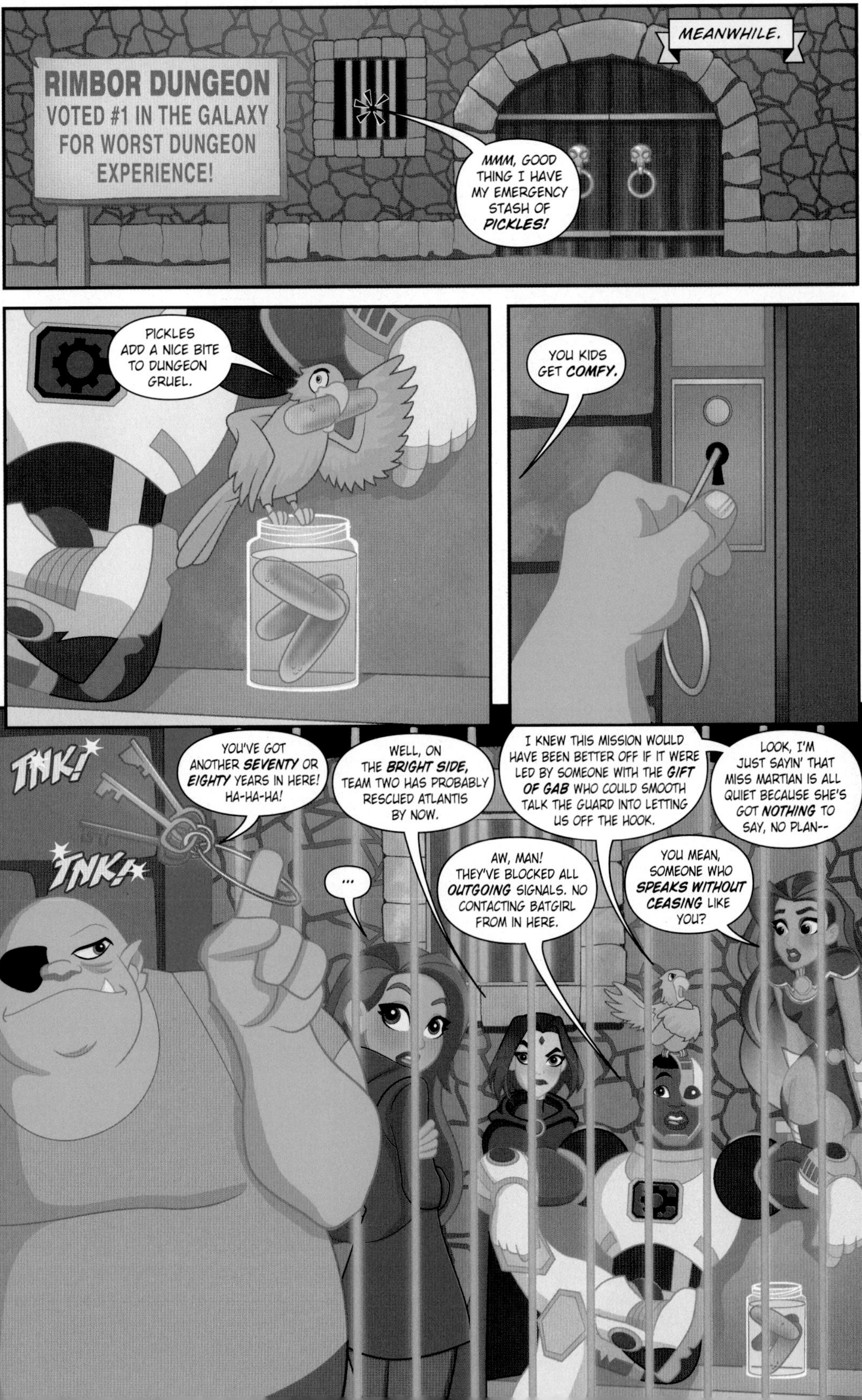
MEANWHILE.
RIMBOR DUNGEON
VOTED #1 IN THE GALAXY FOR WORST DUNGEON EXPERIENCE!
MMM, GOOD THING I HAVE MY EMERGENCY STASH OF PICKLES!
PICKLES ADD A NICE BITE TO DUNGEON GRUEL.
YOU KIDS GET COMFY.
TNK!
TNK!
YOU'VE GOT ANOTHER SEVENTY OR EIGHTY YEARS IN HERE! HA-HA-HA!
WELL, ON THE BRIGHT SIDE, TEAM TWO HAS PROBABLY RESCUED ATLANTIS BY NOW.
...
AW, MAN! THEY'VE BLOCKED ALL OUTGOING SIGNALS. NO CONTACTING BATGIRL FROM IN HERE.
I KNEW THIS MISSION WOULD HAVE BEEN BETTER OFF IF IT WERE LED BY SOMEONE WITH THE GIFT OF GAB WHO COULD SMOOTH TALK THE GUARD INTO LETTING US OFF THE HOOK.
YOU MEAN, SOMEONE WHO SPEAKS WITHOUT CEASING LIKE YOU?
LOOK, I'M JUST SAYIN' THAT MISS MARTIAN IS ALL QUIET BECAUSE SHE'S GOT NOTHING TO SAY, NO PLAN--

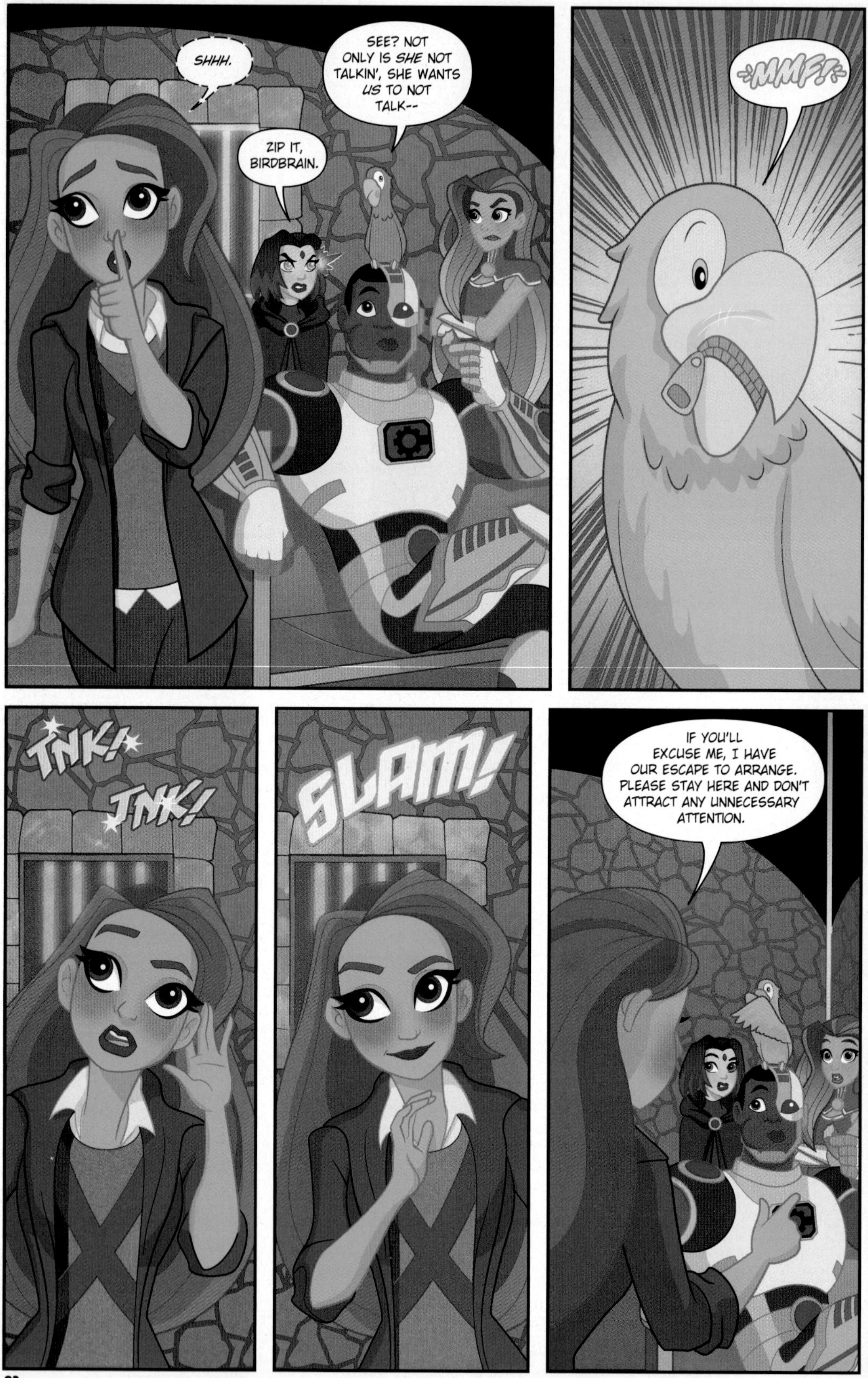
SHHH.
SEE? NOT ONLY IS SHE NOT TALKIN', SHE WANTS US TO NOT TALK--
ZIP IT, BIRDBRAIN.
MMF!
TNK!
TNK!
SLAM!
IF YOU'LL EXCUSE ME, I HAVE OUR ESCAPE TO ARRANGE. PLEASE STAY HERE AND DON'T ATTRACT ANY UNNECESSARY ATTENTION.

IT APPEARS THAT MISS MARTIAN WAS NOT BEING *SILENT* IN *WEAKNESS*, BUT BECAUSE SHE WAS *LISTENING* IN ORDER TO BEST FORM A PLAN.

WHA-WHA-WHAAAAAA...

NEVER UNDERESTIMATE THE *QUIET KID*.

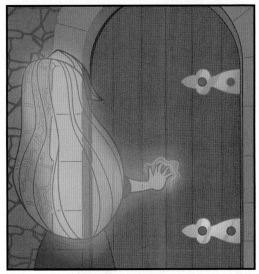

FROM THE SECOND I LAID MY EYE ON YOU, SUGAR-FACE, I'VE THOUGHT YOU WERE MORE BEAUTIFUL THAN A WHOLE BUCKETFUL OF *WORMS*!

AW, SWEETIE!

TNK!

TNK!

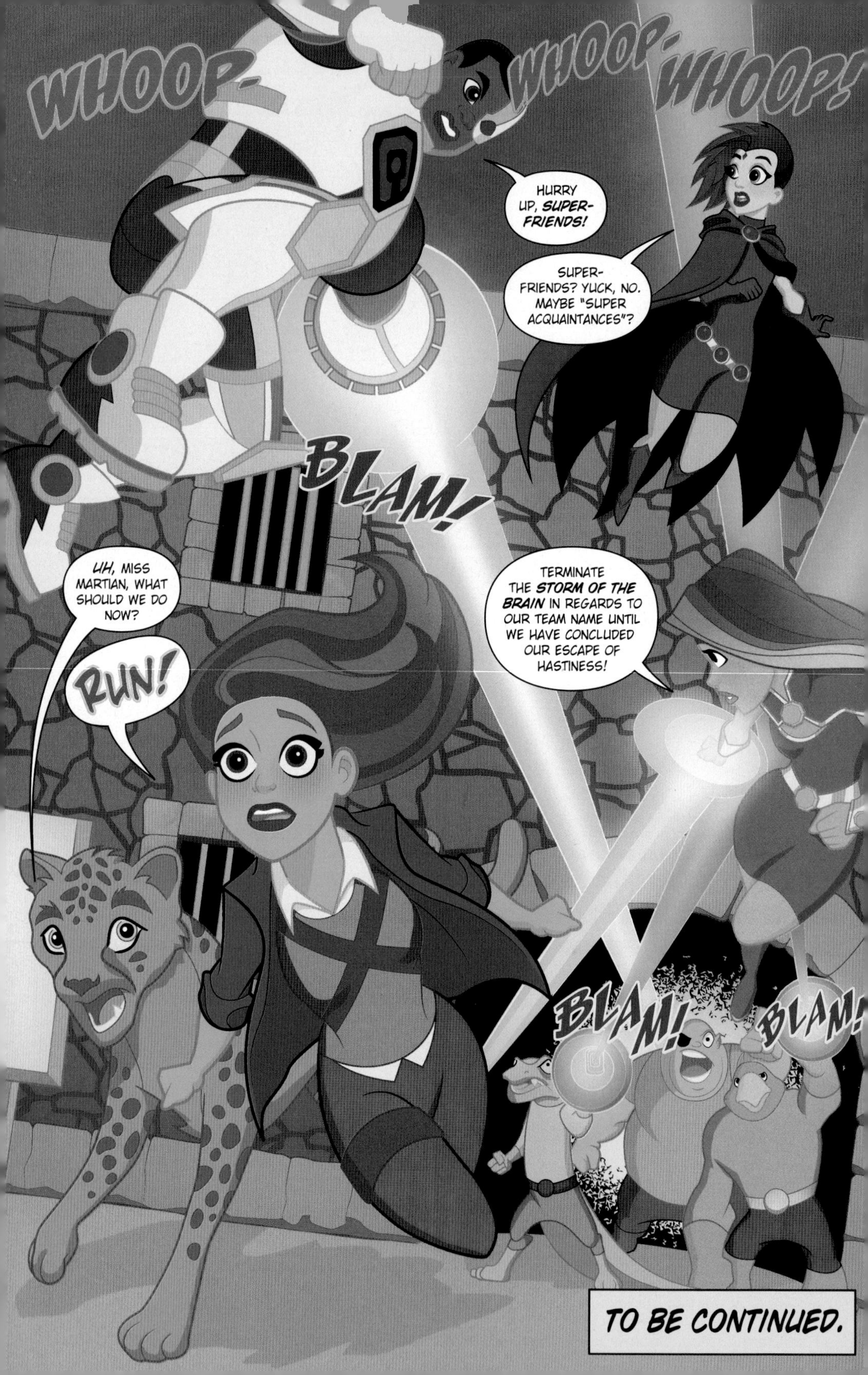
WHOOP-WHOOP-WHOOP!
HURRY UP, SUPER-FRIENDS!
SUPER-FRIENDS? YUCK, NO. MAYBE "SUPER ACQUAINTANCES"?
BLAM!
UH, MISS MARTIAN, WHAT SHOULD WE DO NOW?
TERMINATE THE STORM OF THE BRAIN IN REGARDS TO OUR TEAM NAME UNTIL WE HAVE CONCLUDED OUR ESCAPE OF HASTINESS!
RUN!
BLAM!
BLAM!
TO BE CONTINUED.

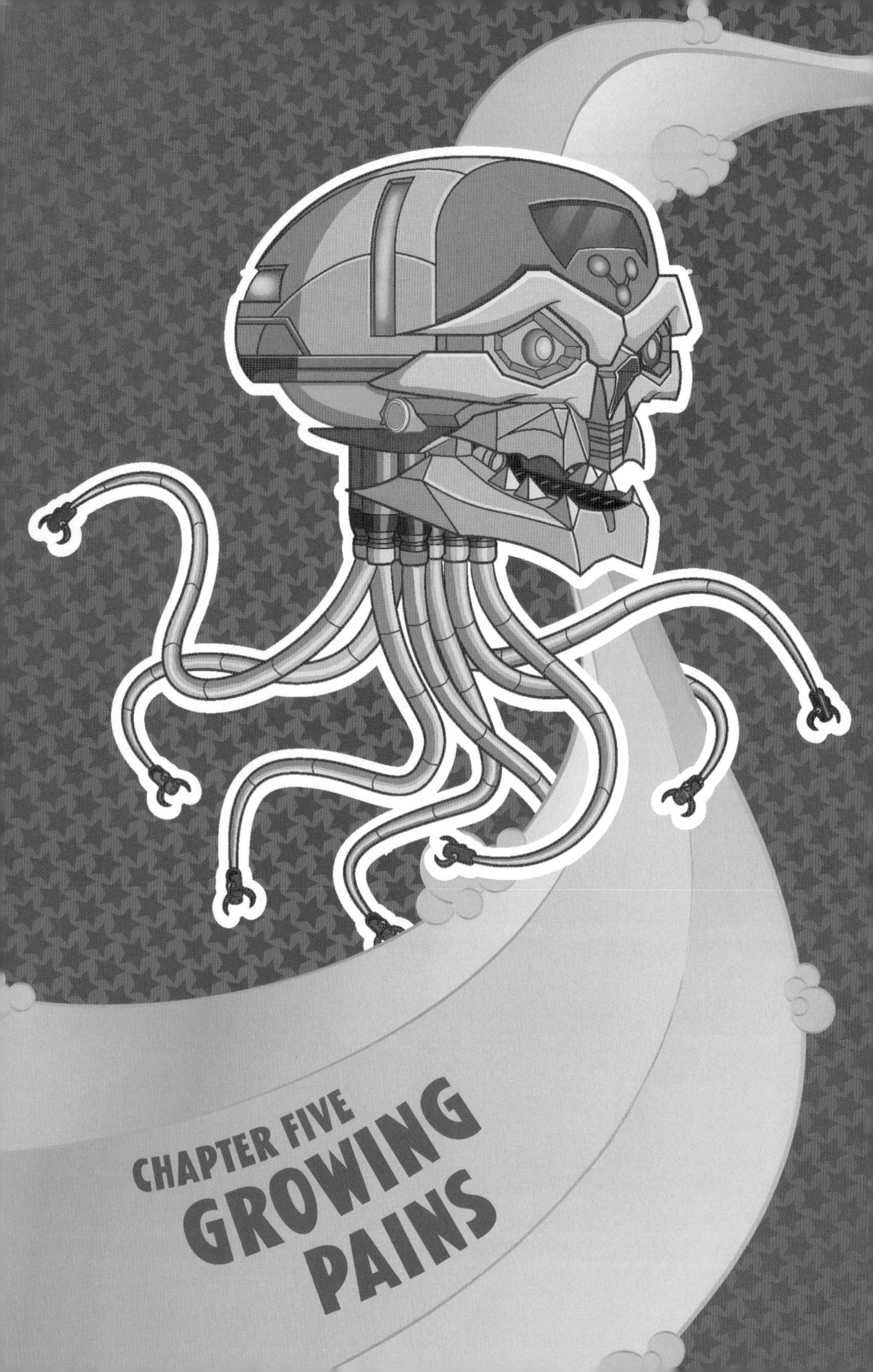

CHAPTER FIVE
GROWING PAINS

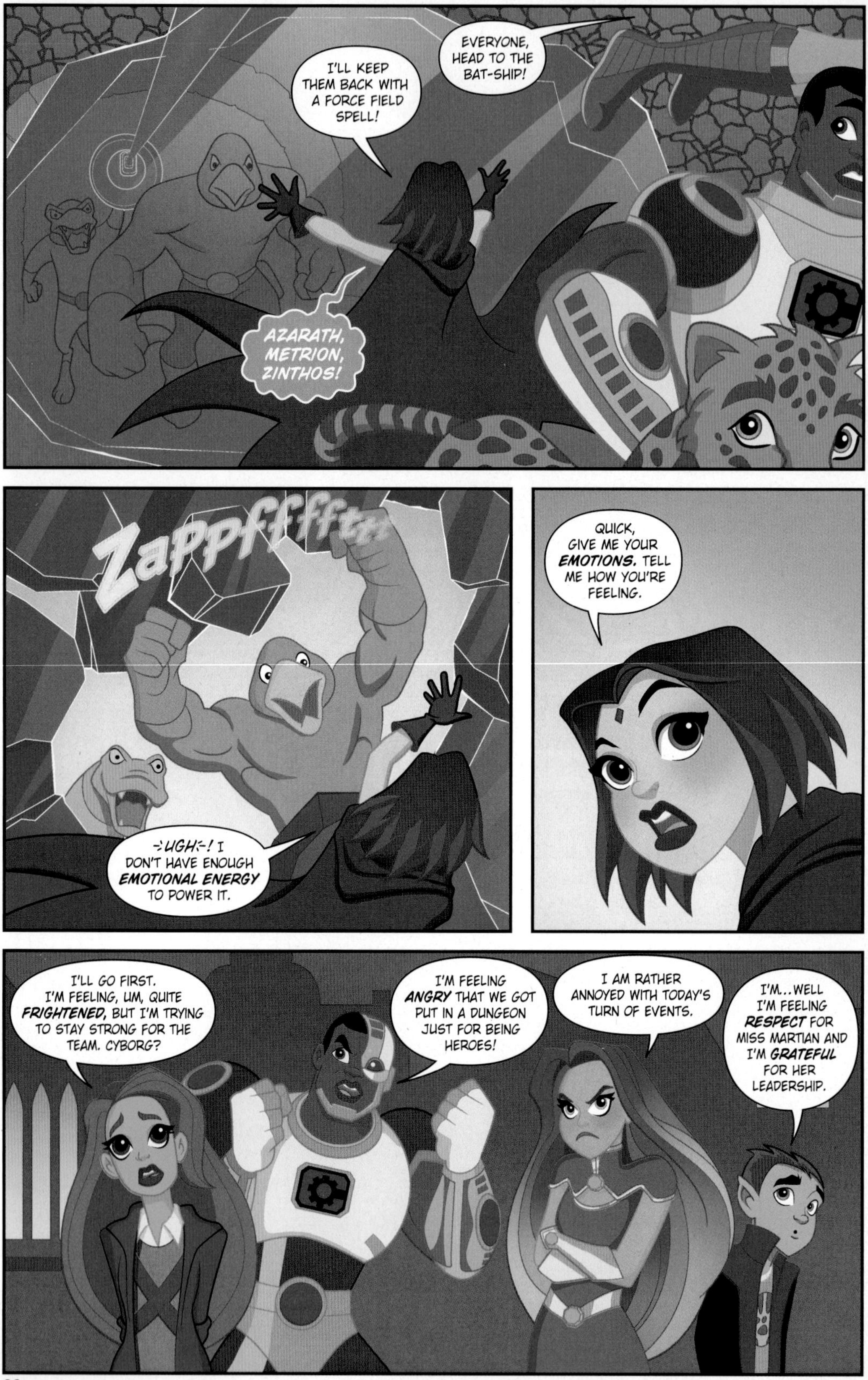
EVERYONE, HEAD TO THE BAT-SHIP!
I'LL KEEP THEM BACK WITH A FORCE FIELD SPELL!
AZARATH, METRION, ZINTHOS!
Zappfffftt
UGH! I DON'T HAVE ENOUGH EMOTIONAL ENERGY TO POWER IT.
QUICK, GIVE ME YOUR EMOTIONS. TELL ME HOW YOU'RE FEELING.
I'LL GO FIRST. I'M FEELING, UM, QUITE FRIGHTENED, BUT I'M TRYING TO STAY STRONG FOR THE TEAM. CYBORG?
I'M FEELING ANGRY THAT WE GOT PUT IN A DUNGEON JUST FOR BEING HEROES!
I AM RATHER ANNOYED WITH TODAY'S TURN OF EVENTS.
I'M...WELL I'M FEELING RESPECT FOR MISS MARTIAN AND I'M GRATEFUL FOR HER LEADERSHIP.

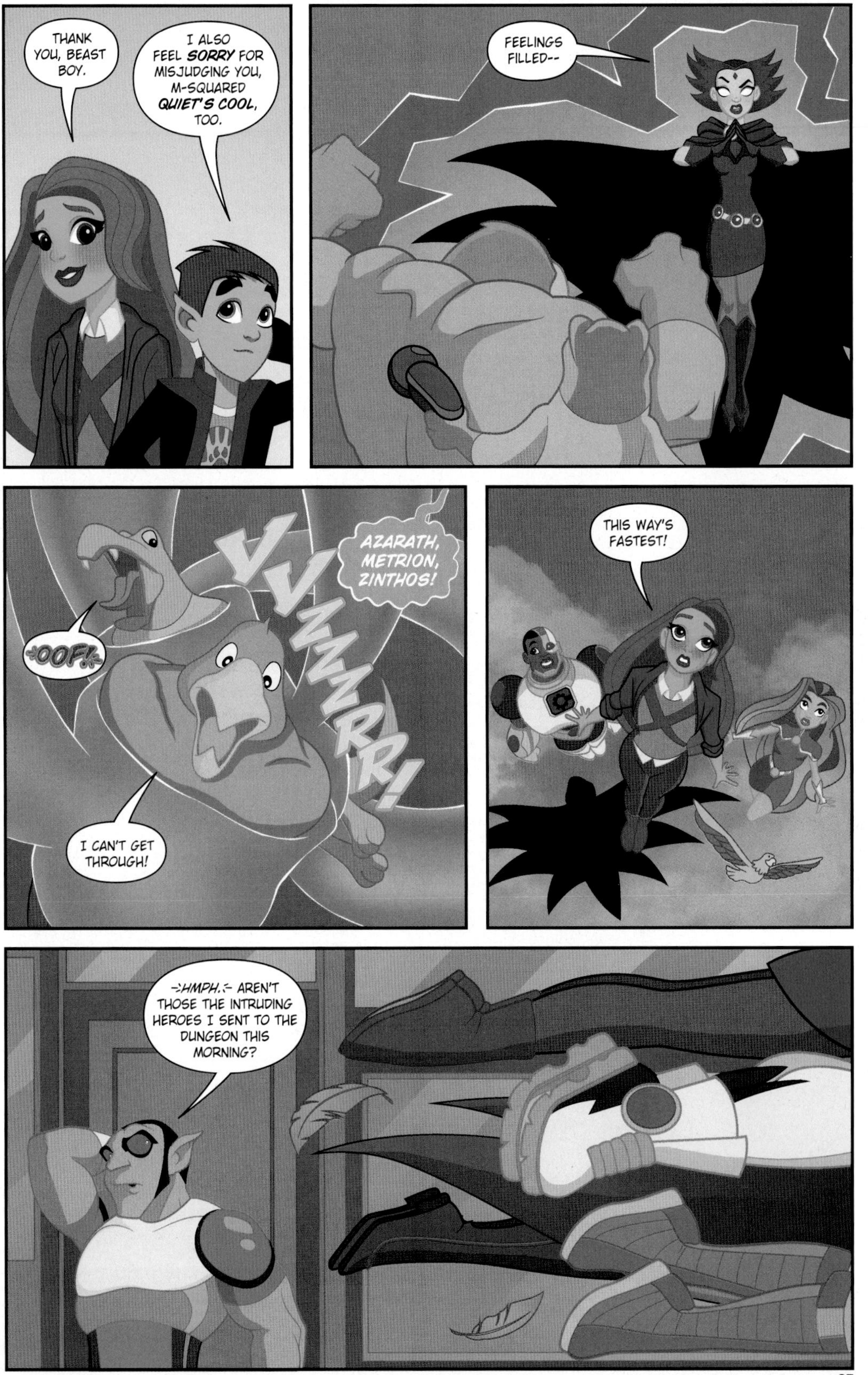
THANK YOU, BEAST BOY.
I ALSO FEEL SORRY FOR MISJUDGING YOU, M-SQUARED QUIET'S COOL, TOO.
FEELINGS FILLED--
AZARATH, METRION, ZINTHOS!
VVZZZRR!
OOF!
I CAN'T GET THROUGH!
THIS WAY'S FASTEST!
HMPH. AREN'T THOSE THE INTRUDING HEROES I SENT TO THE DUNGEON THIS MORNING?

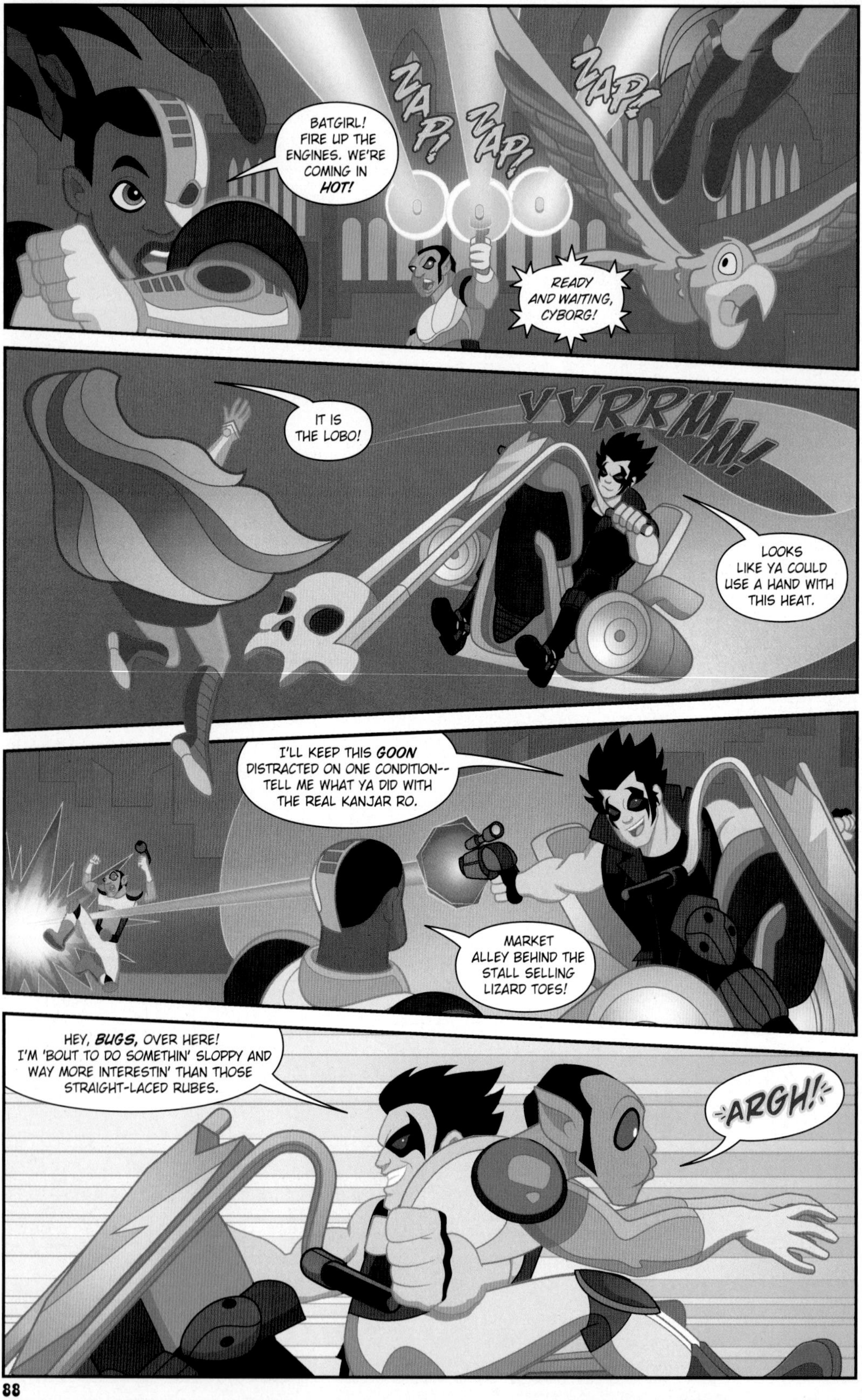
BATGIRL! FIRE UP THE ENGINES. WE'RE COMING IN HOT!
ZAP! ZAP!
ZAP!
READY AND WAITING, CYBORG!
IT IS THE LOBO!
VVRRMMM!
LOOKS LIKE YA COULD USE A HAND WITH THIS HEAT.
I'LL KEEP THIS GOON DISTRACTED ON ONE CONDITION--TELL ME WHAT YA DID WITH THE REAL KANJAR RO.
MARKET ALLEY BEHIND THE STALL SELLING LIZARD TOES!
HEY, BUGS, OVER HERE! I'M 'BOUT TO DO SOMETHIN' SLOPPY AND WAY MORE INTERESTIN' THAN THOSE STRAIGHT-LACED RUBES.
ARGH!

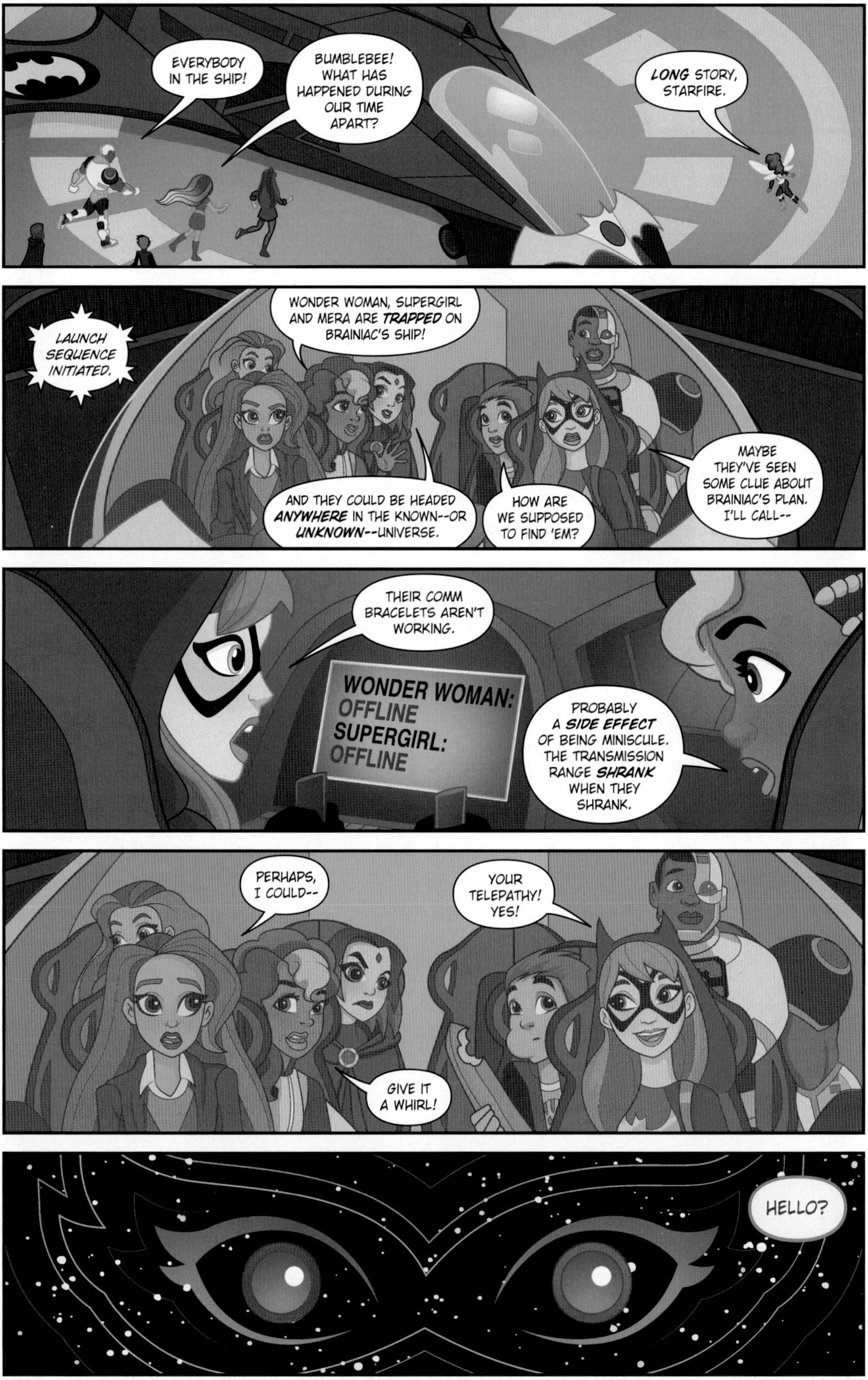
EVERYBODY IN THE SHIP!
BUMBLEBEE! WHAT HAS HAPPENED DURING OUR TIME APART?
LONG STORY, STARFIRE.
LAUNCH SEQUENCE INITIATED.
WONDER WOMAN, SUPERGIRL AND MERA ARE TRAPPED ON BRAINIAC'S SHIP!
AND THEY COULD BE HEADED ANYWHERE IN THE KNOWN--OR UNKNOWN--UNIVERSE.
HOW ARE WE SUPPOSED TO FIND 'EM?
MAYBE THEY'VE SEEN SOME CLUE ABOUT BRAINIAC'S PLAN. I'LL CALL--
THEIR COMM BRACELETS AREN'T WORKING.
WONDER WOMAN: OFFLINE
SUPERGIRL: OFFLINE
PROBABLY A SIDE EFFECT OF BEING MINISCULE. THE TRANSMISSION RANGE SHRANK WHEN THEY SHRANK.
PERHAPS, I COULD--
YOUR TELEPATHY! YES!
GIVE IT A WHIRL!
HELLO?

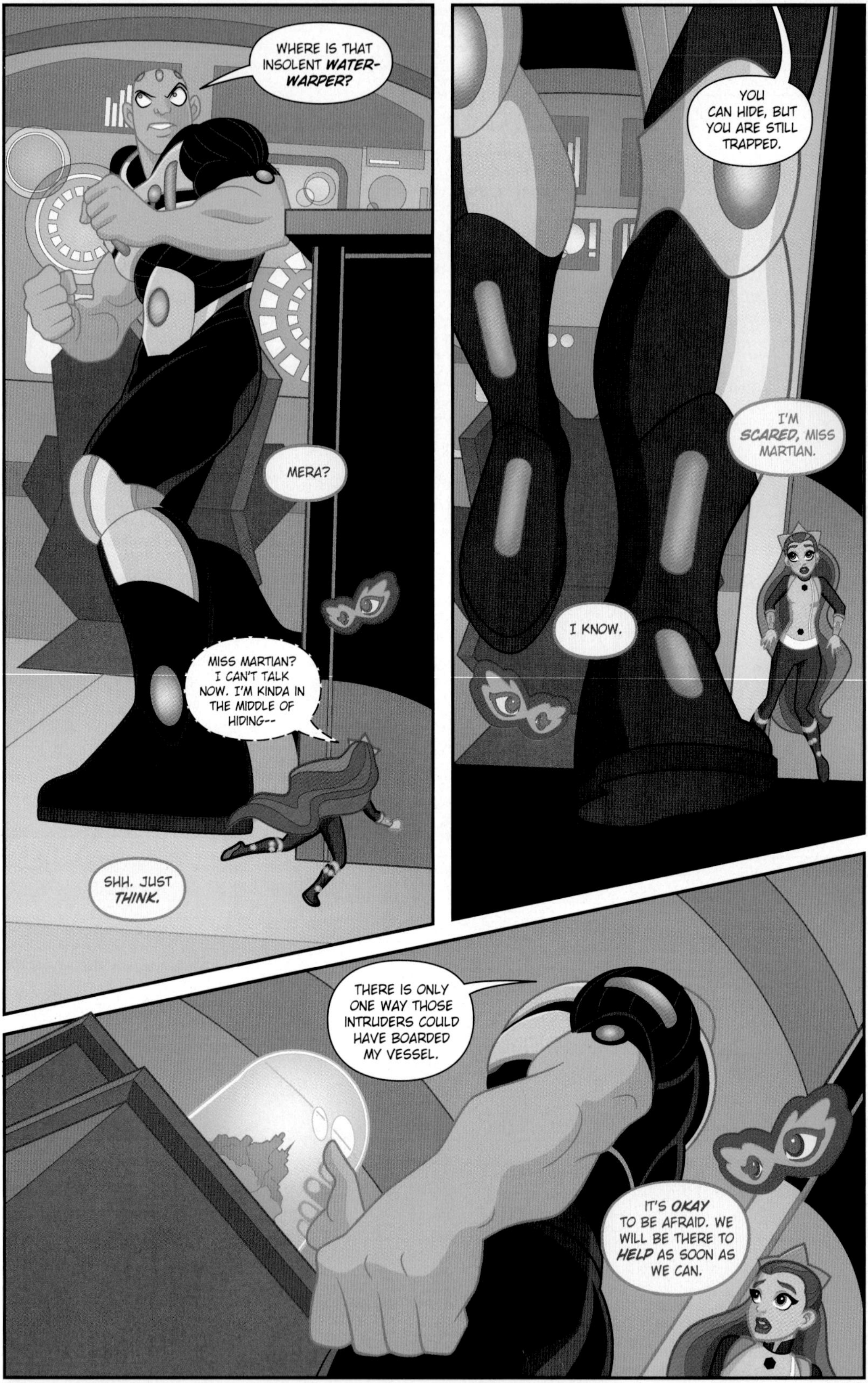
WHERE IS THAT INSOLENT WATER-WARPER?
MERA?
MISS MARTIAN? I CAN'T TALK NOW. I'M KINDA IN THE MIDDLE OF HIDING--
SHH. JUST THINK.
YOU CAN HIDE, BUT YOU ARE STILL TRAPPED.
I'M SCARED, MISS MARTIAN.
I KNOW.
THERE IS ONLY ONE WAY THOSE INTRUDERS COULD HAVE BOARDED MY VESSEL.
IT'S OKAY TO BE AFRAID. WE WILL BE THERE TO HELP AS SOON AS WE CAN.

DO YOU KNOW WHERE BRAINIAC'S HEADED?

A *COUNTERFEIT!*

SMASH!

SET COURSE FOR SPACE SECTOR 2814! I PAID FOR THEMYSCIRA AND NOW HUMANITY MUST REPAY ME!

EARTH. HE'S GOING TO EARTH!

MERA, YOU HAVE TO GET OUT OF THERE SO WE CAN STOP HIM WITHOUT HURTING YOU.

I'LL *TRY.*

THAT ARROGANT PLANET WILL BE MINE. PIECE BY PIECE, CITY BY CITY, COUNTRY BY COUNTRY...

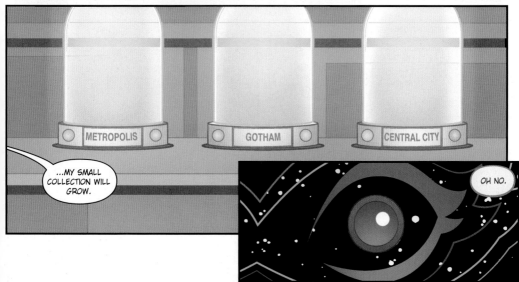

METROPOLIS

GOTHAM

CENTRAL CITY

...MY SMALL COLLECTION WILL GROW.

OH NO.

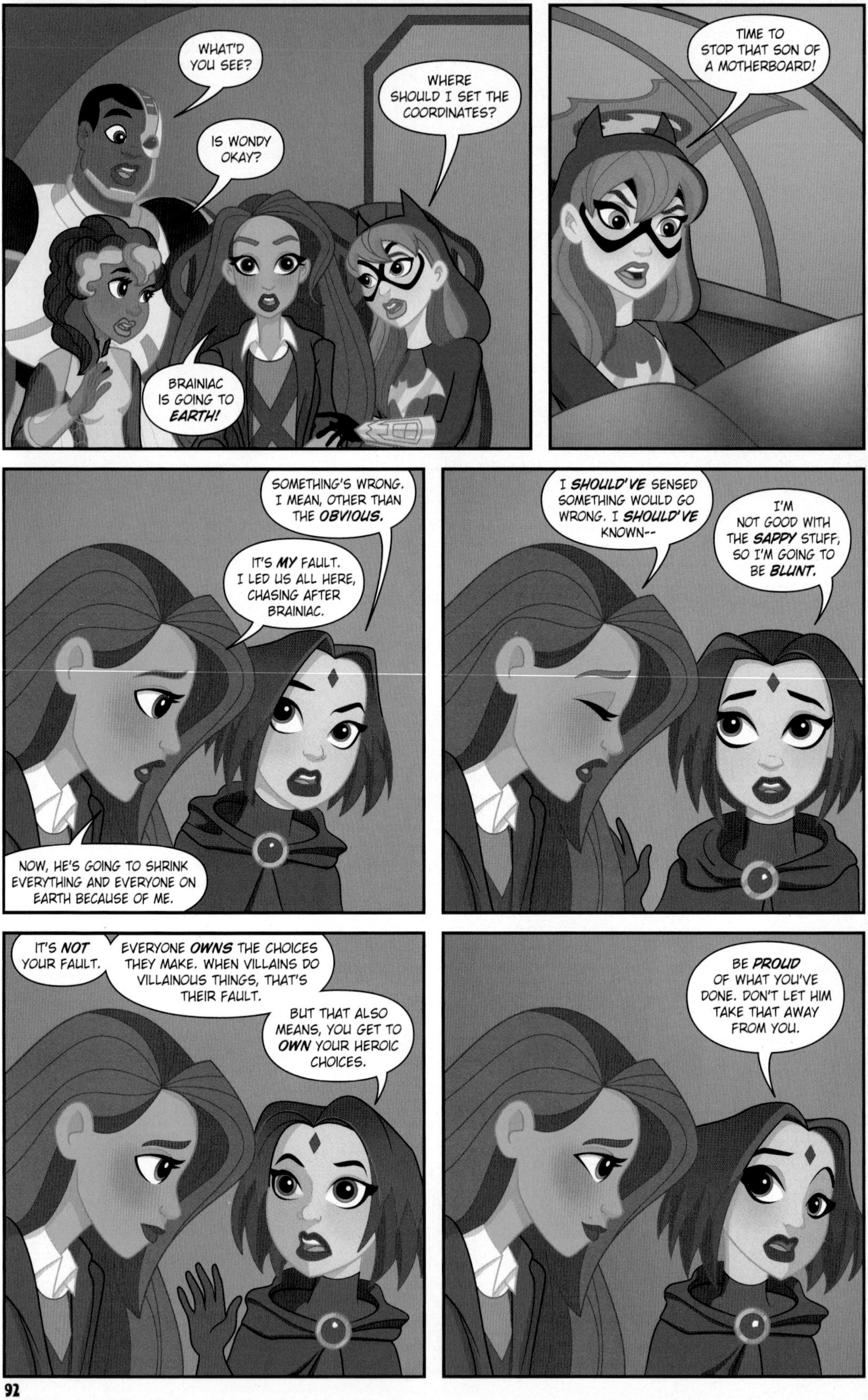
WHAT'D YOU SEE?
IS WONDY OKAY?
WHERE SHOULD I SET THE COORDINATES?
BRAINIAC IS GOING TO ***EARTH!***
TIME TO STOP THAT SON OF A MOTHERBOARD!
SOMETHING'S WRONG. I MEAN, OTHER THAN THE ***OBVIOUS.***
IT'S ***MY*** FAULT. I LED US ALL HERE, CHASING AFTER BRAINIAC.
NOW, HE'S GOING TO SHRINK EVERYTHING AND EVERYONE ON EARTH BECAUSE OF ME.
I ***SHOULD'VE*** SENSED SOMETHING WOULD GO WRONG. I ***SHOULD'VE*** KNOWN--
I'M NOT GOOD WITH THE ***SAPPY*** STUFF, SO I'M GOING TO BE ***BLUNT.***
IT'S ***NOT*** YOUR FAULT.
EVERYONE ***OWNS*** THE CHOICES THEY MAKE. WHEN VILLAINS DO VILLAINOUS THINGS, THAT'S THEIR FAULT.
BUT THAT ALSO MEANS, YOU GET TO ***OWN*** YOUR HEROIC CHOICES.
BE ***PROUD*** OF WHAT YOU'VE DONE. DON'T LET HIM TAKE THAT AWAY FROM YOU.

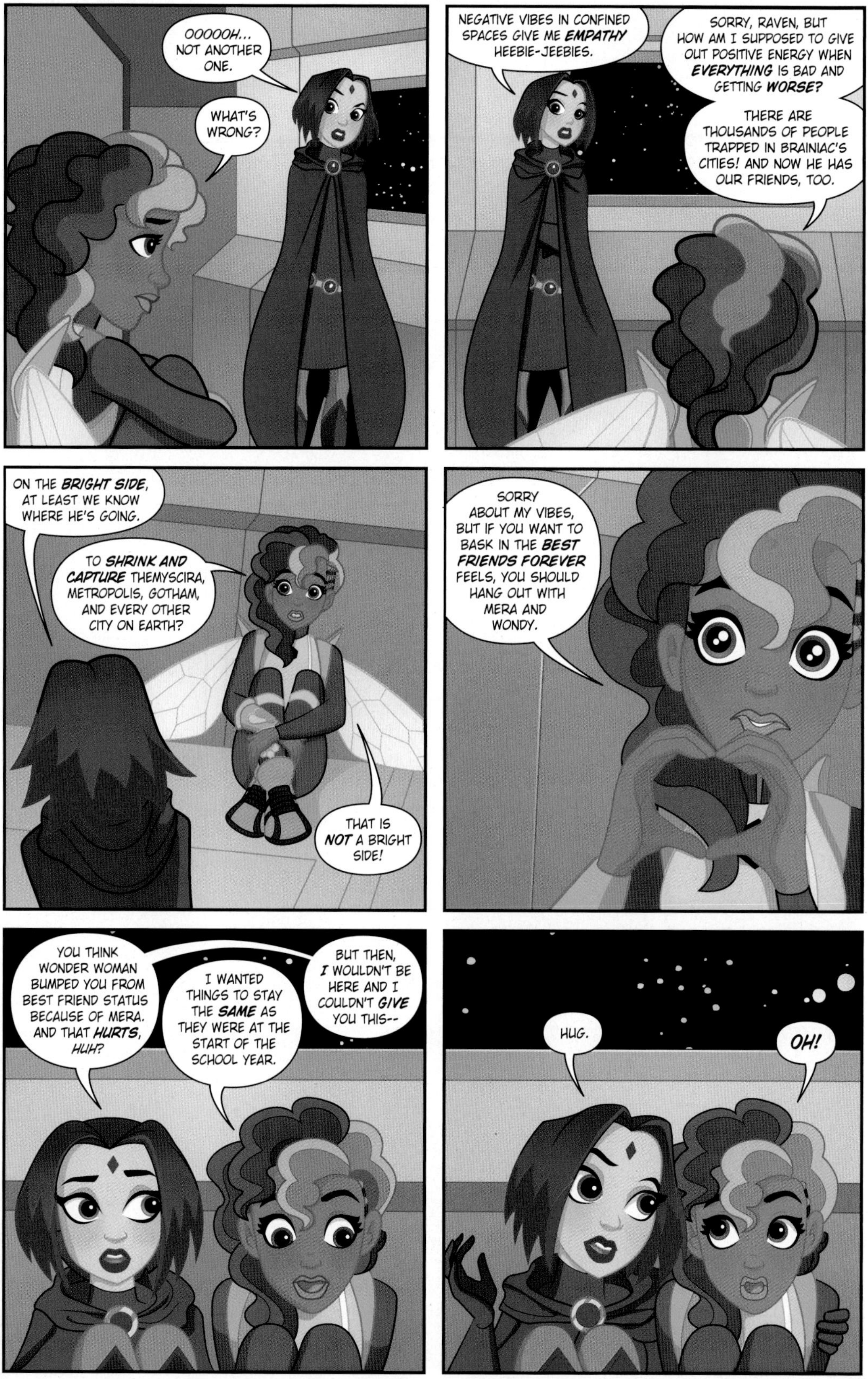
OOOOOH... NOT ANOTHER ONE.
WHAT'S WRONG?
NEGATIVE VIBES IN CONFINED SPACES GIVE ME EMPATHY HEEBIE-JEEBIES.
SORRY, RAVEN, BUT HOW AM I SUPPOSED TO GIVE OUT POSITIVE ENERGY WHEN EVERYTHING IS BAD AND GETTING WORSE?
THERE ARE THOUSANDS OF PEOPLE TRAPPED IN BRAINIAC'S CITIES! AND NOW HE HAS OUR FRIENDS, TOO.
ON THE BRIGHT SIDE, AT LEAST WE KNOW WHERE HE'S GOING.
TO SHRINK AND CAPTURE THEMYSCIRA, METROPOLIS, GOTHAM, AND EVERY OTHER CITY ON EARTH?
THAT IS NOT A BRIGHT SIDE!
SORRY ABOUT MY VIBES, BUT IF YOU WANT TO BASK IN THE BEST FRIENDS FOREVER FEELS, YOU SHOULD HANG OUT WITH MERA AND WONDY.
YOU THINK WONDER WOMAN BUMPED YOU FROM BEST FRIEND STATUS BECAUSE OF MERA. AND THAT HURTS, HUH?
I WANTED THINGS TO STAY THE SAME AS THEY WERE AT THE START OF THE SCHOOL YEAR.
BUT THEN, I WOULDN'T BE HERE AND I COULDN'T GIVE YOU THIS--
HUG.
OH!

THANKS, RAVEN. THAT DID HELP ME FEEL BETTER.

SEE? *CHANGE* CAN BE ALL RIGHT.

I GUESS I HAVE WORK TO DO.

IF I CAN *CHANGE* UP MY TECH, I CAN *GROW* EVERYONE BACK TO NORMAL SIZE AFTER WE FIND THEM!

WHATEVER. JUST DON'T TELL ANYONE I DID THAT *HUG* THING. IT'LL RUIN MY REPUTATION.

EMERGENCY TECH SUPPLIES

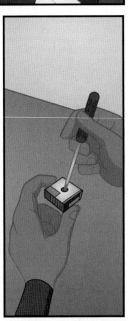

YEAH, HONEY!

94

EARTH.

POP!

THE OCEAN IS BELOW US. I CAN *FEEL* IT.

MERA TO THE RESCUE!

IF I EVER GET BACK TO ME-SIZED, I WILL *NEVER* AGAIN FEEL AWKWARD ABOUT BEING *TALL!*

YOU TWO HANG ON TIGHT.

WE'LL DO OUR BEST, BUT WE'RE IN YOUR HANDS. *LITERALLY.*

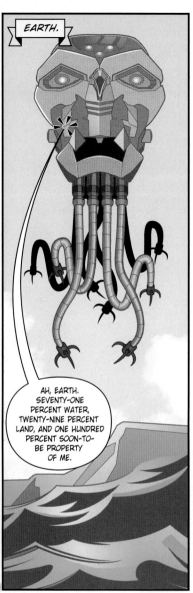

AH, EARTH. SEVENTY-ONE PERCENT WATER, TWENTY-NINE PERCENT LAND, AND ONE HUNDRED PERCENT SOON-TO-BE PROPERTY OF ME.

THIS SUIT BETTER BE JUST LIKE BUMBLEBEE'S BECAUSE HERE GOES SOMETHING *COCONUTTY--*

--ELECTRIC STING!

WHAT IS--

ZAP!

95

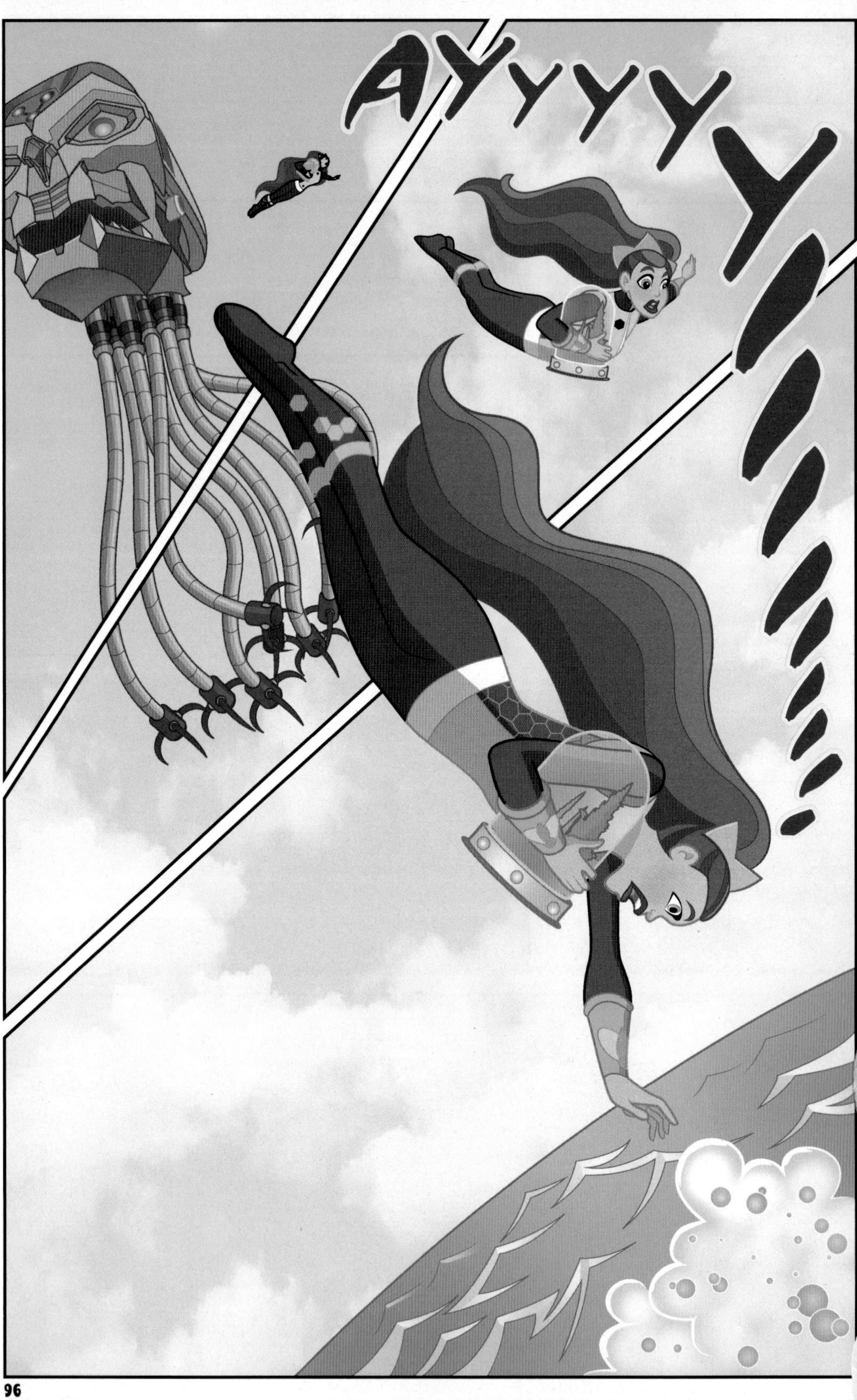
AYYYYY!!!!!!!

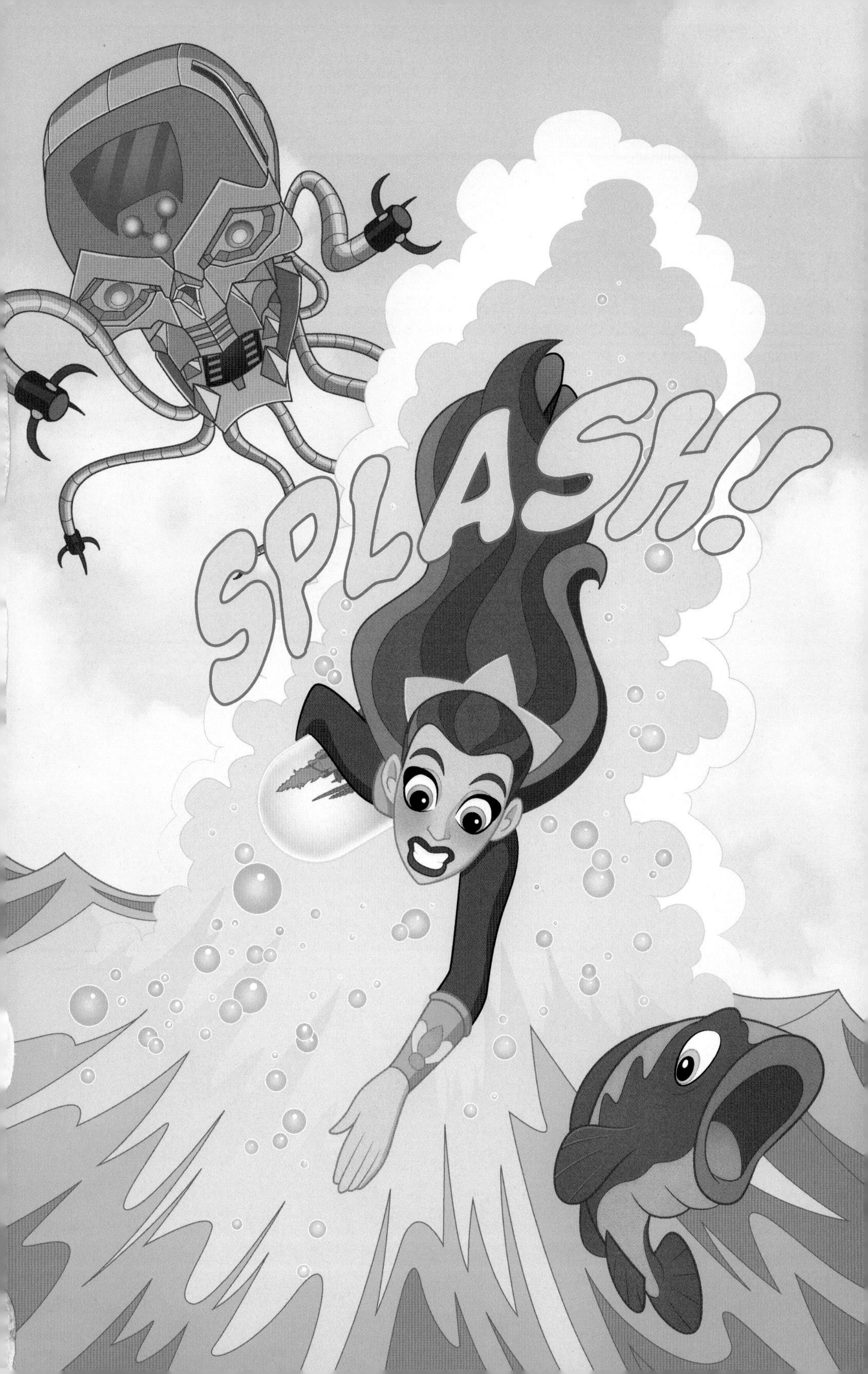
SPLASH!

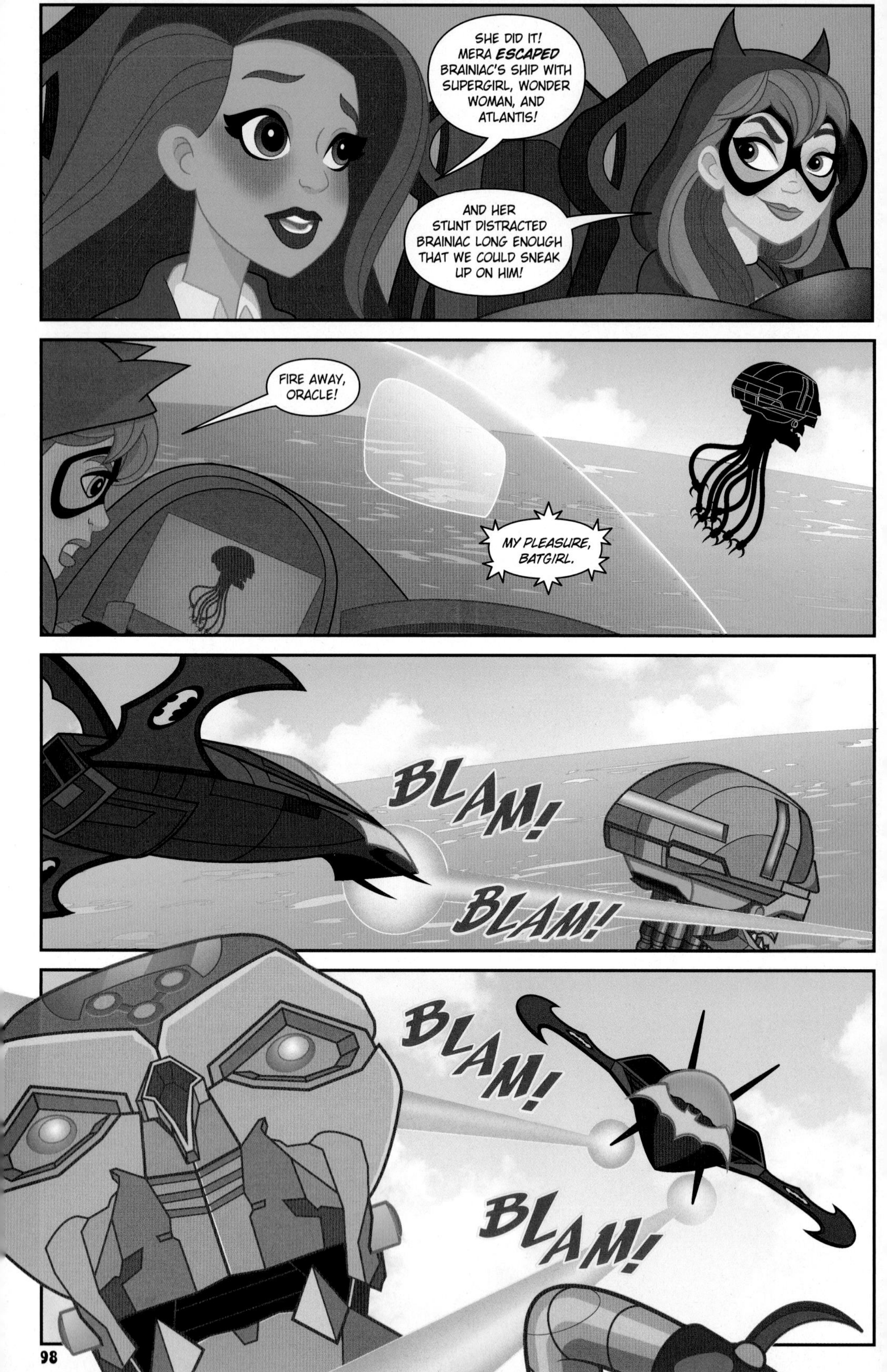
SHE DID IT! MERA ESCAPED BRAINIAC'S SHIP WITH SUPERGIRL, WONDER WOMAN, AND ATLANTIS!
AND HER STUNT DISTRACTED BRAINIAC LONG ENOUGH THAT WE COULD SNEAK UP ON HIM!
FIRE AWAY, ORACLE!
MY PLEASURE, BATGIRL.
BLAM!
BLAM!
BLAM!
BLAM!

YOU *INSOLENT* HEROES.

HEY, WHO TURNED OUT THE LIGHTS?

THAT'S BRAINIAC'S VOICE!

ORACLE, *HOW* IS BRAINIAC IN MY COMPUTER?

THAT SNEAKY *RAT'S* ON OUR SHIP?

-EEP!-

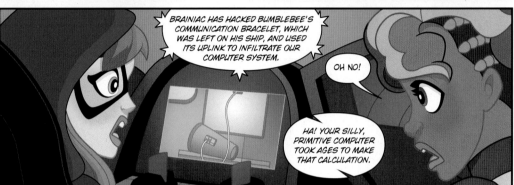

BRAINIAC HAS HACKED BUMBLEBEE'S COMMUNICATION BRACELET, WHICH WAS LEFT ON HIS SHIP, AND USED ITS UPLINK TO INFILTRATE OUR COMPUTER SYSTEM.

OH NO!

HA! YOUR SILLY, PRIMITIVE COMPUTER TOOK AGES TO MAKE THAT CALCULATION.

CONTROL-ALT-DELETE!

I CAN MAKE *TRILLIONS* OF COMPUTATIONS EACH SECOND, AND I HAVE CALCULATED THAT THE BEST CHANCE TO ADD YOUR PRECIOUS PLANET TO MY COLLECTION IS TO AVOID YOUR INTERFERENCE.

CLACK-CLACK-CLACK!

SO...

GOOD-BYE, SUPER HEROES

AAAAGH!

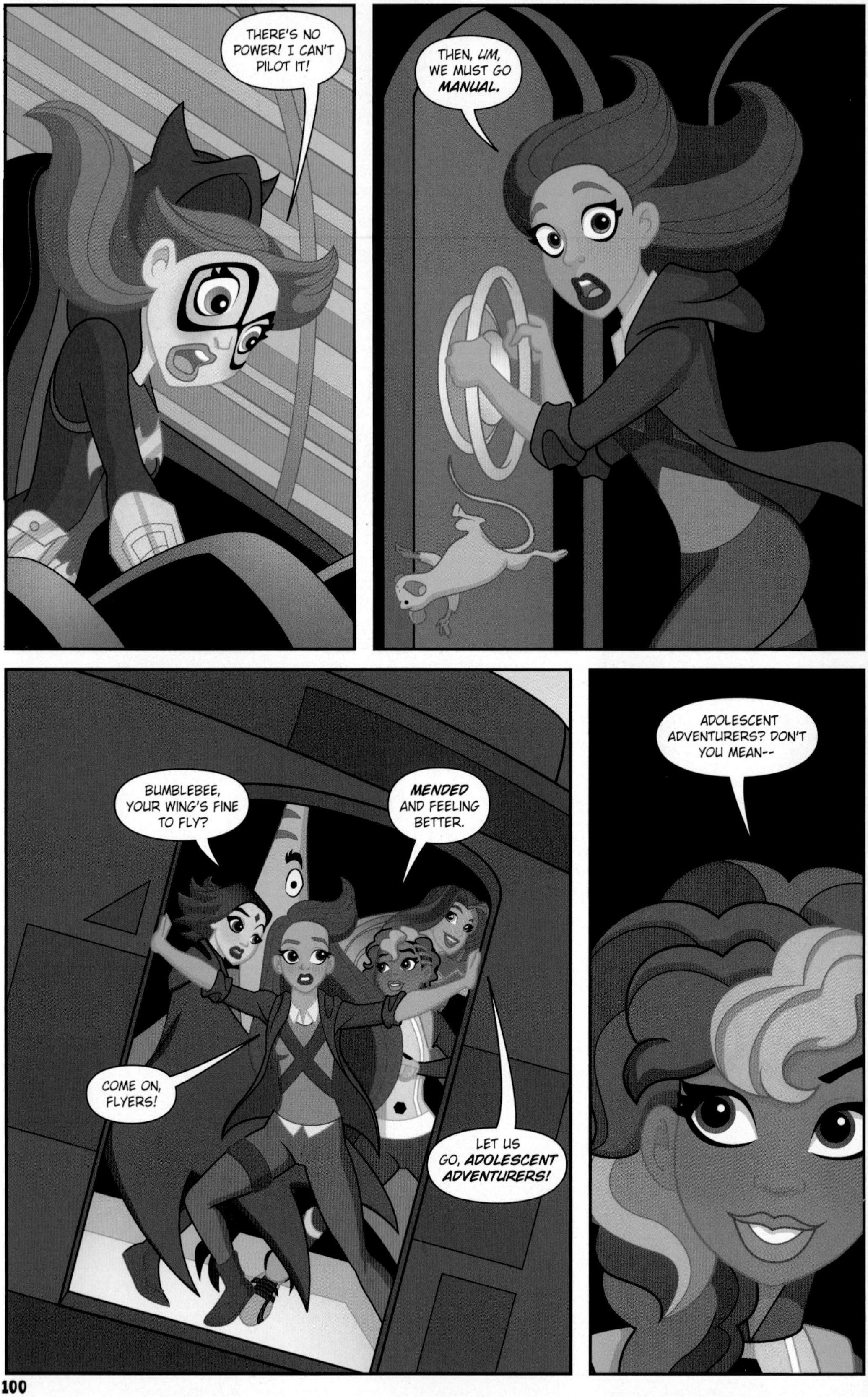
THERE'S NO POWER! I CAN'T PILOT IT!
THEN, *UM*, WE MUST GO ***MANUAL.***
BUMBLEBEE, YOUR WING'S FINE TO FLY?
MENDED AND FEELING BETTER.
COME ON, FLYERS!
LET US GO, ***ADOLESCENT ADVENTURERS!***
ADOLESCENT ADVENTURERS? DON'T YOU MEAN--

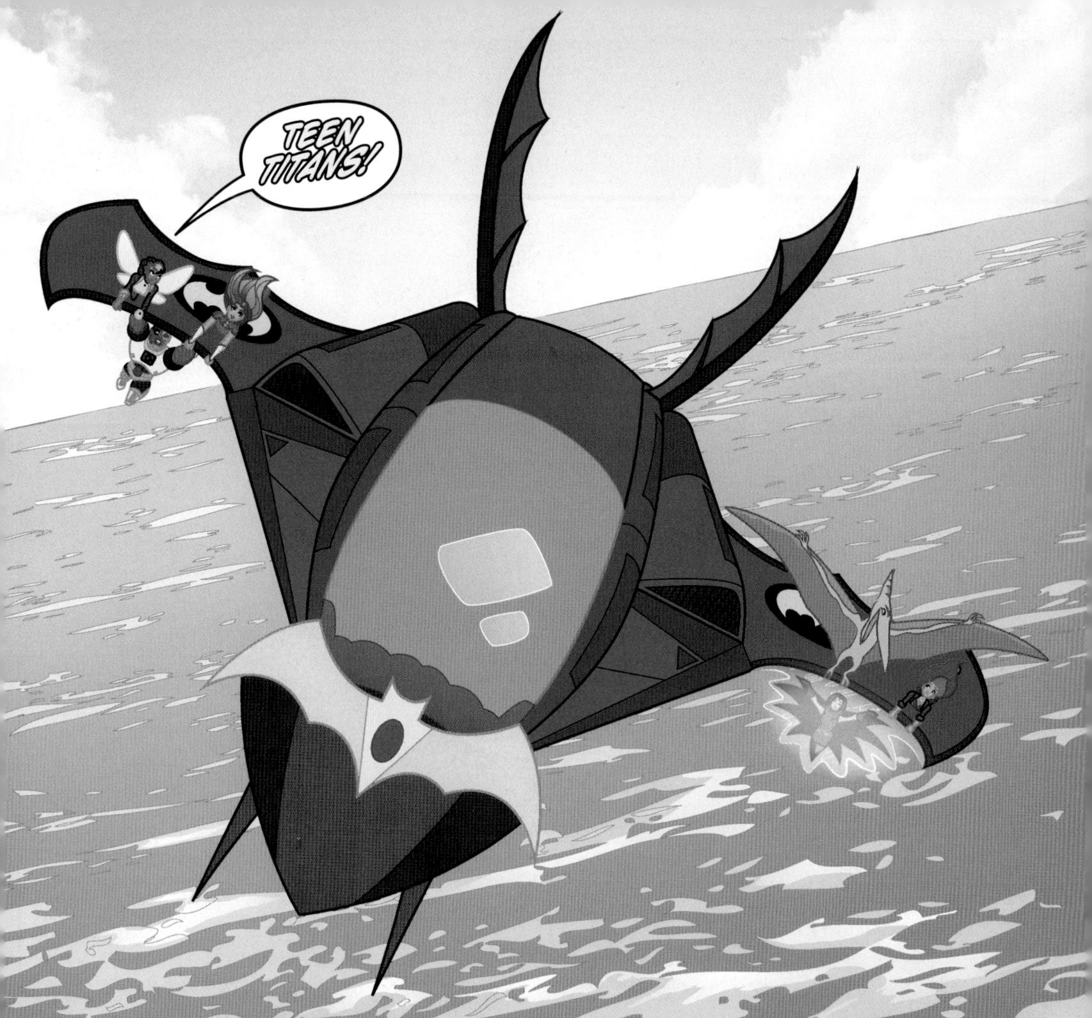
TEEN TITANS!

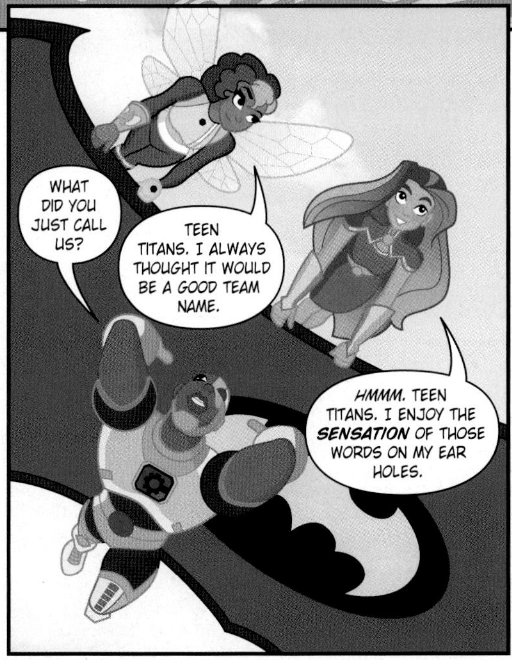
WHAT DID YOU JUST CALL US?
TEEN TITANS. I ALWAYS THOUGHT IT WOULD BE A GOOD TEAM NAME.
HMMM. TEEN TITANS. I ENJOY THE ***SENSATION*** OF THOSE WORDS ON MY EAR HOLES.

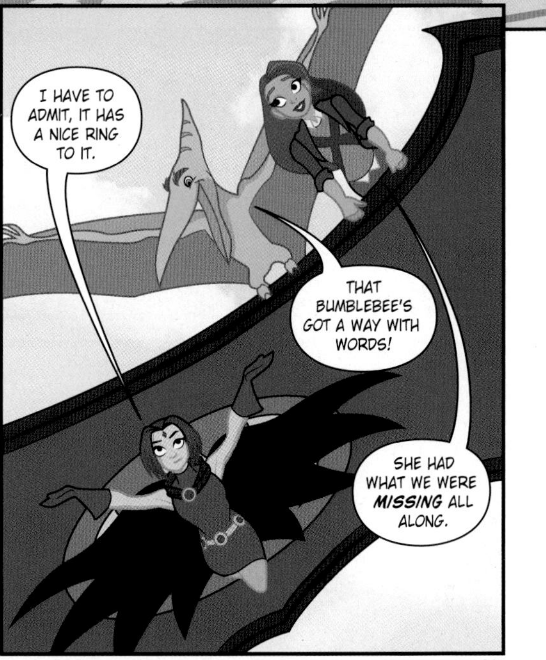
I HAVE TO ADMIT, IT HAS A NICE RING TO IT.
THAT BUMBLEBEE'S GOT A WAY WITH WORDS!
SHE HAD WHAT WE WERE ***MISSING*** ALL ALONG.

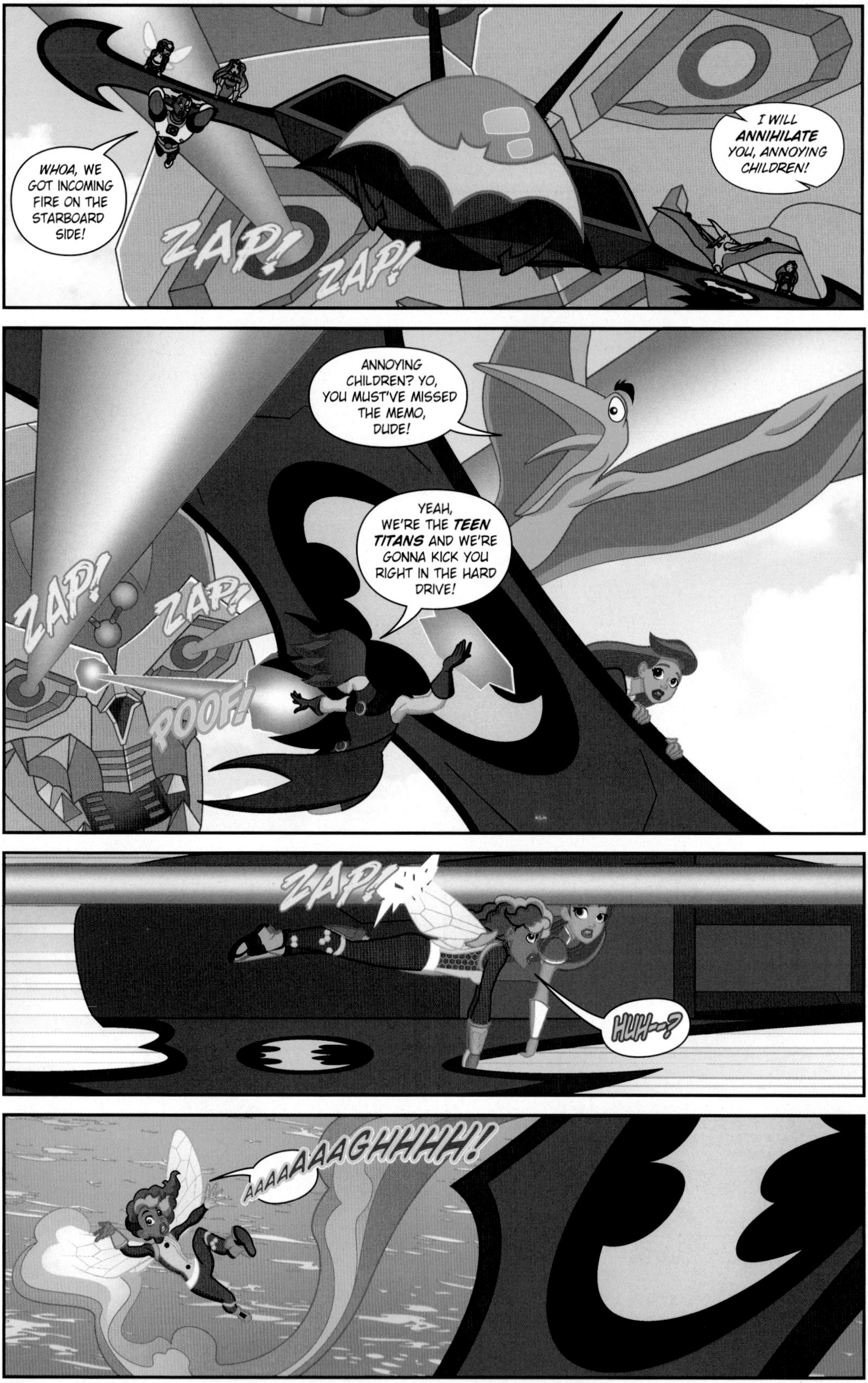
WHOA, WE GOT INCOMING FIRE ON THE STARBOARD SIDE!
I WILL **ANNIHILATE** YOU, ANNOYING CHILDREN!
ZAP! ZAP!
ANNOYING CHILDREN? YO, YOU MUST'VE MISSED THE MEMO, DUDE!
YEAH, WE'RE THE ***TEEN TITANS*** AND WE'RE GONNA KICK YOU RIGHT IN THE HARD DRIVE!
ZAP! ZAP!
POOF!
ZAP!
HUH--?
AAAAAAAAGHHHHH!

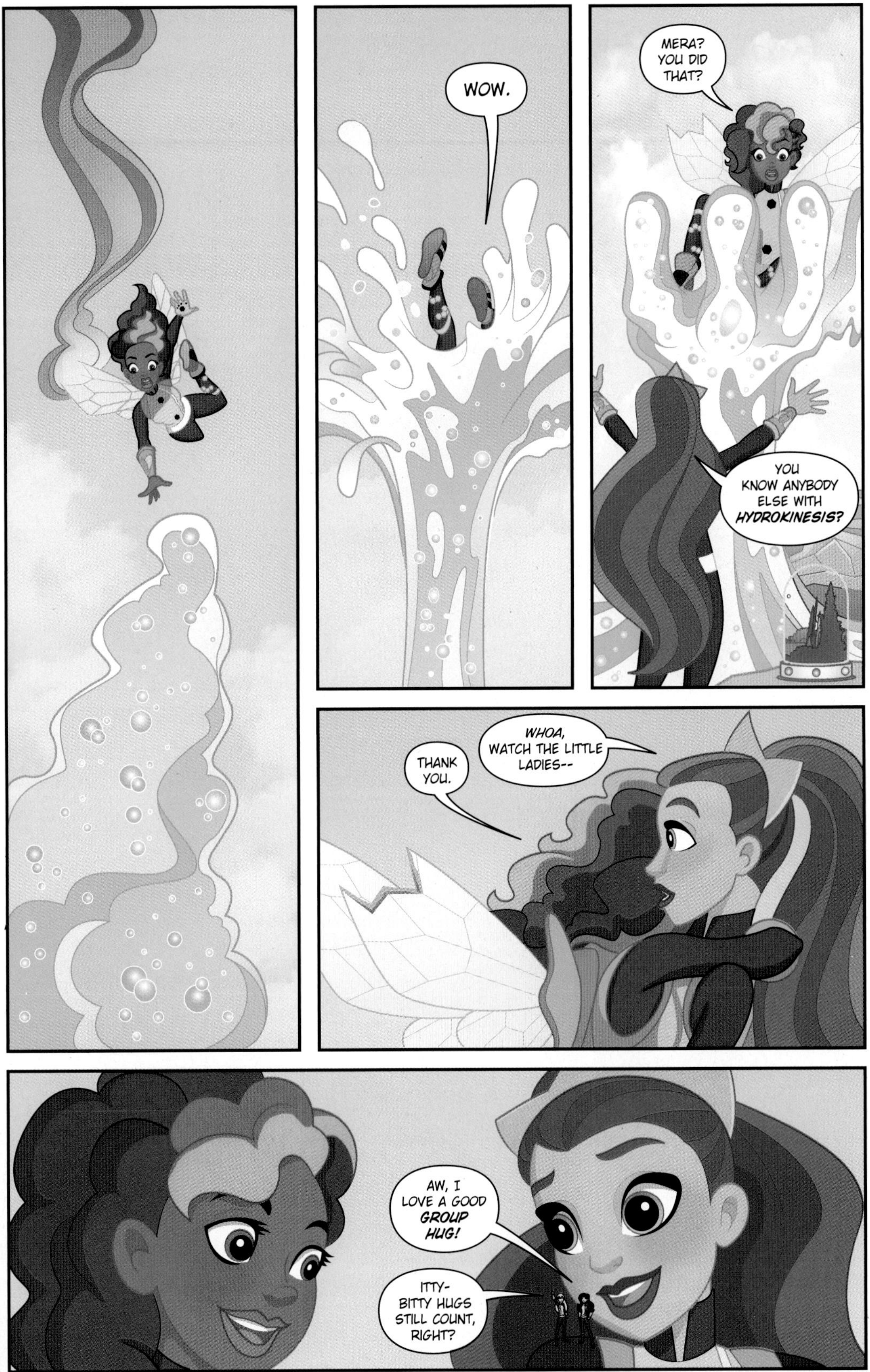
WOW.
MERA? YOU DID THAT?
YOU KNOW ANYBODY ELSE WITH *HYDROKINESIS?*
THANK YOU.
WHOA, WATCH THE LITTLE LADIES--
AW, I LOVE A GOOD *GROUP HUG!*
ITTY-BITTY HUGS STILL COUNT, RIGHT?

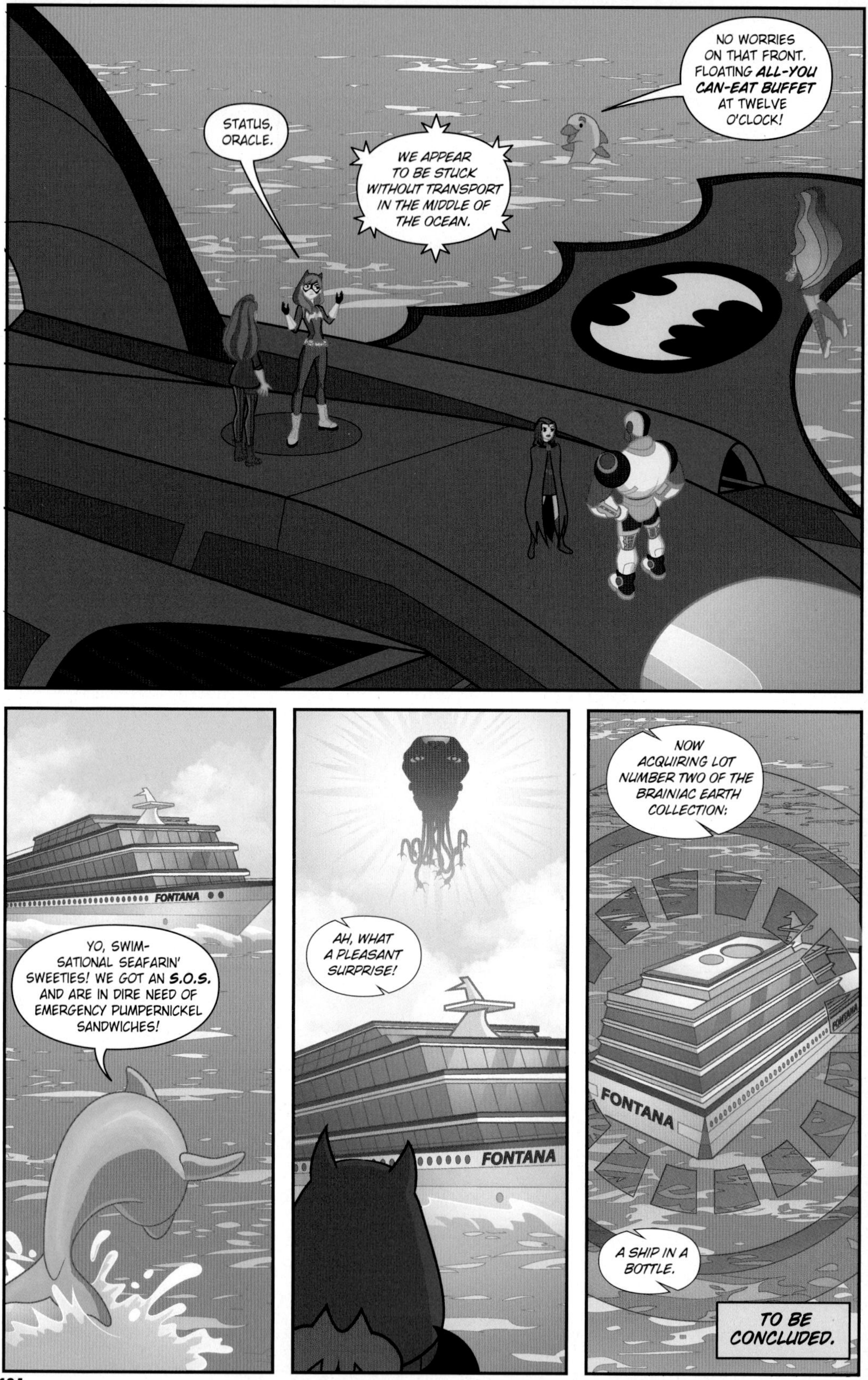
STATUS, ORACLE.
WE APPEAR TO BE STUCK WITHOUT TRANSPORT IN THE MIDDLE OF THE OCEAN.
NO WORRIES ON THAT FRONT. FLOATING **ALL-YOU CAN-EAT BUFFET** AT TWELVE O'CLOCK!
FONTANA
YO, SWIM-SATIONAL SEAFARIN' SWEETIES! WE GOT AN **S.O.S.** AND ARE IN DIRE NEED OF EMERGENCY PUMPERNICKEL SANDWICHES!
AH, WHAT A PLEASANT SURPRISE!
FONTANA
NOW ACQUIRING LOT NUMBER TWO OF THE BRAINIAC EARTH COLLECTION:
FONTANA
A SHIP IN A BOTTLE.
TO BE CONCLUDED.

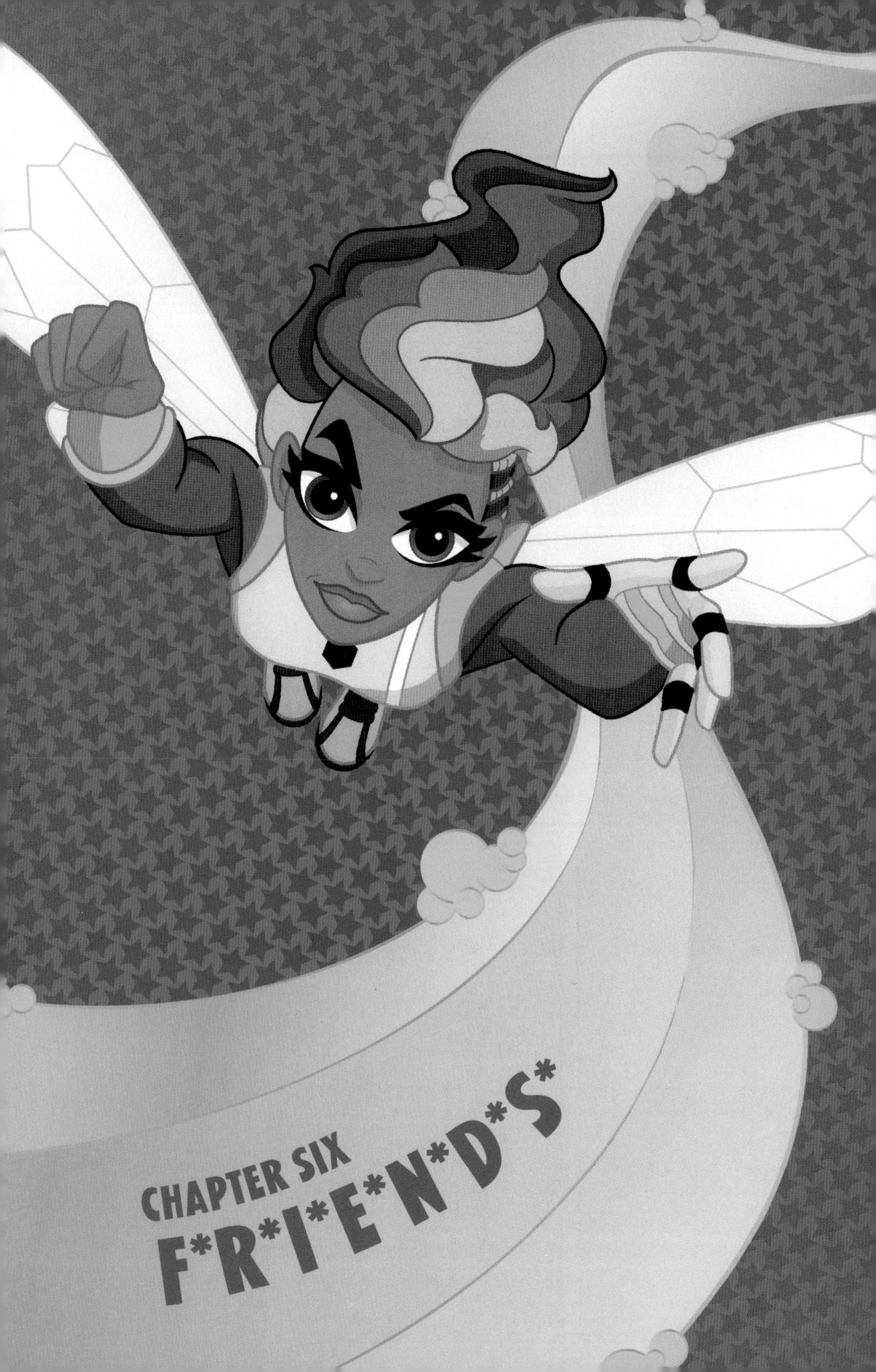

CHAPTER SIX
F*R*I*E*N*D*S*

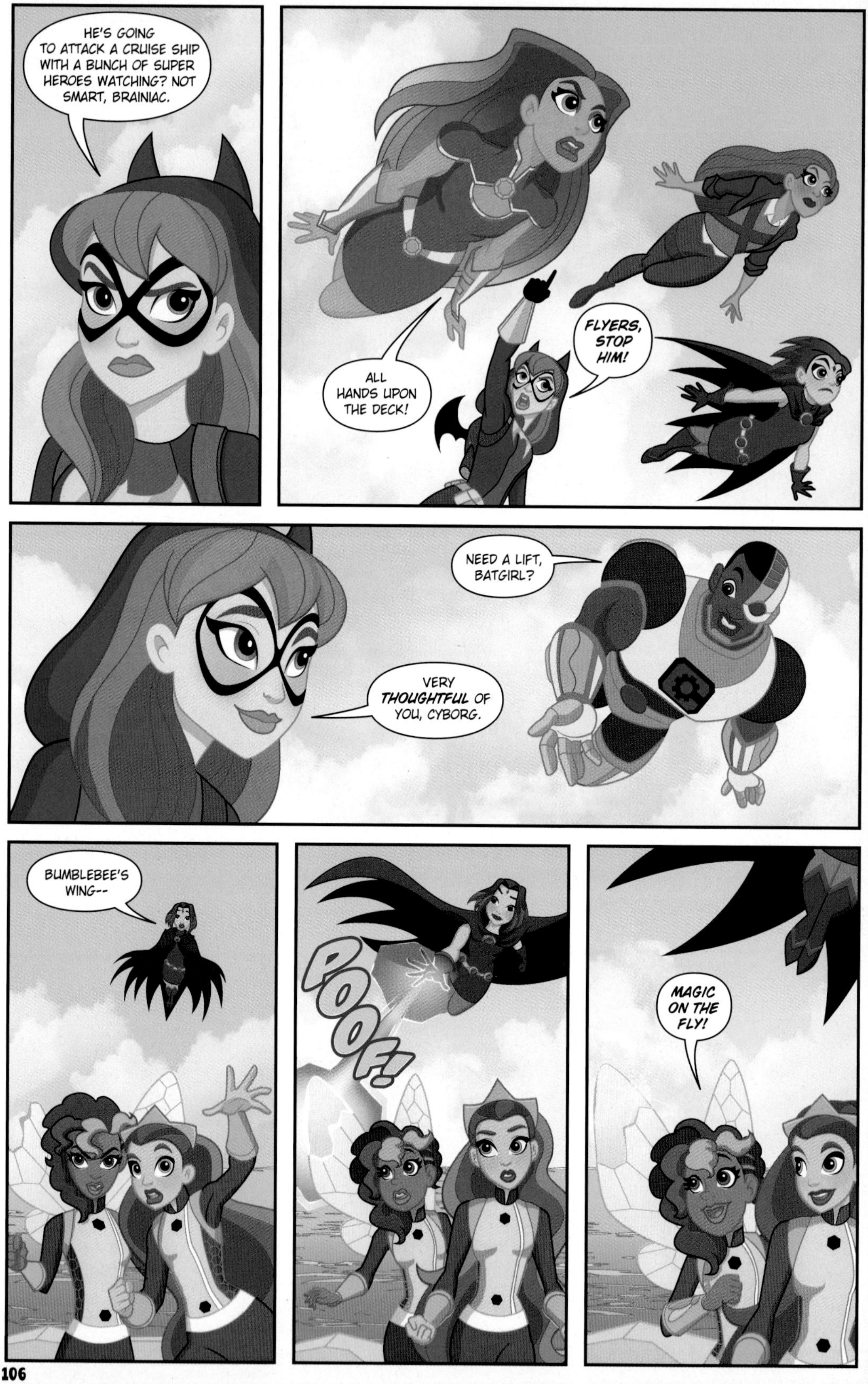
HE'S GOING TO ATTACK A CRUISE SHIP WITH A BUNCH OF SUPER HEROES WATCHING? NOT SMART, BRAINIAC.
ALL HANDS UPON THE DECK!
FLYERS, STOP HIM!
NEED A LIFT, BATGIRL?
VERY THOUGHTFUL OF YOU, CYBORG.
BUMBLEBEE'S WING--
POOF!
MAGIC ON THE FLY!

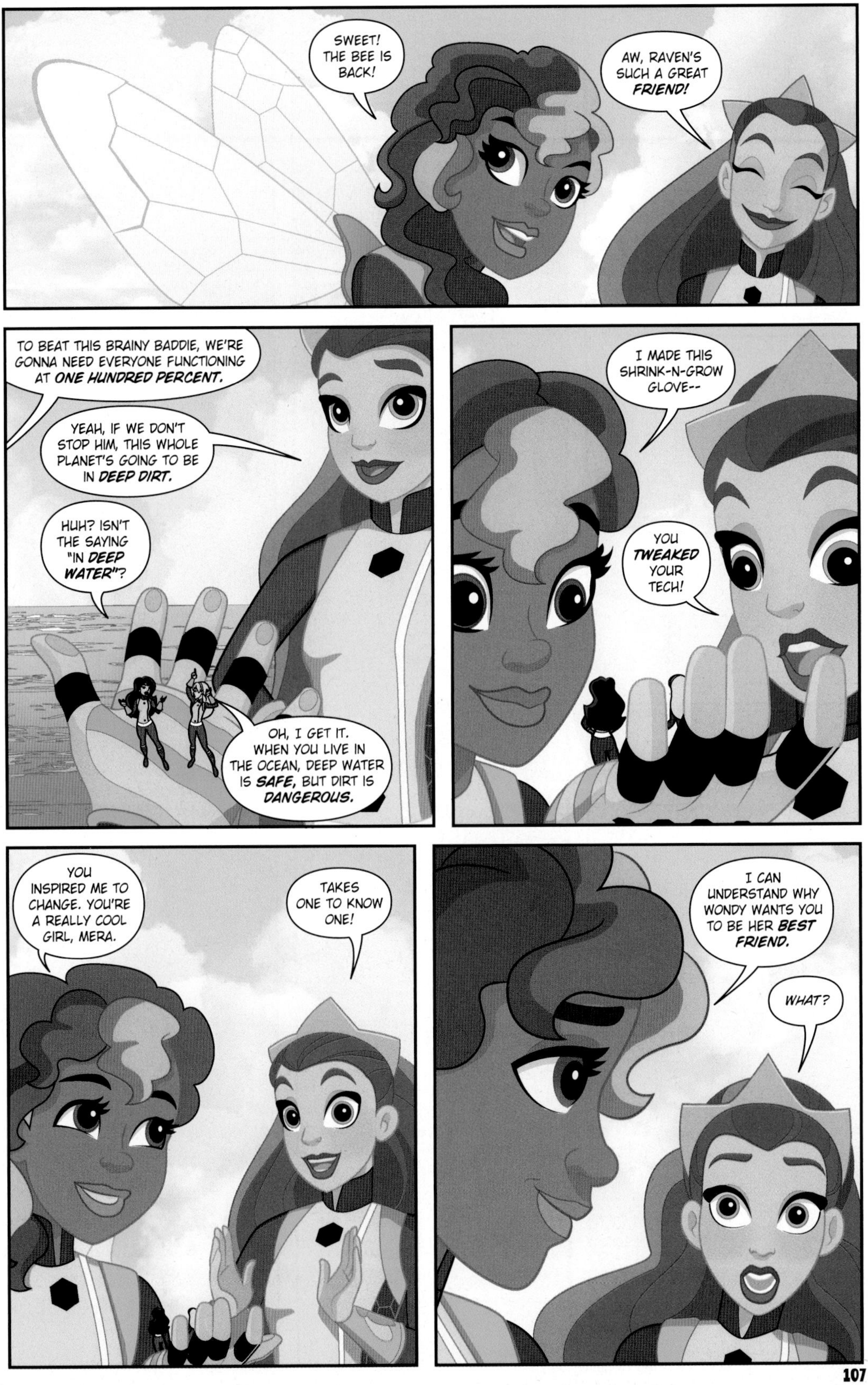
SWEET! THE BEE IS BACK!
AW, RAVEN'S SUCH A GREAT FRIEND!
TO BEAT THIS BRAINY BADDIE, WE'RE GONNA NEED EVERYONE FUNCTIONING AT ONE HUNDRED PERCENT.
YEAH, IF WE DON'T STOP HIM, THIS WHOLE PLANET'S GOING TO BE IN DEEP DIRT.
HUH? ISN'T THE SAYING "IN DEEP WATER"?
OH, I GET IT. WHEN YOU LIVE IN THE OCEAN, DEEP WATER IS SAFE, BUT DIRT IS DANGEROUS.
I MADE THIS SHRINK-N-GROW GLOVE--
YOU TWEAKED YOUR TECH!
YOU INSPIRED ME TO CHANGE. YOU'RE A REALLY COOL GIRL, MERA.
TAKES ONE TO KNOW ONE!
I CAN UNDERSTAND WHY WONDY WANTS YOU TO BE HER BEST FRIEND.
WHAT?

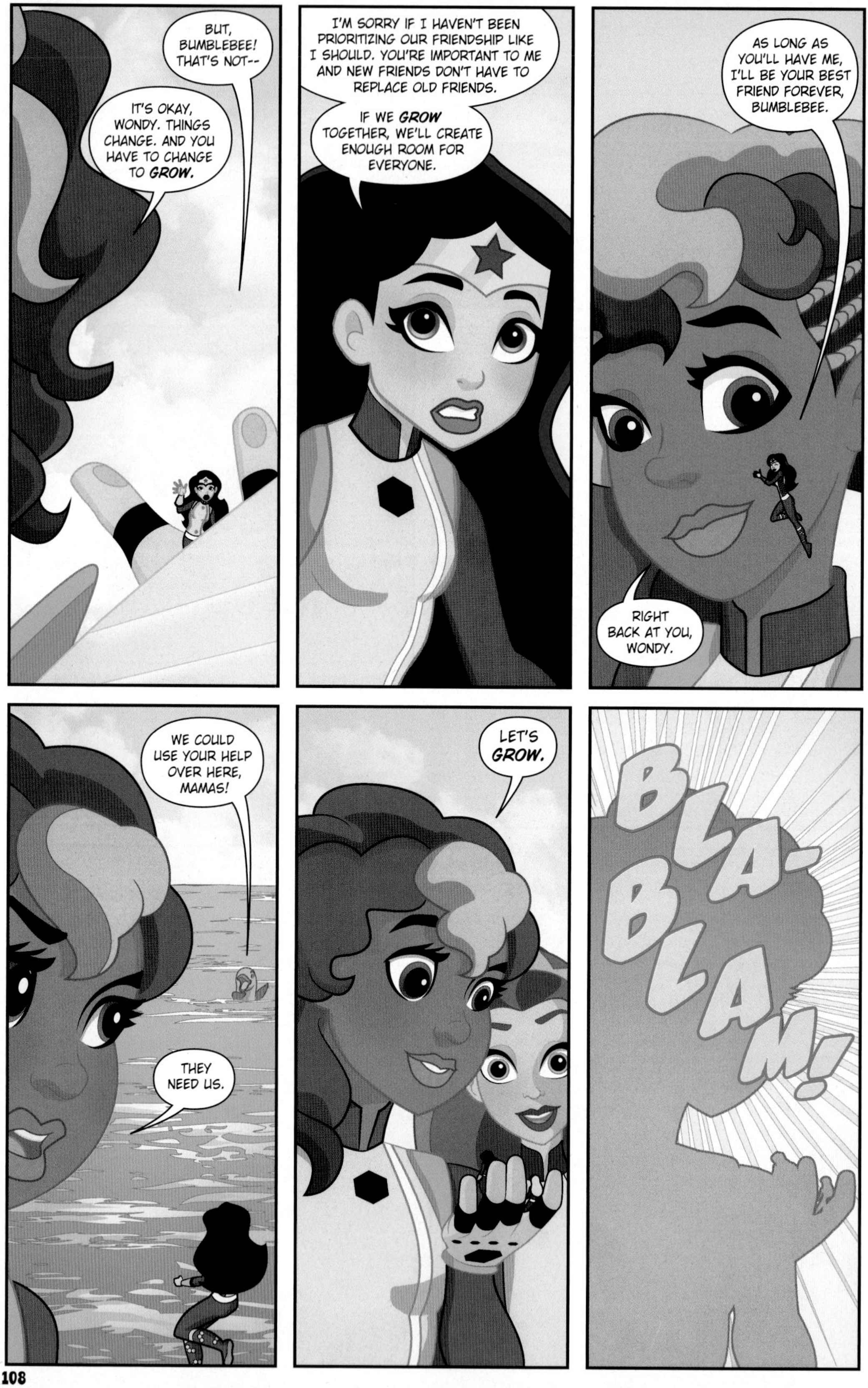
BUT, BUMBLEBEE! THAT'S NOT--
IT'S OKAY, WONDY. THINGS CHANGE. AND YOU HAVE TO CHANGE TO **GROW.**
I'M SORRY IF I HAVEN'T BEEN PRIORITIZING OUR FRIENDSHIP LIKE I SHOULD. YOU'RE IMPORTANT TO ME AND NEW FRIENDS DON'T HAVE TO REPLACE OLD FRIENDS.
IF WE **GROW** TOGETHER, WE'LL CREATE ENOUGH ROOM FOR EVERYONE.
AS LONG AS YOU'LL HAVE ME, I'LL BE YOUR BEST FRIEND FOREVER, BUMBLEBEE.
RIGHT BACK AT YOU, WONDY.
WE COULD USE YOUR HELP OVER HERE, MAMAS!
THEY NEED US.
LET'S **GROW.**
BLA-BLAM!

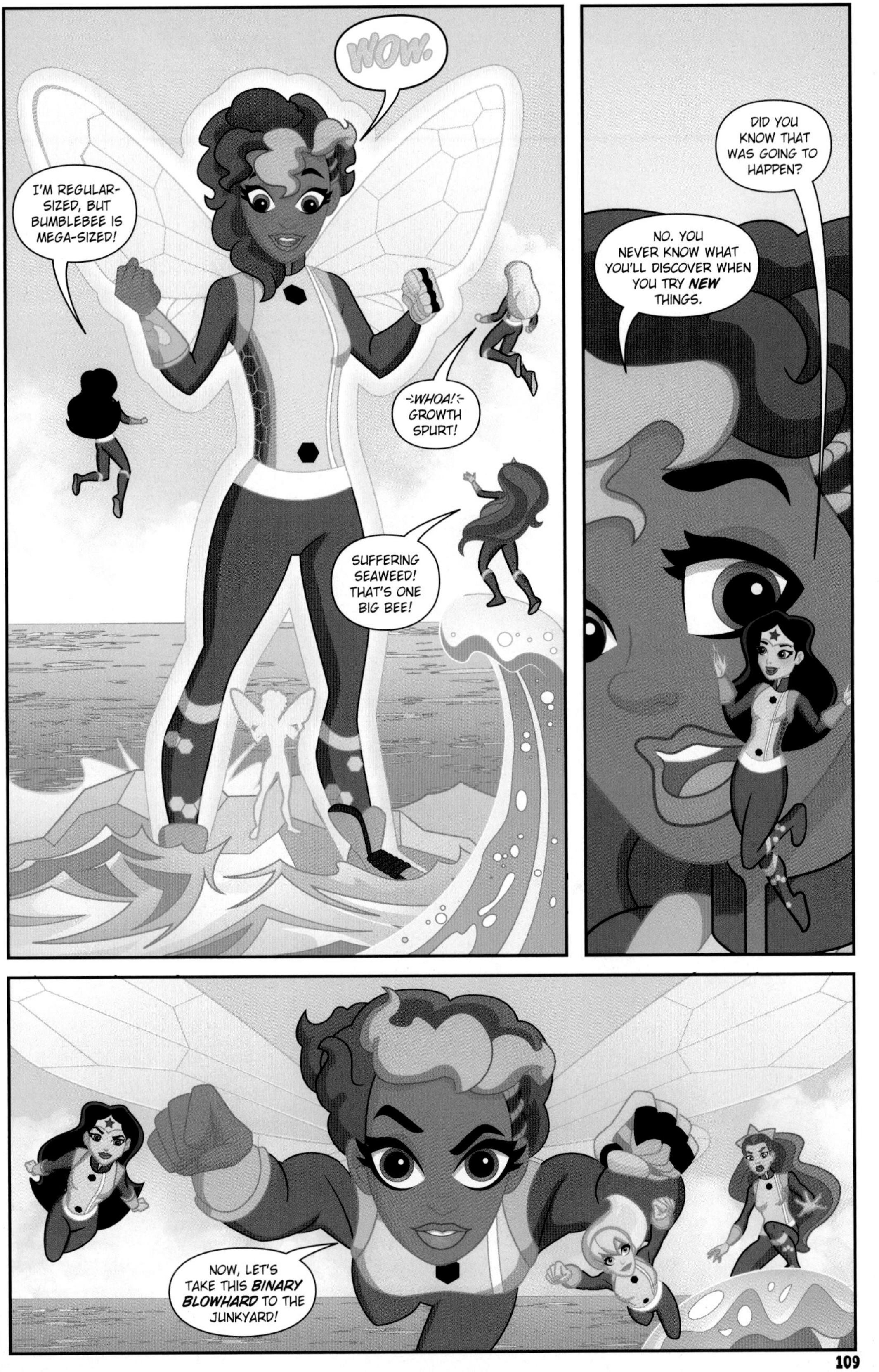
WOW.
I'M REGULAR-SIZED, BUT BUMBLEBEE IS MEGA-SIZED!
-WHOA!- GROWTH SPURT!
SUFFERING SEAWEED! THAT'S ONE BIG BEE!
DID YOU KNOW THAT WAS GOING TO HAPPEN?
NO. YOU NEVER KNOW WHAT YOU'LL DISCOVER WHEN YOU TRY **NEW** THINGS.
NOW, LET'S TAKE THIS **BINARY BLOWHARD** TO THE JUNKYARD!

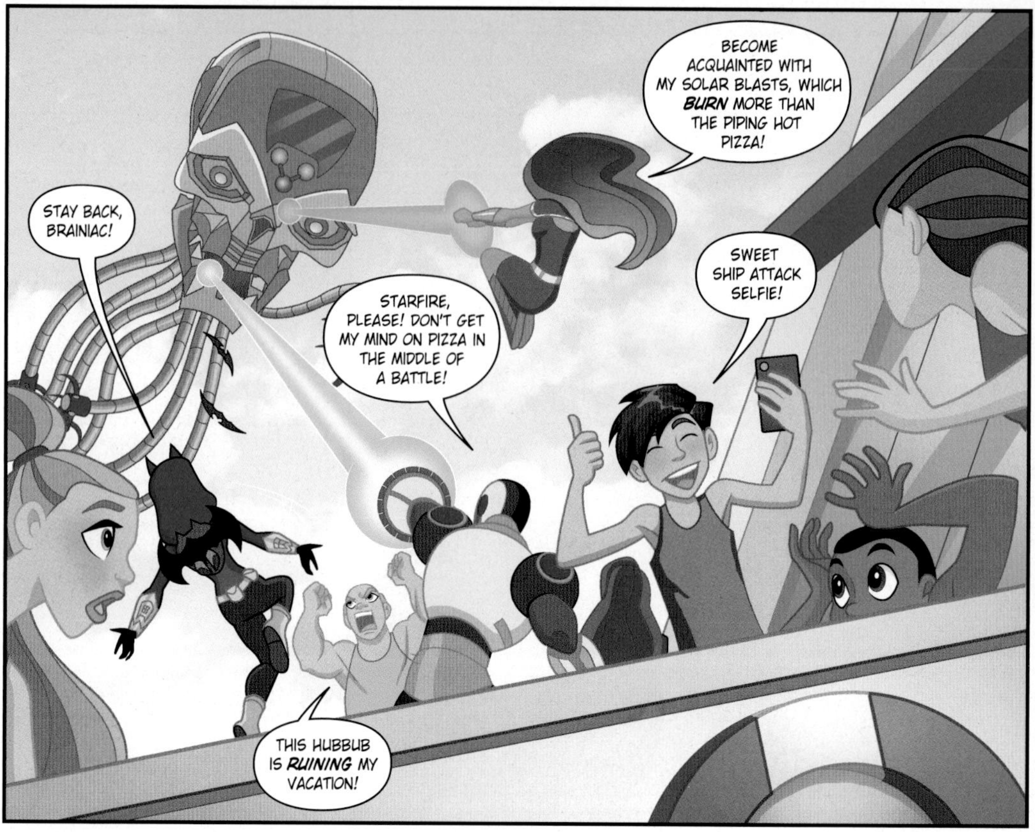
STAY BACK, BRAINIAC!
BECOME ACQUAINTED WITH MY SOLAR BLASTS, WHICH **BURN** MORE THAN THE PIPING HOT PIZZA!
STARFIRE, PLEASE! DON'T GET MY MIND ON PIZZA IN THE MIDDLE OF A BATTLE!
SWEET SHIP ATTACK SELFIE!
THIS HUBBUB IS **RUINING** MY VACATION!

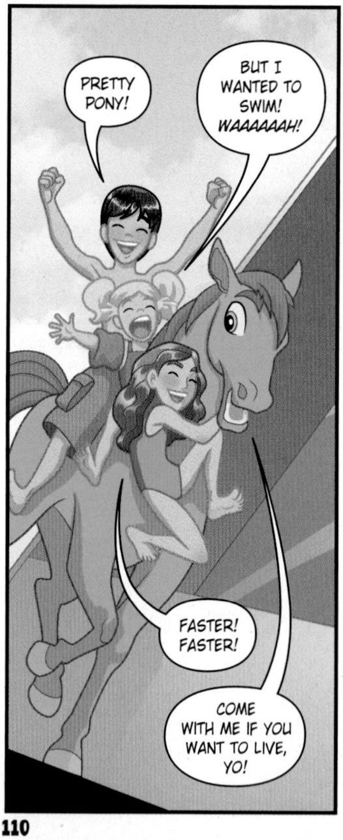
PRETTY PONY!
BUT I WANTED TO SWIM! *WAAAAAAH!*
FASTER! FASTER!
COME WITH ME IF YOU WANT TO LIVE, YO!

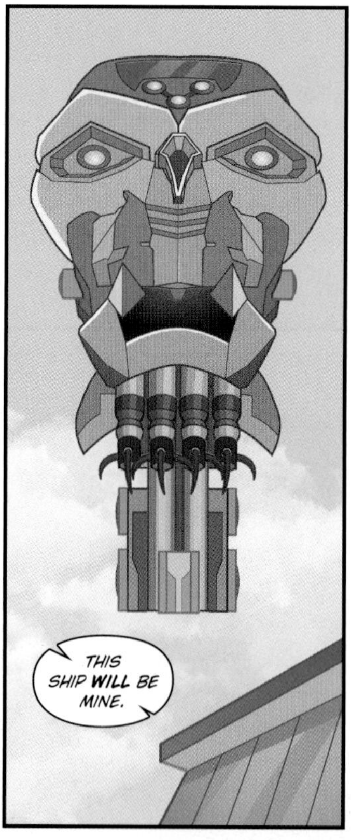
*THIS SHIP **WILL** BE MINE.*

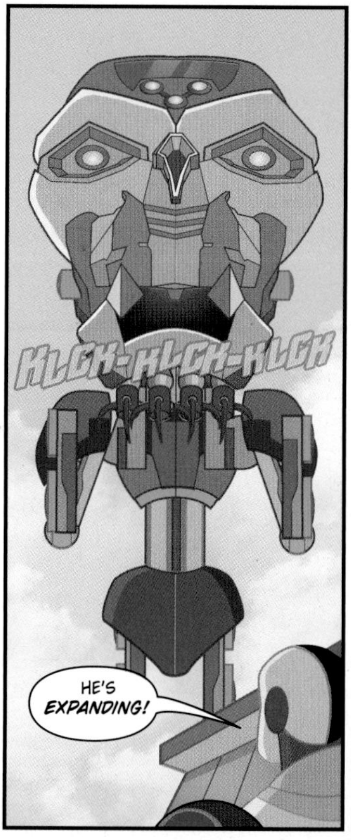
KLCK-KLCK-KLCK
HE'S ***EXPANDING!***

AH. IT FEELS GOOD TO **STRETCH** MY LEGS.

THIS DUDE IS MADE OF SOME **TOUGH** STUFF.

PLINK!

~UNH!~ MY DIAMOND-EDGED BATARANG DOESN'T EVEN **DENT** THE METAL.

TING!

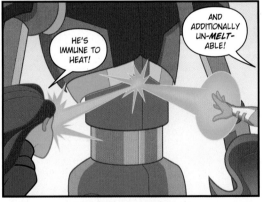

HE'S IMMUNE TO HEAT!

AND ADDITIONALLY UN-**MELT**-ABLE!

~UGH~, MAGIC-DEFYING **SHIELD**. LAME.

SMASH!

ANA

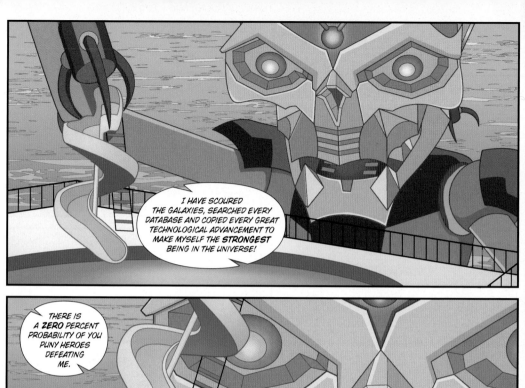

I HAVE SCOURED THE GALAXIES, SEARCHED EVERY DATABASE AND COPIED EVERY GREAT TECHNOLOGICAL ADVANCEMENT TO MAKE MYSELF THE **STRONGEST** BEING IN THE UNIVERSE!

THERE IS A **ZERO** PERCENT PROBABILITY OF YOU PUNY HEROES DEFEATING ME.

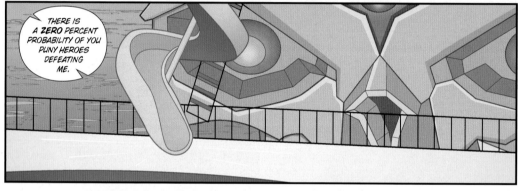

PLEASE... PLEASE DON'T HURT ME.

HEY, BRAINY-BOT!

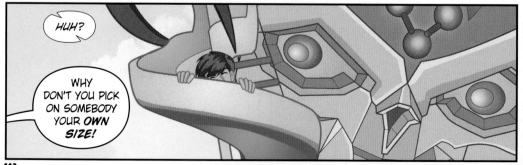

HUH?

WHY DON'T YOU PICK ON SOMEBODY YOUR **OWN** SIZE!

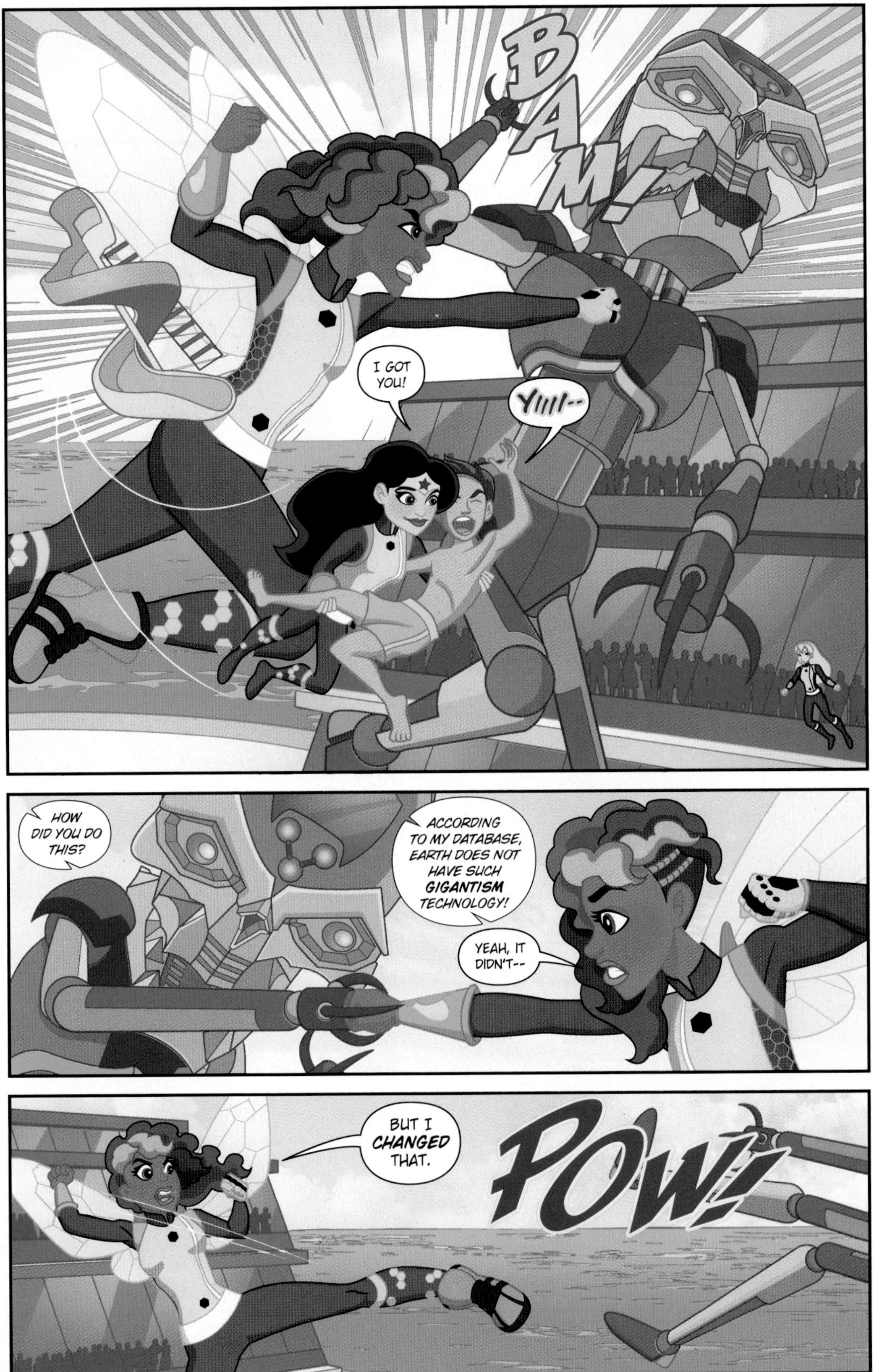
BAM!
I GOT YOU!
YIIII--
HOW DID YOU DO THIS?
ACCORDING TO MY DATABASE, EARTH DOES NOT HAVE SUCH **GIGANTISM** TECHNOLOGY!
YEAH, IT DIDN'T--
BUT I **CHANGED** THAT.
POW!

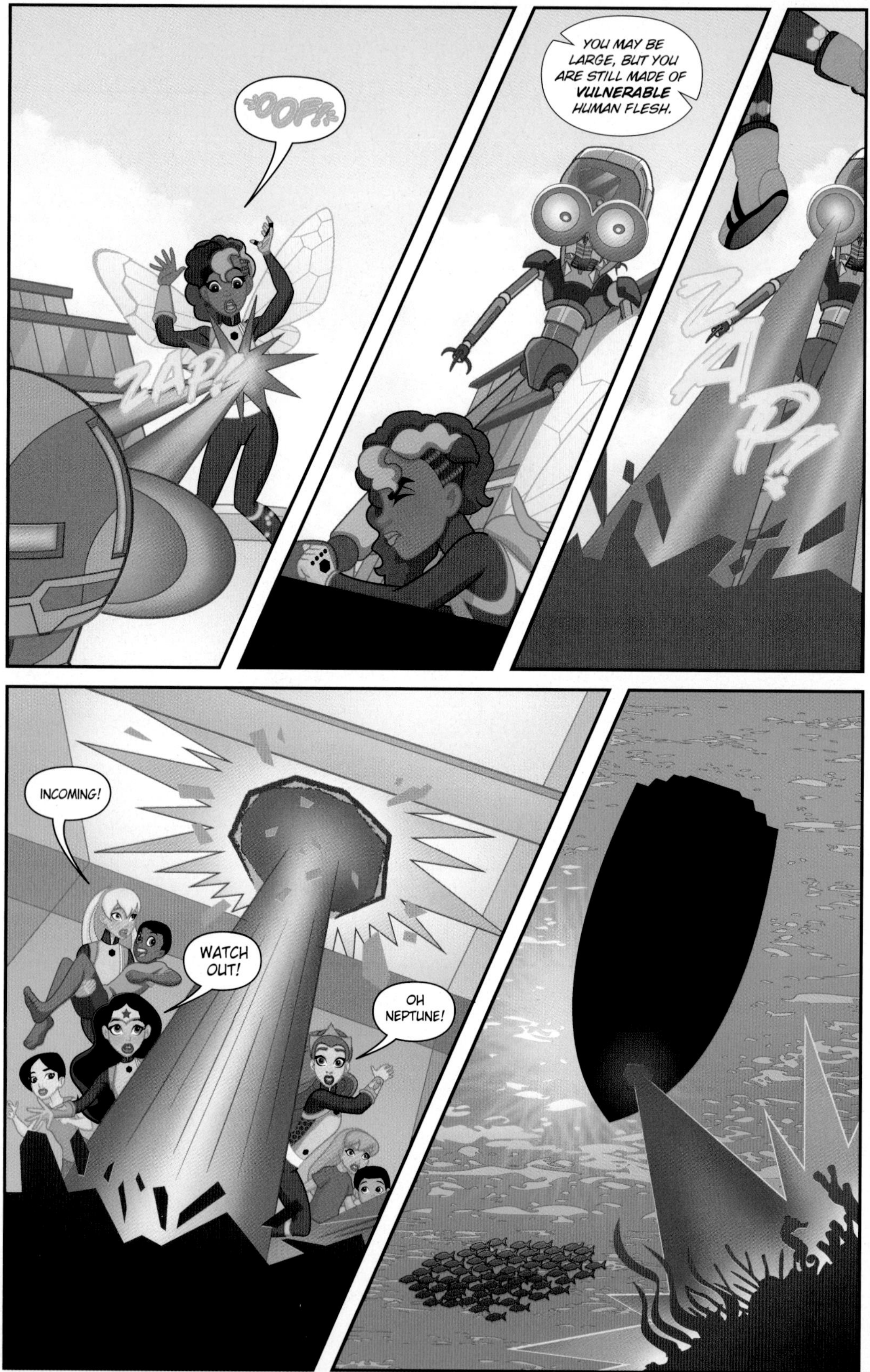

OOF!!
ZAP!!
YOU MAY BE LARGE, BUT YOU ARE STILL MADE OF **VULNERABLE** HUMAN FLESH.
ZAP!!
INCOMING!
WATCH OUT!
OH NEPTUNE!

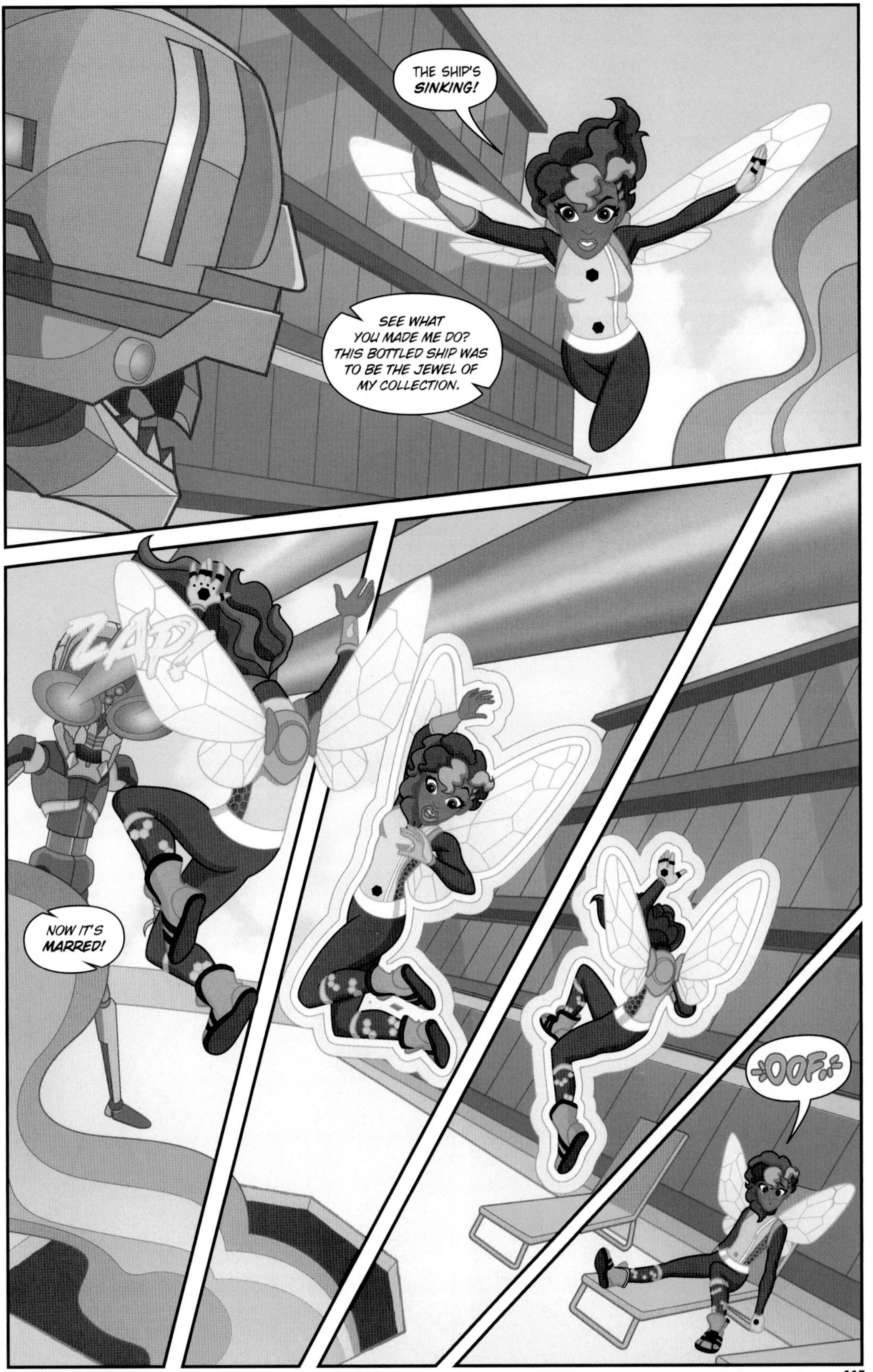
THE SHIP'S SINKING!
SEE WHAT YOU MADE ME DO? THIS BOTTLED SHIP WAS TO BE THE JEWEL OF MY COLLECTION.
ZAP!
NOW IT'S MARRED!
OOF!

THIS IS NOT THE RELAXING VACATION THE BROCHURE PROMISED!

SIR, THE SHIP'S *SINKING.* WE HAVE TO GET YOU OUT OF HERE.

I'M NOT GOING ANYWHERE UNTIL MY SIX DAYS, FIVE NIGHTS ARE UP!

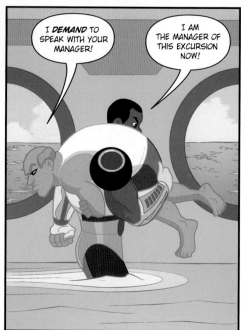

I *DEMAND* TO SPEAK WITH YOUR MANAGER!

I AM THE MANAGER OF THIS EXCURSION NOW!

HOLY HULL HOLE!

IF I COULD CREATE A BUBBLE--

PLAN "NO H2O" IS A WATER WIN!

FWOOSH!

I HAVE A REAL *WHALE* OF AN IDEA! EVERYBODY ABOARD THE BEAST BOY!

THESE ACCOMMODATIONS SMELL LIKE FISH!

SIR, FOR THE LAST TIME, I AM TRYING TO SAVE YOUR LIFE.

DON'T MAKE ME CHANGE MY MIND!

BUMBLEBEE! YOU'RE... *REGULAR!*

BEING GIANT WAS FUN WHILE IT LASTED, BUT I DON'T THINK I'M CUT OUT TO BE THE *NEXT BIG THING.*

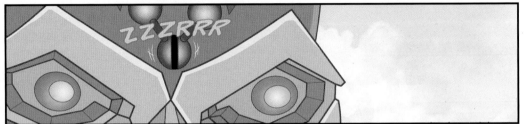

ZZZRRR

WHAT'S HE DOING?

SOMETHING'S COMING OUT OF HIS HEAD, BUT I CAN'T SEE IT--

MAYBE I COULD HELP?

MISS MARTIAN?

I HAVE, UM, *TELESCOPIC* VISION.

IT'S, UM, IT'S--

IT'S HIS *SHRINK RAY!*

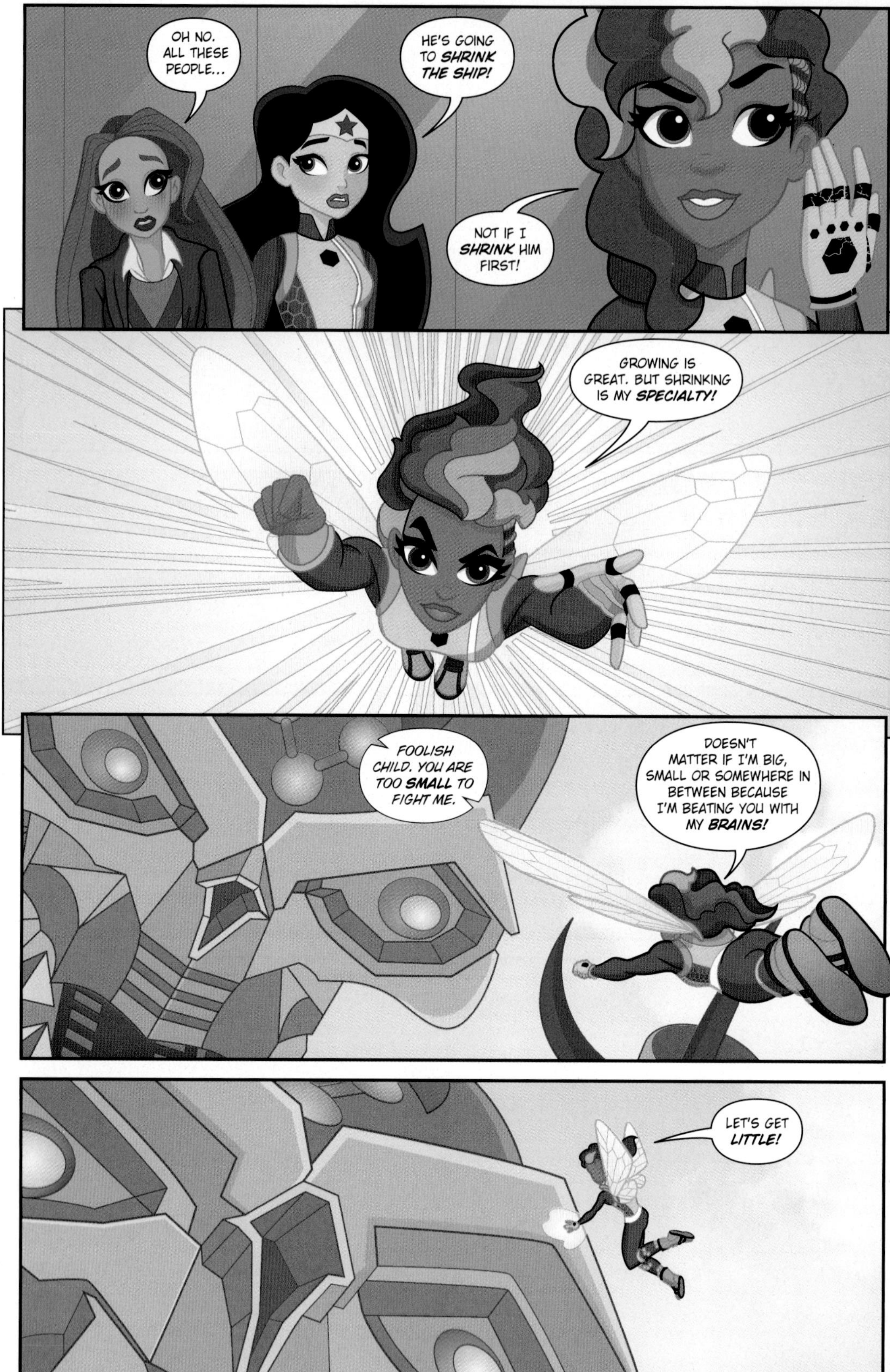
OH NO. ALL THESE PEOPLE...
HE'S GOING TO SHRINK THE SHIP!
NOT IF I SHRINK HIM FIRST!
GROWING IS GREAT. BUT SHRINKING IS MY SPECIALTY!
FOOLISH CHILD. YOU ARE TOO SMALL TO FIGHT ME.
DOESN'T MATTER IF I'M BIG, SMALL OR SOMEWHERE IN BETWEEN BECAUSE I'M BEATING YOU WITH MY BRAINS!
LET'S GET LITTLE!

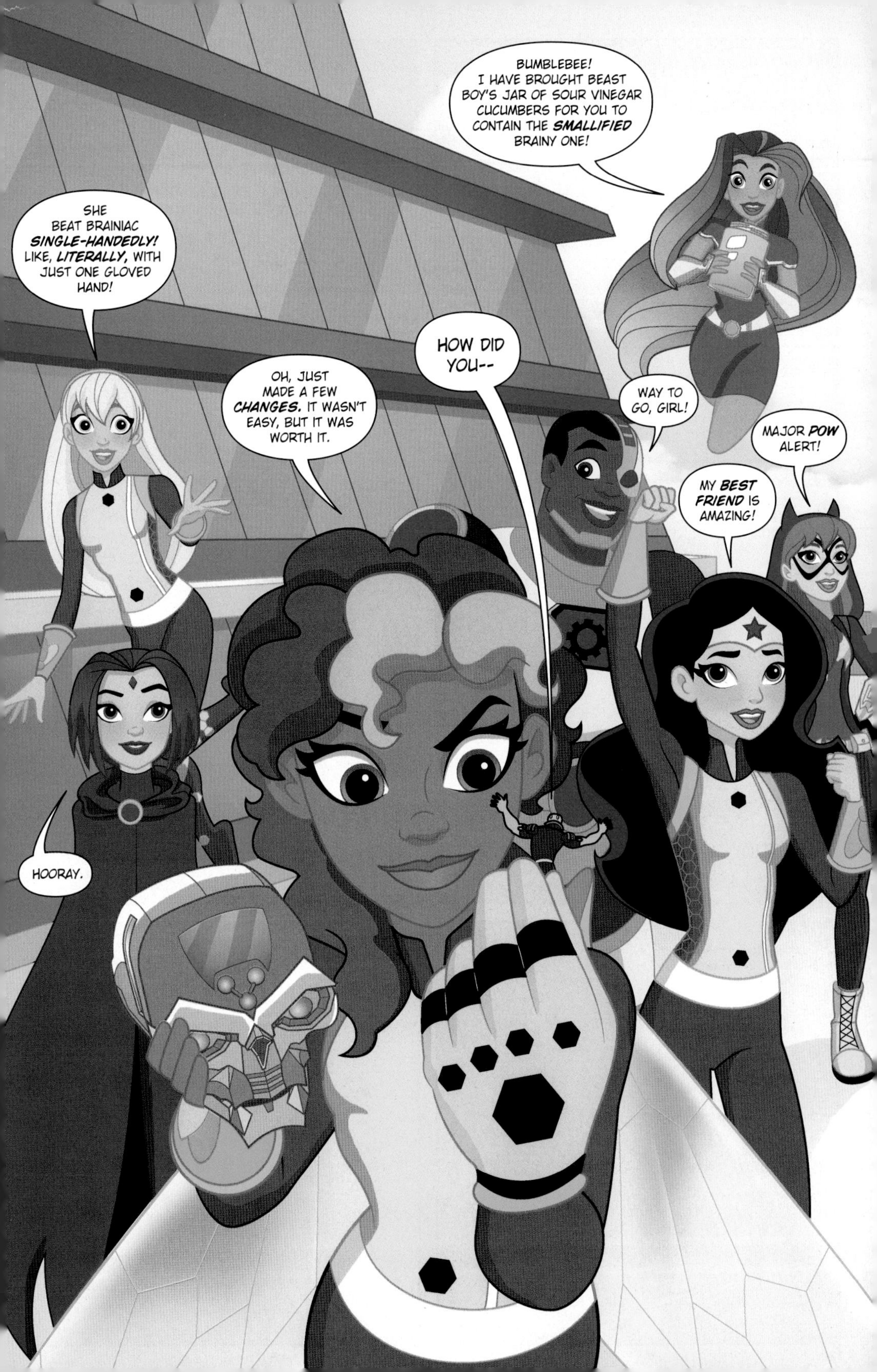

SHE BEAT BRAINIAC SINGLE-HANDEDLY! LIKE, LITERALLY, WITH JUST ONE GLOVED HAND!
BUMBLEBEE! I HAVE BROUGHT BEAST BOY'S JAR OF SOUR VINEGAR CUCUMBERS FOR YOU TO CONTAIN THE SMALLIFIED BRAINY ONE!
OH, JUST MADE A FEW CHANGES. IT WASN'T EASY, BUT IT WAS WORTH IT.
HOW DID YOU--
WAY TO GO, GIRL!
MAJOR POW ALERT!
MY BEST FRIEND IS AMAZING!
HOORAY.

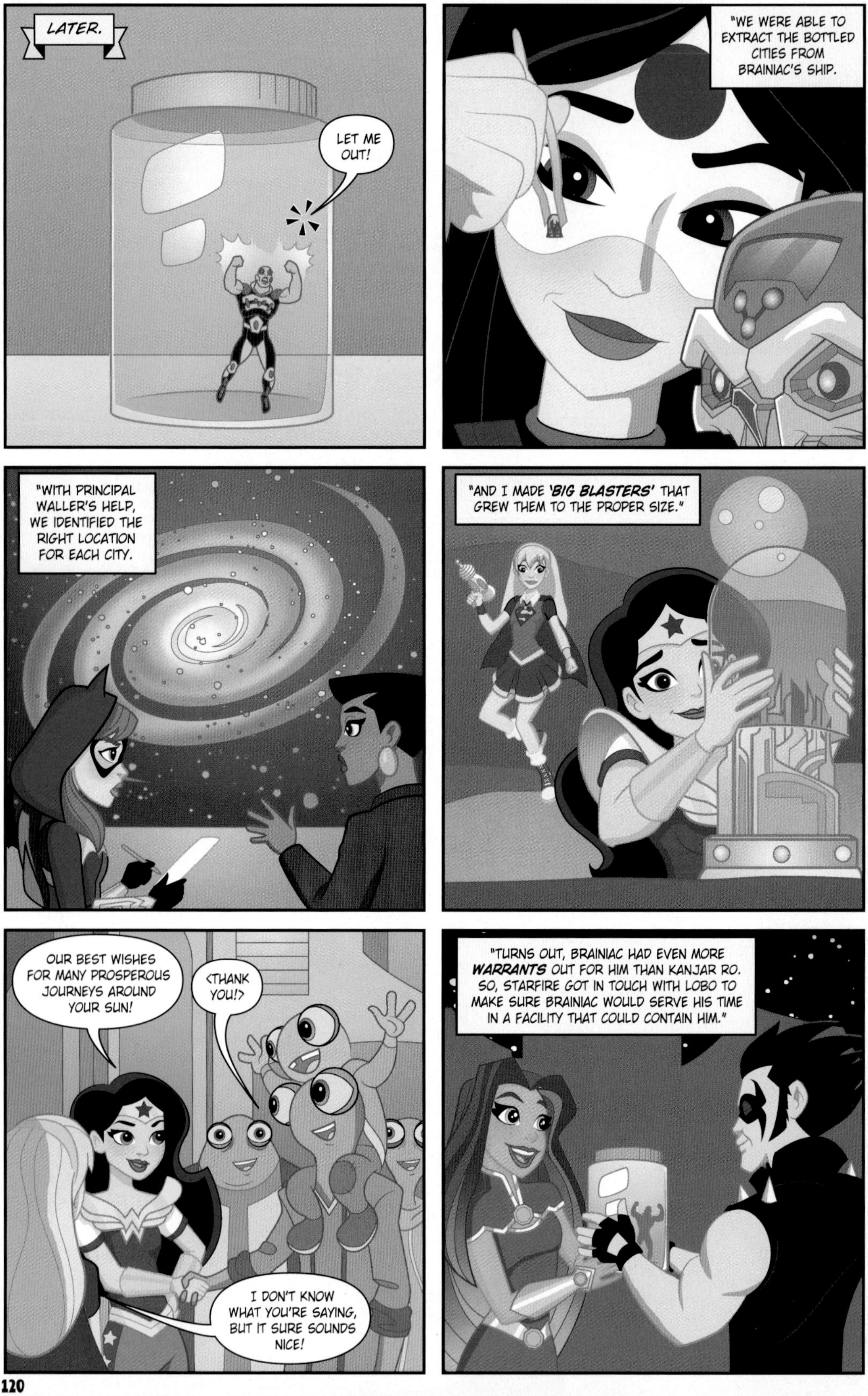
LATER.
LET ME OUT!
"WE WERE ABLE TO EXTRACT THE BOTTLED CITIES FROM BRAINIAC'S SHIP.
"WITH PRINCIPAL WALLER'S HELP, WE IDENTIFIED THE RIGHT LOCATION FOR EACH CITY.
"AND I MADE 'BIG BLASTERS' THAT GREW THEM TO THE PROPER SIZE."
OUR BEST WISHES FOR MANY PROSPEROUS JOURNEYS AROUND YOUR SUN!
<THANK YOU!>
I DON'T KNOW WHAT YOU'RE SAYING, BUT IT SURE SOUNDS NICE!
"TURNS OUT, BRAINIAC HAD EVEN MORE WARRANTS OUT FOR HIM THAN KANJAR RO. SO, STARFIRE GOT IN TOUCH WITH LOBO TO MAKE SURE BRAINIAC WOULD SERVE HIS TIME IN A FACILITY THAT COULD CONTAIN HIM."

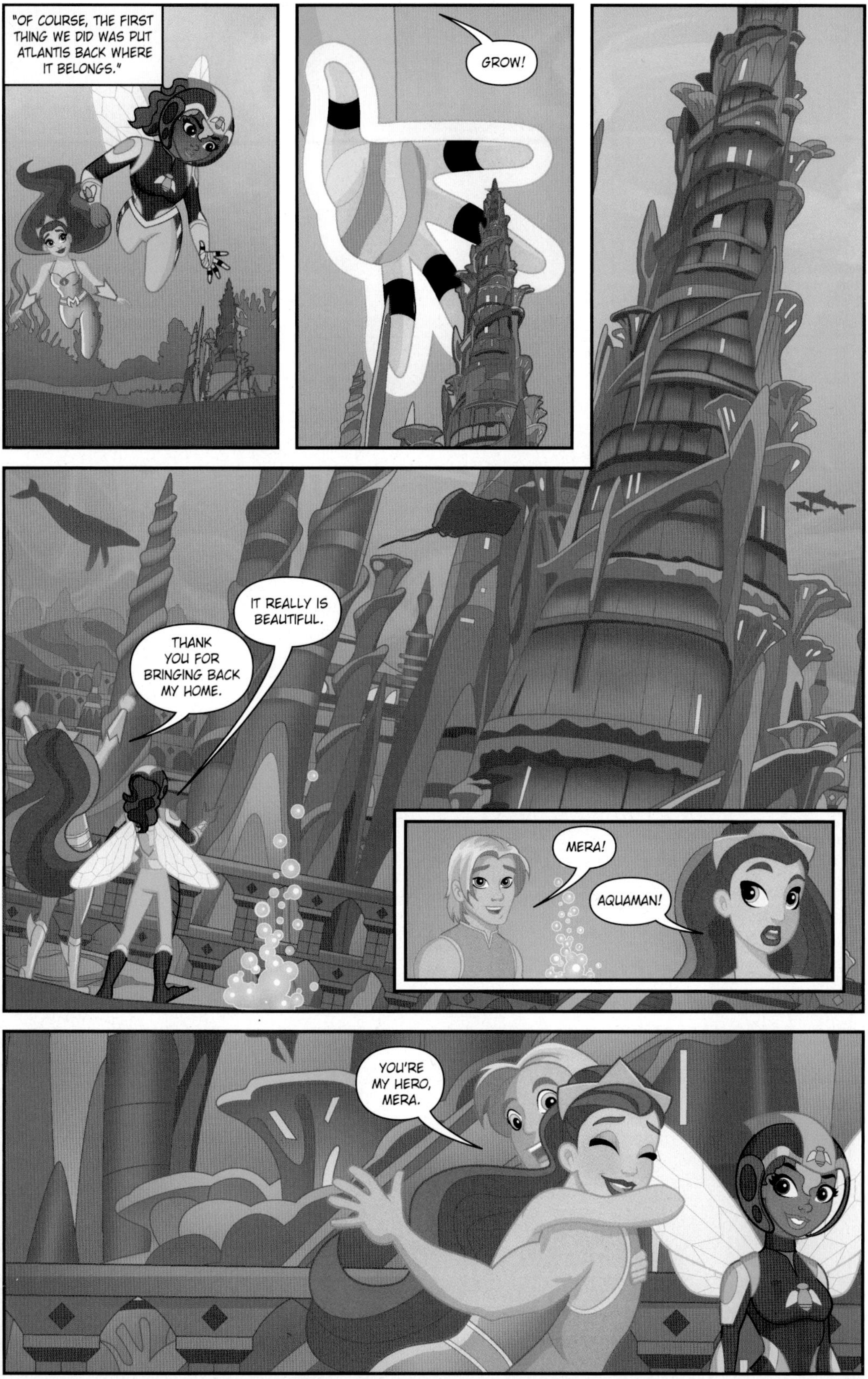
"OF COURSE, THE FIRST THING WE DID WAS PUT ATLANTIS BACK WHERE IT BELONGS."
GROW!
IT REALLY IS BEAUTIFUL.
THANK YOU FOR BRINGING BACK MY HOME.
MERA!
AQUAMAN!
YOU'RE MY HERO, MERA.

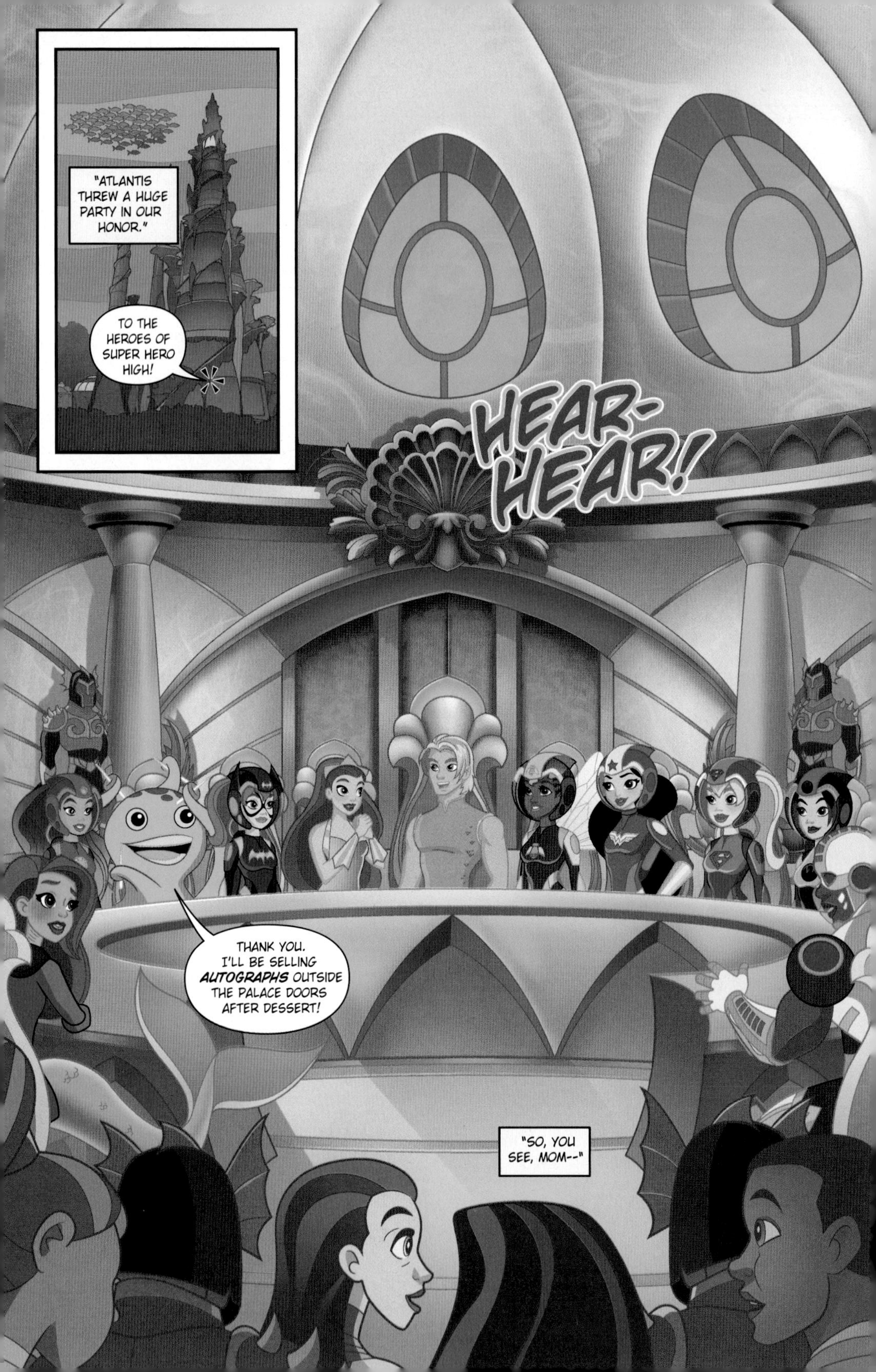
"ATLANTIS THREW A HUGE PARTY IN OUR HONOR."
TO THE HEROES OF SUPER HERO HIGH!
HEAR-HEAR!
THANK YOU. I'LL BE SELLING AUTOGRAPHS OUTSIDE THE PALACE DOORS AFTER DESSERT!
"SO, YOU SEE, MOM--"

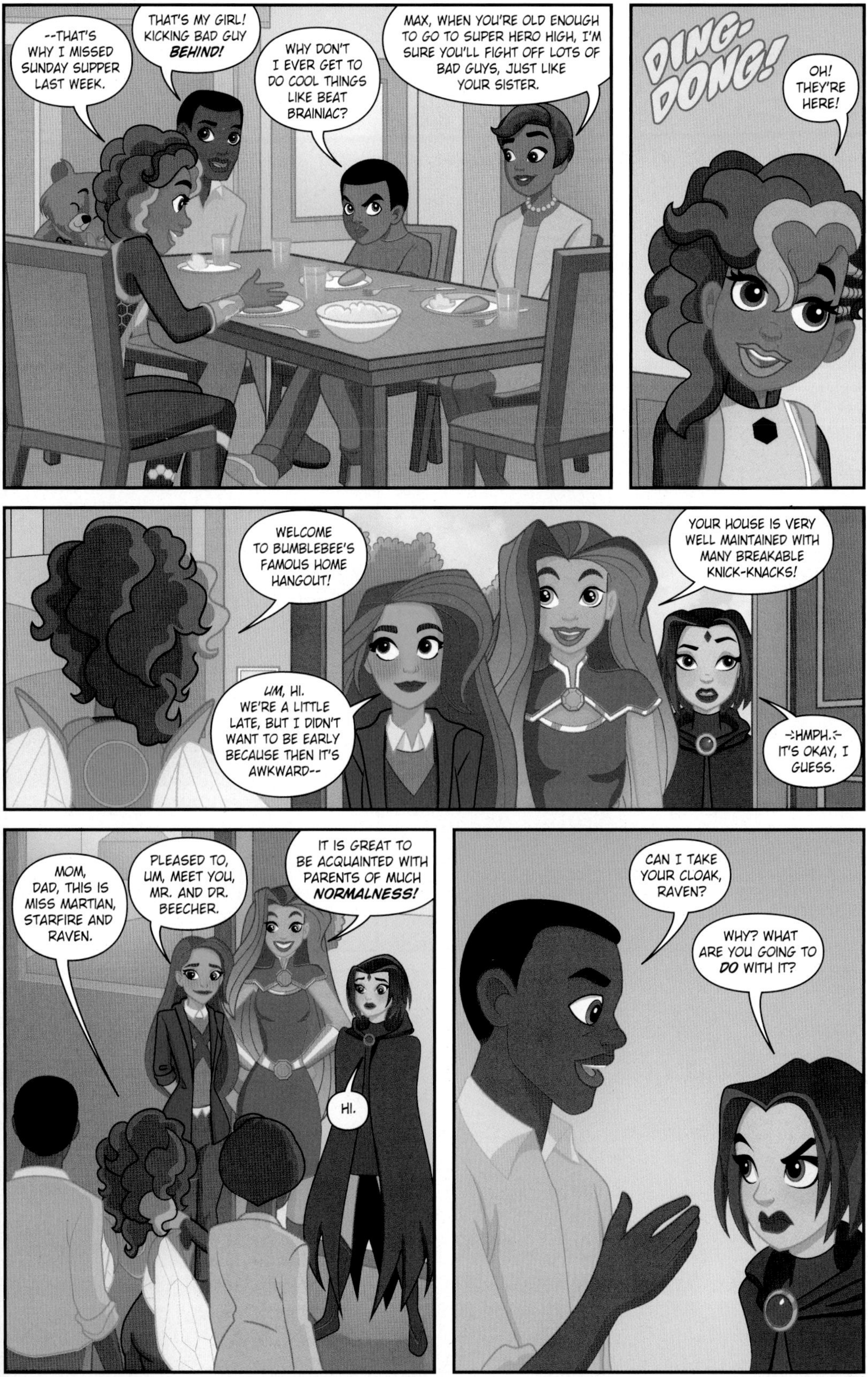
--THAT'S WHY I MISSED SUNDAY SUPPER LAST WEEK.
THAT'S MY GIRL! KICKING BAD GUY BEHIND!
WHY DON'T I EVER GET TO DO COOL THINGS LIKE BEAT BRAINIAC?
MAX, WHEN YOU'RE OLD ENOUGH TO GO TO SUPER HERO HIGH, I'M SURE YOU'LL FIGHT OFF LOTS OF BAD GUYS, JUST LIKE YOUR SISTER.
DING-DONG!
OH! THEY'RE HERE!
WELCOME TO BUMBLEBEE'S FAMOUS HOME HANGOUT!
YOUR HOUSE IS VERY WELL MAINTAINED WITH MANY BREAKABLE KNICK-KNACKS!
UM, HI. WE'RE A LITTLE LATE, BUT I DIDN'T WANT TO BE EARLY BECAUSE THEN IT'S AWKWARD--
-HMPH.- IT'S OKAY, I GUESS.
MOM, DAD, THIS IS MISS MARTIAN, STARFIRE AND RAVEN.
PLEASED TO, UM, MEET YOU, MR. AND DR. BEECHER.
IT IS GREAT TO BE ACQUAINTED WITH PARENTS OF MUCH NORMALNESS!
HI.
CAN I TAKE YOUR CLOAK, RAVEN?
WHY? WHAT ARE YOU GOING TO DO WITH IT?

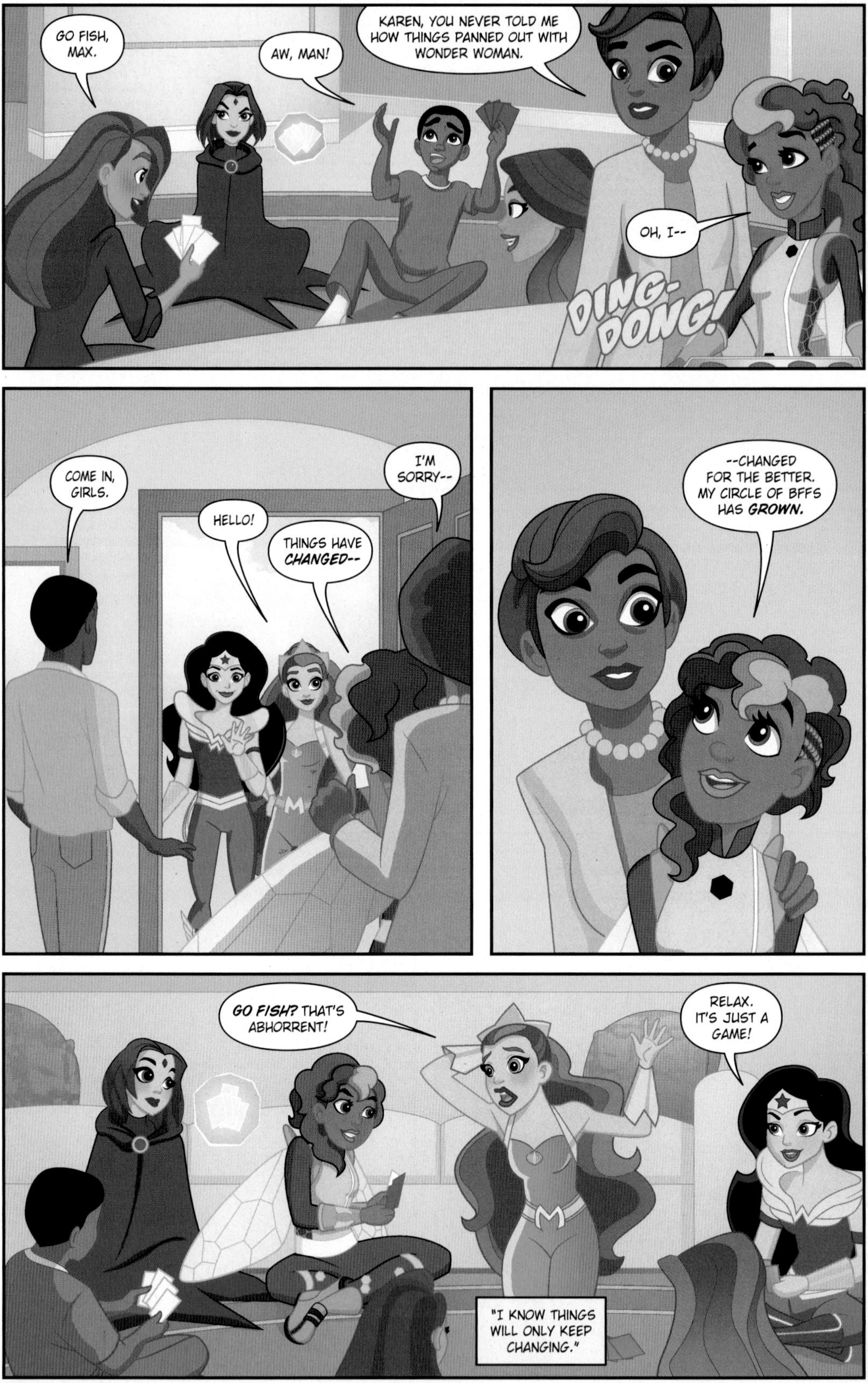
GO FISH, MAX.
AW, MAN!
KAREN, YOU NEVER TOLD ME HOW THINGS PANNED OUT WITH WONDER WOMAN.
OH, I--
DING-DONG!
COME IN, GIRLS.
HELLO!
THINGS HAVE CHANGED--
I'M SORRY--
--CHANGED FOR THE BETTER. MY CIRCLE OF BFFS HAS GROWN.
GO FISH? THAT'S ABHORRENT!
RELAX. IT'S JUST A GAME!
"I KNOW THINGS WILL ONLY KEEP CHANGING."

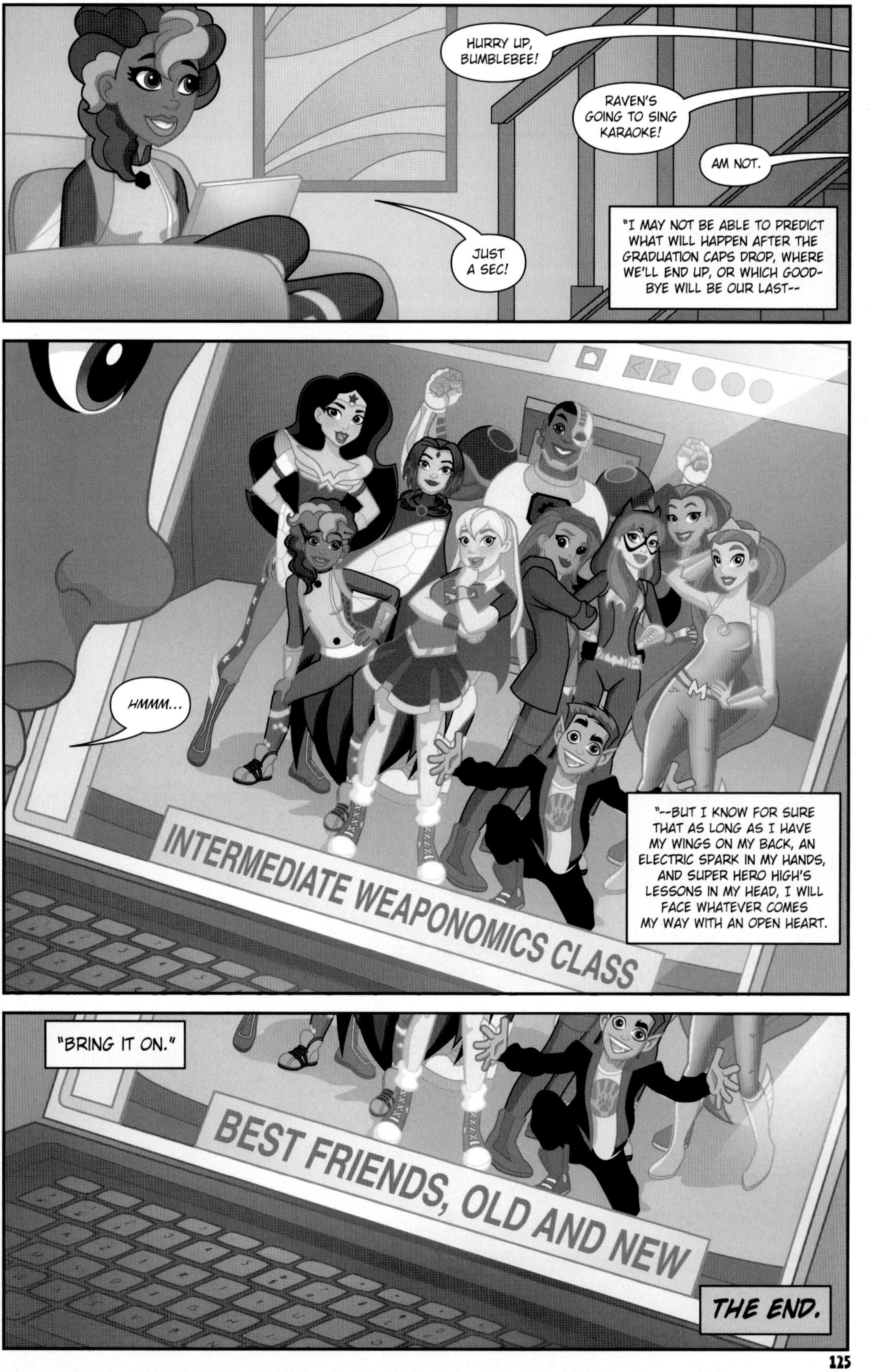
HURRY UP, BUMBLEBEE!
RAVEN'S GOING TO SING KARAOKE!
AM NOT.
JUST A SEC!
"I MAY NOT BE ABLE TO PREDICT WHAT WILL HAPPEN AFTER THE GRADUATION CAPS DROP, WHERE WE'LL END UP, OR WHICH GOOD-BYE WILL BE OUR LAST--
HMMM...
INTERMEDIATE WEAPONOMICS CLASS
"--BUT I KNOW FOR SURE THAT AS LONG AS I HAVE MY WINGS ON MY BACK, AN ELECTRIC SPARK IN MY HANDS, AND SUPER HERO HIGH'S LESSONS IN MY HEAD, I WILL FACE WHATEVER COMES MY WAY WITH AN OPEN HEART.
"BRING IT ON."
BEST FRIENDS, OLD AND NEW
THE END.

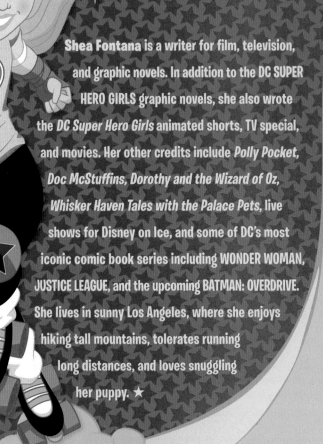

Shea Fontana is a writer for film, television, and graphic novels. In addition to the DC SUPER HERO GIRLS graphic novels, she also wrote the *DC Super Hero Girls* animated shorts, TV special, and movies. Her other credits include *Polly Pocket*, *Doc McStuffins*, *Dorothy and the Wizard of Oz*, *Whisker Haven Tales with the Palace Pets*, live shows for Disney on Ice, and some of DC's most iconic comic book series including WONDER WOMAN, JUSTICE LEAGUE, and the upcoming BATMAN: OVERDRIVE. She lives in sunny Los Angeles, where she enjoys hiking tall mountains, tolerates running long distances, and loves snuggling her puppy. ★

ABOUT THE COLORIST
Monica Kubina

has colored countless comics, including super hero series, manga titles, kids' comics, and science fiction stories. She's colored *Phineas and Ferb*, *Spongebob*, *THE 99*, and various *Star Wars* titles. Monica's favorite activities are bike riding and going to museums with her husband and two young sons.

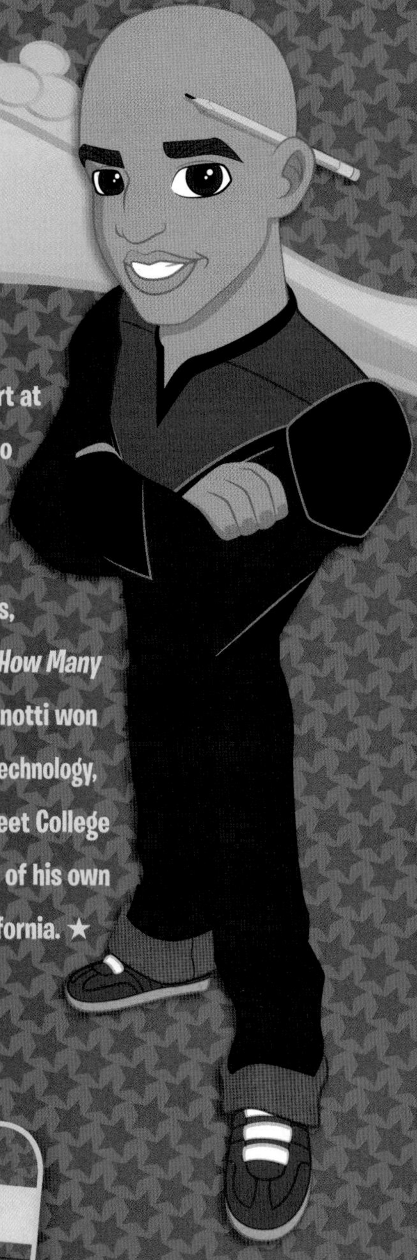

Yancey Labat got his start at Marvel Comics before moving on to illustrate children's books from *Hello Kitty* to *Peanuts* for Scholastic, as well as books for Chronicle Books, ABC Mouse, and others. His book *How Many Jelly Beans?* with writer Andrea Menotti won the 2013 Cook Prize for best STEM (Science, Technology, Education, Math) picture book from Bank Street College of Education. He has two super hero girls of his own and lives in Cupertino, California. ★

ABOUT THE LETTERER

Janice Chiang

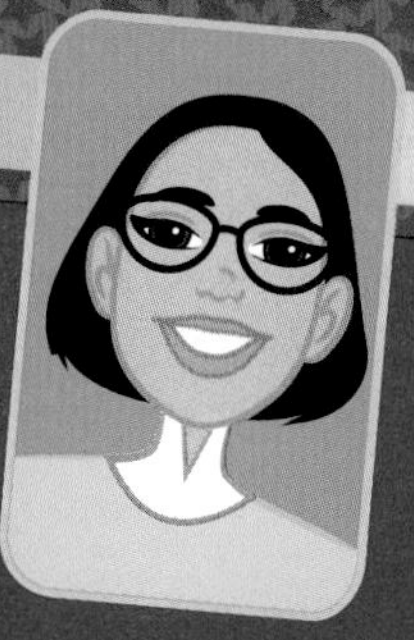

has lettered *Archie*, *Barbie*, *The Punisher*, and many more. She was the first woman to win the Comic Buyer's Guide Fan Award for Best Letterer (2011), and was designated an outstanding letterer by ComicsAlliance (2016), and Best Letterer (2017) by ComicBook.com. She likes weight training, hiking, baking, gardening, and traveling.